STONED ON SEX

Daniel, the genius Broadway actor who gave his greatest performance in bed . . . *Francine*, the cool woman executive who adored being an after-hours slave . . . *Rick*, the famed TV talk-show host who kept very quiet about his private life . . . *Eleanor*, the much-married man eater who knew a million ways to make a guy moan "I love you" . . . *Bob*, a master of mating obsessed not with pleasure but *pleasing* . . . *Betty*, a lovely-looking topless dancer with the most startling sexual secret in New York, which meant the world . . . *Peter*, a lover who wanted to have it both ways . . .

. . . and above, below, and around them all, the star of this drunk-on-love coterie, Jean, a gorgeous painter out to turn her life into a work of erotic art. . . .

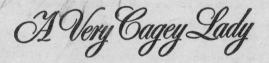

A Very Cagey Lady

Big Bestsellers from SIGNET

A Very Cagey
Lady
Joyce Elbert

A SIGNET BOOK

NEW AMERICAN LIBRARY

TIMES MIRROR

To Eileen, Uranus, and Agatha Christie

I would like to thank Sy Mann for his invaluable
assistance on the subject of toxic poisons.

PUBLISHER'S NOTE

NAL BOOKS ARE AVAILABLE AT QUANTITY DISCOUNTS
WHEN USED TO PROMOTE PRODUCTS OR SERVICES. FOR
INFORMATION PLEASE WRITE TO PREMIUM MARKETING DIVISION,
THE NEW AMERICAN LIBRARY, INC., 1633 BROADWAY,
NEW YORK, NEW YORK 10019.

SIGNET TRADEMARK REG. U.S. PAT. OFF. AND FOREIGN COUNTRIES
REGISTERED TRADEMARK—MARCA REGISTRADA
HECHO EN CHICAGO, U.S.A.

SIGNET, SIGNET CLASSICS, MENTOR, PLUME, MERIDIAN AND NAL
Books are published by the New American Library, Inc.,
1633 Broadway, New York, New York 10019

First Printing, June, 1980

1 2 3 4 5 6 7 8 9

PRINTED IN THE UNITED STATES OF AMERICA

Monday, February 27

❧ 1 ❧

The minute Jean opened her eyes, she knew that something terrible had happened. Her eyes felt heavy, as though she'd been crying, and her body ached. She lingered in that comatose state between sleep and waking, trying to forestall the dreaded knowledge as long as possible.

Outside on her terrace, seventeen floors above the grinding bustle of Manhattan, icicles hung from a barren willow tree and the sky was a cold February gray. She shivered even though it was warm in her beautiful, gorgeous, luxurious, disgustingly lonely bedroom, pulled the covers up to her chin, and looked at the clock on the Victorian nightstand. It was eight-thirty, time to get up, put the kettle on, brush her teeth, do her exercises, feed the dog...

Right on cue, Clark Gable trotted into the room and gazed yearningly at his mistress. A black standard-size poodle, he'd been extremely handsome in his youth, and Jean had named him posthumously after the famous movie star. Now at the age of fifteen, Clark Gable had cataracts in both eyes and there were gray hairs mixed in among the black.

"Neither one of us getting any younger," Jean said to him. "Before I know it, I won't be able to wear a bikini. It's my thighs. I have painter's thighs. I.e., fat."

Clark Gable wagged his tail and let out a short happy

1

bark. Then he retreated into the kitchen, having done his morning's work.

Jean switched on the radio. It was set to WPAT, whose mindless music was about all she could risk at such an early vulnerable hour. A female voice was singing: *I've grown accustomed to his face, he always makes my day begin. . . .*

Daniel's face came into view. It was a sort of lopsided face that looked best in profile, with its aquiline nose, soft blond hair that fell naturally across the forehead, penetrating blue eyes. Yesterday they had pierced her with cruelty, yesterday she had cried herself to sleep alone . . . Yesterday . . . Jean now remembered the terrible thing that had happened. Daniel had left her, fat thighs and all.

"Oh, my God," she said out loud. "I can't face this without a drink."

And yet she had to.

Jean Neelie had been sober for one year, two months, three weeks, and four days. Or as one of her AA friends said, "Who counts?" and everyone ruefully laughed, because like Jean they counted their sobriety time almost down to the minute. They couldn't help it, they didn't want to help it; it was a fierce, self-conscious ritual among people who'd seen hell and survived it. The single most important thing in their lives (as they were fond of saying at Clean Slate meetings) was their sobriety. It was something to be guarded, treasured, boasted about. Only recently O'Brien had bragged: "People on the outside would think I was nuts if I said that even though I've lost my wife, my kids, my house, and my business, I consider myself a very lucky man because *today* I am sober.

Today. Now. One day at a time.

The immediacy of the present was stressed over and over again at AA, where the past was treated as something you couldn't change and the future as something

2

that hadn't yet happened. All of which was logical enough, even if you weren't a drunk. But at Alcoholics Anonymous, it was gospel. When members complained of problems, they were told not to pick up a drink that day and to get to a meeting. As simplistic as it sounded, it was how they were taught to deal with their problems. And the incredible thing was that it actually worked.

At least, it had worked for Jean Neelie until now.

She inched her way over toward the pack of Camels on the nightstand, lit one, and inhaled deeply. Smoking in bed was decadent, dangerous, and addictive, but since she stopped drinking she'd been doing a lot of it. Outside of bed, too. Her feeling on the matter was: better lung cancer than food and a lot of flab. Even when she was drinking her brains out, she had managed to remain relatively slender (except in the thigh department). It wasn't hard; she didn't eat. Which was about all she didn't do because alchohol made her truly crazy, wild, and she did just about everything else, from passing out in the Rose Room of the Algonquin with her face buried in the red spaghetti sauce, to falling asleep on toilet seats in strange bathrooms with her panties down around her ankles, to screwing a one-eyed cab driver in the back seat of his taxi somewhere near the East River, to tapdancing the length of a longshoremen's bar on Eleventh Avenue before the bouncer threw her out.

"The dizzy broad thinks she's Shirley MacLaine yet!"

Jean forced her unruly thoughts back on the track. Daniel. She still could not believe that their relationship was over, that he'd ended it to return to his wife. Yet he had, and there was nothing she could do about it except not pick up a drink and go to meetings.

She frowned, thinking of the day ahead.

In less than four hours Clean Slate would meet, as it did every weekday, in the basement of an old brownstone in the East Fifties. Ordinarily, this would have given Jean hope, something to hang onto, but there was a catch—a particularly ironic one. Daniel himself would be at the meeting. Like her, he was a recovering alcoholic, and it was at Clean Slate that they first met last year. Daniel and his wife, Laura, had been separated at the time, intent upon getting a divorce (he said), when Jean rushed impetuously, naively into love.

In retrospect those first few weeks of passion and loving commitment seemed to her the most beautiful time she had ever known with a man, her marriage notwithstanding. She and Daniel had been like children, innocently sharing all secrets, exposing all wounds, trusting each other in a way that was painstakingly honest for both of them. But now Jean was sorry that she had revealed so much of herself, fearful that Daniel would pass along her innermost thoughts to Laura and the two of them would laugh at her.

He would undoubtedly tell Laura that what she liked most in bed was having her thighs kissed. Kissing was a sign of approval, Jean logically felt, and therefore it meant her thighs weren't as repellent as she believed them to be. Daniel didn't mind kissing and licking them—he said the trail led to interesting juicy places, dribble slurp. He would undoubtedly tell Laura that the reason he couldn't eat zucchini any more was because Jean had once masturbated with one.

"It was young and tender," the traitor would say, "and broke off right in the middle. Don't ask how we got it out."

Was it possible that the gentle man she still loved could prove so heartless?

Why not? He'd been heartless enough yesterday when he showed up after a three-month absence, to inform her that it was all over. He arrived at her apartment around noon, with a bag of bagels and the Sunday *Times*, looking absolutely marvelous ("Why is it," Jean's friend, Betty, has asked, "that when *they* leave you, *they* always

4

look marvelous?"), and talking about the Midwestern tour he'd just completed with *The Iceman Cometh*.

"Playing Willie Oban was like occupational therapy. Can you see me in the role of a shaking, twitching, hungover lush after all those months on the wagon?"

"Were you tempted to drink?"

"No, just the opposite. I've never been so turned off booze in my life. It's a long play, and the whole thing takes place in this dirty, depressing, rundown saloon where everyone is bombed. The set was amazingly realistic. After the final curtain, I just wanted to get away from that sick atmosphere. And then I went to a lot of meetings in the Midwest, which helped keep me sober. So all in all it was a terrific three months, except for . . ."

Because Daniel was an actor and a good one, Jean was forever suspicious of his theatrical posturing. When he paused, she felt that he was playing to the back row.

She fed him his cue. "Except for?"

His expression changed to one of uneasiness, regret. "Except for us."

He didn't have to go on. She knew then and there what his next words would be. Perhaps she had always known, right from the start, that she would never be able to hold a man as magnetically attractive as Daniel. Women like her rarely could, Jean thought, as despair began to mount. They were too shy, too unsure of themselves, too willing to be taken under the wing of a more dominant personality who in time would tire of them. It was almost inevitable that Daniel should leave her for a more exotic, flamboyant creature (Jean was only flamboyant after fifteen martinis), and in a way she couldn't blame him. She wondered who the lucky woman was.

"It's Laura," Daniel said, as gently as possible. "While I was on the road, I realized that I still loved her. Maybe I always have, I don't know. What I do know is that our marriage was ruined by alcohol, and now that we're both sober I think we have a chance to make it work. At least I want to try. I hope she does, too."

Jean was stunned. She felt like running out to the nearest bar and getting bombed.

Laura!

Daniel's estranged wife was hardly her idea of an exotic, flamboyant creature; far from it. Jean knew Laura casually since they both attended the same twelve-thirty Clean Slate meeting, and if anything, Laura was even more ordinary than she. Except for a seductive Southern accent, Laura was a tall, gangly brunette who seemed ill at ease in her own body. She had large hands, large feet, and—Jean realized now, for the first time—a large curved mouth.

The sexual connotations of Laura's mouth flooded into view, embarrassing Jean by their explicit graphicness. She wondered if Daniel had spent the night with Laura, and came here straight from her bed. He seemed flushed and excited as though by lovemaking, and again the erotic possibilities of Laura's mouth presented themselves. Jean's late husband taught her everything she knew about the pleasuring of penises, but he had gone to his grave wistfully disappointed in her expertise.

"For an oral type, honey—!"

She remembered him shrugging in resignation, not even bothering to finish his dismal but emphatic critique. And now she longed to ask Daniel whether he had fallen out of love with her because she was no good in bed. Or was it something else? If so, what? Was she unamusing company? Didn't he like her looks, the way she painted, the way her thighs quivered when he kissed them? Wasn't she slim enough, smart enough, witty enough, fascinating-intriguing-dynamic enough?

She needed to know precisely what had made him tire of her, yet she could not bring herself to ask. It was awful to be cursed with shyness—you never learned what people truly felt about you unless they volunteered the information themselves. And Daniel did not seem about to. Why should he? It was easier to talk about his plans for the future.

"What I'm going to do," he said, biting into a buttered bagel, "is take Laura out for brunch next Sunday. A week from today. It's her birthday, and I'm going to ask her to come back to me."

Jean felt like throwing up. "Do you think she will?"

"I'm very hopeful. She wrote to me in Chicago, saying that she was still in love with me and wanted to try again."

"I see."

"I know what you're thinking." The sunlight filtering into the living room caught the gold of his hair. "Why didn't I tell you all this before I returned? Why did I wait so long to let you find out?"

"That did cross my mind."

"The reason is quite simple. I didn't want to put it in a letter. It seemed so cold, so heartless." He smiled one of his most engaging, least heartless smiles at her. "I really felt you deserved better than that."

She didn't know what to say. *This* was his idea of better! More moral, he meant, more ethical. All that crap they taught you at AA, she thought bitterly. It sounded okay in the abstract, that spiritual do-good business, but when it came down to real life it plain stank. How much kinder it would have been had he told her the ghastly news by mail. Then she could have wept in private, cursed his guts, and shouted obscenities alone on her gardened terrace; she could have had the luxury of instant rage. Now she would have to wait until he was gone in order to indulge herself. Like just about everything else that had happened to her recently, it wasn't fair, Jean decided.

"Aren't you going to wish me luck?" Daniel asked, flashing another one of those smiles.

7

She ached to scream at the top of her lungs "Go to hell!," but as always good manners and diffidence prevailed.

"I hope you're happy," she said, feeling like a hypocrite. "And now I have to get back to my painting. I started an abstract landscape yesterday."

He beamed, thinking his mission eminently successful.

"I knew you would understand, Jean. Only another alcoholic can appreciate what Laura and I have been through."

She saw him to the door, Clark Gable furiously wagging his tail behind them. Clark Gable liked Daniel and had no idea this would be the last time he saw him. Lucky Clark Gable. Because it occurred to Jean that unless she switched to another AA group or Daniel went on tour with another play, she would have to go on seeing him day after day.

"You're a terrific painter!" he blurted out, just before she slammed the door shut.

"Drop dead."

It was easy to be courageous once he was out of earshot. So she was a terrific painter, was she? Marvelous. She kicked a Sheraton chair. Suddenly a familiar craving started to take possession of her and the distinctive black-and-white Jack Daniels bottle danced into view, warm, inviting, seductive. *Drink me and forget your troubles, drink me and be happy, drink!*

Fortunately, there was no alcohol in the apartment; she had poured it all down the sink when she joined AA. And liquor stores were closed on Sunday. But there were always bars, restaurants, even fast-food chains were now offering beer and wine with their meals. Booze was everywhere, goddamn it, so accessible, so tempting, so easy to walk into the discreet Szechuan restaurant a few blocks away and ask for a Jack Daniels on ice. With angostura bitters, of course, so the bartender (who couldn't care less) should not get the idea that she was a garden-variety drunk.

Oh my, no, that would never do. Even in alcoholic stupor she used to try to retain the vestiges of correct, ladylike behavior, which was why her more outlandish exploits appalled and horrified her so the next day.

"Did I actually rip off my blouse after six banana daquiris at Trader Vic's, and throw it in the waiter's face when he refused to serve me a seventh?"

(Yes, whispered a small, embarrassed voice.)

Jean walked over to the terrace and stared south at the pale Manhattan skyline. The wind was blowing so hard that an icicle fell from one of her willow trees. She had to mulch some of the trees and plants again, or they would surely die in this weather. Outside, an antique wrought-iron table sat next to a Brevoort vase in frozen isolation, waiting for summer. Then the terrace was a thriving garden of foliage, beautiful, abundant. She even grew her own herbs and tomatoes, people complimenting her on her green thumb.

And he'd left her, anyway.

"God help me not to take a drink today," she said, swaying a little in prayer.

A moment later she realized that the telephone was ringing.

$\circledcirc 2 \circledcirc$

It was Betty Lathrop, Jean's sponsor, friend, and AA conscience.

"Hi, kid. You okay?" Betty's husky voice rang with concern. "You once told me that you had a real hate thing for Sundays."

Leave it to Betty to remember, to care. Jean was grateful.

"I do," she said. "Sundays really stink."

"What's wrong? I mean, except for an overwhelming desire for sixty-three bloody marys?"

"Make that Jack Daniels."

"I thought you used to be a vodka person."

"Not exclusively. Vodka was only one of my phases; I'd drink anything that was eighty proof. Once when I was desperate I drank two bottles of cough syrup. But I've got the bourbon bug today. I can't imagine why."

Yes, she could. Daniel had said that when he was lapping it up, Jack Daniels was his drink.

"At this very moment, I would cut off both my arms for a good stiff drink," Jean confessed.

"No arms, no hands, no paintings. Look at it that way."

"I'd paint with my nose, if I could just have a drink. Or my toes."

"Eat honey."

"I don't want any goddamned honey."

"I know. I love it when they tell you that at Clean Slate. It's such dumb advice. *Want a drink? Eat honey, instead.* What are you supposed to do if you're walking along the street? Take a jar of honey out of your handbag and start spooning it down your throat in public?" Betty's laugh was like her voice, deep, hearty. "What touched you off, kid?"

"Daniel." It even hurt to say his name. "I just saw him. It's all over. Finished. Kaput. The end."

Betty whistled. "Shit. No wonder you're feeling so low. Hey, I thought that lover-boy was in the Midwest spouting O'Neill. When did he get back?"

"This morning."

Jean had to remind herself that Betty had never met Daniel. Betty moved to New York after Daniel went on tour, and although she asked Jean a lot of questions about him, Jean was always reluctant to reveal too much. She felt that by discussing Daniel, she would be betraying their love, cheapening it.

"You'll see how marvelous he is when you meet him," was all she used to say.

"I can hardly wait. He sounds too good to be true." Betty's skepticism turned out of be more on target than Jean's own foolish optimism. What an idiot she had been!

"You didn't mention that he was coming back today," Betty said now, surprised.

"That's because I didn't know, myself. He wasn't due to return for another week."

"I'll bet he just couldn't wait to get his ass to New York and tell you the rotten news. *Men.*"

Betty was a topless dancer who worked in a kinky East Side club, where she wiggled down a fake leopard-skin runway to disco music several times a night. A tall curvaceous redhead with a narrow waist, full hips, and breasts that owed a great deal to silicone implants, Betty had a hard-nosed attitude toward men. Which didn't stop her from falling in love with them. At the moment she was involved with a Clean Slate member, Peter, several years her junior. Jean could not understand their relationship, for as much as she liked Betty, she suspected her friend gave Peter a hard time. Why did sweet, hand-some, *nice* Peter stand still for it?

"It turns out that Daniel is going back to Laura," Jean said. "Can you believe it?"

Betty whistled like a truck driver. "Speak of adding insult to injury! Jesus Christ! He sounds like a guy I knew back in Detroit, an inventor. We called him 'the mad genius.' "

"What did he invent?"

"Lots of things. Reversible colored pantihose, dolls that made love, tennis rackets for cheating, and the invisible exit. He disappeared in the middle of the night with

11

my best friend. The last I heard they were living in L.A., where he was working on an iron supplement for women. You spray it up your vagina."

"Laura doesn't even know the good news yet."

"Daniel *is* a self-confident bastard, isn't he?"

To her surprise, Jean began to cry. First softly, then louder. She had never been able to cry in front of another person in her life, and in a sense she still couldn't. The telephone acted as a barrier, shielding her from Betty's scrutiny.

"I couldn't believe it when he told me about Laura," she managed to say between embarrassing sobs. "The last I heard on the subject, they were getting divorced."

"Who told you that?"

"Daniel."

"Of course," Betty said, sarcastically. "If you had asked Laura, you can be sure *she* wouldn't have said so."

"But I didn't ask her, I believed him. Daniel always insisted that divorce was the only solution. I never would have gotten involved with him if I thought otherwise. Never. It was an awfully big step for me, you know."

Jean's husband, Frank, had been dead six months when she guiltily started the affair with Daniel. In spite of the unforgivable way Frank treated her while he was alive, Jean had old-fashioned ideas about windows and mourning. But Daniel made it easy, telling her he loved her, telling her he would soon be a free man, telling her not to be afraid. Still, she *was* afraid. Daniel was exactly the sort of man she had spent her life avoiding—an actor, unconventional, unreliable, egotistical. Jean knew about men like him from an early age.

She had grown up in Greenwich Village, the only child of wealthy, bohemian parents, both of them from socially prominent families, both of them well-established portrait painters. Because most of her parents' friends were in the arts, divorce and adultery were treated as natural occurrences and did not carry the social stigma they would have in a more conventional environment. Passionate liaisons and casual affairs flourished openly, proudly, dramatically, attesting to the self-indulgent appetites of their practitioners. More often than not, they ended in disaster. Jean still recalled a poet friend of her parents' stabbing himself in the chest when the ballet dancer he loved ran off with a notorious playboy. His greatest regret afterward was that he had not died.

By the time Jean was a teenager, she had seen enough of bohemian unhappiness to make her wary. She vowed that if she married it would be to a solid, conservative, professional man. And on the surface, Frank was exactly that. A graduate of Harvard Law School with a respectable, if not elegant, New England background, he seemed just what the doctor ordered. How could she have guessed that he would turn out to have the morals and scruples of an alley cat?

In retrospect, she did not think she was being too hard on Frank. Her own easy-going parents would have been offended by his sordid extramarital affairs, outraged by his cynical, callous attitude. Fortunately, her parents were not around to witness Jean's humiliation. They had long since gone to their graves, confirmed romantics.

"Married men are the pits," Betty said now. "That's what I get at the club, these horny married creeps who love their wives but-oh-you-kid. They stink. Daniel and his lies stink. Practically every man I've ever met stinks."

Jean blew her nose. "Even Peter?"

Betty's lover was an actor, like Daniel. In fact, Peter and Daniel had known each other many years before they both ended up at AA. They once had a falling out over a part in a play, but later patched it up and became friends again. Jean now wondered whether Betty's fierce condemnation of Daniel was not somehow caused by jealousy and resentment that Daniel knew Peter longer than she did, and perhaps better.

"Peter is superior to most men," Betty declared. "A

13

recovering alcoholic has a lot of sensitivity going for him, he's faced himself, seen the flaws. Which is more than can be said of ninety-nine percent of the male population."

"Daniel is a recovering alcoholic," Jean pointed out.

"Daniel gives alcoholism a bad name."

"Why are you so hard on men, Betty? I know it's fashionable these days, but why? Why do you run them down?"

There was a slight pause. When Betty spoke again, her voice was more subdued, her anger more quiet.

"Because I know them so well. Maybe too well. I've lived among them . . ." She reverted to her familiar mocking tone. "The trouble with you is you idealize the bastards. You think they're something special. That's why you get hurt all the time."

"Probably." Jean could feel the tears well up inside her again. "Still, you have to admit that the men you come into contact with in your work aren't exactly typical."

"That's where you're wrong, kid. They're typical, all right. They're just being honest and showing their true crummy colors for a change."

In spite of Daniel's rejection, Jean found Betty's downbeat attitude depressing and unfair.

"If you feel that hostile toward men, why don't you quit your job and get something else? Something that's not so demeaning?"

It was a question Jean had wanted to ask before, but always hesitated, telling herself she didn't know Betty well enough to pry into unsavory motives. They'd only been friends for a couple of months, since Betty moved east from Detroit where she had worked at a number of fly-by-night jobs: waitress, cab driver, summons server, lab assistant, door-to-door saleswoman, makeup demonstrator, and the like. Jean often marveled at their friendship, because aside from alcoholism they seemed to have nothing in common. And yet, the bond of affection was strong.

"The reason I don't quit the club," Betty said, "is because I'm a born exhibitionist, always have been. I love being the center of attention. I enjoy shaking my tits at all those panting guys. I like to make them hot, knowing they can never lay their hands on me. Sometimes I get depressed that I like it so much, but I earn damned good money doing it. Oh, Jesus! Look, it's okay so long as I don't drink. If it weren't for AA, I'd never be able to keep that job *and* my sanity. But sober, I can handle the whole scene. Sober, it's cool."

Invariably everything came back to booze, Jean thought. If you were an alcoholic. Because as rotten and punched-out as she felt, as hurt as she was by Daniel's rejection, she didn't want him back right now, all she really wanted was a drink. It didn't even have to be Jack Daniels anymore, any drink would do the trick. The trick being to blot out reality, kill the anguish, lift her to a plateau of indifference, invulnerability, *joy*. That was the one thing people overlooked when they tried to understand alcoholics, the one thing they somehow failed to grasp: how blissfully happy you became when you drank, how alcohol shielded you from pain.

What you did feel was a godlike sense of self-sufficiency, it was marvelous, euphoric. You absolutely needed nobody and nothing, except the bottle, of course. The bottle took the place of friends, lovers, husbands, wives, parents, children, jobs, recreation, ambition, conversation, money, lust, passion, self-respect. As long as you had that bottle, you were safe from the assaults of a hostile world. No wonder alcoholics clung so desperately to their addiction. It gave them so much pleasure.

Until it started to give them so much misery.

And even then, the resistance to stop drinking was monumental. Jean had felt that she could not survive without alcohol, that after Frank's death it was the only thing that kept her going, kept her from blowing her brains out. She sat in this apartment day after day, the drapes closed against the light (which hurt her eyes), playing Billie Holiday records and sobbing into her glass of straight vodka/bourbon/scotch/gin/sherry/ whatever was around. Now she was terrified of repeating the same pattern.

"Hey, are you still crying?" she heard Betty ask. "Do you want me to come over?"

"No, thanks. I'll be okay."

"We could go to a movie, or better yet a meeting."

Clean Slate, their regular group, did not meet on weekends and Jean wasn't in the mood to face new people. Alcoholics or not.

"I've planned on painting this afternoon," she said.

"Are you sure?"

"Positive."

But she stumbled over the word. She was shaking.

"Betty, what am I going to do? I love him so much. I really thought we had it made, Daniel and I. We were going to be happy, we understood each other, loved each other. It's a nightmare, I tell you. First losing Frank in that freak auto accident, and now losing Daniel to Laura."

"I'll be right over. You stay there. Don't go anywhere." *Don't go looking for booze*, was what Betty meant. "Are you listening to me, Jean?"

There was urgency in that voice, authority. Jean could count on Betty to help her get through this terrible day. Betty had strengths Jean did not possess, emotional resources that Jean could draw upon. Sometimes she wondered how she'd stayed sober for as long as she did without Betty to lean on. Betty was the sister she'd never had, the mother she'd always wanted. Her own mother was too busy painting portraits of the rich and the celebrated to pay much attention to her.

"I'm listening," Jean said dully.

"You're going to be all right. Just don't pick up that first drink."

"I won't."

"Promise?"

"Yes, goddamn it!"

She could feel the pain rush out of her and turn into hatred, anger, rage. It was a good feeling, it had been a long time coming. Death claimed Frank before she had a chance to vent her anger upon him. Frank thought she didn't know about his women, and she helped him maintain that convenient illusion. She never said a word. Oh, she was so accommodating, so fearful of conflict, so fucking polite. And then came that head-on collision. How angry could you get at a barely living thing lying on a white hospital bed, covered in bandages from head to toe? How angry could you get at a corpse?

But Daniel was alive and healthy and going back to Laura.

"I hate him," Jean said into the telephone. "I'd like to kill him."

"We'll talk about it when I get there," Betty said. "In the meantime, don't do anything foolish. Okay?"

Dead. She would like to see Daniel dead. How could she know that within forty-eight hours her wish would come true?

☙ 3 ❧

That was yesterday and somehow, with Betty's help, Jean survived it. Today looked like it might be even more difficult. Today she would have to face Daniel at Clean Slate and not go to pieces.

It had snowed heavily last night, the third largest snowfall of the season. New Yorkers were tired of it and up until yesterday, so was she. Today the weather didn't seem to matter. Hot, cold, lukewarm. What difference did it make? She shivered not because it was February, but because Daniel had left her.

The doorman tipped his hat and smiled.

"Morning, Mrs. Neelie."

"Good morning, Albert."

Here in this solid, prestigious building where every tenant owned rather than rented, she still retained an outward sense of identity. Unless she remarried, here she would always be Mrs. Franklin K. Neelie. A widow, youngish, respectable (except for her zonked-out periods in the past, now discreetly overlooked), she could be expected to do the proper thing. Which was why her affair with Daniel had surprised the doorman. He didn't expect that kind of behavior from her so soon after her husband's death. Then Daniel went on tour and the doorman looked relieved, thinking that that nice Mrs. Neelie (the reformed drunk in 17-A) had come to her senses. Now she was the respectable widow again.

Jean stopped at the corner of Park Avenue and childishly stamped her foot. Why did she care what the doorman thought? Why did she want to please the entire world? Why was it necessary that everyone had a high opinion of her? Why did she have such a low opinion of herself that everyone else's approval mattered so much?

Regretfully, she did not know the answers. All she knew was that until she quit drinking a little over a year ago, she would never have thought to ask the questions. Then she simply took her diffidence and passivity for granted. They were part of her, like her thick ash-brown hair and hazel eyes. She might not like them, but she was stuck with them.

Besides, in the past if anything bothered her too much all she had to do was to take a drink. To calm her down, soothe her anxieties. After Frank died, she needed a lot of calming down, a lot of drinks. She felt that had he

18

lived, she would never have become an alcoholic. His sudden, grisly death was the turning point in her life, it pushed her over the edge of social drinking. She couldn't identify with those people at AA who admitted they were born alcoholics, who said that no matter what happened sooner or later they would have become drunks. Jean did not feel that way about herself, not at all. She was able to look back upon her descent into compulsive, uncontrollable drinking with a clear eye and see the justification for it. At the age of forty, her husband was a successful, healthy, vibrant man with a keen zest for life. Given the traumatic circumstances of his demise who *wouldn't* have become a lush?

By the time she got to the small brownstone that housed Clean Slate, Jean's cheeks were flushed and her spirits improved. As usual the door was unlocked and the smell of coffee, strong, reassuring, floated in the air. Several people stood grouped around the large coffee urn in the darkly lit anteroom. They were talking and laughing, cigarette smoke curling over their heads.

"The drunks coming into AA are getting younger all the time," she heard someone say. "Pretty soon the ten year olds will be taking over."

Jean smiled at the familiar sight. The people themselves might vary from day to day, but the tableau remained the same. Coffee, cigarettes, and laughter. If she had to pinpoint three qualities that typified these meetings, those were the ones she would have named. An intense, dark-eyed man approached her.

"Hello, Jean. How're you doing?"

"No complaints," she said, stoically. "Except the usual ones about the weather. How was your weekend?"

"Rough."

He was wearing a Spanish cowboy hat and looked as though he should be on horseback in the Argentinian pampas. Yet his name was O'Brien and his ancestors came from Cork. He held a white plastic cup of steaming coffee in his hand.

"Can I get you some of this poison?" he asked.

"No, thanks. I never drink it here."

Upon giving up alcohol, a lot of recovering alcoholics had become addicted to coffee and were fussy about its preparation. Jean was one of them, but not O'Brien.

"I'll drink any slop," he admitted. "It's my Irish-shanty background. We never got around to the finer things in life, which I'm just starting to appreciate—now that some of them are taboo. Like French champagne. I had to go to a wedding yesterday and it was sheer torture steering clear of all that Dom Perignon. Do you think there'll ever be an end to this insatiable craving?"

"I hope so. It would be hell to go through life wanting something you can't have."

She was thinking of Daniel as much as alcohol.

"It's hell *right now*," O'Brien said emphatically. "I get an urge for a belt at least ten times a day. Don't you?"

"Maybe more," Jean said, grateful that he was taking her into his confidence. "I even dream that I'm drinking."

Since becoming involved with Daniel, people here had begun to accept her as one of their own. Before, they avoided her. She knew that the impression she gave at Clean Slate was the same one she'd given everywhere all of her life: aloof, standoffish, superior. The fact that she was painfully shy went undetected. But Daniel was the best-liked person in the group, and by virtue of his popularity she had started to bloom too, expand, show an interest in others, ask questions. And they responded in kind.

"You used to act like you were too good for us peasants," Vanderbilt told her recently. "I'm glad that Daniel made you come down off your high horse. What the hell, we drunks have got to stick together."

She wondered what would happen when they discovered that she and Daniel had broken up, that he was going back to Laura. It wouldn't take them long to find out, and she was afraid they would drop her. Without Daniel for support, she could easily retreat into her old shell of frozen isolation and stay there indefinitely, friendless except for Betty.

"Some alcoholics have a relatively painless time of it," O'Brien was saying. "Maybe it's because they stopped drinking before they hit rock bottom. We didn't and that makes recovery even harder."

Jean felt a kinship to O'Brien. His sobriety was as difficult as her own, and his story a lot worse. He used to own a Third Avenue pub that catered to New York's beautiful people, but as his drinking habits deteriorated so did the popularity of his pub, until he was forced to declare bankruptcy. Shortly afterward, his wife sued for divorce and got custody of the children. O'Brien ended up on the Bowery. Now he worked as a bartender, saving his money for the day he could once more open his own place.

"I've been sober for nearly five years," O'Brien said, "and I still find it hard to forget about booze."

"So do I."

She had found it particularly hard yesterday. Perhaps later during the discussion period, she would talk about it. At Clean Slate you were encouraged to share your feelings, ask questions, complain, above all not to hold back, not to let resentments and problems build up. Sharing was very therapeutic, and every time she did it she felt better. There was only one problem now, she suddenly realized. Daniel. He would be at today's meeting and she didn't want him to know how much she'd suffered on his account. She would be too embarrassed to describe how she tried to fill the hours yesterday with endless activity, in a desperate attempt to remain sober.

She and Betty had gone ice-skating at Rockefeller Plaza, stopped off to see the new English art exhibit at the Met, had a leisurely dinner at a French restaurant, then walked back to Jean's place through the softly falling snow.

"Do you think you can sleep?" Betty asked her.

"Yes, I'm exhausted."

"Good. That was the idea."

Jean felt touched. "Thanks."

She tried to kiss Betty on the cheek, but the other woman pulled away, embarrassed by this display of gratitude.

"See you tomorrow, kid," Betty said gruffly, heading for home.

Yet when Jean got upstairs, she found that sleep would not come. After much tossing and turning, despair began to set in, then anger and the craving for a drink. The craving was so intense that she could taste the bourbon on her lips, smell its smooth bouquet, feel it go down her throat and warm the tips of her toes. It was then that she decided to call Daniel.

She didn't know what she was going to say, she merely wanted to talk to him, feel him near her. Anything was better than lying there fantasizing about alcohol, was how she rationalized it as she dialed his number. Daniel lived in Greenwich Village, not far from where she grew up. Jean had never been to his apartment. Daniel said it was a mess, he wanted to get some furniture before he invited her there.

"Hello."

It was a woman's voice, crisp and clear. Jean knew it couldn't be Laura, who was from Savannah and had a distinct Southern accent. She stopped, confused.

"Hello!" the woman said. "Is anyone there?"

"Can I please speak to Daniel?"

"He's taking a shower," said the coolly efficient woman. "Would you like to leave a message?"

Jean hung up, trembling and perplexed. Who could the woman be? What was she doing in Daniel's apartment at midnight? There seemed only one obvious conclusion, but it made no sense. Daniel said he was going back to Laura, that he loved Laura, that all he wanted was to make his marriage work. Could he have been lying? Jean never thought of him as duplicitous, frivolous (promiscuous?), and she didn't want to think of him that way now. But something was wrong. She turned out the light in the bedroom again, praying sleep would come quickly.

5

Jean was now aware of movement. People were leaving the anteroom and filing into the larger adjoining room, where meetings were held. Normally they tended to wait until the last second to take their seats, which meant that the scheduled speaker must be a good one. She wondered who it was. Because of the heavy snowfall last night, Clean Slate was only half full. Jean spotted Laura seated up front, her black hair shining in the artificial light of the basement.

She had never gotten friendly with Daniel's wife, and she was sorry now. She would like to know what Laura was thinking, feeling. All Jean knew about her was that she worked as a writer for an early-morning television show, and was still in love with Daniel. In less than a week they would be reconciled, unless the woman on the telephone . . . No. Jean hastily blocked her out of the picture. Daniel couldn't possibly be involved with someone else (*she* was the someone else!). There had been some sort of mistake. The woman on the telephone did not exist. Daniel never invited women to his apartment.

FIRST THINGS FIRST

EASY DOES IT

A DAY AT A TIME

BUT FOR THE GRACE OF GOD ...

Unlike the woman on the telephone, the framed signs were comforting and familiar. Jean had laughed when she first saw them (trite, childish, was her contemptuous reaction), but she soon discovered that their advice was not so easy to follow. She was still trying to follow it. Beneath the signs were two chairs facing the audience. Constance, the current chairwoman, sat in one looking impatiently at her watch. She was a deftly made-up blonde with a cool executive manner. The seat next to her, reserved for the speaker of the day, was empty.

"Do you know who's going to talk?" Jean asker Marcel beside her.

"I believe it's our good friend Daniel."

"*Daniel?*"

"Due to the bad weather, the scheduled speaker had to cancel. And Daniel volunteered." The Frenchman winked. "You should know, *chérie*."

Jean was about to say that Daniel's actions no longer concerned her, but she hesitated. Marcel and the others would find out soon enough that she and Daniel had broken up, and then her day in the sun would come to an end.

"Here he is now," Marcel said.

Daniel was moving down the aisle, smiling and shaking hands with friends he hadn't seen in months. The conquering hero, in a wheat-colored turtleneck and custom-made jeans. People's faces lit up at the sight of him. Phrases like "Good to see you again" and "How've you been, you bastard?" and "The bad penny returns" filled the long room.

If there had been any doubt of his popularity, today's reception quelled it. Just as Jean was contemplating a speedy exit, someone sat down in front of her conveniently cutting off her view of Daniel. It was that snotty art director, Bob, who acted as though he had invented sobriety. At least now she could barely see the object of her love, misery, and deep disappointment.

"My name is Constance and I'm an alcoholic," the chairwoman said, rapping up front for silence. "Welcome to the Monday, twelve-thirty meeting of Clean Slate. This is an open discussion meeting. I will read the preamble and then introduce today's speaker.

"*Alcoholics Anonymous is a fellowship of men and women who share their experience, strength, and hope with each other that they may solve their common problem and help others to recover from alcoholism. . . .*"

As Constance continued reading the preamble, Jean felt a vague undefined sense of uneasiness. She looked at the woman in front of the room for a clue, but all she saw was an attractive well-dressed blonde whose training as an executive secretary made her ideally suited for this job.

"And now here to share his experience, strength, and hope with us is Daniel."

Everyone applauded. Daniel smiled and began his speech.

"My name is Daniel and I'm a grateful recovering alcoholic. As most of you know, I've been out of town for the past few months. What you may not know is that I was touring with Eugene O'Neill's play, *The Iceman Cometh*. In it, I played the part of a man who shared certain similarities with me. He had gone to Harvard Law School which was one of my early ambitions, and he was a seriously disturbed drunk." Daniel grinned. "How's that for impeccable type-casting?"

A ripple of laughter spread across the room as people visibly relaxed. Next to Jean, Marcel lit his pipe. Like the others, he knew he was safe for the next half hour, his attention secured by a good storyteller.

Only Jean fidgeted in her seat. Daniel's reminiscences evoked too many memories. She knew that his early ambition was to become a criminal trial lawyer, but something happened in college to make him change his mind and he enrolled in drama school instead.

"An actor and a criminal trial lawyer are not so dissimilar as they may seem," Daniel had said at the time. "Basically, they're both showoffs."

Frank had been a lawyer too, not criminal law, though; he represented large corporations. There was a big difference between the two, Daniel once pointed out, and Jean agreed. She could not imagine two men more unalike than Frank and Daniel. They had only one thing in common: each, in his own way, had abandoned her.

"I always had an extremely vindictive nature," Daniel was saying now from the speaker's chair. "I find it difficult to forgive someone who's harmed me. and even worse I can't forget old grievances. Instead, I tend to bide my time until I can show that person what I really think of him."

He appeared to be addressing these remarks to Peter, Betty's lover. Peter had the kind of husky, all-American, football-hero good looks that made people trust him instantly. Yet in 1971, when he and Daniel had been up for the same part in a Broadway play, *That Championship Season*, Peter tried to hustle Daniel out of it. According to Daniel, by exceptionally underhanded, unscrupulous means. Even though Peter finally lost the part to a third actor, Daniel hated him for a long time afterward. Jean was surprised to discover that Daniel still secretly harbored grievances, despite the fact that the two men now appeared to be friends.

"This vengeful quality is one that I'm not very proud of," Daniel was saying, "which is why I'm talking about it. Because I sincerely hope to change, to develop some humility, and with God's help I will. But I haven't gotten there yet, not by a long shot."

As he went on, Jean realized how much she loved him. Not because he was trying to become a better person, but just because he was Daniel. She loved him exactly the way he was, vengeful or not, without improvement. Was that the way Laura felt, too? Then she remembered that Laura did not yet know her marriage was going to be saved, her prayers answered ("I still love you," she had written Daniel in Chicago), that she was going to get her husband back.

Jean felt tears come to her eyes, and once more the inviting prospect of a drink swam before her. At that moment she envied everyone in the room who was happily, romantically involved. She envied Betty and Peter sitting together; they looked so serene, their heads almost touching, their lives so much less troubled than hers. She envied Marcel next to her, smoking his pipe, still married to the woman he met when he worked in the Resistance; Marcel claimed that she stuck by him through the many turbulent years of his alcoholism.

Jean did not envy the much-married, much-divorced Eleanor who was industriously knitting a scarf a few seats away. Jean knew that whenever Eleanor met a new man, she began a new scarf (in a new color). It was possible to chart the success of each romance by the length of the scarf. Most of them never saw completion. This one was bright red, and Jean idly wondered who it was for.

"I want to thank everyone in this room who has helped me stay sober," Daniel was saying. "Thank you all, dear people."

Hearty applause followed his speech.

"There are no dues or fees at AA," Constance announced. "But there are expenses. Please try to give generously."

She began to pass the basket around for contributions.

"And now we'll continue with the discussion part of the meeting. If there is anything you would like to say, just raise your hand. For those of you who might be new, remember there are no foolish questions at AA, so don't hesitate to speak up."

Jean felt her stomach clench and her mouth go dry. There was something familiar about Constance, something she couldn't put her finger on, something disturbing. Directly in front of her, Bob's hand shot up. The good-looking art director invariably had a testy comment to make.

"Thank you for your qualifications, Daniel. I was very interested in your remarks about revenge, because I happen to disagree with them. I fail to see why we should be so ready to forgive when we've been hurt. Doesn't the Bible itself preach an eye for an eye? If a person harms you, doesn't he deserve to be paid back in kind? Justifiable revenge is only human, only fair."

Bob had moved forward in his seat, so now Jean could see Daniel more closely. Above his turtleneck sweater, his face looked drawn, his eyes haggard. She wondered why. When he left her yesterday, he was in excellent spirits, full of plans for the future, buoyant. Now an air of defeat seemed to hang over him, and she realized that his entire speech echoed a kind of wistful unhappiness. For one mad moment, Jean's thoughts began to race. What if he had decided that he still loved her? That it was a mistake to go back to Laura? What if he had changed his mind since yesterday? Later he would telephone and beg her forgiveness.

"*Darling, I made a mistake,*" he would begin.

Daniel's voice at Clean Slate jerked her back to reality.

"I'm not opposed to justifiable punishment, Bob. What I mean is that I feel it's wrong to *harp* upon revenge, to enjoy it for its own sake, to revel in it. That's my problem, it's what I still do." Daniel's eyes darted quickly to Peter. "When I was out in the Midwest I had a lot of time to think about my behavior and I found myself looking at the Fifth Step, studying it."

AA's program of recovery as outlined by its founders, relied heavily upon a series of guidelines called The Twelve Steps. Members were asked to learn about these basic principles of conduct and to practice them.

"In the Fifth Step, we admit the exact nature of our wrongs," Daniel said. "We confess our mistakes. That's all I'm trying to do today. Confess my mistakes, get them off my chest, start over again with a Clean Slate." He smiled wanly at the audience. "That's what this group is called, isn't it?"

The discussion period continued.

Jean longed to share yesterday's alcohol temptation with the others, in the hope that she would not be so sorely tempted to drink today. But every time she thought about raising her hand, she resisted, afraid of what she was liable to blurt out directly to Daniel: "*I want to drink myself to death and it's all your fault, you lousy, hypocritical bastard!*"

But was it, an inner voice asked? Or was she using Daniel's rejection as an excuse to get drunk? A strange thought crossed her mind: just as she had used Frank's death? A chill went through her, a foreboding of danger. She did not know in what area the danger lay nor when it would strike, only that it was there somewhere in the shadows, hiding, waiting.

Then the sixty minutes were up, and people were getting to their feet.

"We will close with the Serenity Prayer," Constance said.

Jean shivered without knowing why. She felt Marcel

put his hand in hers. Everyone in the room had joined hands, bowed their heads, and were starting to speak in unison. Suddenly, she broke her clasp with Marcel. Her head straightened, her mind was racing. The woman who answered Daniel's telephone last night . . . that cool, crisp voice . . . it belonged to Constance!

"Is something wrong?" Marcel whispered.

"Yes." Jean could barely breathe. "Terribly."

Tuesday, February 28

✺ 1 ✺

Daniel was murdered the next day.

What started out as an ordinary Tuesday turned into a nightmare for Jean. She had bad dreams the night before; someone was chasing her through a dark alley in a strange country threatening her with death. She woke up covered with sweat, and aching for a brandy to calm her down. It was a relief when morning came.

Daniel was still on her mind. Just before she left Clean Slate yesterday, she walked over and told him how much she enjoyed his speech. It was a lie, but she was trying to behave normally around him, not allow his presence there to overwhelm or inhibit her. She needed Clean Slate, Daniel or no Daniel, if she was to retain her sanity, her sobriety.

"Thanks," he said, looking uncomfortable. "Very kind of you."

Peter and Betty were right behind her.

"Hey, buddy!" Peter clapped Daniel on the back. "I thought you and I had buried the hatchet a long time ago. Why all the talk about revenge? You're not still mad at me?"

"How could I stay mad at *you*, amigo?" Daniel said.

Betty held back, letting the men enjoy their reunion. Jean realized that Peter would want to introduce Betty to Daniel, and possibly the three of them would go somewhere for lunch. She was afraid that if she hung around, they might feel obligated to ask her to join

31

them. She hurried out, telling Betty she would talk to her later.

She never did. She'd been too busy.

After a sandwich, she went to her life class at the Art Students League where she had been studying for the past year. When she got home she plunged into work on the unfinished landscape and painted all evening. Her favorite painter was Edward Hopper whose scenes of America revealed a lonely, alienated mood that matched her own. Hopper and his wife, who used to live on Washington Square North, had been friends of Jean's parents and she remembered the gifted man with awe and respect. If she could only be one-tenth as talented, she would be satisfied.

It was snowing again on Tuesday when she set out for Clean Slate, a soft wet snow that tickled her face. Everything felt wet today. She had gotten her period early that morning, and the flow was exceptionally heavy. Was that why she felt so uneasy? No, it wasn't the onset of menstruation that troubled her, it was Daniel. Why had he ever returned to New York? More importantly, what was she going to do about him?

She decided to ask Betty to have lunch with her that afternoon; maybe they could make up for missing yesterday's talk. She wanted to ask Betty how to deal with Daniel's continued attendance at meetings. What should she do? Switch to another AA group and avoid him? Or stick it out and hope that in time she would adjust to his being there? She had no way of knowing that in a while, death would relieve her of these problems.

The darkly lit anteroom was its usual bustle of pre-meeting activity. At the center of it all were Betty, Peter, Laura, and Marcel. They stood around the coffee urn, their heads engraved in a broken semicircle. In days to come Jean would remember the four of them grouped that way, vividly, suspiciously. The semicircle appeared broken because someone had temporarily left it, marking the place with a soggy pack of Salems on the table. Daniel smoked Salems, four packs a day. Jean helped herself to coffee, and wondered where he was.

"I thought you never drink the stuff here," O'Brien said, putting his cowboy hat in the closet.

"I'm making an exception today."

"Slumming?"

She laughed uneasily. O'Brien once admitted that when he owned his pub, he was forever in awe of the fashionable men and women who patronized it. Having grown up poor himself, he was easily impressed by people with money. It had taken Jean awhile to realize that O'Brien considered her a person with money. When she pointed out that Eleanor was far more wealthy than she, O'Brien waved this remark aside.

"It's not the same thing," he said. "Eleanor got her money through marriage, husbands, alimony. You inherited yours."

"What's the difference? Money is money."

"No, inherited money is like land . . . real, solid. You grow up feeling secure if you have it. It makes you different. All Eleanor ever felt was anxious about how to grab her next rich husband. Five divorces and she's only thirty-eight! No wonder she used to guzzle scotch sours for breakfast."

Jean was about to say that she hadn't grown up feeling particularly secure, when she tasted the Clean Slate coffee.

"God, this is terrible. How can anyone drink it?"

"It takes our minds off the hard stuff," Daniel said, emerging from the bathroom. "That's how, my sweet."

He stationed himself at the center of the little group, lit a Salem, and started telling an amusing anecdote about his recent Midwestern tour. The others hung on his words, laughing in all the right places. It wasn't that he said anything terribly funny, Jean thought; it was the way he drew them into his exclusive world and made them charter members.

All except Laura. She was dabbing at her eyes with a blue Kleenex, clearly disturbed about something. But the others didn't seem to notice her, they were too caught up in Daniel's story. Then Laura dropped the Kleenex into the wastebasket beneath the table and wordlessly walked off to the meeting room.

Jean wondered what Laura could have to be unhappy about, now that Daniel was returning to her. Then she remembered that Laura did not yet know. How foolish of Daniel to wait for her birthday next week, to break the good news. Why didn't the fool speak up now? He probably didn't even realize that his wife was unhappy. *Men* (as Betty had so accurately said).

Across the room Jean spotted Eleanor approaching her, with a distressed look in her eyes. Eleanor had a habit of walking around with that look whenever she met a man unsuitable for marriage (by *unsuitable*, Eleanor meant *poor*), and Jean was not in the mood to hear about her latest romantic catastrophe. She was still too immersed in her own.

"I must do something with my hair," she said, ducking hastily into the bathroom.

&2&

Eleanor was hurt. She knew that the others in Clean Slate were sick of listening to her woes, but she thought she could count on Jean to be sympathetic. Since getting cozy with Daniel, Jean had started to act human, vulnerable, receptive to the problems of others. Before, she had displayed the emotional capacity of an iceberg.

"I've fallen in love again," was what Eleanor wanted to tell her. "And this time he's dead broke."

In the past she had no scruples about sleeping with such a man, but marriage? Never. She had been a poor child from a lower-class Italian family, growing up in Staten Island at the end of the Depression. Ever since she was very young, Eleanor's dream was to marry a rich man and be waited on hand and foot. The fact that it wasn't a very original goal did not bother her in the least. She used to fantasize about the gifts her husband would bring her, glittering and costly, every one of them proof of his deep affection and love. She felt convinced that only a rich man could give her the assurance that she was truly loved. And she married five such men, each of whom eventually left her. Her last husband, a Wall Street banker many years her senior, summed up the feelings of the others.

"I'd gladly give you all the rubies and sables in the world, if I thought they would make you happy. But nothing is ever enough, you always want more. And you always will. The fact is that your hunger is bottomless, you'll never be satisfied. You just can't believe anyone really loves you." He sighed. "Actually, I used to."

And now for the last few weeks, all she thought about was marrying a man who could give her nothing. Yet if he said he loved her, she would believe it in a second. The trouble was that he had not committed himself, and his silence was driving Eleanor crazy. Did he care for her at all? She couldn't tell; he was too enigmatic, and she was afraid to ask directly. Jean might have a clue, or help her find out. Eleanor needed an intermediary between herself and her penniless Clean Slate lover.

Just then she heard an outburst of laughter from the little group surrounding Daniel, and her mouth twisted in bitter memory of him. She doubted if anyone knew of their brief encounter which took place several months ago, before Daniel became so enmeshed with Jean. He showed up at her Park Avenue duplex late one evening, saying he had a yen for her trim little body. Then he coaxed her into bed, spent five dizzying hours devouring her, and was never heard from again outside of Clean Slate.

What hurt the most was that afterward he behaved as though nothing had happened. Once upon a time Eleanor would have been able to get them both off the hook (her easy acquiescence, his insulting rejection) by blaming it all on their being drunk and not accountable for their actions. But now even that time-honored rationale was denied her. In a gesture of feeble retaliation, she abandoned his scarf after three rows of impassioned cable-stitching.

She had avoided Daniel ever since. She hated Daniel ever since. People who didn't know better thought that Eleanor's main concern was money. It wasn't. Money was an important, powerful, vital second. First and foremost was her ability to hold any man she fancied, for as long as she fancied him, and to hear him say, "I love you." Because she was exceptionally agreeable toward her lovers, devoted to their whims, solicitous to their needs, and because she had schooled herself carefully in the art of lovemaking (she still practiced vaginal contractions whenever she went to the bathroom), she usually succeeded. She was shameless about how she dragged those three heavenly words out of them, there was no level to which she would not sink. Before she married her fourth husband, they were caught in a raging storm off the coast of Cuba. Convinced their sloop was going to capsize, Eleanor said: "Quick! Before we die, say it!"

"I love you," the terrified man croaked.

It was enough for her.

That she had failed to coax these words out of Daniel came as a cruel and humiliating blow.

"You don't have to mean it," she urged him, "just say it."

"You give great head."

36

That he had walked out of her life without so much as a backward glance was an unforgivable insult. People also thought she was an easy-going, good-natured, sort of Lorelei Lee gold-digger. Again, they were wrong. Eleanor's feelings ran deep. She didn't forget so readily and she didn't forgive; she had ways of getting even that were so effective nobody ever dreamed she was responsible. People underestimated her. But she'd be damned if she would tell anyone how clever she was, and she sure as hell wouldn't tell that rich bitch, Jean Neelie, who felt too goddamned superior to even listen to her latest dilemma.

☜ 3 ☞

When Jean emerged from the bathroom, everyone was gone. The meeting had started, and she made her way inside just as the guest speaker launched into her talk. Later she would never be able to explain to the police why she sat down next to Daniel. There were a lot of vacant seats in the room that she might have chosen. The weather was still keeping people away, and the entire row behind her was empty except for a drunk she had never noticed before.

The guest speaker was a woman named Renee. She looked like someone's grandmother, her gray hair pulled back in a bun, her lined face devoid of makeup. Her soft voice explored the whys and wherefores of her descent into alcoholism. Despite her homey appearance, she turned out to be a printing executive whose career took off just about the time her husband of many years left her for a young divorcee. The combination of suddenly finding herself an abandoned woman and a corporate officer drove Renee to the bottle in a big hurry. She began with a double shot of vodka in her morning tea.

As Jean listened to the familiar story, she noticed that Peter was seated on the other side of Daniel. Betty was up front by herself. Even though seating arrangements at AA were arbitrary, it struck Jean as strange that they weren't together. She glanced at Daniel beside her. He seemed totally absorbed in Renee's tale as he sipped his coffee, oblivious to Jean's presence. How could he have forgotten her so quickly, so completely?

"I thought I was being very clever about my drinking," Renee said. "I thought I had everyone at the office fooled, but they were wise to me the entire time. Alcohol *smells*. Yes, even breathless vodka."

Jean's attention drifted around the room.

Bob was sitting diagonally in front of Daniel, his broad shoulders hunched forward. Next to Bob was an Eurasian girl new to Clean Slate. There were several newcomers here today. Frequently a speaker from another AA group, like Renee, brought her own friends with her for moral support. Not that Renee needed any, there was barely a rustle in the room. Eleanor's knitting needles, busily clicking away, made the only sound. People nodded as Renee talked, a good sign, it meant they were identifying—both men and women. It seemed to Jean that one of the few nice things about alcohol was that it broke down the barriers of prejudice between the sexes. "Alcohol doesn't discriminate," O'Brien once said, "it's an equal-opportunity employer."

Now Renee was saying: "Despite all the strides that have been made by the feminist movement, people are still more discriminatory against women drinkers than against men. I knew that unless I did something about my vodka consumption, I was going to lose my job. And that job was all I had."

Jean heard a gagging sound next to her. She looked at Daniel, shocked by the sudden change in him. His face had broken out in a cold sweat, his hands shook, and he appeared to be gagging.

38

"Daniel," she said. "What is it?"

His eyelashes fluttered wildly. He opened his mouth and one word came out: *Jean.* She was vaguely aware that Bob had turned around and was staring at them. Then Daniel slumped over in his chair, inert, the plastic coffee cup falling from his hand, coffee streaming all over the floor. Jean was stunned to see that he had wet his trousers.

"Someone get a doctor!" she cried. "Daniel's fainted."

Renee stopped talking and total confusion set in. People left their seats and moved to Daniel's side, crowding around him. Nobody was a doctor, but everybody had an opinion. O'Brien was heard to say, "Too bad we can't administer brandy."

Peter, who was taking Daniel's pulse and listening for his heartbeat, finally said: "I think he's dead."

This brought forth an uproar of protests, questions, and suggestions. No one could believe it.

"It's not possible." Jean was talking more to herself than anyone else. "I was sitting right next to him. He was fine a few seconds ago."

"Someone call the police," Peter said, his boyish face gone pale. "Where's Laura? Where's his wife? Jesus Christ, what a nightmare."

"I'm here." Laura was white and trembling, a large white fish. "Is he really dead?"

"I'm afraid so." Peter gently closed Daniel's eyes. "Did he have a heart condition?"

"No, not that I know of."

"He was choking on something," Jean said.

Hugh dumbly said: "Maybe he choked to death."

People just stood there, their mouths hanging open, horror written plainly on their faces. Eleanor's knitting had dropped to the floor. Jean caught a glimpse of Constance, ashen. Constance didn't say a word, she looked as though she were beyond speech. Laura had begun to sob. Only Bob seemed to grasp the essentials of the situation.

"I'll call the police," he said. "Someone get Laura a cup of coffee. She looks awful. Where the hell is the telephone?"

"In the anteroom," Jean said.

He gave her an odd look, his eyes flashing angrily. "I'll be right back. Don't you go away."

"Where would I go?"

She glanced at Daniel's lifeless form still in the chair, and shivered. She had never before been at the actual scene of death. Her parents and Frank had all died in their sleep, her parents peacefully (only months apart), Frank under heavy sedation from his wounds. She never realized how lucky she was to have missed this grim ritual.

"The police will be here shortly," Bob announced a few seconds later. "They don't want anyone to leave until they arrive. And they don't want anyone to touch anything. So I guess we might as well sit down."

Again he shot an angry look at Jean but now she realized that it was an accusing look as well. What was he accusing her of? What had she done? The possibility that Daniel might have been murdered still hadn't occurred to her. Like the others, she thought it was a heart attack. Later Bob would tell her that he suspected foul play right from the start, conceding that he had an ugly mind. Later when they were lovers, he would tell her a lot of things. Right now she only knew that she disliked him. He seemed to take charge of the situation too readily, he was too assertive, too filled with his own sense of importance, too handsome (Alain Delon came to mind). They were qualities that reminded her of her husband.

As everyone returned to their seats, they steered clear of Daniel. Even those who had been sitting near him before, now made sure to keep their distance. It was as though death were contagious, Jean thought. She herself moved back to the fourth row where the anonymous drunk was seated. He was the first person she had ever seen show up at a meeting smashed out of his mind, reeking of alcohol. He was an elderly man and his clothes were skimpy. He had probably come in here to get out of the cold snowy weather, and would rather be somewhere else drinking.

Strangely enough, Jean didn't want a drink. She couldn't imagine why not. The man she loved was dead. *Daniel was dead.* Why wasn't she more upset? But it didn't seem to register. All the talk she had ever heard about shock and delayed reactions buzzed through her mind. That was undoubtedly it, she thought, she was too stunned to feel anything, it had happened too fast. It would hit her later. Suddenly, the drunk got to his feet.

"I can't hang around here all day," he cried in a panic-stricken voice. "I've got to get a shot. A man's dead, for Christ's sake. I need a shot!"

"Take it easy, Pop," Peter said.

"*You* take it easy," the drunk said contemptuously. "And don't call me Pop. I'm not your father."

He was heading for the door when Bob stopped him, urged him to sit down, offered him a smoke, spoke softly to him, persuasively. The drunk's hands were shaking (like Daniel's at the end, Jean thought, feeling sick), and he kept repeating: "I've got to get a shot. I'm a very sick man. Don't anyone understand?"

She understood. Everyone in the room understood. They were all sober.

☜4☞

By the time the police got around to questioning Jean, the room was buzzing with talk of murder. It started with Renee who was the fifth person to be interrogated.

The police had roped off the section in which Daniel was sitting when he died, asked everybody to wait in back, and then a detective began to talk to each person separately using the small kitchen at the rear. Afterward, people left immediately. Without exception they all came away looking furtive, as though they'd been asked not to reveal something important. Only Renee broke the vow of silence.

"Murder at AA!" she said indignantly, on her way out. "No place is safe anymore in this rotten city."

"*Murder?*" Jean said.

But Renee had rushed by, her rougeless cheeks flushed with excitement, leaving behind a horrified group of people. Now almost two hours later a police photographer was taking pictures of the room, lab technicians milled around dusting for fingerprints, uniformed men were stationed inside and out, chalk marks had been made on the floor surrounding the chair where Daniel's body still remained, grotesquely slumped over. Why hadn't it been taken away yet, Jean wondered. When she tried to go to the bathroom a few minutes before, a policewoman in plain clothes was asked to accompany her.

"What for?" Jean wanted to know.

"To make sure you don't flush anything down the toilet that you oughtn't to," was the answer.

For a moment Jean did not understand. Then slowly, it became clear. Since Daniel had not been shot, knifed, or strangled, he must have been poisoned, but the search for evidence to that effect had so far revealed nothing. She noticed one of the cops methodically going through the contents of the wastebasket in the anteroom, the same wastebasket in which Laura had thrown that tear-soaked Kleenex.

Daniel was alive then. Jean could not get it through her head that he was dead, that she would never see him again. The door to the kitchen swung open, and Marcel came out. The familiar pipe was clamped between his

42

teeth, and he was shaking his head, muttering something in French. His eyes carefully avoided Jean's as he headed for the front door. She was next in line and she turned to Betty.

"If I don't get a chance to talk to you afterward, why don't you and Peter meet me at the coffee shop?"

Betty nodded gravely. "Sure, kid. We'll be there as soon as we can."

Peter did not glance up; he stared at the floor as though the shock of Daniel's death was too much for him to comprehend. He looked even younger and more boyish than usual. Behind him were six people waiting to be questioned. Most were familiar faces that Jean saw every day, and she found it hard to believe that one of them might shield a murderer. Yet it was possible. She looked at them closely. Laura, Constance, Vanderbilt, Hugh, and two total strangers.

Laura had been crying earlier. Perhaps she harbored grievances toward Daniel that nobody guessed at, grievances which could have culminated in murder. Jean once read that the police always suspected members of the victim's immediate family first.

Constance might have been the woman in Daniel's apartment late Sunday night. If so, her relationship with him went far beyond the casual one they assumed at Clean Slate. How much did Daniel actually mean to Constance? Enough to kill him, if she realized she had lost him?

Vanderbilt was the group's only black regular. He had a militant past, and claimed he was just starting to get rid of his prejudice. But what if he was lying? Before Daniel went on tour, Vanderbilt lashed out at him derisively calling him "the tall blond god," and saying that whities like Daniel, with all of society's advantages, made niggers like him mad. Mad enough to turn violent?

Hugh was a fashionable hairdresser, who resembled Woody Allen. He puzzled Jean because he did not seem to belong at AA. He almost never spoke about his problems or shared his successes. At times, Jean suspected he wasn't an alcoholic at all. Then why did he attend meetings every day? Had he passed himself off as an alcoholic in order to be near someone he had it in for? Daniel?

The two strangers were an unknown quantity. One was a short, stocky, tired-looking businessman. The other was the drunk. *Any one of them could have done it*, Jean thought. Bob was not among them. He must have spoken to the police and left while she was in the bathroom. She remembered him turning around in his seat when Daniel said *Jean.* She also remembered the angry accusation on his face right after Daniel died. Surely, Bob didn't suspect her of . . . ?

The detective in charge was a tall, good-looking Puerto Rican named Rodriguez. Seated next to him, taking notes, was the policewoman who had accompanied Jean to the bathroom. Rodriguez introduced her as Detective Adams. They were both in plain clothes, and Adams' purse lay open on the table in front of her, a revolver clearly visible. The two police officers were drinking coffee. Jean sat down at the formica table, suddenly aware that her heart was pounding.

"How long did you know the deceased?" Rodriguez asked, after announcing that anything she said could be used in evidence.

"A little over a year."

"Would you tell me how you happened to meet him?"

"He was here the first time I came to a meeting. My husband had died recently and I'd been drinking a lot. So I decided to join AA. And Daniel was here," she finished lamely.

"What did your husband die of, Mrs. Neelie?"

"He was killed in a car crash."

"I see." Rodriguez spoke softly. "I imagine that a lot

44

of people were here that first day. What brought you and the deceased together?"

Jean stared at the revolver in the policewoman's purse, wondering if she had ever used it. "I don't understand the question."

"How did you and the deceased happen to become friends?"

"He was the first person to speak to me when I walked in here. I was very nervous, and Daniel—Mr. Streatham—tried to put me at ease. He'd been in the program for a number of years, and he understood what I was going through. He was being kind."

"I see."

Jean doubted if he could. Could anyone who was not an alcoholic possibly appreciate those first few moments of terror, when by your very presence you were publicly admitting your addiction? Admitting it and willfully, painfully, regretfully abandoning it? She didn't think so. Only another alcoholic knew how much guts that took, and how much fear was involved.

"So you and the deceased became friends."

The way Rodriguez said it, it was a question.

"Yes."

"*Just* friends, Mrs. Neelie?"

"At the beginning, yes. Later, our relationship changed."

"Go on."

She swallowed. "Eventually, we became lovers."

"When was that?"

"About six months ago."

Detective Adams was writing it all down. Jean felt as naked as she had earlier in the bathroom, when she changed the tampon in front of her.

"Please continue," Rodriguez said. "You became lovers six months ago. And then what?"

"Three months ago Daniel went on the road with a play. I imagine you know he was an actor. I didn't see him again until he returned to New York this past weekend."

"Did anything significant take place over the weekend?"

"We broke up. Daniel told me he was going back to his wife. They had been separated, I thought they were getting a divorce. Anyhow, he said he was going back to her, and it was all over between us. His wife's name is Laura—"

"I'm aware of that. On which day did the deceased tell you it was over?"

Jean wished he would stop calling Daniel "the deceased." It sounded so morbid.

"Sunday," she said.

"Did you have any communication with him after that? Aside from Clean Slate, that is?"

She thought of the telephone call she'd made to Daniel late Sunday night, when the woman sounding like Constance had answered. Constance had not yet spoken to Rodriguez, she was still waiting outside.

"No," Jean said. "There was nothing further to say."

Suddenly, Rodriguez' tone changed. It was no longer soft and insinuating. "Jean, do you have any idea why the deceased spoke your name just before dying?"

She felt as though she had been punched in the stomach. Who had told Rodriguez? Who, besides her, heard Daniel? Bob.

"I can't possibly imagine," she said.

"Then you admit that the last thing he said before losing consciousness was *Jean?*"

"Yes."

"And you were the only person present by that name?"

"Yes. At least I think so. There were a couple of newcomers at the meeting. Daniel might have meant *Gene,* a man's name."

"We're aware of that, but it doesn't seem to be the

case. And it suggests nothing to you? The deceased speaking your name with his last breath?"

She shook her head helplessly. "Nothing at all. It's very mysterious."

"Mysterious," the detective said. "Okay, here's an easy one. Would you say the deceased was a heavy smoker? Light smoker? Moderate?"

"Could you please stop calling him that? Daniel was a very heavy smoker. Four packs a day. I tried to get him to cut down, but he refused."

"Did you love him?"

Rodriguez sure didn't crap around, she thought.

"Yes."

"And how did you feel on Sunday, when he told you it was over?"

"How do you think?" To her surprise, tears had come to her eyes. "I was very angry, very hurt."

"Did you kill him, Mrs. Neelie?"

"No. I most certainly did not."

"Thank you. We may have to speak to you again."

Jean stood up.

"Oh, just one more thing. Did you help yourself to coffee before the meeting started?"

"Yes, I did."

"And do you normally drink coffee at Clean Slate?"

"No, not normally."

"You can go."

Jean felt Rodriguez' eyes on her as she walked out of the room. She was drained, yet her mind was racing with questions. Why had the detective wanted to know about Daniel's smoking habits? About her coffee habits? Had it been Bob who told the police that Daniel said *Jean*, or someone else sitting nearby? Did Rodriguez really think she killed Daniel? The fact that he was killed at all was astonishing. Daniel never appeared to have enemies, only friends, well-wishers, fans. She had been his biggest fan, but even fans could turn against the

47

love object in cold destruction. She herself had confessed to Betty on Sunday that she would like to kill Daniel. And now he had been killed, coldly, carefully, and the killer was walking around.

When she emerged into the meeting room, Daniel's body was gone, but the investigation was still going on. Police were everywhere, examining, measuring, removing. The murder would be in all the papers and on TV, she realized, looking at the people who still remained on line. Betty seemed tired, disheveled from the strain of waiting. One stocking was ripped and her lipstick had been chewed off.

"How was it?" she asked.

"Not too bad." Jean laughed unsteadily. "They haven't arrested me yet."

Betty did not laugh. Neither did Peter. One look at Jean's face, and he said: "He really was knocked off, wasn't he?" As though up until then, he hadn't been able to grasp it.

Betty was watching her with concern, afraid that Jean intended to walk into the nearest bar and get smashed.

"I feel like it," Jean admitted. "But I'm not going to do it. I promise."

"We'll see you at the coffee shop," Betty said. "Just as soon as we get through here."

Peter seemed too lost in his own grief to say anything more. He was taking his friend's death especially hard, Jean thought. She felt sorry for him.

⋐ 5 ⋑

Daniel would have gotten the part if he hadn't been killed. That's what Peter was thinking as he watched Jean leave. *The son of a bitch would have beaten me out of the part. Easily!*

48

Yesterday morning, both actors had auditioned for the lead role in a brilliant new play scheduled for Broadway that fall. And as much as Peter hated to admit it, Daniel's reading was flawless, blessed with magic, magnetic. In comparison, his own was merely competent. The two men had left the theater together to walk over to Clean Slate.

"You were great, old buddy, simply great," Peter told him. "Your name will be up in lights before long."

Daniel looked at him, surprised. "Do you really think I was good? I felt kind of rusty after hibernating in the Midwest."

Peter couldn't believe it. When it came to women, Daniel's self-confidence was limitless, but professionally he had no idea of his own worth. Peter was the exact opposite, he now realized, feeling slightly sick at the thought, the guilt, at what he tried most of the time not to think about: the fact that nice, handsome, talented Peter might be gay. His relationship with Betty only compounded his worst doubts because he knew that a lot of people figured she was a lesbian, and what if (back at home base) she *were*? What did that say about him?

But in terms of his career, Peter had a much surer grasp on himself, and while he might not be an inspired actor he knew he was good. That was why the rivalry with Daniel doubly frustrated him. *Good* was not the same as *great*, and Peter suspected that if he worked his tail off for the next hundred years, he would never be able to touch Daniel's genius. It was something you were born with, the sages said, and he felt convinced now they were right. Daniel sure as hell had been born with it.

"I should be so rusty," Peter had said, laughing.

But secretly, he didn't think it was very funny. He was envious, jealous; he wanted that part so badly there was nothing he wouldn't do for it. Well, almost nothing. Parts like that were gems, rare and infinitely desirable.

What's more, the queen who was going to direct the play was an old friend and owed him. Peter knew that if it were at all possible, the grateful director would have given him first chance at it. And queenie had plenty to be grateful to Peter for.

When queenie's young lover walked out on him some years before, Peter had walked in and virtually kept him from blowing his brains out. Peter took over the household; he cooked, cleaned, and saw to it that queenie ate three meals a day and slept at night without pills. Peter tried not to think about the fact that he had also kept the director satisfied sexually, and when he did he blamed it on booze. He was still drinking at the time and gin did strange things to him, made him even more passive than he generally was. It was pleasurable to lean back and just let queenie do his stuff, feed queenie in more ways than one, keep queenie from going totally berserk, *save another human being's life*, was how Peter looked upon it as he drunkenly, philosophically, came in queenie's mouth.

But now that Daniel had showed up in New York several days ahead of schedule, the possibility that queenie would honor old debts was a dim one. For the fact was that the director had always been a respected pro, and as such would realize that Daniel was the actor he needed to catapult this play to Broadway success. Daniel said he read about the play in *Variety* and returned from the Midwest expressly to audition for it. There was no doubt in Peter's mind that, barring a catastrophe, Daniel was as good as cast in the lead right now.

"I should have been more restrained in that scene with my father," Daniel was saying, as the two of them trudged along. "I think I hammed it up too much, don't you?"

"You were the epitome of restraint," Peter truthfully replied. "Your tone was perfect."

Daniel clapped him on the back. "You weren't so bad yourself, amigo."

Peter still felt guilty about the way he had finagled and maneuvered the last role away from Daniel in *That Championship Season*, only to lose it later to another actor. He didn't blame Daniel for getting angry at him, for not talking to him all those years. They probably would still not be talking if their mutual alcoholism hadn't brought them together at Clean Slate. Peter now wished they'd never become friends again—it was harder to hurt a friend, much harder. But he wanted that part, and he was sure he could get it if Daniel were eased out of the running.

Barring a catastrophe, he had thought yesterday, and today that catastrophe had occurred. A passive kind of catastrophe, a passive murder: poison was used by passive people. And as Peter stood patiently in line waiting to be questioned by the police, he wished that he were able to feel more guilty about Daniel's death but he couldn't. He merely felt relieved as hell. The lead role was now virtually his.

৯ 6 ৫

A surprise was waiting for Jean when she got outside. Television crews had set up their cameras and were photographing the exterior of the Clean Slate brownstone. Several reporters rushed up to her, mikes in their hands.

"Can you tell us what happened?"

"How well did you know the murdered man?"

"Has there ever been a murder at AA before this?"

"Was Mr. Streatham a personal friend of yours?"

"Do you believe that alcoholics have especially violent personalities?"

Jean brushed them aside, refusing to answer any of the

questions, and hurried down the street. The coffee shop which the group used as a hangout after meetings was, fortunately, not far away. When she got there, Marcel and O'Brien had taken a table along with the Eurasian girl Jean noticed earlier, and Eleanor who was knitting again.

The four of them waved to Jean, but despite the fact that there was room at their table they didn't invite her over. She wondered if they knew that Daniel had dropped her, and was planning to go back to Laura when he died. Could that possibly account for their coolness? She hoped not. She didn't want to believe they were insensitive enough to penalize her twice for losing him, once in life and again in death.

She sat down at a booth and looked at the menu, but her mind wasn't on food. She watched the others across the room. *Any one of them could have done it.*

Marcel had been an active member of the French Resistance during the Second World War, and had first-hand knowledge of killing. He said that everyone in the maquis was prepared to swallow a deadly poison if picked up for questioning by the Nazis. So beneath Marcel's charming Maurice Chevalier facade lurked a ruthless personality familiar with violence.

Eleanor might have been secretly attracted to Daniel and tried to entice him into an affair. If he rejected her (as Jean felt certain he would), could Eleanor have become vindictive enough to kill him? It seemed farfetched, and yet Eleanor's life was spent in the snaring of men . . . if not for marriage, then for sex. Failure in either department might result in violent retribution.

O'Brien had lost everything he valued because of alcohol. His wife and children, his business. Jean suspected that beneath his disgruntled exterior, O'Brien was seething with unexpressed rage. Did he want to get back at the world? Was murder a way?

The Eurasian girl was a newcomer, but even so not

above suspicion. The very fact that she was present at today's meeting meant she had as much opportunity to kill Daniel as anyone else.

Jean put her menu down and walked over to their table, uninvited. It was not like her to take such a bold step, except in the old days when she drank. Once she approached a group of Arabs at Studio 54 and asked them all to dance with her. As they courteously refused, she started to feel faint, dizzy, and slowly crumpled to the floor in front of them, smashed out of her mind on brandy alexanders.

"I imagine you've been talking about the murder," she now said to the table of four. "Does anyone have an idea who did it?"

"Not a clue," O'Brien replied. "The problem is going to be motive. Who'd want to knock off *Daniel?* That handsome, charming, charismatic man? The cops are going to have a hell of a time solving this one."

"I hope not," she said, surprised by the underlying resentment in his voice.

He went blithely on. "Did you know that if a large-city homicide isn't wrapped up within the first forty-eight hours, the odds against it being solved go down to practically zero? There are so many murders in New York, some even go unreported."

"That will not happen in this case," Marcel said. "Not with all those television people outside Clean Slate, pushing and shoving. They even tried to interview Francine."

He introduced Jean to the Eurasian girl, who was wearing a pair of very unusual drop earrings, made of silver and stained glass. When she moved her head, they tinkled.

"Francine designed them herself," Marcel pointed out. "She is a talented jewelry designer, though anyone who has Oriental blood in this country is automatically considered untrustworthy and suspicious."

"Especially if you've converted to Judaism," Francine

53

said. "Then you're looked upon as some kind of religious freak. Rodriguez really gave me a hard time—you'd think *I* had poisoned Daniel! What puzzles me is how the killer managed it, with all those people present."

"Perhaps he slipped the poison in Daniel's coffee when nobody was looking," Marcel suggested. "It's possible."

"Somebody is always looking," O'Brien said.

Eleanor glanced up from her knitting. "What I don't understand is why Daniel was murdered at all, if he doesn't have any money. I thought people were usually murdered for financial gain. It's the only reason I can imagine for killing someone."

"Or for marrying him," O'Brien remarked.

"Whoever killed Daniel had something on his mind besides money," Jean said thoughtfully. "I would love to know what it was. I still can't believe this has happened. It means that one of us is not what he or she pretends to be."

The four of them stared at her expressionlessly. Whatever they were thinking, they were intent upon keeping it to themselves. Jean's worst fear about being relegated to the sidelines once more seemed to be coming true. Without Daniel, she simply did not count. She started to walk back to her booth.

"The empty aspirin bottle," Francine whispered. "Hasn't she heard all the commotion about it?"

"Pipe down," O'Brien said.

☜7☞

O'Brien wished he'd never made that snide remark a few minutes ago about Daniel being charming and charismatic. He didn't like the way Jean looked at him, as though she sensed the depth of his resentment. Well, it was too late now to take it back, too late to take *any-*

thing back, he thought . . . what's done, was done. And if he wanted to be truly honest, he didn't regret his hasty actions. Why should he? Daniel had shown himself to be a real prick when he turned down O'Brien's heartfelt request for a three-hundred-dollar loan this past Christmas. Three hundred stinking dollars, and the self-righteous bastard refused him.

O'Brien had hesitated to call Daniel in Chicago, but after thinking it over, he decided that Daniel was the only person he knew who had the money and should be willing to help out a fellow alcoholic. Also, actors were used to living on a financial seesaw and could appreciate it when others fell on hard times. At least that was O'Brien's reasoning before he put the call through. And it wasn't as though he wanted the money for himself, it was to buy Christmas presents for his three kids who lived with their mother in Seattle.

His guilt about not being able to support his family as he would have liked to was always gnawing at him, and never more so than when the holiday season rolled around. He knew how much it meant to kids. But he was still paying off debts he had incurred during his alcoholic period—enormous, burdensome, never-ending debts—and he had just enough money left over to scrape by without starving. Last Christmas he'd been reduced to sending his kids a load of cheap toys, and he felt like a creep. This year he wanted to go to F.A.O. Schwartz and buy the joint out.

"I'm sorry, old buddy," Daniel said over the crackling wires. "But since sobering up, I've quit lending money. The only reason I did it in the past was because I felt so damned guilty about my drinking. Hell, I used to throw the green stuff around as though I could buy back my self-respect with it. Now I feel that unless it's a matter of life and death, I don't have to pay all that penance."

"But it *is* a matter of life and death," O'Brien had

pleaded. "You don't have kids, you don't know how low a father can feel—"

At that strategic moment they were cut off. O'Brien waited at home for Daniel to call back—he knew that Daniel had the number (all AA people had each others' numbers for emergencies)—but the call never came. Daniel hadn't even cared enough to make that simple decent gesture of goodwill, and then O'Brien wondered whether Daniel had deliberately hung up on him. He stewed for weeks afterward, just thinking about the actor's heartlessness. This past Christmas O'Brien's children received another batch of cheap toys that were probably broken by now. And yesterday, when he saw Daniel for the first time in three months, all the bastard said was: "I like your cowboy hat, old buddy. Someone give it to you for Christmas?"

O'Brien had wanted to kill him.

❧ 8 ❧

Jean had ordered lunch and was wondering what Francine meant about an empty aspirin bottle. She remembered seeing one of the policemen going through the contents of the wastebasket in the anteroom. Had he found an empty aspirin bottle? Was that what the commotion was about? Jean wished she knew. She wished she were not sitting here alone by herself, dying for a drink. Francine and the three others had just left (without so much as a good-bye) when Betty and Peter finally arrived. Jean had never been so glad to see two people in her life.

Once after Frank died, she made a luncheon date with two women she knew whose husbands were also corporate lawyers. She had never been especially friendly with them while Frank was alive, but she decided that it would be good to get out of the apartment, see people, try to become social again. Both women were driving in from Mamaroneck, and unfortunately traffic was very heavy that day.

Jean arrived at the restaurant ahead of them and ordered a sherry while she waited (sherry presented a respectable front, while packing the wallop of a double scotch). When she finished the first drink, her friends still had not arrived and she ordered another. It wasn't until the fifth sherry that she began to get nervous about them, her mind flashing to automobile accidents, injuries, hospitals, death. She was so lost in catastrophic thought that she didn't realize they were finally standing before her taking off their fur coats.

"I'm so glad to see you." she said, unsteadily getting to her feet to embrace them. She noticed that they drew back, a suspicious look on both their faces.

"What have you been drinking, dear?" the older of the two asked.

"Only a little sherry."

They exchanged knowing glances.

"We'd better get some food into you," the younger woman said. "Foolish girl, drinking on an empty stomach."

"It was only sherry," she said weakly.

She never saw them again. Three weeks later she joined AA.

Betty and Peter now sank down opposite Jean, exhausted from the police interrogation.

"And I still have to work tonight," Betty said. "I don't know how I'm going to *stand* on my feet, let alone dance. It never occurred to me before, but after meeting Rodriguez I've decided that there must be a lot of Puerto Rican overachievers floating around New York. I'm just sorry that one of them was assigned to this case."

"Did he say anything about an empty aspirin bottle?" Jean asked. "I understand one turned up."

They exchanged quizzical glances.

"What does aspirin have to do with Daniel's murder?" Peter asked.

"It's the bottle, not the aspirin, that I was thinking of. Francine, that Eurasian girl, just mentioned it."

"Oh, is that her name?" Peter's solemn freckled face came to life. "I've never seen her before. Who is she?"

Before Jean could reply, Betty began to discuss the menu in elaborate and painstaking detail. Was she simply jealous of a beautiful stranger, Jean wondered, or did she want to deroute the conversation for another reason? The murder seemed to have affected her strongly; she looked tense, on edge, her usual good humor gone.

"Perhaps the murderer filled an empty aspirin bottle with poison," Jean suggested, "dumped the poison in Daniel's coffee, and then threw the bottle away. The police could have found it in that wastebasket we keep in the anteroom. You know, underneath the long table."

Betty glanced at Peter, and went pale.

"That's an interesting theory," he said. "But why would the killer leave the evidence lying around? Now if it were me, I would have flushed it down the toilet. Much smarter."

"Not if the bathroom were occupied," Jean said.

As it had been, she now realized, first by Daniel and then by herself escaping from Eleanor.

"Even if someone were in the bathroom—" Peter began when Betty abruptly cut him off.

"I've been listening to this kind of morbid talk for hours, and I can't stand anymore. Enough is enough. I'm terribly sorry that Daniel has been killed. I know how much he meant to both of you, but frankly I'm bored. Can we please talk about something else?"

But Betty did not look bored. she looked uneasy, nervous. Why was she so anxious to change the subject? In contrast, Peter appeared guilelessly anxious to go on dissecting the murder that had just taken place. Somewhere Jean had read that the killer always wanted to talk about his crime, and felt frustrated because he couldn't. A long time ago Peter and Daniel had been deadly enemies, professional rivals. Was it possible that the old competition recently flared up again, and exploded into violence?

She stole a glance at Betty's pinched face. Did Betty have reason to believe that Peter had killed Daniel?

It was a startling notion.

৯9৩

That evening Jean dined at home, alone. The table, an elegant Hepplewhite which seated six, had been inherited from Jean's mother as had most of the other furniture in the room. In Baltimore where Jean's mother grew up, dining was considered a formal affair and Jean still clung to the tradition. In her drinking days she'd clung to it even more tenaciously, as though trying to prove to herself that as whacked out as she was on booze she could still go through the motions of gracious living.

Once she started sobbing uncontrollably in the middle of the first course (coquilles st. jacques) for reasons she could not explain to a startled Thelma. But after gulping down three glasses of Rhine wine, she felt better and was able to continue with the meal. Another time she fell off the chair and hurt her dignity. But it was only when she ended up eating peach melba underneath the table, in a fit of paranoia, that Thelma became worried.

Tonight Thelma had prepared beef stroganoff with green noodles, a mixed salad, and fruit compote. Jean absolutely adored having Thelma come in three days a week to cook, clean, and generally take care of her. She had grown dependent upon Thelma's cooking, with the enormous portions for leftovers the next day. But tonight she felt so hungry that she finished everything and even gorged on gingersnaps and ice cream afterward.

Clark Gable followed her into the paint-splattered studio when she was through. Her mind still on the murder, Jean stared blindly at the unfinished canvas. It was a night view from her terrace with buildings disappearing into a starless sky and no sign of people anywhere. She had used a lot of heavy, somber colors in an attempt to show a rather haunting picture of New York, but it didn't work. And at the moment, she couldn't think how to make it right. She had turned on the six o'clock news earlier, and sure enough Daniel's murder was a television highlight. With the Clean Slate brownstone in the background, a reporter was trying to question several emerging people. Two of them (she recognized Bob and Constance) held their hands over their faces, not wishing to be identified. Vanderbilt, though, seemed delighted to answer questions.

"What's happening inside?" a reporter asked.

"A lot of confusion, man. A lot of nervousness. Everybody is looking at everybody else and wondering if the other guy is a dangerous killer." Vanderbilt laughed, enjoying this unexpected publicity. "Me, I'm a lush, I don't deny it. But murder just isn't in my league. I hope they catch the (bleep)."

"Do you think the police are close to an arrest?"

"Not yet, man. But it had to be someone in that room. Nobody left the meeting, and nobody came in after we were all seated." Vanderbilt laughed again. "It had to be one of us recovering drunks. We got a lot of violence in our souls when we come off the sauce."

It was an interesting point, Jean thought. Getting drunk was a way of releasing hostility and aggression. People who were used to having that outlet at their disposal would feel frustrated without it. It wasn't hard to

60

see how, in desperation, murder could occur. Betty's inexplicable behavior at the coffee shop still troubled her. There was one possible explanation for it. Betty was the murderer. That would account for her turning white at Jean's mention of the aspirin bottle. It would explain why Betty had been so anxious to change the dangerous subject.

There was only one hitch.

Betty had no motive. Jean corrected herself. Betty didn't have *much* motive. All Jean could see was that Betty disliked men, particularly men like Daniel who treated women unfairly. Was Betty a psychotic who imagined that death was what Daniel deserved for having thrown Jean over? It was possible, but unlikely. Peter didn't have much of a motive either. His old feud with Daniel had been patched up a long time ago, and from what Jean observed just yesterday, the two men appeared to be the best of friends. Yet Betty plainly knew something, suspected somebody.

A minute later, the obvious truth hit Jean. Betty suspected her! What an idiot she was not to have realized it before. Betty knew how upset she was on Sunday after she'd seen Daniel, how hurt and vengeful.

"*I hate him. I'd like to kill him,*" Jean had said.

And then Daniel *was* killed. How natural to assume that Jean had done it. How foolish, but how absolutely human. That was why Betty didn't want to talk about the murder. She was trying to keep Jean from breaking down and confessing the terrible truth in front of them. It all made sense now. She sprang to her feet and went into the living room to dial Betty's number at home. She should either be there or at Peter's.

The line was busy.

Betty had told Jean that she was planning to live with Peter after she'd been sober for an entire year. It was one of the restrictive tenets that AA members were strongly urged to consider: not to make any drastic changes in their lives during the first year of sobriety. The reasoning was that change brought pressures, which might cause the recovering alcoholic to start drinking again. It always amazed Jean that Betty had been sober for less time than she, but handled it so well that Jean turned to her for guidance. Before moving to New York, Betty had taken care of a terminally ill mother and Jean often wondered whether it was that experience which gave her the fortitude Jean relied upon so much.

She tried the number again, and Betty answered.

"I've been trying to figure out your screwy behavior this afternoon," Jean said, "and it finally hit me. You think I killed Daniel, don't you?"

There was a long awkward pause, and then Betty softly said: "I wish you hadn't asked."

"I knew it. My hunch was right. Please don't feel bad, Betty. I understand why you jumped to that conclusion."

"Bad? I feel like shit. You have no idea what it's like to accuse your best friend of murder."

"Stop worrying. I didn't do it."

Betty's voice was peculiar. "Sure."

"No, you don't understand, I really didn't do it."

"What the hell difference does it make?" Betty said angrily.

"What difference does *what* make?"

"I understand your reasons. How hurt you were, how much you loved the guy, what a bastard he turned out to be. Believe it or not, kid, I am sympathetic. Look what Marge Farber did to Cappolino when he ditched her."

"Who?"

"Don't you remember the famous Carl Cappolino murder case back in the late sixties?"

"No."

"Never mind. It's not important."

"It is if you think that because Daniel ditched me, I went crazy and killed him."

"It wouldn't be the first time it happened."

"Betty, you're not listening. I repeat. I did not kill Daniel Streatham."

For a moment there was absolute silence.

"Are you serious?" Betty asked.

Jean felt her patience give way. "Do I look like a murderer? What's the matter with you? I thought you knew me better than that."

"Take it easy. I'm sorry if I hurt your feelings, but I was convinced you were guilty."

"Well, I'm not. Okay?"

"Then how come you knew about the aspirin bottle?"

Jean resented having to defend herself to her best friend. Was it so hard for Betty to believe in her innocence?

"I told you," she said. "I overheard Francine mention it. Besides, it might not have happened like that."

"I don't follow you."

"I don't know for sure if the poison was in an aspirin bottle or a milk bottle. I was just theorizing this afternoon."

"Theorizing?" Betty sounded incredulous. "Look, kid, you don't have to lie to me."

Betty really and truly thought she had killed Daniel! The knowledge of her friend's suspicions hurt Jean more than she would have imagined. It was as though Betty had never understood her at all.

"I'm not lying," Jean said.

"Then are you saying that that *isn't* how Daniel was killed?"

"Since I didn't kill him, how the hell should I know!"

"There's no need to shout."

"I'm sorry."

But she wasn't. She was angry, hurt.

"Wouldn't it be funny if it turns out that was what

JOYCE ELBERT

actually happened?" Betty said. "Just the way you imagined it?"

"Very funny. Hilarious."

Jean slammed down the receiver and looked at the antique Terry clock over the fireplace. It was a few minutes past nine, and she couldn't think of what to do for the remainder of the evening. She had been going to paint, but now she didn't feel like it. She was too angry. How could Betty have misunderstood her so completely? If their conversation had taken place in the old days, she would have poured herself a cognac and turned on TV. Several cognacs later, she would be crying and feeling sorry for herself because her best friend thought she was a murderer. By the time the cognac bottle was empty, the television screen would be a square of snow and the evening long since over.

Drinking consumed a great deal of time. In fact, she never realized how much until she stopped and joined AA. One of the first questions that plagued her was how she was going to fill the hours, now that she was sober. Like all alcoholics, Jean relished the time-consuming ritual of drinking . . . buying the bottle, unwrapping it, getting out the ice, selecting a glass, deciding upon a mixer, pouring, tasting, adjusting, and finally (bliss!) drinking. And then doing it all over again. And again.

Her mind drifted when she drank, she visited foreign lands, had imaginary conversations, was witty, charming, gorgeous, and breezily self-confident. Virtues, God knew, she did not normally possess. Television was more interesting when she drank, Johnny Carson was funnier, sitcoms were livelier, movies were never dull, even commercials didn't bother her. Nothing bothered her when she was drinking, because nothing existed outside of her drink. It alone was real. That liquid inside the glass. Nothing else mattered, other things were only adjuncts that could be dispensed with if they happened to interfere in any way with her mood while she was drinking.

How often had she experimented to try to capture just the right mood, and hold it forever? Keep it suspended in time, exquisitely, infinitely, her very own gossamer secret? But the right mood continued to elude her. She was still looking for it when Thelma found her over a year ago, at two o'clock in the afternoon, passed out in her new John Kloss nightgown, reeking of Polish vodka.

Jean winced at the painful memory. Alcohol was disgusting, it turned you into an animal. Then why did she still want that cognac? Courvoisier VSOP. She could almost taste it.

"Come on, Clark Gable," she said, resolutely. "We're going to bed."

Whenever Jean became drink-crazy, she either called someone at AA to talk it out or reread chapter five of AA's Big Book.

Tonight she decided upon the latter procedure. Once she was safely under the covers, she opened the familiar blue book and turned to page fifty-eight. *Rarely have we seen a person fail who has thoroughly followed our path.* She read until she could keep her eyes open no longer, then turned out the light and sighed in the darkness.

"Thank God for Alcoholics Anonymous."

Wednesday, March 1

❧ 1 ❧

It was clear and sunny the next morning, yet Jean felt immensely depressed. She could not shake off the uneasiness about Daniel's death, the nasty way in which he had died.

The killing was a personal affront to every Clean Slate member who had expressed love, trust, and compassion for his fellow sufferer. To realize that a crass murderer had wandered into their midst, corrupting and defiling the essence of their self-help program by this terrible act, not only frightened Jean, it made her mad as hell. It was like spitting in her face, telling her there was no good in this world, telling her that evil could ultimately triumph. She refused to believe it.

"ACTOR DIES AT AA."

The murder had made the front page of the Daily News. There was a large gruesome photograph of Daniel's body covered by a white sheet being taken away to the morgue. Inside were photos of Daniel at a younger age, looking very handsome, plus a recounting of what happened yesterday. The News strongly hinted at poison as means of murder. *A Mickey Finn in the Java?* read the caption.

In *The Times*, the story was on the first page of the Metropolitan Section. *Suspicion of murder* was as far as that august paper would go. It said that Daniel was thirty-six, had played in an off-Broadway revival of *A Moon for the Misbegotten*, and after the autopsy his body would be flown home to Ohio for the funeral. Surviving him were his wife and parents. Girlfriends weren't mentioned in obituaries, Jean thought wryly, as the telephone began to ring. She hoped it would be Betty, apologetic about last night, but it wasn't. Instead a woman who refused to identify herself, said: "Daniel lied to you. He never intended to go back to Laura."

Before Jean could utter a word, the mysterious woman had hung up. She remember the woman in Daniel's apartment Sunday night, and wondered if they were one and the same. This voice had been deeper, but if it was Constance she could have tried to disguise it. *Daniel lied to you.* It was like a voice from the grave bringing him back to hurt her again, and when she left for Clean Slate she found herself walking slowly, listlessly.

In a little while a strange thing happened. Instead of turning down her regular street, she kept on going until she realized that her feet were taking her to the Museum of Modern Art. She didn't have the vaguest idea why. For many years the museum had been her stamping grounds, her refuge. She used to escape there after painting and haunt the cluster of rooms upstairs for sustenance, survival. Frank had been indifferent to art, rarely expressing a preference for anything, including her own work. A mild diversion, was his attitude toward painting, nothing to get excited about.

Was that why she had returned today? Because she was filled with self-doubts . . . about her artistic ability . . . about her ability to hold a man . . . *Daniel lied to you . . . ?*

Lichtenstein's *Drowning Girl* still hung on the left near the windows that overlooked the sculpture garden. The garden was shivering in the cold, Moore's gigantic pieces covered with snow. In Lichtenstein's pop painting, the girl had blue hair and tears in her eyes. She was saying: "I don't care! I'd rather sink than call Brad for help!"

Behind it was Andy Warhol's famous silk-screen

painting of Marilyn Monroe with her garish green eye-shadow. Jean felt a nostalgic affection for MM, having been nineteen and studying full-time at the Art Students League when Marilyn died in 1962. She met Frank that year at a party given by one of the girls in her anatomy class. The party was held in the Dakota, in a huge oak-paneled apartment which delighted Jean by its elegance. She had just accepted a glass of champagne from the waiter when Frank appeared, put her glass on a table, and wordlessly drew her out to the dance floor.

That was how it all began.

She wondered what he saw in her, why he fell in love with her, and most curious of all why he asked her to marry him. In fact, the longer they remained married the more quizzical Jean became. They had practically nothing in common except for one of those fierce, unexplained chemical attractions. The sex was riveting, magnetic right up to the end. Yes, even when he was cheating on her. Still it was not a basis for marriage, and it now occurred to Jean (as she climbed the stairs to the second floor) that she never really had a marriage in the true sense of the word. What she'd had was a fifteen-year fuck.

She smiled to herself.

Most people wouldn't complain about a thing like that. It probably sounded okay. What the hell, women were always bitching about their sexual problems. They were unsatisfied, unfulfilled, unrealized. Well, Jean had been realized. And although it was nice that Frank turned out to be such a spectacular lover, it was a thing set apart. It was like being married, say, to a man who played the piano expertly. While he was playing the piano, everything was fine—terrific, in fact; yet it had nothing to do with any other area of their life together (he couldn't play the piano *forever*). That was what she objected to, and what Frank didn't understand. He called her a puritan.

"A puritan in thought, a wildcat in the sack," was his amused summation.

Jean couldn't explain that at times his erotic skills dismayed her. They seemed so technical, so impersonal, so disconnected with her. And that's exactly what they were, she realized after a while. That was why he could make love to any number of women and still come home and screw her too. And expect her to be happy.

"Most women would give their right tit to get a guy like me," was his immodest self-appraisal. "I don't have any problem getting it up, I'm always raring to go, and I give great head. What the hell more do you want? A string quartet in the background?"

At the top of the museum stairs was a Picasso oil: *The Studio*. The colors were bright, heartening. Jean liked it. What she especially liked was that you could never mistake a Picasso, except for certain paintings done during his Cubist period which looked like Braques. Otherwise you always knew it was Picasso, his style was unique. The same could be said of Edward Hopper, there was no possibility of confusion, ever. Their personalities were too strong, too exceptional, to possibly be confused with anyone else's. That was their genius.

The museum was crowded with people on their lunch hour. It was one o'clock. The speaker at Clean Slate would have finished talking about his alcoholism by now, and the group would be into the discussion part of the meeting. Jean wondered if anyone missed her. She wondered what it was like to have a nine-to-five job and try to absorb a little culture on your lunch hour. She never had a job in her life. Even if she hadn't married Frank, she wouldn't have been compelled to work. Her parents had thoughtfully set up a handsome trust fund for her.

"You're a golden girl," Frank said to her once, angrily. "You know shit about struggle, about what really goes on out there in the jungle. And you don't care. I envy you. You're the best kind of snob there is. A natural one."

She never understood what he was talking about.

When she left the museum, she walked north until Fifty-ninth Street, going past the heraldic St. Moritz Hotel and into the warm gemütlich confines of Rumpelmayer's. The restaurant, with its display of stuffed animals, was a long-time favorite of Jean's. Her parents used to take her here for toasted cheese sandwiches and hot chocolate with swirls of whipped cream when she was a child. And that was exactly what she wanted now. Then she would go to the movies.

She accepted the menu from the waitress with a feeling of guilty pleasure. This was like playing hookey from school, this leisurely, self-indulgent, carefree day. The restaurant was thinning out and Jean savored her lunch more than any in recent memory. Why didn't she do things like this more often? The museum, Rumpelmayer's, a movie. She had forgotten that these simple pleasures existed, were so readily available.

The movie Jean chose was *An Unmarried Woman.* She hadn't read the reviews, but she could identify with the title. The film was under way a few minutes when Michael Murphy told Jill Clayburgh that he had fallen in love with someone else and was leaving her. Jean didn't like that very much. She thought about Daniel telling her on Sunday that he was leaving to go back to Laura, that it was Laura he loved. Jill Clayburgh's face on the screen was exactly how Jean imagined she must have looked when Daniel said that: lost, dazed. She didn't stay for the rest of the movie. As she emerged into the bright wintry day, she felt lost. Where should she go now? What should she do?

It was times like this that Jean wished she and Frank had had a child. She would now be able to pick up a darling little boy or girl after school and have companionship, purpose. She knew it was an irrational way to look at their deliberate decision not to become parents.

"I just can't see you coping with a child," Frank had said. "You have your hands full with Clark Gable."

And she had accepted his judgment without argument, without comment. She wasn't even a real person then, merely a shadow of her dynamic decision-making husband. And yet he had died, and she—the weak one—lived on, with all of her problems rising to the surface as soon as he was gone. She was sorry now that she had skipped Clean Slate today. She missed hearing about problems similar to her own. She needed the daily reminder that she was an alcoholic, in order to stay sober.

It was getting colder. Jean stood at the corner of Fifth Avenue and shivered. Suddenly the image of a large scotch floated before her eyes, warm, inviting. She dug into her purse for the piece of chocolate she carried with her for just such moments, but she'd eaten it at the movie. The bar at the Plaza came to mind. How she longed to walk in there and order a drink. Just one. One lousy scotch to make up for *An Unmarried Woman*.

It was an old alcoholic trick of hers, to "reward" herself with a drink after something unpleasant or disappointing had happened. In the old days something disappointing was always happening. Once when she failed to receive any mail on Saturday and had nowhere to go that evening, she bought two bottles of Pouilly-Fuissé as an extra-special treat. She had a beastly hangover the next day which necessitated switching to something with a bite to it. For her depression, of course. Four martinis later, she wasn't depressed any longer. She was drunk again.

"Jean. I thought it was you. Where have you been?"

She looked up into the eyes of Bob, the accusing art director. But today those eyes were concerned and tender. A bright blue shirt and paisley tie could be seen beneath the narrow flaring coat he wore. In one hand he

carried the status L.L. Bean canvas bag, the other hand
touched the lapel of her mink cape. He really was very
attractive, she thought; he had a fabulous smile. She
never noticed it before.

"I went to the movies," she said, feeling childish. "Did
I miss anything?"

"I'll say. The cops showed up again." The light
turned green and he took her by the arm. "Do you have
time for a cup of coffee? I want to talk to you."

"What were the cops doing there?"

"That's what I want to talk about. There's something
you should know. Come to think of it, I'd rather have a
Perrier. Let's go the the Plaza." He turned her around,
then retraced their steps. "I hope you don't mind bars. I
rather like them myself, now that I'm off the sauce."

"What is it I should know?"

"It looks like you're the number-one suspect. Off the
record, so to speak."

There was no escape, Jean decided. Not in drinking
and not at the movies. Eventually, everything had to be
faced.

"What am I suspected of?"

Up ahead the wide impressive facade of the Plaza
beckoned.

"Killing your boyfriend," Bob said.

❧ 2 ❧

Detective Charles Henry Rodriguez paused at the corner of Fifth Avenue and Fifty-ninth Street, holding a
small blue Tiffany's shopping bag in one hand.

With the other hand, he unconsciously flicked a piece
of nonexistent lint off his black raincoat. He always felt
like a damned peasant in that elegant store, with its
snotty sales clerks who acted as though they were as

wealthy as the people they waited on, and a few minutes ago he had softly cursed his wife for being a sucker for prestige gifts. But now that he had caught a glimpse of the two people heading for the plaza, he redirected his ignoble thoughts about his wife and felt positively grateful to her for having a birthday in March.

Off in the distance Jean Neelie turned toward Bob Edwards, as they walked up the steps of the fashionable hotel. Interesting, Rodriguez thought with grim satisfaction, immensely interesting.

Earlier that afternoon he had found Jean's unexplained absence at Clean Slate highly suspect. And he still did. Where the hell was she, he had wondered at the time? None of her compatriots seemed to know, and except for Betty none seemed to care. When he asked them where they *thought* she might be, they just shrugged and said they had no idea, Jean was a very private person, she didn't confide in others. Rodriguez found that illuminating, but it didn't answer his question. Jean wasn't at home (he had rung her apartment). She wasn't detained at an office (she didn't have a job). And she hadn't been called to some school emergency (she was childless).

Yes, she could have had an appointment with a doctor, dentist, or psychiatrist, there was always that possibility. But after speaking to everyone at Clean Slate, Rodriguez came away with the feeling that unless it was literally a matter of life and death, recovering alcoholics never made appointments that conflicted with their AA meetings. Providing they took their sobriety seriously, AA was their first and foremost priority. What was it O'Brien had said only a few hours ago?

"They'd have to run me over with a Mack truck before I'd miss one of these meetings. I used to think I was a pretty tough, pretty independent character, but I'll tell you frankly that AA has become my lifeline to sanity. I haven't skipped a meeting in two years. I wouldn't dare."

The private statements of the others backed him up (except for Hugh, but he was a special case). And Jean Neelie certainly seemed to be taking her sobriety seriously, she hadn't touched a drop in more than a year. When Rodriguez pinned down her friend, Betty, she admitted that Jean was zealous about going to Clean Slate. *Why then had she stayed away today?* There was one strong possibility: Jean had killed Daniel, and the prospect of returning to the scene of her crime so soon after the fact made her feel queasy, uncomfortable.

Someone with less police experience than Rodriguez might have argued the point, saying: "But the murderer would never intentionally stay away. It would make her look too conspicuous, too obviously the murderer. It's the last thing in the world she would do."

Rodriguez knew better. He knew that no matter how much premeditated murderers congratulated themselves upon their neat, tidy, logical minds, logic and murder did not go hand in hand. The reason that Rodriguez knew this was very simple: murderers were amateurs. Okay, maybe they had successfully had one shot at killing before, but even so what were two murders compared with Rodriguez' fifteen years of tracking down killers for the NYPD? In terms of hard experience, just about nothing. And experience was what counted; without it carelessness resulted.

Furthermore, Rodriguez doubted that Daniel Streatham's killer had ever struck before. He felt relatively certain that although this had been a premeditated crime, it was also a crime of passion (the only question was *whose* passion?), and that meant the murderer was emotionally unstable. Daniel had not been killed for money or any other kind of financial gain. He was killed either because Jean Neelie hated him for leaving him, or

74

because Bob didn't know that Daniel had left her, or because Constance . . .

The third possibility drifted out of Rodriguez' mind as he watched the good-looking couple disappear into the Plaza. He wondered how accidental their meeting was. The only accidents Detective Charles Henry Rodriguez believed in were of the automobile variety, and that reminded him of something. He took out his pad and made a note: *double-check suspect's story of husband's death.*

Of course it would be downright stupid to lie to a cop about an easily traceable fact like that, but Rodriguez had heard of odder things happening when people were under pressure. Much odder. He flicked another piece of nonexistent lint off his black raincoat and started walking east to Constance's apartment. Constance hadn't been at today's meeting either, but he'd already spoken to her and was pretty sure he understood the reason why. Grief, plain and simple.

Unlike Jean Neelie who had just waltzed into the Plaza on the arm of a handsome man (they seemed to be her specialty), Constance was at home overcome with grief, the grief of a . . . Rodriguez stopped himself just in time for his hard-nosed, professional skepticism to set in . . . unless Constance had lied earlier on the telephone. He didn't think so, she seemed too shrewd to lie, but it was always best to keep an open mind in a case like this.

"Amateurs," Rodriguez mumbled to himself, as he started to walk faster.

❧ 3 ❧

" '*Where is Jean Neelie? Has she arrived yet?*' That's what Rodriguez kept shouting at us every ten minutes," Bob said. "He'd pop his head out from that kitchen room after speaking to someone, and say, '*Is Jean Neelie here yet?*' It was as though he was determined to make you appear guilty by virtue of not showing up."

The Oak Room of the Plaza was nearly deserted except for the two of them seated at the bar. Jean hadn't been at a bar since she stopped drinking, and it was an odd sensation. In the past, she had equated drinking with romance . . . champagne for two, a handsome couple silhouetted at a cozy corner table, their glasses clicking, inhibitions laughingly shed. . . . This sophisticated picture was glaringly at odds with her last sojourn at the Plaza, when Frank had to carry her to a taxi and she had no recollection of the ride home. The next morning, she couldn't even remember where she had been. Frank stared at her oddly as she admitted this unusual memory loss.

"I don't understand why Rodriguez was so eager to see me," she said now, sipping Perrier with lime. "I told him all I knew yesterday. How can he possibly think I killed Daniel? I loved him."

Bob flinched as though he found it painful to hear her talk about her former lover, and she couldn't help comparing the two men. Their appeal was totally different. Daniel had been taller, huskier, with more expressive features. Bob was restrained compact, his energy centered. Unlike Daniel's easy-going charm which people found so engaging, Bob radiated intensity. Seated only inches apart, Jean could feel its electric charge. Her previous dislike of him evaporated in a flash, and to her amazement she found herself wondering whether he made love in a different way from Daniel, a more explosive way perhaps. What was wrong with her? She was a suspect in a murder case, and all she could think of were two men's prowess in bed.

"Rodriguez never directly accused you of being the murderer, but he sure asked a lot of strange questions," Bob said. "He wanted to know what you were doing yesterday before the meeting started, whether you normally drink coffee at Clean Slate, whether it was customary for you to sit next to Daniel, whether I knew that you and Daniel had broken up over the weekend. Etcetera. In my opinion, he wanted us to think you were the prime suspect."

"Really?" she shivered at the thought. "Why?"

"Maybe because if you had enemies, they would then feel free to run you down. And anyone who was fond of Daniel would become outraged, talkative. It's Rodriguez' way of getting information."

"But *everyone* was fond of Daniel."

Yet even as she said it, she thought of Vanderbilt's tirade against whities, O'Brien's resentful manner at the coffee shop, Betty's explicit denouncement of Daniel, Peter's old feud with him.

"Rodriguez hoped to stir up the group's feeling against you," Bob said. "It's a rotten thing to do, but it usually produces results. Groups can be manipulated."

He drained his Perrier and motioned authoritatively for another. She recalled the assertive way he had taken charge of matters after Daniel died, and realized that this mode of behavior came naturally to him. As an art director, he was used to giving direction. Daniel, as an actor, was used to taking it. Yes, their styles of making love would be totally different.

"I can't say that I'm crazy about Rodriguez' methods," Jean mused, "but he must be desperate to solve this case. I hope nobody at Clean Slate paid any attention to him."

"I'm afraid they did."

She felt her mouth go dry. "What do you mean?"

"Everyone now thinks you killed Daniel."

She remembered Betty's grotesque suspicions last night.

"But that's crazy. They know I'm not a murderer. They know I'm not capable of—"

She stopped in midsentence as she realized they did

77

not know her at all. How could they? Up until recently she had kept her deepest thoughts and opinions to herself, buried her emotions, concealed her fears, not spoken about what mattered the most. *Feelings.* And even when she began to unwind emotionally (as she had only since her involvement with Daniel), it was on a limited and reserved basis, as though she didn't fully trust the group with her secrets. She used to marvel at the outpourings of other alcoholics; it seemed so easy for them to bare their souls. She wished she could bare hers, but her goddamned shyness stood in the way, trapping her again. She felt suddenly furious. Would she never escape its smothering influence?

"Did Betty say anything in my defense?" she asked.

"Not that I recall."

"So the verdict against me was pretty unanimous."

He avoided looking directly at her, sensing her hurt.

"I'm afraid so, Jean."

She couldn't believe it. Being suspected by her peers upset Jean far more than being suspected by the police. In a way, she knew that was irrational. Her peers could not arrest her, they could not put her in prison. Still she needed their approval and esteem, if she were to remain sober. And she needed it badly.

"I told them they were being unfair," Bob assured her. "I said they were letting themselves be manipulated by Rodriguez, but this murder has angered them. They want a scapegoat."

"And I happen to be handy."

"I'm sorry I had to be the one to tell you this."

She smiled at him, grateful for his kindness, appreciative of his finely chiseled good looks. The shirt he wore was a beautiful deep blue. She had forgotten how attractive that color was on men with brown eyes. Both Daniel and her husband were blue-eyed. At that moment Jean knew that she and Bob were going to have an affair. It was not a hope or a wish, merely a recognition of

78

fact. She wondered how she was going to manage it without alcohol to relax her. Yet she hadn't needed alcohol with Daniel, she'd been in AA for six months when they became lovers. Why wasn't she nervous then?

Oh, yes, now she remembered what happened. She'd been sick with the flu and a temperature of 102 when Daniel came over one afternoon to see how she was doing. The next thing she knew he had climbed into bed with her and was taking off her nightgown ("I don't think your thighs are too fat," he said, "I think they're perfect"), while a few doors away Thelma was making chicken marengo in the kitchen. Between Daniel's outrageousness and her own feverish condition, she was both too drugged and too dumbstruck to be nervous.

"You have a strange smile on your face," Bob said. "What are you thinking of?"

"Whether I'll be nervous when you make love to me."

"You don't pull any punches, do you?" But he looked pleased, flattered. "Why should you be nervous?"

"I'm afraid of new situations, they terrify me. Like finding out I'm a murder suspect. I don't know how to handle it. What am I supposed to do? Catch the murderer myself, to prove I'm innocent?"

Instead of laughing at the idea, he said: "You might have to. If you care so much about the group's opinion."

"I do care. It might seem foolish to you, but since my parents and Frank died they're the first real family I've had. How they feel about me means a great deal."

"What about how *I* feel?"

"That means even more."

"I'm glad." He put his hand in hers, it felt warm and friendly. "I'm convinced you're innocent, even though you had a seemingly strong motive. A woman scorned."

She jerked her hand away. "Who told you that?"

"Rodriguez."

"That bastard."

79

"I'm sorry, Jean, but everyone knows by now that Daniel was responsible for the breakup. Not you."

"And I'm supposed to have been so miserable and grief-stricken that I killed him, in order to prevent Laura from having him? Is that it?"

"In a nutshell."

She was sorry now that she told Rodriguez about the breakup, but she'd been afraid to conceal evidence, afraid that if she didn't tell him Betty might and it would look even worse for her. If she hadn't mentioned this entire business to Ms. Betty Lathrop to start with, she would not be under suspicion this very minute. And yet it wasn't fair to blame Betty, who had only done what Jean would have if the situations were reversed.

Bob's eyes rested apprehensively upon her. "Did you love him very much?"

"Yes, I did. I loved Daniel more than I've ever . . ." She stopped, feeling as though she were being a traitor to Frank's memory. "I was crazy about him."

"No wonder Rodriguez considers you a likely suspect. Still, he doesn't have any hard-and-fast evidence to convict you. There weren't any fingerprints on the aspirin bottle. It was either wiped clean afterward, or the killer wore gloves."

"Aspirin bottle?" Jean was startled. "You mean, the poison was actually *in* it?"

"Sure was. You shouldn't have skipped today's meeting. It was very informative. It seems as though that aspirin bottle is the only clue the cops have."

Wouldn't it be funny if it turns out that that was what happened? Betty had said last night. *Just the way you imagined it?*

Jean wished that her hunch hadn't proven so deadly accurate. It reflected badly on her. Her own innocence was beginning to appear less and less credible with everything Bob told her, and she could feel the noose of accusation tighten around her neck.

"But if I were the killer, I would have flushed the aspirin bottle down the toilet," she said hastily. "I was the last person to use the bathroom. I had the perfect opportunity to get rid of the evidence. Don't you see? The fact that I didn't should prove I'm innocent."

"Not if you were a very cagey lady. You might have tried to outsmart the police. You might purposely not have flushed it away, thinking that would throw suspicion off you. It would be a daring thing to do, leaving the evidence in that wastebasket. But murder *is* daring."

Jean laughed in spite of herself. "The most daring thing I've ever done in my life is go on the roller coaster at Palisades. Still I can see how it must look to others. I was in love with Daniel. I was sitting next to him. I had the motive . . . and he spoke my name before he slumped over."

Bob turned pale at mention of this last fact. She remembered that he had turned around when Daniel said *Jean*. The only reason she'd forgotten Bob staring at them was because of the chaos that immediately followed Daniel's collapse, the confusion.

"It was you who told Rodriguez what Daniel said."

"No Jean, I didn't. I swear it."

"Who then?"

"I don't know. Does it matter? Whoever spoke up was only doing his duty. You can't blame him."

"I guess not."

By the same token, why *hadn't* Bob mentioned that rather important fact to the police? It seemed strangely irresponsible of him. Unless he was trying to protect her. God knows, she needed all the protection she could get.

"I'm glad you believe in me, Bob."

It helped to know that someone did, that at least one person was on her side. One person, she said to herself, or Bob in particular? Her question was answered a few minutes later when he asked her to have dinner with him that evening. All the way home she found herself won-

dering if he had ever been married, had children, objected to women painters, liked the color red. She was
going to wear her knockout red chiffon dress tonight,
the dress she'd bought to celebrate Daniel's first evening
back in New York.

Yes, she wanted her ally to be Bob in particular.

Almost as much as she wanted Daniel's murderer to be
found and her own innocence firmly, irrevocably es-
tablished.

☙ 4 ❧

Detective Rodriguez was waiting in the lobby when
Jean got home.

"I'm sorry I missed you at today's meeting, Mrs.
Neelie. Any reason you weren't there?"

All of Jean's warm feelings about the evening ahead
suddenly evaporated. It must be serious if Rodriguez
came here.

"I decided to go to the Museum of Modern Art instead. I go there quite frequently. I'm a painter, remember?"

"May I come upstairs with you? There are a few
things I'd like to talk to you about."

When they got to her apartment, Clark Gable nearly
knocked the two of them over, leaping and wagging his
tail.

"Nice dog," Rodriguez said, patting his head. "What's
wrong with his eyes?"

The detective certainly didn't miss a trick.

"He has cataracts."

"Too bad. Anything you can do about it?"

"No. Unfortunately, dogs can't wear glasses."

Rodriguez sat down on the Duncan Phyfe sofa and lit
a cigarette. The room was filled with costly antiques,

mostly contributed by Jean's parents with one exception. A Boston rocker that Frank had brought with him from Harvard. Even though it was glaringly at odds with the rest of the furnishings, Jean refused to get rid of it. The rocker was all she had left to remember Frank by.

"Can I get you something?" she asked. "A cup of coffee? Tea?"

"You don't happen to have any scotch, do you?"

"I'm afraid not. It's too dangerous to keep alcohol around. I'm liable to be tempted."

The sofa was a graceful Directoire, vintage circa 1820, which she had reupholstered in a fine French silk, and the tall Puerto Rican detective looked decidedly out of place in it. He kept his black raincoat on. Jean wished that Rodriguez hadn't mentioned scotch. It was that time of day. The happy hour when people were getting out the ice, glasses, stirring drinks. . . .

"How long have you been sober, Mrs. Neelie?"

"Fifteen months."

"What do you think of AA? Good organization?"

"The best. I never could have come this far without it. Members are extremely supportive of each other." Then she remembered that everyone at Clean Slate suspected her of murder. "When it comes to keeping each other sober, that is."

"But not when it comes to covering up for murder suspects? Is that what you were thinking?"

It had been a long tiring day, and the last thing she felt like right now was to answer Rodriguez' insinuating questions.

"I don't know what you mean," she said.

"I thought Mr. Edwards might have filled you in?"

"Mr. Edwards? Who's that?"

"I keep forgetting that AA doesn't use last names. Perhaps you know him as Bob."

It took Jean a moment to absorb this information.

"Have you been following me?"

It was the first time she had seen Rodriguez laugh. He had very small, very white teeth. They reminded her of rodents' teeth.

"Nothing so melodramatic, Mrs. Neelie. You've been watching too much television. I was coming out of Tiffany's when I spotted you and Mr. Edwards crossing Fifth Avenue. That's how I happened to know that the two of you were together today."

"We ran into each other," she said, wondering what the hell Rodriguez was doing at Tiffany's. "It was purely accidental, although I doubt if you'll believe me."

"Why shouldn't I? Accidents happen all the time."

She couldn't tell if he was being sarcastic.

"What do you think of Mr. Edwards?" he asked.

"He seems very nice," Jean said carefully. "I barely know him, though."

"Then you aren't friends outside of AA?"

"Not at all. Today was the first time we had a real conversation. He invited me to dinner this evening."

"Has he asked you out before?"

"No, never. Why?"

"I was just wondering whether he was attracted to you for a long time."

"You mean, and didn't do anything about it because Daniel was in the picture?"

"It's a possibility."

"Are you suggesting that Bob considered Daniel a rival for my affections? Enough of a rival to kill him?"

"That, too, is a possibility. You're a very alluring woman, Mrs. Neelie."

Alluring.

It was a word that would be used to describe someone like Greta Garbo, and Jean found it hard to accept about herself. Sometimes when she got drunk she did used to feel alluring; she'd wear more eye makeup and dress in bolder colors then. Once when Frank was away on a business trip, she picked up a ventriloquist at an East Side hotel bar. She was wearing the one purple dress she

owned (purchased when she was blotto, of course), and
the ventriloquist invited her upstairs to his room. It was
only after she got there that she began to panic and tried
to escape. When she returned home (her honor miracu-
lously intact), she threw the purple dress down the incinerator. One entire sleeve had been ripped off by the
ventriloquist's dummy.

"So you went to the Museum of Modern Art today,"
Rodriguez said. "And then you ran into Mr. Edwards? Is
that correct?"

"Not exactly. After the museum, I went to Rumpel-
mayer's for lunch. Then I went to see *An Unmarried
Woman*, but I didn't like it so I left. *Then* I ran into Mr.
Edwards."

"What didn't you like about *An Unmarried Woman*?"

Jean realized that if she'd been lying, she would not be
able to answer that question.

"What I didn't like was Jill Clayburgh's husband leaving her for another woman."

"Did that remind you of Daniel leaving you?"

At least he wasn't calling him "the deceased" anymore.

"As a matter of fact, it did. It was very unpleasant. I
couldn't have chosen a worse movie if I tried."

"I've changed my mind, Mrs. Neelie. I'll take you up
on that cup of coffee after all."

Jean led him into the attractive spotless kitchen, and
put the kettle on to boil. Then she emptied a small
amount of coffee beans into the grinding machine, and
turned it on. The loud whirring sound lasted only a few
minutes. She fitted a Melita filter over the top of her pyrex coffeemaker, emptied the ground beans into the filter, and poured boiling water over them. When Betty
watched her go through this procedure a few months
ago, she said it revealed a lot about the difference between them.

"I'd never go to all that trouble," Betty said. "Not
when there's Instant around."

"I've tasted your Instant."

"It might not be fabulous, but it's convenient. The trouble with you is you're exacting and perfectionistic."

"I also brew good coffee, and it's hard to make a mistake this way."

"You probably even squeeze oranges for juice," Betty said. "Serve croissants with coffee. Men must love you."

"What do you give Peter?"

"Tang and cornflakes."

Now Rodriguez seemed impressed. "I hope it tastes as good as it smells. Do you make coffee like this every day?"

"Yes, I much prefer it to any other method."

"You normally don't drink the coffee at Clean Slate, do you?"

"No, but I know what you're going to say. Why did I drink it yesterday when Daniel was killed?"

"I must admit it seems odd. Why did you?"

"I was feeling tired. I had just gotten my period and I needed something to perk me up. I couldn't afford to be choosy. It's as simple as that."

"If you say so."

He was looking at her curiously. Did he believe her? Or did he think she had gone over to the coffee urn because that's where Daniel happened to be? So she could stand next to him, and when nobody was looking slip the deadly poison into his cup? It occurred to her that she did not know what kind of poison it was. Back in the living room, she asked Rodriguez.

"I'm not at liberty to divulge that information," he said. "However, there is something I can tell you. It's in reference to Daniel leaving you. You claimed he was going back to his wife. I'm afraid that doesn't check out."

"Excuse me?"

"He wasn't going back to his wife. Laura. That's his wife's name, isn't it?"

Jean could barely speak. "Yes."

86

"It's just not true. There never had been any idea of a reconciliation between them. I've spoken extensively to Mrs. Streatham about this."

"She must be lying," Jean said, dazed.

"Why? What possible reason would she have to lie?"

"I don't know. But it can't be. I mean, if he wasn't going back to Laura, then why did he—?"

"Leave you?" Rodriguez finished her question.

Jean nodded.

"Well, Mrs. Neelie, that part is exceptionally interesting, if I do say so myself. Your Daniel was quite a ladies' man—yes, quite a ladies' man." He chuckled in that obnoxious way men had when they were talking about another man's sexual prowess. "It seems he was heavily involved with someone else."

Jean thought of the anonymous phone call that morning, warning her. *Daniel lied to you.*

"Someone else? Who?"

"The chairwoman at Clean Slate."

She could feel the blood drain out of her face. "*Constance?*"

"That's right. In fact, Daniel was planning to go to the Dominican Republic and get one of those quickie divorces so they could be married. They even set a date."

Rodriguez consulted a small blue notebook. "Here it is. I've just come from Constance's home. She wasn't at today's meeting either. Too upset. They were going to be married on March seventeenth. It seems that's Constance's birthday."

Jean stared at Rodriguez wordlessly. Daniel said he was planning to take Laura out for brunch on *her* birthday, to ask her to come back to him. But according to Rodriguez, he was really planning to marry Constance on *her* birthday. The only thing Daniel seemed to be consistent about were women's birthdays. Maybe if she had had a birthday coming up soon, he would have married her. How foolish she was to have just celebrated one last month.

"I can't believe it," she said at last. "I thought he and Constance were only casual acquaintances. This is shocking."

"Is it?"

"What does that mean?"

"It means I only have your word for it that Mr. Streatham said he was going back to his wife. His wife denies it. She says she agreed to the divorce. Constance denies it. And unfortunately, we can't ask Mr. Streatham."

Jean felt her patience give way. "What exactly is your point, Detective Rodriguez? Are you accusing me of murder?"

Rodriguez put his coffee cup down on the Queen Anne end table. As he did so, Clark Gable jumped off the sofa and went into the bedroom. The dog hated unpleasantness almost as much as Jean. The only difference was that she had no means of escape.

"I'm not accusing you of anything," Rodriguez said. "But how about the following possibility? Strictly theoretical, you understand."

Jean was curious. "Go ahead."

"Let's say that Daniel was two-timing you before he left on that road tour. He was making love to you and Constance. Somehow you found out about it, and were properly enraged. He'd tricked you, played with your affections, etcetera. Then Daniel returns to New York three months later and realizes he cannot go on with the farce. He shows up here on Sunday to tell you that he's asked his wife for a divorce so he can marry Constance. You become hysterical. You plead with him not to do it, you say you still love him. He doesn't listen, and he leaves.

"You're miserable, frantic. You've been rejected by the man you loved and trusted, the only man you've been involved with since your husband's death. Then you see Daniel the next day at Clean Slate. He's happy, smiling, the same popular Daniel as always. But you're not happy, you're not smiling, Mrs. Neelie, you're even more frantic than you were on Sunday. The thought of having to face Daniel and Constance day after day is too much for you to bear. You decide that if you can't have him, no one will.

"You make your plans carefully. When you go to Clean Slate on Tuesday, you break your usual pattern and pour yourself a cup of coffee. That way, you can be standing next to Daniel. It's easy for you to put the poison in his cup when nobody is looking. Daniel makes it easier by conveniently going to the bathroom and leaving his cup on that long table. Then everyone files into the meeting room, but you have to go to the bathroom. Now, do you flush the empty poison bottle down the toilet? No, you're too clever for that, too cagey. It would be too much of a giveaway, since you're the last person to use the bathroom. Someone might suspect that's what you did, and the bottle could be retrieved through the drainage and implicate you. Instead you daringly throw it away in the wastebasket, in the anteroom.

"Why not, you figure? It doesn't have your fingerprints on it, you were wearing gloves because it was so cold. How can anyone prove you did it? There were fourteen other people present besides you and the victim. Any one of them could be the killer. In the meeting room, you even sit down directly next to Daniel to make sure he drinks his coffee. He does. But then he does something you hadn't counted on. He speaks your name just before dying. Francine clearly heard him say *Jean*. Think about it. A man knows he's dying. He knows he has enough breath left to say the name of the person who killed him. And that's exactly what Daniel does, makes a feeble attempt to nail his murderer. You hadn't anticipated that, had you, Mrs. Neelie?"

Jean could not speak.

"You overlooked one important consideration, however. I'm sure you thought about it, but not being able to see a way around it you went ahead with your plan anyway. What you overlooked was motive. Nobody at Clean Slate had any reason to kill the deceased except you. At least, from what we've gleaned so far. You were the only one with a bona-fide motive. Now what do you say, Mrs. Neelie?"

Jean felt as though some cruel joke were being played on her. And yet the way Rodriguez described the sequence of events, it was very plausible. It could have happened precisely as he said—only it hadn't.

"Is this what you've told them at Clean Slate, Detective Rodriguez? To turn them against me?"

"Not in so many words."

"That's disgusting! Contemptible! How *could* you?"

"Calm down. I'm only doing my job."

"Then start looking elsewhere for the murderer. Because I'm innocent."

Instead of challenging her or belaboring the point, he lit another cigarette. "Do you have any idea who did it?"

His nonchalant turnabout came as a second shock.

"So you don't think it was me, after all. You were just trying it on for size."

"I wouldn't go quite that far. At the moment you're my main suspect, but I don't have proof to convict you. Therefore, the case remains open. Any suggestions?"

"Laura."

"Oh? Why?"

"If what you said about Daniel and Constance is true, then wouldn't his wife have sufficient motive to want to see him dead? The same motive, in fact, that you ascribed to me. Revenge? Jealousy?"

"Apparently not. Laura amicably agreed to the divorce."

Jean remembered Laura crying into that blue Kleenex before yesterday's meeting started. She certainly hadn't acted like a woman who was amicable to a divorce.

"How do you know she agreed?" Jean asked. "You only have her word for it."

Rodriguez smiled. "It's interesting you should say that. That's the way a cop thinks. Most people tend to believe what they're told point-blank. No, Mrs. Neelie, I don't just have Laura's word for it. I also have her lawyer's word. He confirms her statement that she was willing to give Daniel his freedom. There was even correspondence between Daniel and Laura to that effect while he was touring. Laura saved his letters. It's very clear that she had no interest in trying to salvage their marriage. According to Laura, it had ended quite a while ago—even before he became involved with you."

Then everything Daniel said about Laura writing him in Chicago saying, *I love you,* was a lie. What Laura had written was that she no longer cared about him, that he could have his divorce, that they were through. *Why, Jean asked herself? Why had Daniel deemed it necessary to tell her such an outrageous lie?*

"Most men are cowards when the crunch comes," Rodriguez said, as though reading her mind. "Daniel was probably too ashamed to admit he'd been two-timing you with Constance. It was easier for him to say he was going back to his wife; it sounded more conventional, more acceptable. He must have figured you'd be less hurt that way."

Just as he figured she'd be less hurt if he told her about Laura in person, rather than putting it in a letter? So he came over here on Sunday and handed her a pack of lies. And all to make her feel better!

"But Daniel knew I would find out the truth before very long," she said. "I saw him and Constance every day. It was such a stupid, senseless lie."

"You wouldn't have been seeing them much longer.

They were planning to move to the West Coast. Daniel felt there were more opportunities for actors there. Constance said that even the wedding was going to take place in California."

Jean didn't know which surprised her more. The fact that Daniel had worked out his future so carefully, or the fact that he'd been too much of a coward to tell her she had no part in it. What hurt more than anything was having believed for so long that he was honest, that they kept no secrets from each other, that he never cheated on her. Frank had cheated, too. The only difference was that with Frank it was many women, and with Daniel only Constance. Still, infidelity was infidelity. Even though Jean started dating in the permissive sixties, there had been only two men in her life, Frank and Daniel (she refused to count the one-eyed cab driver), and both turned out to be duplicitous and unfaithful. She wondered what that meant about *her*.

"In light of this new information regarding Daniel and Constance, do you still insist that you never phoned his apartment Sunday night?" Rodriguez asked. "Because Constance recognized your voice."

"Very well, I lied. I did call but I didn't speak to Daniel. The woman who answered said he was taking a shower, and I hung up."

"Didn't you realize it was Constance?"

"Not at the time. I thought it might be, when I heard her voice the next day at Clean Slate. But it seemed so unlikely, I couldn't imagine what she would be doing there at midnight. Naturally, I had no idea they were ... lovers."

Then she told him about the anonymous telephone call she had received that morning. *Daniel lied to you.*

"And you don't think it sounded like Constance?" he asked.

"No, the voice was deeper, different. And yet, I can't imagine who else knew what was going on."

"This is an interesting case all right," Rodriguez said, getting up. "It's the kind of case that I, personally, find very challenging. Murder at Alcoholics Anonymous. It's a unique situation. Stimulating. Don't you worry, Mrs. Neelie, we'll find the killer."

"It would be a relief to me."

"I'm sure it would."

He looked at her as though to say that he wasn't fooled by her wish to see someone, *anyone*, arrested for the crime so she would be off the hook. Then his gaze shifted outside to her desolate garden on the wrap-around terrace. Jean decided to prune the rosebushes and mulch the two willows first thing tomorrow morning. It was too dark to do it now. It would feel good to get her hands into the earth again, to work at something simple and basic instead of trying to follow the labyrinthian trails leading to Daniel's murderer.

"What kind of insecticide do you normally use?" she heard Rodriguez ask.

"I don't believe in insecticides. In the summer I spray my plants every day with soapy water."

"An environmentalist, are you?"

"Yes, you could say that."

"Don't your rosebushes attract aphids?"

"Not if I put garlic around the base?"

Rodriguez seemed impressed. "Garlic? That's a new one."

Jean walked him to the door. "Why all this sudden interest in my garden, Detective Rodriguez?"

"My wife is an enthusiastic gardener. I like to pick up a few tips for her whenever I can. That's all, Mrs. Neelie." Jean doubted that was all, but she didn't say anything.

"Garlic," Rodriguez repeated on his way out.

⚫5⚫

Peter was in the IRT subway, and the damned train was stalled between Columbus Circle and Seventy-second Street.

He glanced at his watch: seven o'clock. If this train didn't move soon, he would be late to his uptown appointment and he didn't want to keep the man waiting. No, the meeting was too important.

The other IRT passengers seemed glazed with resignation, as the train stood infuriatingly still. Peter cursed to himself. After wrapping up this next piece of business, he wanted to window-shop at the jewelry stores along Sixth Avenue before joining Betty at Sardi's. Reason told him to skip the jewelry stores tonight (he could just as well look at engagement rings tomorrow), but he didn't feel especially reasonable at the moment. He felt excited, turned on, willful. If only this rotten train would start to move, he'd be able to squeeze everything in, including a proposal of marriage to Betty over dinner.

Peter had decided that his bothersome homosexuality would be most effectively laid to rest if he got married. The fact that his first marriage hadn't settled the matter did not deter him now. He attributed its failure to the fact that his first wife had been a middle-class bore. Betty was different—gutsy, ballsy—maybe like him she dug a little action on the side, so what? That suited Peter just fine.

He felt a sudden jolt and realized that the decrepit train was moving at last. Thank God. When he got out at Seventy-second Street, he walked quickly to the address he'd memorized. He would only be a few minutes late.

6

It was seven-fifteen, and O'Brien was getting anxious. He couldn't concentrate on AA's Big Book no matter how hard he tried; he had read the same words over and over again (*We admitted we were powerless over alcohol—that our lives had become unmanageable*), and at last he closed the book, shifted in the dilapidated easy chair, and decided to give his third visitor of the day a few more minutes. Traffic was heavy at this hour, he reminded himself.

Still he couldn't wait forever, he had to go to work soon. In his plaid shirt, faded cords, and Spanish cowboy hat, he was dressed for the long night ahead. O'Brien had taken to wearing the hat whenever he was awake. It gave him a certain sense of security, identity, hell, it made him feel different from the masses. Now he tightened the string under his chin, as though he were tightening and putting the break on his own apprehension.

"Cool it," he cautioned himself. "The doorbell's going to ring any minute."

His first two visitors had separately come and gone, each with a different and elaborate theory as to who killed Daniel, and why, and O'Brien listened like the good bartender he was even when he was off duty and relaxing at home. Listen, look, be alert, and shut up. That was the ticket, all right. Consequently, he hadn't interrupted or contradicted or told them who the murderer really was. His next fucking visitor, that's who— and O'Brien was the only person in the world who knew it, the only one smart enough to have kept his bartender's eyes open at Clean Slate and actually spotted the poisoner in the act.

Now as he got out of the easy chair and walked into the kitchen to make some coffee, he wondered if traffic had in fact detained the son of a bitch. Maybe no one was coming, maybe he was being stood up. No. O'Brien looked around at the depressing dark green walls and vetoed that unpalatable possibility. God, how he despised this filthy hole.

O'Brien's apartment on Amsterdam Avenue was an untidy affair, consisting of three small rooms with no doors separating them. Just crummy archways that needed plastering. He had considered knocking down the green walls and turning the place into one large, breathable room (instead of the three rabbit hutches that he felt suffocated in), but that was before Daniel had been so conveniently murdered yesterday.

Yes, it had been a lucky break for O'Brien. And now that he was about to come into a windfall, the first thing he intended to do was move out of this rotten apartment and into something really classy on Sutton Place or the Upper East Side. His eyes shone at the thought of his projected move, and he loosened the string of the Spanish cowboy hat. He had carried the AA book with him into the kitchen. He put it down on the stove, next to where the kettle was boiling.

Although O'Brien didn't like violence any more than the next guy, he also felt that if anyone had it coming to him it was that tight-fisted creep, Daniel Streatham. *Why* he had it coming from this particular person made no sense to O'Brien, no sense at all. Still, he wasn't going to knock himself out trying to unravel slippery motives, or consider the possibility that the killer was plain nuts, or anything murky like that.

Screw that shit, was the way O'Brien felt as he dumped a tablespoon of Nescafé into a large mug and poured boiling water over it. What he was going to do, instead, was concentrate upon the lovely ten grand that was about to fall into his lap any second now. It was the first of a series of payments that the murderer would make to him (he had decided yesterday), and actually he wasn't asking for a lot of money to keep his mouth shut and not go blabbing to the police. He was being . . . well, *fair* about it. . . .

O'Brien grinned as he took a sip of the scalding coffee. Extremes in temperature did not bother him as much as they did the average person—extremes in anything for that matter—which was why he felt he had made a tremendous concession in his moderate and fair request for ten grand. Of course, the murderer didn't know that was only for openers, at least couldn't be certain; well, perhaps suspected it was, but so what?

O'Brien patted the small thirty-two automatic concealed in his trouser pocket. *He* was calling the shots now, not the murderer. O'Brien was about to move up in the world. Maybe he would get an apartment with a terrace overlooking gardens . . . that was a thought: this sudden image of himself sitting on an attractive terrace in the early evening—like right around now—enjoying a leisurely cup of coffee, before going off to tend bar for the rest of the night.

Hell, what was wrong with him? Everything had happened so fast that he hadn't had a chance to figure out all his future plans. But it seemed likely that if he played his cards right, he would be going to work for himself again before too long . . . his own saloon, a fashionable pub like the one he lost because of his irresponsible boozing. Yes, his own pub once more, and this time he would stay sober and hang onto it. He could see his name spelled out in lights above the entranceway, he could envision the rich mahogany of the bar itself, the expensively dressed crowd it would attract, he was an experienced pub-keeper, he would know just what to do, maybe he would even have a neon outline of his Spanish cowboy hat right alongside the pub's name, *his* name.

The sound of the doorbell startled O'Brien. He nearly dropped his cup of coffee before he pulled himself together and walked the few steps to open the worn, dark green door.

"I thought maybe you had decided to stand me up," he nervously greeted his visitor.

"That never entered my mind."

"Glad to hear it. Come on in."

"Thanks."

"Is the dough in there?"

O'Brien's visitor tapped the small black attaché case. "Sure is."

"You're being very smart, you know," O'Brien said, hoping his relief wasn't visible.

"What choice did I have?"

O'Brien grinned, a little more relaxed now. "None."

"That's what I figured, too." The person's eye went to the AA book, lying on the stove. "I see you're reading our Bible."

"Yeah, I shlep it with me everywhere. Hey, how about a cup of coffee?"

"Why not?"

O'Brien turned his back to light the stove with a match. When he moved into his gleaming new apartment on Sutton Place, the stove would be an automatic, technicolored *Better Homes & Gardens* marvel; he would have a microwave oven, two freezers, Baccarat crystal, Egyptian tiles in his kitchen if he felt like it.

Those were O'Brien's last thoughts before the five-inch steel knife went smoothly, noiselessly into his plaid-shirted back. As he sank to the cheap linoleum floor, the string of his Spanish cowboy hat loosened even more under his chin. But the hat did not fall off.

7

Jean arrived at the restaurant first. She waited at a table for a few minutes before Bob got there at eight-fifteen, breathless and apologetic.

"Can you ever forgive me? My goddamned watch stopped."

His smile was engaging and he seemed flustered, truly sorry.

"Consider yourself forgiven."

"Thanks. I'm usually very punctual."

The restaurant he'd chosen was small, French, candle-lit, and on the Upper East Side.

"In *our* neighborhood," he informed her now.

Jean was happily surprised to learn that he lived only a few blocks away from her, yet up until the time she joined Clean Slate she had never laid eyes on him. They both agreed, over *carré d'agneau*, that it was one of the things they liked best about New York: not having to be chummy with your neighbors if you didn't feel like it.

It was the reason Jean had not gone to an AA group close to home; she felt apprehensive about running into someone she knew. Clean Slate was far enough away to be safe, and not too far to be inconvenient. Bob went there at lunchtime because his office was just around the corner.

"I'm working on an ad campaign for a large distiller," he said as dinner passed pleasantly, uneventfully. "Liquor is hard to photograph, tricky. We had to substitute strong tea for scotch today. The scotch didn't look amber enough."

Jean had deliberately not told him about the visit from Rodriguez, and by the time dessert arrived she began to wonder why. Was she afraid that he might start to doubt her innocence? Or was she disturbed by Rodriguez' intimation that Bob himself had reason to kill Daniel?

"Gin tends to photograph yellow," he was saying. "We often replace it with water for the camera. Would you believe that I've built up a reputation in this business by being an expert on *booze* accounts?"

"Why not? You're certainly familiar with your product."

She didn't think it any coincidence that Bob was good at liquor advertising, any more than it was a coincidence that O'Brien worked as a bartender. Even in sobriety, the alcoholic was drawn to the source of his addiction.

"I saw you and Constance on the news last night," she said. "You were coming out of Clean Slate and you both had your hands over your faces."

He seemed horrified. "You mean, you *recognized* me?"

"Is that bad?"

"It's terrible. I'd lose my job in three seconds flat if my boss found out that I belong to AA, and so would Connie. Most people have a very distorted idea about AA, they think it's strictly for skid-row winos."

Jean realized how lucky she was that she had no employer to account to, yet she knew what he meant about people having distorted ideas. The few friends she'd made when she was still married to Frank had looked at her strangely when she told them she had joined AA, and after a while they dropped her altogether. Later she realized they had never been friends at all. Her social life now revolved exclusively around other AA people.

"No wonder Connie didn't come to work today," Bob said. "The TV exposure must have made her nervous. Ironically, her boss is a prime candidate for AA but he won't face it. He's the account supervisor on this liquor campaign."

Jean knew that Constance was an executive secretary,

but she hadn't realized it was in the advertising field any more than she realized that Bob called her Connie.

"So you and Constance work for the same agency," she said.

"That's right. Wonderful girl, Connie. Smart. Hard worker."

She was a hard worker, all right, Jean thought. She had worked Daniel away to herself.

"Did you know that Daniel and Constance were in love?" she asked. "That they were planning to be married?"

"*Married?*" Bob appeared flabbergasted. "That's impossible. I mean, it's very suprising. I thought Daniel was in love with you."

"So did I."

He put down his dessert spoon. "Are you saying that all the time he was involved with you, he was also involved with Connie?"

"That's exactly what I'm saying."

"It's the best-kept secret at Clean Slate. How did you find out?"

"Rodriguez told me." She decided to get it all off her chest. "He stopped by my apartment earlier this evening. He thinks that when I found out about Constance, I went crazy and killed Daniel."

"I just can't believe it." There was a dazed, faraway expression in Bob's eyes. "Daniel and Connie. She usually confides in me when she gets involved, asks for my opinion, relies upon my judgment. Daniel wasn't even her type."

"What type is that?"

She had never seen a man blush before. "It's hard to explain," he said.

"People don't necessarily have any one set type. I don't. My husband and Daniel were quite different. And you're different from both of them."

He thanked her with his eyes for making it easy for

him. He, too, had thought about going to bed. Maybe he'd thought about it long before she did, fantasizing what she would be like if he were fortunate enough to have her to himself, without Daniel, with Daniel dead. Apparently men found her desirable at the beginning. Frank did. Daniel did. And now Bob. Alluring, was how Rodriguez described her. The word itself connoted an unknown quality, a mystery. But when they got to know her better, they left her. They had unraveled the mystery. Obviously, she wasn't so alluring without it.

"Check, please," Bob said.

He paid for dinner with a credit card. The name on the plate was E. Robert Edwards. Jean idly speculated what the letter "E" stood for. Edward? Ernest? Eugene? Suddenly she felt herself go cold as her mind raced back to Daniel slumping over in his seat, one word coming out of his mouth. *Jean*. Or was it *Gene?* As they were waiting for the receipt, she asked Bob about his first name.

"It's Edwin," he replied easily. "Why?"

"Just curious. How come you don't use it?"

"It was my father's name, and I hated being Edwin Junior. I started calling myself Bob at an early age, and it caught on."

"I see."

☙ 8 ❧

Bob had plunged his hands into his pockets, so she couldn't notice them trembling. That was a close one, he thought, impressed by how well he handled it. He knew that before long the police would find out his name was really Eugene, but he hoped they'd have made an arrest by then. In the meantime, there was no point in alarming the lovely and desirable Jean Neelie. If he told her the truth, he doubted that she would let him make love to her tonight, she would be too scared. And there was nothing about him to be scared of, as he used to tell The Rabbit.

"But that's what I don't like about you," The Rabbit would object. "You're too meek, too passive. Don't you understand?"

No, he didn't. Since The Rabbit was aggressive enough for both of them, why couldn't she let him curl up at her feet and be her slave? The Rabbit, however, had different ideas and left him finally out of boredom. She didn't mind seeing him occasionally after the divorce, but only if he didn't interfere with her active sex life. Oh, he wouldn't interfere with his beloved Rabbit, particularly since he expected them to be together again one day. Not that he would ever push for it (pushing wasn't his style); he would simply dream of an eventual reconciliation, idyllic and enduring. He was still dreaming of it when he saw Jean at Clean Slate for the first time last year, and promptly switched his dreams to her.

There was something about Jean's remote and aloof manner that intrigued him right off. The others said she was a cold fish, but he didn't see her that way at all. Oh no, to him she was a lady, well bred, well mannered, and underneath that reserved facade probably seething with a passion that he hoped was . . . cruel. His feelings for her ran so deep that he couldn't even bring himself to talk to her at Clean Slate, let alone look directly at her for fear of what he might blurt out.

All of his dreams came to an abrupt end this past summer when Jean and Daniel started their affair. They were suddenly aglow with love and happiness, and he was suddenly miserable. Daniel had ruined his chances, thrown him back for sustenance upon The Rabbit who was far too busy to cater to his needs. Bob felt that his timing was terrible. He felt that if only Jean had noticed him before she noticed Daniel, he would have asked her to marry him and never thought of The Rabbit again.

But Jean stuck to Daniel like glue. Even when he went off on that tour she was forever talking about the letters he sent her and how she couldn't wait for his return. *Daniel's return.* That was uppermost in Bob's mind these last months at Clean Slate, when he pretended to be listening to heart-rending stories of alcoholic debasement. *Daniel's return.*

He would like to give the arrogant bastard a return he'd never forget, a return to the earth in a gold-trimmed coffin. And then yesterday when he heard the gagging, choking sound behind him and wheeled around to see what was happening, he realized that his dream was coming true at last. Daniel was having a convulsion, he was sick, very sick, he was dying! and Bob was glad. Daniel was sweating and pissing in his pants, and Bob was happy. Daniel was saying *Gene*, as though he knew that Bob had wished him dead for a long time.

✥9✥

"Look!" Jean whispered excitedly. "Look who's sitting there."

They were leaving the restaurant, and there at one of the tables was Hugh, alone. He resembled Woody Allen more than ever, Jean thought, his face pale and vulnerable behind horn-rimmed glasses, his thinning hair sticking out at odd angles. No one would ever guess him a fashionable hairdresser, nor an alcoholic. For he was casually sipping a glass of red wine as though it was the most natural thing in the world. All of her suspicions about him not belonging to AA returned in full force.

"I knew it," she said. "I always thought he was a phony."

They managed to leave without Hugh spotting them. It was cold and a fierce wind blew as they walked the few blocks to Jean's apartment.

"That wasn't an alcoholic having a slip," she said. "There was nothing compulsive or guilt-ridden about the way he was drinking that wine. He's been lying all the time. I wonder if it has anything to do with Daniel's death."

"Daniel's death?" Bob said. "What do you mean?"

"I guess my mind is becoming geared to distrust, apprehension, fear. I don't like it. I don't like Rodriguez coming to my place, trying to incriminate me. I don't like what you said about everyone at Clean Slate thinking I did it. I don't like suspecting Hugh, merely because he's not an alcoholic."

She felt like adding, "And I don't like suspecting you because your first initial is 'E.' "

"I'm afraid that I'll become even more distrustful until the murderer is found."

"Then let's hope he's found very soon," Bob said cheerfully.

"But what if he isn't? Do you realize that if that happened, I would always be suspect? In the eyes of the group, I mean."

"You worry too much about what they think."

"I can't help it. Put yourself in my shoes and imagine what it's like, being under suspicion. Slimy. To know that whenever your friends look at you, they're wondering if you're the person who slipped that poison into Daniel's coffee. It would be hideous if I had to go on sensing their misgivings; I couldn't stand it."

"Then don't miss any more meetings. It doesn't look good if you stay away."

"That's what I mean. Any innocent move I make is automatically open to misinterpretation. It's like having to go through life proving yourself all the time, and never succeeding. That shadow of doubt would always be there."

By the time they reached her building, Jean had made a decision. If Rodriguez failed to come up with Daniel's murderer within forty-eight hours from the time the crime was committed, she would find him herself. But how? Where would she begin? Who would she talk to? The members of Clean Slate, of course. She knew them better than the police did and she had more insight into the workings of an alcoholic's mind, being an alcoholic herself. All of her life she had sat back and shyly let others take the initiative, while she remained passive. Alcoholics were basically passive people, their main activity confined to drinking. By tracking down Daniel's killer, she would not only be exonerating herself of murder (of which she was innocent), but of her abominable shyness (of which she was guilty).

"I'm glad we had dinner this evening," Bob said in the elevator. "I've enjoyed myself very much. I hope you have, too."

"Oh, yes."

"I find you extremely appealing, you know."

"Really?" She smiled at him, pleased. "Why?"

"Because underneath that toned-down facade of yours, I detect a very sensual woman. Are you?"

"I've never particularly thought of myself that way," she lied.

"Those that are seldom do."

Men believed her when she said that, because she looked so ladylike. That was what turned them on, her goody-two-shoes facade juxtaposed by the occasional hint of a deeply erotic nature. If she could only figure out what caused them to tire of her, she'd have it made. Perhaps one day she would figure it out, one day soon, one day with Bob. . . . Perhaps he wouldn't tire of her at all.

A thrill ran through Jean as she opened the door to

her apartment, and switched on the chandelier. The living room gleamed and glowed with rich wood and polished surfaces, soft shades of rose and beige. Jean felt herself inwardly glow with the promise of a passionate adventure about to unfold.

"Where did you get all these fantastic antiques?" Bob asked, as Clark Gable ran happily around. "Is that sofa a real Duncan Phyfe? It's a beauty."

"I'm glad you approve."

"Who wouldn't?" he said incredulously.

"You'd be surprised."

Frank had not approved of the decor but he let her have a free hand, except when it came to the bedroom. There he put his foot down. He absolutely refused to sleep in the elaborate mahogany Chippendale with its corniced canopy, he said it made him feel like a fucking fag. So they bought a macho king-sized bed, very modern, had a stereo installed in the headboard, and Frank felt at home. Jean merely felt disappointed. As soon as he died, she gave the bed to charity and got the Chippendale out of storage. She recovered it with French silk in a delicate blue pattern that tended to make the bed appear less overwhelming. Even so, Daniel said it was too rich for his taste, and a lot of the time they made love on the thickly carpeted floor.

"I'm a peasant at heart," Daniel had confided.

"Is that why you never let me see your apartment? Because it's not grand enough?"

"A queen in a mere humble abode?" he joked. "It would never do."

Did Daniel really regard her as superior? It didn't sound as though he were joking. Perhaps the trouble in her relationship with both Frank and Daniel was that in certain ways she *did* feel superior. It had nothing to do with family or inheriting money. Jean believed that true aristocracy was of the spirit; it lay in appreciative, aesthetic sensibilities. Yet feeling aristocratic was not an attribute that her culture applauded or paid homage to. America was a democracy. At school she was taught that people were supposed to be equal, and the virtues of the common man were forever being praised.

But at home, it was a different matter.

Her parents lived in an artistic world of their own making, where individuality and eccentricity were the rule, not the exception. Her mother wore men's smocks years before it became fashionable, and her father had longish hair and a beard before anyone heard of hippies. At the time, Jean found them peculiar, embarrassing, and wished they would be more "normal" like the parents of other girls. Her mother told her about sex when she was eleven. The explanation came in simple, physical terms sprinkled with an overlay of love as a prerequisite between the two participants. It sounded very pleasant and enjoyable to Jean.

"It's known as lovemaking," her mother said. "For the reason I've just mentioned. If you hear someone talk about it as 'fucking,' disregard that person. He has no soul."

Sometime later at one of her parents' frequent dinner parties, the subject of lovemaking came up. Jean was surprised to hear her father offhandedly say: "Of course we don't bother with it ourselves. We have servants for that."

Everyone laughed at the joke, except Jean. She seriously wondered if it was possible to assign the task of lovemaking to their Polish maid and her husband, who helped with windows and heavy cleaning. Years later when she remembered her earnest conjecturings, she tried to determine how much they had shaped her erotic attitude. Possibly a great deal. Because although she enjoyed sex immensely, it never took on any of the larger-than-life overtones she heard whispered about among other girls. Promiscuity and nymphomania were alien to her. If lovemaking became too much of a burden (she thought), she could always let the servants do it.

"Who painted the still life?" Bob asked. "It reminds me of Matisse."

He had sat down on the sofa in almost exactly the same spot that Detective Rodriguez occupied earlier, and he was looking at one of her watercolors.

"I did," she said. "I was influenced by Matisse at one time. I admired that lush Mediterranean quality of his."

"So you're a painter. I had no idea. That's marvelous. I'm glad we have similar tastes."

"So do I. I'm tired of pretending to be interested in football games when I'd much rather watch the ballet."

He smiled in complete understanding, and then they launched into an enthusiastic conversation about her fine-arts training and his commercial one, about youthful ambitions and subsequent disillusions. Bob had grown up in San Francisco and wanted to study painting at the famous school there, but marriage at an early age forced him into the competitive marketplace. As he described the way he worked himself up the ladder to advertising art director, Jean got a picture of a very shrewd, very ambitious, very calculating man. A man intent upon getting ahead by asserting himself, a man not above stepping on others to achieve his goals. A man not above killing?

They talked for a long time and then realized they had forgotten to watch the news on television, to see whether Rodriguez had made any progress. They were so caught up in trying to explain themselves to each other that they had forgotten about Daniel's murder. They found a comforting bond in the fact that each had been married once.

"I'm divorced, and you're widowed," Bob said. "That means we're kind of on even footing. I like that."

"So do I."

She also liked the fact that he wasn't trying to rush

her off into the bedroom; he understood her need to be courted. He was sensitive to her moods; perhaps they matched his own. He was a *gentleman* in the true sense of the word, she thought, wondering how she could have even considered him capable of killing Daniel. He was too kind to even hurt a fly.

"Are you religious?" she asked suddenly.

"I don't go to church, if that's what you mean."

"No, not that. I meant in a moral sense. Do you believe in right and wrong?"

"Of course. Doesn't everyone?"

Murderers didn't. Jean had never thought about them in that context before, but there was no denying that in the end it came down to a simple question of morality. *Did the person believe in right and wrong?* Or did he assume he made his own laws? It was something to bear in mind when dealing with other Clean Slate suspects, she decided, not even conscious of the fact that she hadn't been gracious enough to give Rodriguez his full forty-eight hours to find the murderer. She would find the bastard herself.

"You're so lovely, so wonderful, so beautiful," Bob murmured, taking her in his arms.

"My thighs."

"Your *what?*" he said between kisses.

"Nothing, it's not important. But I must find out why Hugh pretends to be a drunk."

"Find out tomorrow."

She would. Jean Neelie, painter, window, recovering alcoholic, and (alluring) love object was on the case.

Thursday, March 2

❧ 1 ❧

When Jean woke up in the middle of the night, Bob was sleeping quietly beside her. She smiled at him in the darkness, lit a cigarette, and thought about the lovemaking earlier. One minute they'd been sitting in the living room kissing, and the next minute they were in the bedroom taking off their clothes and he was telling her how lovely she was.

"So beautiful," he kept repeating. "I had no idea."

Frank and Daniel said they'd had no idea either that her body would be so sensual. It seemed that she camouflaged it in clothes, making herself appear thinner and smaller-breasted than she really was. She was unaware of deliberately doing so, but it must be a fact because the surprise of all three men upon seeing her naked appeared genuine enough. She did not like to draw attention to herself. Yes, that would account for the unobtrusive style in which she dressed: Quiet dark colors, clothes that concealed rather than revealed the flesh underneath it.

"Damn!" she said now, in the darkness.

Except for the red chiffon she wore last night, all of her clothes mirrored her shyness. Still, she was not sexually shy. She found it easy to let go with Bob, despite the fact that there wasn't a drink on hand to relax her. She didn't need one. She felt relaxed from the start, and his whispered compliments spurred her on to

111

even more intense passion than she normally would have been capable of the first time.

The only thing that surprised her was his awkwardness. He held back at moments, waited for her to help him out; he faltered . . . it was engaging. Because of his authoritative manner socially, she thought he would be authoritative in bed too. He wasn't. She had the feeling he had not been with many women, and she appreciated that. It meant he was selective (he was too handsome not to have had unlimited opportunities). After Frank and Daniel with their studlike appetites and capabilities, Bob was a refreshing and welcome change.

"Get on top," he had whispered. "I like that. Oh yes, I really like that very much. You can ride me like your very own horse, ride me until I can't stand it any longer, until I'm sore. . . . Make me beg you to stop. . . ."

His orgasm took a long time to come, he had problems with it, he was immensely grateful for it; he covered her with kisses afterward, giving special attention to her thighs which he said he adored.

"They're firm, gorgeous, *strong*," was his comment.

He buried his face between them and she was convinced he would smother to death.

"I'd gladly stay there forever," he claimed.

They fell asleep in each other's arms. She was happy but a little confused. She didn't understand him. He was *different*. . . .

When morning came, Bob was dressed and seated beside her on the bed. He had brought her a tray of juice, toast, and coffee.

"How sweet," she said, touched.

"You're the sweet one. I have to be going now." He kissed her on the mouth, and held her face in his hands as though studying it. "I'll see you later, darling. You will be at Clean Slate, won't you?"

"I promise."

"I'm going to fall in love with you," he threatened.

It was the first time Jean had made love since Daniel went on tour three months ago, and she'd forgotten how sensational her body felt after it was touched and caressed and brought to life by an attentive partner. There was no other feeling like it. Yet when there wasn't a man around, she never missed sex or thought about it. Her erotic cutoff was complete. Only the physical presence of one man she desired could rekindle passion within her, which was why she didn't understand the appeal of pornography. All those impersonal people in improbable positions, they left her cold.

Fantasy, however, was another matter. And there, Jean was not immune. Her own special fantasy figure was Alain Delon, the French movie star. She thought he was sensational, and it occurred to her that he and Bob looked a lot alike. In fact, the resemblance was startling. She smiled to herself as she got out of bed, intrigued by the brilliant (albeit, unconscious) way she had selected her new, made-to-order lover. She took a long time bathing and dressing, savoring her flesh before covering it up for the day ahead.

As she went into the kitchen to feed Clark Gable, she realized that the telephone had been strangely still. She could imagine the people at Clean Slate calling each other and talking about the murder, sharing their grief; talk was natural at a time like this, healthy. But she was being purposely excluded from it. Two days had passed since Daniel was killed, and she hadn't heard a peep out of any of them, not even Betty.

"It's known as the deep freeze," she said to Clark Gable. "I guess I had better get used to it."

Her own calm and philosophical attitude came as a pleasant surprise. In the past, she had no tolerance for any kind of rejection. If the clerk at the art-supply shop looked at her crooked, it was enough to make her get drunk for the rest of the afternoon. Being slightly paranoid to start with, drinking exacerbated that condition to a painful degree.

She went through a pernod phase once, when she was convinced that at any moment a bunch of thieves, rapists, and lunatics were about to come marching through her terrace and do her bodily harm. She couldn't sleep in the bedroom during that phase (which lasted a full week), but would curl up into a fetal position on the sofa and keep a wary vigil all night, praying for her ultimate safety.

The phase finally ended when her supply of pernod ran out on a Sunday, and she switched to vodka. The vodka cleared her head fast and she resolved never to go back to pernod, it was a vicious drink. But a few months later she forgot her resolution and went through another sleepless, vicious, paranoid phase—only worse. She had started mixing pernod with gin, a concoction that kept her absolutely crazed through the entire autumn. . . .

❦ 2 ❦

After a leisurely breakfast, Jean decided to put her thoughts regarding Daniel's death in order. She sat down at the slant-top desk in a corner of the living room and made a list.

MURDER SUSPECTS

Group #1	Motive
1. Laura	Jealous of Daniel's marriage to Constance.
2. Constance	Last-minute cancellation of wedding, by Daniel.
3. Bob	To have clear field with Jean.

Group #2

4.	Betty	To avenge rejection of Jean.
5.	Peter	Old feud with Daniel ignited.
6.	Hugh	?
7.	Drunk	?
8.	Vanderbilt	Hatred of WASPs.
9.	Marcel	?
10.	O'Brien	Resentful of Daniel.

Group #3

11.	Eleanor	?
12.	Renee	?
13.	Francine	?
14.	Businessman	?

She wrote the names hurriedly, off the top of her head, not certain why she put the drunk in the second group and the tired-looking businessman in the third. They both had shown up at Clean Slate for the first time on Tuesday, and should probably be treated equally in terms of suspicion. Still, there was something about the way the drunk made such a spectacle of himself that stuck in her mind as being a little too theatrical to be true. If Hugh wasn't an alcoholic, why couldn't the drunk not be a drunk? Perhaps he'd purposely gotten bombed on Tuesday to have a cover.

The rest of the list seemed logical enough in its priorities. Marcel belonged in the second group only because he had more opportunity to kill Daniel than those in the third group. Jean could still see those four people huddled around the coffee urn waiting for Daniel to rejoin them: Betty, Peter, Laura, and Marcel.

Just having written the list made her feel better. At least she knew where to begin her investigation. With Laura. It was only a few minutes past eleven, which meant that Laura should still be at the network. Jean sometimes watched parts of the daily two-hour TV show *People Talk*, which Daniel's wife wrote for. It was a live, early-morning, news-chat show clearly modeled after *Today*, and she wondered if Laura harbored secret ambitions to follow in the footsteps of Barbara Walters who had also started as a television writer. Somehow Jean pictured Laura more as a behind-the-camera personality. Maybe it was that distinct Southern accent of hers, or the apparent awkwardness.

In the taxi, Jean realized that Daniel's death was the perfect excuse for barging in on Laura at work.

"I apologize for not expressing my condolences sooner," she would begin.

Laura had never once indicated that she was aware of Jean's relationship with her husband, and Jean admired her pride. Would she still be so proud now that she was a widow, and the truth about Constance was going to become public at last? Or would there be triumph in Laura's eyes? The triumph of having prevented Daniel from leaving her for another woman?

People Talk was located in the news department of the network, whose main offices were in an imposing modern building on Fifth Avenue. Jean took an elevator up to the twenty-eighth floor and asked a stunning black receptionist where she could find Laura Streatham.

"You mean, Laura *Roland*," the receptionist said, pushing a button on a sleek vermilion telephone. "Walk down the corridor as far as you can, and turn left."

At AA last names were almost never exchanged, and Jean had forgotten that Daniel's was really Roland. He changed it to Streatham when he became an actor and tried to join Equity. The union already listed a Daniel Roland among its members, and he took his mother's maiden name as the most desirable alternative. There was something very old-fashioned about Laura choosing to call herself Roland. It was as though she were announcing that she was first and foremost a married woman, and secondly a career person. Daniel and Laura had been married a long time, Jean realized, since 1965.

Huge blown-up photographs decorated the walls of the long corridor she found herself in. The photographs were of famous news personalities associated with the network over a period of years. The corridor was thickly carpeted and flanked by offices. Jean noted that the most prominent of these were occupied by the production staff of *People Talk*, and the two stars who co-hosted the popular morning show.

She nearly walked into one of them, a handsome red-haired man called Rick who had made a name for himself in daytime television because of a charming manner combined with an incisive wit. Before he joined the network he had been in a few movies, usually playing second or third lead, but it took *People Talk* to establish him as a superstar.

"Excuse me," Jean said.

Close up, Rick's smile was electric. "My fault."

There was a rumor that he and his co-hostess, an ex-fashion model, were having a hot affair. Jean wondered if the rumor were true. Both Rick and the beautiful ex-model were supposed to be happily married.

"Well, well. And what brings *you* here?"

Laura was standing in front of an opened door, dressed casually in a light blue corduroy pants-suit and a white cashmere sweater. With her gleaming long black hair against the white, she looked almost attractive. But the expression on her face was far from welcoming.

"I hope I didn't get you at a bad time," Jean said. "I'd like to talk to you about Daniel."

"Why not?" Laura shrugged. "Come on in, if you can stand the mess."

Jean saw what she meant.

The office was small, windowless, and cluttered. An old Underwood typewriter sat on the desk alongside a cardboard container of coffee and an ashtray overflowing with cigarette butts. Every inch of desk space was taken by something apparently related to *People Talk:* a glossy photo of Jack Klugman as Quincy, a copy of James Jones' posthumous novel, *Whistle,* a record jacket of Mary Travers' new album, a snapshot of a spectacled blonde taking someone's picture on the golf course. At closer inspection, Jean realized that the "someone" was Bob Hope, and the photographer was Susan Ford. In one corner was a color TV set with the video turned on to a game show, and the audio turned off. Laura ignored it, her eyes firmly focused on Jean.

"What *about* Daniel?" she asked.

Seeing her here in this no-nonsense workaday atmosphere, all visions of languorous Southern belles faded from Jean's mind. Even Laura's accent sounded less drawling. Jean quickly abandoned her stilted condolence speech in favor of something more to the point.

"Detective Rodriguez came to see me yesterday, and what he had to say was pretty upsetting. He told me that Daniel was planning to marry Constance. Is that true?"

"Yes, as a matter of fact it is. Why do you look so surprised?"

"I thought—"

"You thought you were the only woman in Daniel's life," Laura said, finishing the sentence for her. "Well, darling, join the crowd."

Jean tried to ignore the snideness in Laura's voice.

"Are you saying that you were agreeable to a divorce?"

"Why not?" Laura tapped her fingers on the Jack Klugman photo. "I had nothing to lose. There wasn't any money or property involved, and my heart was elsewhere. Quite frankly, a divorce would have been a big relief to me. My marriage ended a long time ago."

According to Rodriguez, it had ended before Daniel and Jean became lovers. Laura seemed to read her mind.

"No, not when you began shacking up with my husband. Way before that. As I said, you were merely *one* of the women in Daniel's life."

"Why does it give you so much satisfaction to remind me of that?"

"It's not a question of satisfaction. I just thought you might want to know about Daniel's crummy Casanova past. Although I guess it's irrelevant now that he's dead, isn't it?"

Laura was trying to hurt her, and Jean was trying not to give her that satisfaction. The woman's venom was almost palpable. No wonder Laura had never acknowledged Jean's affair with Daniel. She loved him too much to admit he was cheating on her, but it was a ferocious, smothering kind of love. Jean could see now why Laura chose to call herself Roland. It was all she'd been able to extract from Daniel—his last name.

"If he was such a Casanova," Jean said, "why do you suppose he planned to marry Constance and settle down?"

Laura laughed joylessly.

"What the hell makes you think that marriage meant settling down to my husband? He never settled down with me, and I strongly doubt if he had any intention of doing so with Constance. Daniel looked upon a wife as a very handy convenience. Someone to cook his meals, take care of the laundry, and be a built-in fuck."

"Since you have such a low opinion of him, why were you in tears on Tuesday?" Jean came back at her. "Are you sure you weren't crying because you knew you'd lost him?"

"My tears had nothing to do with Daniel. Just because you happened to be in love with him, doesn't mean that to everyone else he was the sun, moon, and stars. I couldn't have cared less what he did, or who he married. I was upset for a totally different reason than Daniel, but it's none of your damned business."

"It *is* my business. Rodriguez thinks I killed Daniel,

and I think you did. I think you had provocation to kill him. You loved him, and he was leaving you for another woman."

"That's ridiculous! I had nothing to do with Daniel's death and the police know it. Rodriguez has spoken to my attorney, who told him that I inquired about a divorce months before Daniel and Constance made plans to marry. I'd been thinking about dissolving my marriage for a long time, and for reasons you're not aware of. I just said it was none of your business, but I'll tell you anyway."

Laura paused for full dramatic effect.

"I happen to be involved with the star of *People Talk*, and have been for several years. The reason I was crying on Tuesday was because Rick's wife is giving him a hard time now that she knows he wants to leave her. And in *that* divorce, there'll be a great deal of money at stake."

Laura emphasized this last part, as though to make sure that Jean understood the significant financial difference between her lover and her husband.

"I thought Rick was having an affair with the co-host of the show," Jean said. "That ex-model."

"So you fell for the rumors about him and Monique, too! Good!" Laura clapped her hands triumphantly. "That's exactly what we wanted everyone to think. It's a wonderful smokescreen for us. Also, the make-believe affair is great for ratings whereas I wouldn't be. A lowly television writer, you know. We've even got Rick's wife believing he's banging Monique, which means that she and her lawyer are following the wrong lady and barking up the wrong tree. It couldn't be more perfect except for the inconvenience."

"What do you mean?"

"Rick and I can't spend too much time together, or people would wonder. And since we're in love, it's hard for us to be apart. I've told Rodriguez about all this, which is why he has no cause to suspect me of killing

Daniel. But I should think your motives are more open to question, aren't they?"

Jean felt like slapping the smirk off Laura's mouth. Still, this was only the beginning. The others at Clean Slate would be thinking (if not saying) the same sort of thing, and she had better get used to it. What she would never get used to, though, was someone *wanting* her to be guilty, as Laura so obviously did. Did Laura really think she had killed Daniel? Or was Laura just anxious to divert suspicion from herself?

Jean wasn't sure. If Laura was having an affair with the star of *People Talk*, then she was in the clear. She would have had no motive to kill Daniel. But was she telling the truth? The romance with Rick was a perfect cover because it would be so hard to check. Everyone at the network would deny it whether true or not, but what did that prove? As Laura said, the make-believe affair was the one people wanted to believe, it boosted ratings. *If* it was make-believe, Jean had to remind herself.

"Rick was in here a few minutes ago, when the receptionist buzzed," Laura said, almost coquettishly. "It's barbaric the way we have to sneak our moments together. But all that will be over soon."

"Oh?"

"Yes, indeedy. Things are starting to look up at last."

"I thought you said his wife was giving him a hard time."

"That was Tuesday. But what a difference forty-eight little hours can make. It seems she's finally begun to recognize the inevitability of losing him, even though she assumes it's to Monique. She called her lawyer yesterday, making divorce sounds. That's what Rick came in to tell me when you arrived. So you see, you're looking at a very happy lady."

Or a very shrewd one, Jean thought.

"It's just too bad my dear husband isn't alive to share

my happiness," Laura said, tacking Jack Klugman's photo to the wall. "I certainly hope they catch the son of a bitch who killed him, don't you?"

The thumbtack went right through the center of Jack Klugman's forehead.

◎3◎

Laura was mad as hell at Jean's showing up at the network, probing into her tangled relationship with Daniel. The damned *impudence* of the woman. Who did she think she was, Laura wondered, except another piece of ass in Daniel's life? Constance was a force to be reckoned with, but Jean? Hardly. Still she was a troublemaker, the way she'd accused Laura of killing Daniel!

As the two women walked over to Clean Slate together, Laura silently congratulated herself on cooling the sticky situation by sounding so positive about her future with Rick. The fact was that she had never felt less positive about anyone. Rick was one of the most handsome, sexy men she ever met and women were all over him. They were climbing out of his ears and it had taken her months to get rid of the masses before she was able to claim him for her own.

Only then did she begin to consider the obstacle of his having a wife and two children. She started to hint (delicately) about their getting married someday, and he (just as delicately) agreed it would be wonderful. Yet when she tried to pin him down, he was slippery. She refused to give up and kept after him.

"But, honey, you're married too," he finally said one day. "So why don't we just continue like this?"

"Because I think it's time we started to consider our future."

"There is no such animal." Rick laughed. "I love you right now. In the present. Isn't that enough?"

"It most certainly is not," Laura said emphatically. "I've asked my husband for a divorce, and if you really love me you'll get one too."

"A divorce?" He roared as though it were the most outrageous idea in the world. "You must be out of your sweet Southern mind, sugar."

"But you said it would be wonderful to be married to me."

"Sure. If I weren't already married. That's what I meant. I thought you understood."

Understood! That was two months ago, and Laura had panicked. She felt so positive Rick would do anything she wanted, that in a moment of sublime self-confidence she had indeed written to Daniel asking for her freedom. Daniel happily agreed, saying he was thinking about getting remarried himself. Laura knew what a bitch Constance was, and figured it would serve Daniel right. Then just as things were progressing so smoothly, Rick backed off, leaving her out on a limb, dangling.

Since that time she had tried everything to make him change his mind, but Rick was adamant. He said he was married to a perfectly decent woman and he couldn't ruin his wholesome television image by crassly leaving her and abandoning his children, to boot. He talked about things like Nielsen ratings, while Laura thought about her own premature optimism. What a fool she was to have asked Daniel for a divorce so soon.

There was only one thing to do. Tell Daniel that she had changed her mind and wanted to save their marriage. She didn't want any such thing, she didn't love Daniel anymore, but by remaining married to him she had a better chance of eventually landing the evasive Rick. As an eager, available, single woman it would be hopeless, her position worse than ever.

123

"Absolutely not," Daniel replied to her request. "It's much too late for us to try again. You must realize that."

"I don't. I'm your wife, and that's the way it's going to stay."

"Over my dead body."

Daniel insisted he would get a divorce one way or the other, and if she refused to cooperate there were legal avenues he could pursue. She called him in Chicago saying she would never give him up; she cried, she pleaded, she begged. When Daniel laughed, he sounded like Rick laughing. Laura was beside herself, horrified by the mess she'd made of things. Daniel got back to New York on Sunday, and she went to see him at that filthy apartment in the Village. Once again, she asked him to reconsider his position.

"I wouldn't stay married to a cunt like you if you had eighteen million dollars and were the greatest fuck in the world," said Mr. Wonderful. "Since you're neither, I suggest you get the hell out of here and not bother me again."

Laura slowly walked back home, thinking of her humiliation when everyone at Clean Slate found out he was going to leave her for Constance, thinking of her abysmal stalemate with Rick, thinking, thinking. . . . If Daniel were to fall off the face of the earth, her pride would be saved . . . if Daniel were to drop dead she could hold up her head at Clean Slate and Rick might even be persuaded to change his mind. Widows were much more sympathetic figures than divorcees; men felt protective toward them, tender, they wanted to console them for their tragic loss. . . .

What was it Rick had called her once? *Determined.* Perhaps he was right, because when she saw Daniel's convulsed face on Tuesday and heard Peter pronounce him dead, all she could think of was how much easier it would now be to get Rick to marry her. Why, it wouldn't even affect his Nielsens so badly. Widows were victims of calamitous circumstances, they were noble creatures, respectable, acceptable, appealing. Rick's ratings might even go up!

❦ 4 ❦

When Jean and Laura arrived at Clean Slate together, more than one person turned around to stare at them. But no one spoke to Laura until she had separated herself from Jean; then the others came forward and asked her if she felt well enough to be there, applauded her courage, commiserated with her bereavement. Except for Betty, they all steered clear of Jean.

"Since when did you and Scarlett O'Hara become pals?" Betty asked.

"I'll explain later. What are you doing after the meeting?"

"Nothing. Peter's got an acting class."

"How about lunch?"

"Fine."

Constance rapped on the desk for silence and began to read the AA preamble. Then she announced that she would be today's speaker.

"I need to get something off my chest," she said.

Jean forced her mind away from the unsettling talk with Laura onto Constance, her next suspect in Group #1. If she was lucky, Constance might indicate a last-minute argument with Daniel, something unpleasant that caused him to change his mind about getting married. Daniel was impulsive, hot-tempered. It would not have been out of character for him to angrily cancel their wedding plans just like that. Then in a rage, Constance killed him.

If so, she looked glowingly innocent two days after the fact. Constance was wearing a pale green knitted

125

dress, gold jewelry, and high suede boots. Her blonde hair had been pulled back into a graceful chignon, and on the surface she was her usual well-groomed, self-contained self. Her opening remarks surprised Jean.

"I grew up on a farm in Iowa, but you can forget all those dirty jokes about the farmer's daughter because they didn't apply to me. I was the original hick. Virginal, naive, church-going. Nobody in my family drank, liquor was considered the devil's curse. I didn't pick up my first drink until I was twenty-one and had moved to New York. I still remember it, a sloe gin fizz. . . ."

Constance went on recounting headaches and hangovers, lost jobs and lost friends, all the familiar afflictions of the garden-variety alcoholic. Yet the way she told her story, it was eloquent and moving. About halfway through, Bob walked in and sat down in the back row next to the man who'd been drunk on Tuesday. He was sober now, but blatantly hungover. His hands shook and he was drinking Coca-Cola in long, thirsty gulps. Jean recognized the signs of dehydration that followed a heavy drinking bout, which meant that he was probably a bona-fide alcoholic and not the imposter she had suspected. Still, the fact that he belonged in AA did not mean he was innocent of murder. Jean mentally moved him from Group #2 on her suspect list, to Group #3. His motive remained a question mark.

A moment later Jean realized that O'Brien was absent today, and that Constance had begun to talk about Daniel.

"Despite the fact that the man I loved was murdered here in this very room two days ago, I still have not picked up a drink. I loved Daniel with all my heart and he loved me. He was on the verge of getting a divorce, then we were going to be married. It was all worked out. We had even planned where we were going to live. Southern California. I can tell you this now, and I tell

126

you proudly. I loved Daniel, and a piece of me died when he did."

There was a rustling of surprise in the room as everyone tried to assimilate this startling new information. They had all thought Daniel was in love with Jean. Next to Jean, Laura was scowling with disapproval at what Constance had just said. Laura did not like being upstaged in her role as the bereaved widow.

"Very touching," Laura muttered, staring venomously at Constance. "The fiancée who never got to the altar."

Somehow Jean couldn't believe that Laura was as willing to give Daniel his freedom as she pretended. Laura struck her as far too possessive to let Daniel walk out of her life, marry a beautiful blonde, and move three thousand miles away. Not without one hell of a struggle. A struggle ending in murder?

"I knew that picking up a drink couldn't bring Daniel back to life. Whoever killed him is answering to his own God this very minute, or *her* own God," Constance said, looking at Jean. "But I realize that personal atonement isn't enough. The murderer must be legally apprehended and brought to justice. I can only hope and pray that happens soon. Thank you."

Hearty applause followed Constance's speech. The usual basket was passed around for contributions, and then the discussion period began. Jean raised her hand.

"My name is Jean and I'm an alcoholic. Perhaps the following statement will sound as though I'm protesting too much, but I must say it anyway. *I did not kill Daniel.* I know that many of you believe I'm guilty, and that makes me sad. Like Constance, I loved Daniel and would never have harmed him. I can empathize with what Constance has gone through the last couple of days, and how hard it's been for her not to pick up a drink. It's been hard for me as well. Unfortunately, the worst is not yet over. I mean for all of us.

"As Constance pointed out, Daniel's killer is still at

large. Possibly he is sitting here in this room this very minute, yet none of us knows who it is. Clever. Daring. Unscrupulous. That's the kind of person we're dealing with, and I urge everyone to bear it in mind. There's a lot of trust in this room, and that's one of the reasons the killer has been able to get away with this terrible crime so far. Because of the trust we feel for each other. What I'm saying to you is, *be careful*. Keep your eyes open. Suspect everyone. Thank you."

A stunned silence ensued. It was a strongly felt speech. Then a few people began to applaud, and Betty put her hand up.

"My name is Betty and I'm an alcoholic. Personally, I believe Jean. I realize that being Jean's friend and sponsor, I'm prejudiced, but I also know her pretty well. When something goes wrong, she takes it out on herself, not on others. Her rage turns inward, not outward. Like this past Sunday, after Daniel broke off their affair. I went over to see Jean, and what did I find? A vindictive, spiteful woman? No. I found a hurt, bewildered one who was afraid that if left to her own devices, she'd pick up a drink. Not a bottle of poison to kill someone, but a *glass* of poison to help kill herself.

"Fortunately, I was able to intervene and Jean didn't take that first drink. I well realize that her being sober, doesn't mean she's innocent. But there is something I would like to point out. In this country a person is legally innocent until proven guilty, and no court of law has proven Jean Neelie guilty of killing Daniel Streatham. I suggest we all try and remember that salient fact."

"Thank you'" Constance said. "It's a good reminder."

Jean was impressed by Betty's heartfelt yet effective words. Betty might have been a criminal lawyer defending her client before a hostile jury, and Jean wondered if the others were equally moved. There seemed to be a buzzing of conversation, then a few people turned

128

around to glance at her as though a shifting of viewpoint might be taking place. Marcel, who'd been avoiding her gaze, turned and smiled, his teeth browned from pipe tobacco.

Jean smiled back at him through the haze of smoke, her eye catching Bob's. He was looking at her with devotion, yearning. *I'm going to fall in love with you*, he had said this morning. Why did it sound like a threat instead of a beautiful promise? Probably because of the two terrible experiences she'd had with Frank and Daniel. They had both loved her, they had both betrayed her, they were both dead. Was she afraid that another loving man meant another catastrophe? Perhaps.

Yet she did not want to live in fear . . . that Bob would die in some ghastly and unexpected manner, that her vulnerable heart would die again. No, she didn't want that at all. What she wanted (she suddenly realized) was to be happy, brave, loving, strong . . . and self-assured. It was a funny feeling, wishing to be self-assured, an odd feeling, alien and yet familiar all at once. And somehow she knew she could be, she knew it in a wild kind of way which meant the aspiration had been there for a long time, lying low, waiting for the right moment to make itself known. She had squandered too much energy thinking that the worst was going to happen. Why not think that the *best* would? Why not believe it in the depths of her vulnerable heart? (and maybe it would come true).

"I've been debating whether I should share this with everyone and I decided it can't hurt. It might even help us find the killer."

Jean realized that, next to her, Laura was speaking.

"It's about how Daniel was killed, the kind of poison that was used. Detective Rodriguez didn't want to give me that information, but I managed to convince him that as Daniel's wife I was entitled to know. Well, it was nicotine sulfate. You're probably wondering what that means. All I can tell you is that in large enough quantities, it's a deadly poison. It's also very easily obtainable. Anyone can buy it. According to the police it's one of the principal ingredients in certain insecticides which are for sale at garden stores everywhere."

Assured that she had the group's attention, Laura went on.

"The police found traces of nicotine in the aspirin bottle the killer used. Rodriguez said it's a good thing that bottle was discovered, or Daniel's death might never have been attributed to murder. He was a heavy smoker, and it would have been natural for there to be a large concentration of nicotine in his bloodstream anyway. But thanks to the aspirin bottle, the coroner was looking for *especially* heavy amounts when he performed the autopsy, and he found them."

Some of Rodriguez' questions now made sense to Jean. That was why he asked her whether Daniel was a heavy smoker, and what kind of insecticide she used in her garden. Thank God she didn't use any. But how could Rodriguez be sure of that? He might think that she got rid of the evidence after knocking off her boyfriend. Having a garden, was one more strike against her. Even though anyone could buy an insecticide (as Laura pointed out), wouldn't it be convenient to have the filthy stuff on hand? That would be the cynical attitude of most people, Jean thought, wondering how she could apply her burgeoning optimism to this unpalatable new development.

"Thank you for that information," Constance said to Laura. "Nicotine poisoning. It sounds very clever."

"According to the police, nicotine sulfate has a bitter taste, but then so does coffee," Laura said. "Particularly when it's drunk black, the way Daniel liked it."

Constance looked at her as if to say that she knew perfectly well how Daniel liked his coffee. The hostility between the two women seemed to stick out a mile. The wife and the fiancée, Jean thought, realizing how little she had actually mattered in Daniel's life. It seemed strange that he should have preferred Constance to her, to the wonderful new person she was about to be, strange and disappointing. Perhaps she had overestimated Daniel, just as in the past she had underestimated herself.

Jean had no reason now to doubt Constance's word. Not because Constance was incapable of lying, but because Laura wouldn't be so snide toward her if the wedding weren't real enough. Which meant that Constance had less motive than anyone in the room for killing Daniel. Why would she want to see her future husband dead?

Jean mentally removed Constance's name from Group #1 and put it in a new category, Group #4 ("No longer suspect"), by itself. That left only Laura and Bob in the first group. Jean still considered Laura a prime suspect. Laura was mean, vindictive, and bitchy, and Jean would not put it past her to resort to murder in order to keep Daniel from being happy with another woman. *But only if she herself was unloved and unhappy.* To Jean's mind, Laura's innocence depended a lot on whether or not she was truly involved with the star of *People Talk*. Somehow Jean was going to have to find out if that story were true.

With Bob, the situation was even trickier. For two reasons:

1. His motive of possessive jealousy was far-fetched.
2. She didn't believe him capable of murder.

Remembering last night, every part of her felt electrically charged, and she longed to make love to him again. Maybe she wasn't the greatest judge of character in the world, but she didn't think she could desire a murderer. Her instincts would warn her there was something wrong, wouldn't they? She felt certain she could count on them, she prayed she could. . . . She wanted to be with him this very minute. She wondered if he wanted her as badly. . . .

Then the meeting was over and Bob appeared at her side.

"Are you free for dinner?" he asked.

"I was just going to invite you to my place. Thelma is making a pork roast."

"I wouldn't care if she were making broiled bluefish."

"What's wrong with broiled bluefish?"

"I don't like it."

"I hope you like red cabbage and acorn squash, because that's what she's serving with the pork."

"I can't wait to see you naked again."

They refrained from kissing, conscious of the others milling around. All those innocent-looking faces, she thought, and one of them probably belonged to the murderer. Out of the corner of her eye, she saw Betty motioning to her that she was getting hungry. Lunch with Betty, dinner with Bob, both of them dear to her and both suspects in this terrible case that *she* was going to solve.

There suddenly seemed no doubt in Jean's mind that she would solve it—and soon. Yet here on this cold, crisp, early March day with a handsome man smiling at her lovingly, murder struck her as irrelevant and unreal. It was as though Daniel had never been killed, as though she'd merely had a bad dream. . . .

⊚5⊚

As soon as they had ordered lunch, Betty reached for Jean's hand across the table and squeezed it.

"I'm sorry, kid. What can I say? Daniel was an even bigger bastard than I imagined. All the time he was making love to you, he was making love to Constance too.

And planning to marry her! How low can you get? No wonder somebody poisoned him. The only thing that surprises me is that she didn't do it sooner."

"*She?* Who's she?"

"I don't know. Whoever else he was screwing."

Jean broke off a whole-wheat breadstick, startled by Betty's line of reasoning. They were at a popular health-food restaurant. It specialized in quiches made with naturally incubated eggs and organically grown vegetables.

"You don't believe that Daniel was killed because some mysterious woman decided he was being unfaithful to her, do you?"

"I didn't before today," Betty said. "But I get a much clearer picture of Daniel now that I know what a double-crosser he was. Yes, I think he was murdered because one of his playmates refused to sit still for his crummy behavior any longer. And I don't mean you. I was serious when I said I believed in your innocence. I didn't at first, but I do now."

"One of his *playmates?*"

"Sure. Another gullible gal at Clean Slate that he was screwing around with. She got wise to the fact that she wasn't exactly numero uno in his life, flipped out, and poisoned the prick. Why do you look so surprised?"

Their quiches and alfalfa salads arrived. Jean's quiche was made with artichoke hearts and was probably delicious, but she had lost her appetite.

"*Another* one?" she said incredulously. "You mean in addition to Laura, Constance, and me?"

"Why not?" Betty's appetite did not seem to be adversely affected. "I know this is painful for you, but try to be rational. This could be the missing motive. Daniel was obviously a Don Juan, and if he pulled off that neat charade with you and Constance, why can't there have been a third woman involved?"

"Fourth. You left out Laura."

"Okay, fourth. Tenth. With guys like that, the more the merrier. Aren't you going to eat your lunch?"

Betty might be right. The only reason it hadn't occurred to her before was that the idea was too revolting. Learning about Constance was bad enough. What she had to do was gain entrance to Daniel's apartment, and poke around. She might find something. Also, as soon as she got home she would make a list of the remaining women at Clean Slate and consider them, one by one, in light of Betty's suggestion.

"What made you decide I was innocent?" she asked.

"The way you spoke up at Clean Slate today. I was moved by what you said. I don't think you could have sounded like that if you were lying. No. It's another woman, all right."

"Maybe."

"If I were you, I'd be suspicious of every man I met from now on. Don't believe a word they say."

Jean laughed. "Oh really, Betty."

"You believed Daniel and look where it got you. I hope you don't make the same mistake with Bob."

Jean felt herself blushing. "How did you know?"

"I saw that tender scene between the two of you before, and I'm glad that you're not sitting around playing the ice maiden. But take my advice and be suspicious. If Bob says he's divorced, ask to see the documents. And don't look at me like I'm crazy. The inventor I told you about used to assure every woman he met that he was a free agent. That was another thing he invented: instant, imaginary divorce. He not only had a wife tucked away in the suburbs, he'd been living with her for the last ten years. I'll let you in on a secret. I'm still suspicious of Peter, even after all this time."

"Peter?"

"I know what you're thinking. Who wouldn't trust devoted, honest, freckle-faced Peter? Don't let that innocent look of his fool you, Peter is much sneakier than

134

you might imagine. Like right now. He says he's at an acting class, but I'm keeping an open cynical mind about it. Maybe he is, and maybe he's in some curvy redhead's bed."

"You're a curvy redhead," Jean pointed out. "Has he been unfaithful before?"

"Let's just say I haven't caught him at it."

Betty looked especially attractive today. She was wearing an aquamarine sweater and dyed-to-match wool skirt. Jean had never seen her in trousers. Betty always wore skirts and dresses as though to emphasize her blatant femininity. Her long hair fell over her shoulders in waves reminiscent of Rita Hayworth in the old movies. Betty was a throwback, Jean thought, to the image of the sexy but hard-boiled chorus girl of another day. It was as though the feminist movement and women's liberation had never touched her.

"Speaking of Peter, there's something I want you to know." Betty suddenly seemed nervous. "He's asked me to marry him."

A moment later, Jean regained her powers of speech.

"And you accuse *him* of being sneaky?"

"He just proposed last night, I didn't have a chance to tell you before this. The problem is that he wants to get married immediately, and I want to wait. No, I don't exactly *want* to, but I feel I have to . . . because of the time element. You know, the one-year AA restriction about not making any major changes in your life until you've been sober for an entire year. I've only been sober for seven months. . . ."

"It's not exactly a restriction. It's more of a suggestion. Nobody is compelled to abide by it."

"I realize that, but I'm afraid to take a chance. I've heard such terrible stories about people who did and ended up in detox centers. Or worse. I've worked hard on my sobriety and I don't want to screw it all up now, especially when it's only a matter of five more months. Do you understand, Jean?"

What struck Jean was that after all this time, she still had no idea whether Betty loved Peter. Really loved him. Betty had never committed herself on the subject.

"Does Peter understand?" she said. "That's what you ought to be asking yourself. He should. He's an alcoholic, too. What does he say?"

"That I'm being foolish, that nothing horrendous is going to happen to me if we get married tomorrow, that I'm using this one-year business as an excuse to wiggle out of the wedding."

Jean had the same feeling. "Are you?"

"Of course not," Betty said defensively. "Don't *you* start in on me too. Peter is bad enough. I don't want to lose him, Jean, but neither do I want to go back to drinking again. That awful nightmare. I guess I'll have to work out the answer by myself. It's just that I was so flabbergasted when he popped the question. We were having dinner at Sardi's last night. . . ."

ᘓ6ᘐ

Betty could not stop babbling, even though she saw how disappointed Jean was by her indecision. Jean probably thought that she was unsure of whether she wanted to marry Peter, whether she even *loved* him. Jean would be stunned if she knew the truth. Betty's feelings for Peter were something she never spoke about; they were too special, too deep, too exclusive. Peter was the first man she had ever truly loved; that married inventor in the Midwest barely touched her heart. Peter could break it, if he chose to. Peter made her feel truly female, as opposed to other men who were taken in by that tough exterior of hers and considered her a ballbreaker.

Betty knew what they thought and if it weren't so comical, she would have cried. In private she was the most devoted and loving of helpmates, but because of her deep-seated insecurity she couldn't reveal that side of herself in public. The fact that she was five years older than Peter only made her more anxious to please and take care of him; all of her thwarted maternal instincts surfaced when they were alone. She cooked for him, cleaned his apartment, even ironed his shirts, and secretly called him *baby*.

"Oh, baby, you're such a marvelous actor," she had told him at the beginning of the week. "Why are you so worried about the audition with this Daniel character?"

"Because he's a genius," Peter replied. "You don't know him, you've never met him, you've never seen him on stage. He takes it over and makes it his own. I can't begin to compete, and the bitch of it all is that I want the damned part. God, how I want it! Why the hell did he have to come back to New York *now?*"

"Do you think you'd stand a chance without him?"

"I'm positive of it," Peter said. "The director likes me, we're old friends. But that won't matter when he hears Daniel read. Believe me, it won't matter one tiny bit."

When she saw Peter later on Monday after the audition, it began to seem as though he were right. He told her that although no decision had been made, Daniel's reading was brilliant, inspired. Peter was positive that Daniel would get the part. Betty sat through the Clean Slate meeting listening to Daniel talk, and even though it was not a professional performance she could see what Peter meant. Daniel was compelling, endearing, sympathetic without being pitiable, strong without being insensitive (on the surface anyway). Yes, Betty could see that as an actor he would probably have it all over Peter, and she resented him for it.

Having spent most of Sunday listening to Jean's tale of heartbreak, Betty was prepared to resent Daniel anyhow.

The fact that the same man was lousing up the lives of the two people she cared for most was something that Betty Lathrop did not take lightly. She wanted Peter to have that part. She wanted Jean to be happy. She hated and despised Daniel even before he invited her and Peter to lunch after Monday's meeting.

And during lunch, her hatred grew. Daniel was the sort of man who used his not-inconsiderable charm to get whatever he wanted, who stepped over others less forceful than he, who would stop at nothing to have his own way, fulfill his greedy and self-indulgent desires. Her father was like Daniel. He cheated, lied, connived, and ruined her mother's health. It was because of her father that she found it so hard to trust men until Peter came along . . . sweet, well-intentioned, easily taken advantage of by people like Daniel. Daniel had cruelly taken advantage of Jean too, pretended to love her. . . .

Betty never knew she was capable of so much hatred until that Monday at lunch, when she listened to Daniel say how wonderful he thought she was for Peter. It was obvious he thought nothing of the kind; Daniel didn't like her, his sarcasm and patronizing remarks cut through her like a blade, and it was then that she wished he were dead. If Daniel were to die, Peter would probably get that part. If Daniel were to die, Jean would have a chance to forget him and be happy.

She hated Daniel so much that the next day she refused to sit near him at Clean Slate. She told Peter she would go up front by herself, rather than be near that monster.

"But, Betty, he's my best friend," poor, sweet, misguided Peter said.

"Then *you* sit next to him."

Silly as it sounded, it was their first argument. Caused by that troublemaker, Daniel. When he died less than an hour later, Betty was not hypocrite enough to pretend to feel sorry or upset. The only thing she was sorry about was that Peter took it so hard, he started to flirt with Francine in an attempt to forget his grief. Betty had felt jealous of Francine—tired from that long police interrogation, drained—but mostly she felt relieved that Daniel would never hurt anyone again. . . .

☜7☞

As soon as Jean got home, she sat down at the slant-top desk and made a list of all the women who'd been at Clean Slate on Tuesday. She wanted to see if she could figure out with whom Daniel might have had an affair. Aside from herself, Laura, and Constance the list was short:

1. Eleanor
2. Francine
3. Renee
4. Betty

Except for Francine, she couldn't imagine Daniel going to bed with any of them. Eleanor was too aggressively desperate, Renee was too old, and Betty was too involved with Peter. But Francine was beautiful, young, and exotic enough to appeal to Daniel. And Francine knew about the empty aspirin bottle before anyone else, Jean suddenly remembered. At least she had mentioned it first.

Clark Gable came over and was trying to get her attention by placing his paws on the legs of her pants-suit. She wondered if Clark Gable would like her so much if she were a man. Were dogs attracted to people of the opposite sex, just as people were? People who were not homosexual, she amended, glancing at the list of women

139

again. But what if it hadn't been another woman in Daniel's life? What if it had been another man?

She thought of Hugh sipping wine at the restaurant last night. Could Hugh have been posing as an alcoholic in order to see Daniel every day? It seemed unlikely, but so did the idea of a person without a drinking problem going to AA meetings. What if Daniel was bisexual? The possibility hadn't occurred to her before, and she needed time to consider it. She would work on her original plan first, and if nothing came of that, then she would consider a male lover.

The next step was to get into Daniel's apartment and see if she could find any evidence that he had known Francine intimately. That was going to be difficult. The police had undoubtedly been there and removed anything that might have a bearing on the case. They might even have put a padlock on the door to discourage snooping people like herself.

"Be inventive," she said out loud. "Be daring."

Clark Gable thought she was talking to him and began to bark in reply, which brought Thelma in from the kitchen. Thelma's hands were streaked purple from cutting cabbage, and her face was steamy.

"Did you call, Mrs. Neelie?"

"I'm sorry, Thelma. I was thinking out loud."

"Just so long as I'm not hearing things. What time shall I serve dinner?"

"At eight. As usual."

"I hope your guest likes pork. Some people don't. He's not Jewish, is he?"

Thelma always became anxious when Jean invited someone new to dinner, and she was used to it by now.

"I really don't know what Mr. Edwards' religion is, but he seemed very happy when I mentioned pork."

"Then he's probably not Jewish."

"Stop worrying. I'm sure it will be a great success."

Thelma shook her head uncertainly. "I don't like the looks of those squash."

A few minutes later as Jean was trying to figure out how to get into Daniel's apartment, the telephone rang.

"Wait until you hear the latest," Betty said breathlessly.

"They've found Daniel's murderer."

"No. They found O'Brien stabbed to death."

๑8ฎ

Rodriguez mechanically checked Betty Lathrop's name off the alphabetical list of Clean Slate suspects, and looked at the next name. Jean Neelie. He wondered how the attractive and alluring Mrs. Neelie was going to account for her whereabouts last night at the time O'Brien was murdered. She'd better have a damned good alibi, he thought, better than that of her new boyfriend.

"I was home, shaving," Bob had snidely said just a little while ago. "And no, I cannot prove it."

Sitting on a blotter, on Rodriguez' desk, was the blue AA book that the police had retrieved from O'Brien's apartment. The killer had carefully propped up the book on the floor next to the murdered man, so that the entire bottom of the book was soaked clear through with his blood. The book was obviously O'Brien's own copy (only his fingerprints marked the pages), which meant that the killer had worn gloves throughout. When the police got to Amsterdam Avenue late that morning, the blood was still slightly wet. Rodriguez grimaced and dialed Jean Neelie.

"Betty just told me the shocking news," Jean said. "Do you have any idea who did it?"

"That's why I'm calling you."

"Me?"

"Where were you last night between seven and seven-thirty?"

"Right here. I was taking a bath. Then I changed clothes before going to meet Bob for dinner."

"Do you have proof of that?"

"Of what? That I was taking a bath?"

"Don't be cute, Mrs. Neelie. That you were home at the time?"

She hesitated. "No, I don't. My cook doesn't come in on Wednesdays. I was alone."

"Nobody called you on the phone? You didn't call anybody? You didn't see a neighbor? Nothing like that?"

"Nothing like that."

"That's too bad."

"You don't really suspect *me* of killing O'Brien, do you?" she asked incredulously.

"At this point, I suspect everyone who doesn't have an airtight alibi for last night."

"Yes," she said thoughtfully. "Of course. You mean, everyone at Clean Slate, don't you, Detective Rodriguez?"

"That's right."

"How do you know that a stranger didn't kill O'Brien? A burglar? A junkie?"

"Because nothing appears to have been stolen from the apartment. The police checked very carefully, all of O'Brien's possessions were in order. Nothing had been touched. And there was no sign of a forced entry. Apparently, O'Brien let the person in himself. It was somebody he knew, somebody he was friendly with."

"I see. When did you find the body?"

"This morning. The guy who tended bar with O'Brien called us. When O'Brien didn't show up for work last night, this guy just figured he was off on another binge. But when there was no maudlin, apologetic telephone call today, he became suspicious. He went around to

O'Brien's building and the super let him in. They found the poor bastard lying in a pool of blood on the kitchen floor, a knife wound clear through his back. How do you like them apples?"

"Ghastly." He could hear her intake of breath on the other end of the telephone. "You think it's the same person who killed Daniel, don't you?"

"It seems likely." He hadn't been going to mention the bloodstained AA book, but now he changed his mind. "Do all of you people have a copy of this book?"

"I don't know about the others, it's optional. I have one. Why? What are you getting at?"

"I thought perhaps you could shed some light on the murderer's actions. Why he chose to prop up the book alongside the victim's body. It didn't serve any practical purpose. Is there any symbolism involved? Does it suggest anything to you, Mrs. Neelie?"

"Yes, it suggests that we're dealing with a lunatic. At one point Betty said she was afraid the murderer might be systematically planning to kill everyone at Clean Slate. And now that I've spoken to you, I think she has a point."

"I don't," Rodriguez said emphatically.

"Why not? If this monster could have murdered two innocent people, then why not three? Six? Ten?"

"I have reason to believe that is not going to happen." Rodriguez hoped he sounded convincing. "You take it easy now, Mrs. Neelie. I'll be in touch."

He hung up and put a big red question mark next to Jean Neelie's name. The restaurant she'd met Bob at last night was only a few blocks from her apartment. She could have stabbed O'Brien to death at, say, seven-fifteen, gone home (crosstown) to change her clothes, and still had time to meet Bob at eight. Easily. The same was true of Bob, of course.

Rodriguez sighed and lit a cigarette.

He had more Clean Slate suspects to call, more alibis

to check out, a lot more work to do before this damned case was going to be solved. Daniel's death had seemed a relatively simple matter, but O'Brien complicated things. Like Betty, Rodriguez wondered if they were dealing with a mass murderer, perhaps someone who had a psychopathic grudge against alcoholics. He looked at the next name on his list. Hugh Paderewski. Or, Mr. Hugh, as his illustrious clients called him.

Rodriguez suddenly remembered what Hugh told him about his family's history. In light of O'Brien's murder, he found it extremely interesting. . . .

೩9೮

It was several months since Jean had been in the Village, and she tried not to compare the way it was now with the way it used to be when she was growing up. The area suffered so much by comparison.

All of the old leisurely charm that she remembered from her childhood had been replaced by a frenetic, circuslike atmosphere, and the people she passed on the streets were self-consciously dressed and made up. Everyone seemed to be trying hard for individuality but, they all came out looking alike. She walked through Washington Square Park, not far from where she and her parents had once lived, and over to Thompson Street.

The only reason she came down to the Village these days was because of the art galleries that had started to flourish in Soho in recent years. Daniel's apartment on Thompson Street was just north of Soho. She located the building easily, it was a renovated tenement wedged between an Italian restaurant and a chess shop. The telephone call from Rodriguez had given her the idea of how to get into Daniel's apartment.

All of the bells were arranged vertically on the outside of the building, with the name of the occupant next to each one. She noted the number of Daniel's apartment, then rang the one marked "Superintendent." A young man with a beard opened the front door.

"Yes?" he said. "Can I help you?"

He was wearing sneakers, blue jeans, and a T-shirt. The shirt said *University of Miami* in red letters against a yellow background. Jean had expected to be greeted by an elderly Italian who spoke broken English. That was the kind of superintendent who would have been employed there in the old days.

"I was told that apartment 5-C is for rent," she said. "I'd like to look at it."

"Who told you that?"

"Mr. Streatham's wife. She's a friend of mine." Jean paused delicately. "When I read about the death of her husband, I called to say how sorry I was. Then I asked about the apartment. She said that as far as she knew, it was available."

The bearded man scrutinized her doubtfully, and Jean realized it was a mistake to have worn her mink cape. She should have put on her old duffle coat, but she'd been in such a hurry to get here that she didn't think.

"I'm not supposed to show these apartments to anyone who doesn't come through the real estate agency," the bearded man said. "If they found out, I could lose my job."

She took a ten-dollar bill out of her purse and handed it to him. "I'll only be up there a few minutes."

He put the bill in the back pocket of his jeans.

"I suppose I could sneak you in. Nobody's there right now. But the painters are coming first thing in the morning, and Miss Caruthers is due to drop by in about an hour to pick up Streatham's stuff."

"Miss Caruthers?"

145

"She was sort of his girlfriend. A dishy-looking blonde."

It took Jean a moment to realize that he meant Constance. She had arrived just in time. Daniel's belongings should still be intact. She followed the bearded man into a tiny elevator, and they moved slowly upward.

"Did you know Mr. Streatham well?" she asked.

He pushed a button and the elevator came to a standstill. Jean had the uncomfortable feeling they were between floors.

"Are you a newspaper reporter? Because if so, lady, out! And I mean it. You'd better level with me."

"I'm not a reporter, I swear it. I'm just a struggling painter, looking for a place to live."

"You don't look like a struggling anything," he said, appraising the mink.

"It's my mother's," she apologized.

"Why the interest in Streatham?"

"I met him once and thought he was kind of cute. I'm surprised to hear he had a girlfriend. His wife told me that he liked to play the field."

The bearded man still looked suspicious. "You the fuzz?"

"I told you, I'm a painter. But I can't help being curious about the way Mr. Streatham died. I mean, it *was* murder. It's very exciting, particularly since they haven't found his killer yet."

The elevator started up again. He had tabbed her as a dumb sensation-seeker, with a crush on Daniel Streatham.

"Streatham was a real stud," the bearded man said. "There were so many chicks waltzing in and out of this building, that if I had charged admission I'd be a rich man today."

It was an effort to keep her voice even. "Did Miss Caruthers visit him very often?"

"More than the others. Some were strictly one-shot

146

deals. In, out, and never to be seen again. But fabulous-looking. That guy had taste. As for who killed him, it could've been anybody he was banging. Although the actual murder didn't take place here, he was poisoned at one of those AA meetings. It makes you wonder about giving up booze, doesn't it?"

They got out on the fifth floor and the bearded man opened the door to 5-C.

"It's not much. Only one room, kitchenette, and a john. Lousy view."

Jean entered the apartment hesitantly, not knowing what to expect. The furniture was makeshift. A few canvas chairs, a double bed covered with an Indian spread, a cheap drop-leaf table and two unpainted chairs, a chest of drawers. Then she gasped. In a far corner of the room was a long, theatrical dressing table with an enormous beveled mirror that reached almost to the ceiling. Along both ends of the mirror and across the top and bottom were bare electric bulbs, spaced at careful intervals. Scotch-taped to the sides of the mirror were photographs of women. All kinds of women.

Jean flicked on the electric switch, and the border of light brought the women blindingly to life . . . blondes, redheads, brunettes, women who were semi-clothed, women profiled in tight sweaters, women looking over their shoulders at their bare asses, women touching themselves, women cut off below the neck smiling into the camera, women cut off above the neck, women sprawled lewdly on fur rugs, women with granny glasses and no makeup doing things with dogs, women with women, women with men, women with Daniel.

And among the appalling gallery of photographs was one of her, barely recognizable. Jean remembered when Daniel had taken it. They were walking through Central Park on a beautiful fall day and he asked her to pose against a tree. She'd been wearing a suede jacket, and from the way he cropped the picture she could still see the jacket's lapels. But her hair was much shorter then and curled, and at a quick glance nobody would identify her. Obviously, the bearded man did not.

"Some collection, huh?"

Jean felt sick to her stomach. No wonder Daniel had refused to let her visit him. And yet according to her bearded informant, Constance came here frequently. Jean did not understand how Constance could have been witness to this display of vulgarity and still gone on seeing Daniel, loving him, planning to marry him. If she lived forever, she would not understand it.

"Streatham sure didn't go for any one particular type," the bearded man pointed out. "He liked them in all sizes, shapes, and colors."

It was then that she spotted the photograph of Francine. Her slanted eyes were very heavily made-up, and she was wearing the same pair of silver and stained-glass drop earrings that she'd worn the day of Daniel's murder. Her body was clothed in a slinky black ankle-length gown, with one shoulder bared and both nipples visible. If there were photographs of Constance or Laura, Jean didn't see them. Maybe they were the ones cut off from the neck up. Suddenly, she knew she had to get out of there or she would be sick.

"Hey, don't you want to see the kitchenette?"

But she was out the door and running down the five flights of stairs as fast as her feet could carry her. At the corner of West Third Street she hailed a cab and asked the driver to turn on the heat. There were goosebumps all over her skin, and she had to clasp her hands to keep them from shaking. She'd been in love with a stranger, a liar, a monster.

It was after five when she got home, still reeling from shock. She couldn't wait to get out of her clothes and take a long hot bath, cleanse herself from the contamination of Daniel's photo gallery. In less than two hours Bob would be here for dinner, and she mustn't let him see that anything was wrong. Daniel's gross infidelities brought back memories of Frank and all the women he played around with.

She had chosen two faithless, careless, heartless men. Why? Didn't she think she deserved better? Even if that had once been true, it still did not excuse *them.* Only recently she would have attributed their vile behavior to some lack, or flaw, or inadequacy within her, but no longer. She was tired of blaming herself for everything. She was sick of making herself the scapegoat. It was with a great deal of satisfaction that Jean now awarded both Frank and Daniel posthumous medals for being total and utter shits.

A large glass of scotch suddenly appeared before her eyes and for a second the old desire lingered, then it drifted away. No, she didn't want a drink. What had happened? She'd been sober for more than a year, and this was the first time that she could dismiss alcohol so easily from her mind. Instead of wanting the scotch, she realized that she was hungry. Lunch had been light and she didn't eat a thing afterward.

She also realized something else. She hadn't craved a drink since deciding to track down Daniel's murderer. Could there be a connection between the two facts? Was an assertive, active participation in life a deterrent to boozing? She wondered. True, she made that decision only twenty-four hours ago, yet up until today she would have had a repeated succession of drink-cravings within that time period. In the past, barely an hour went by that she didn't feel like throwing down a belt of something.

Once before joining AA, she became so disgusted with her drinking that she tried to stop on her own. She chose a particularly bad day for it. She had a horrible hangover, but nonetheless was determined to quit cold turkey. *Not another drink*, she said firmly to herself, *not now, not ever!* To prove that she meant it, she poured every bottle of alcohol down the kitchen sink, then marched into the living room and tried to watch a movie on TV. Within an hour she was shaking, and her hands felt clammy.

Still determined, she went out for a walk. It was summer in New York, humid, sweltering, and she impulsively got on the Fifth Avenue bus going downtown. She didn't have a destination, she just wanted to get away from herself, be distracted. She looked around at the other passengers, sweating and dripping, the pores on their faces gleaming with perspiration, and then suddenly she felt ill. The window next to her was open and to her mortification, she started to throw up. People quickly moved away from her, murmuring among themselves, noses sniffling in distaste, as she continued to heave. She stumbled out at the next stop and hurried into the nearest bar.

"A gin and tonic," she said to the bartender. "Make it a double, please, with a lot of ice. I've never felt so terrible in my life."

She realized later that she had been sober for less than three hours. . . .

⊚ 10 ⊚

By the time Bob arrived, Jean had calmed down from that afternoon's shock. She even enjoyed a bitter laugh at her own expense, remembering her fear that Daniel might be bisexual. Not likely! The lurid picture gallery made her think that Betty had originally been on the right track: there must be a lot of women who hated Daniel enough to kill him. Whether Francine was among them was something she would have to find out. Jean now understood why Rodriguez was chuckling yesterday when he called Daniel "quite a ladies' man." It all made her sick.

"I'm crazy about long clingy dresses like that," Bob said. "Don't tell me what you're wearing underneath. Let me suffer until I can discover it for myself."

"You're a strange man."

"Just honest, darling."

He was dressed casually in a brown tweed jacket and velour sweater, and he had cut himself shaving. She forgot how exceptionally good-looking he was, his features almost perfect. *He* was perfect; the way he turned up in her life when she needed a man so bady, fallen in love with her on the spot, was gazing at her right now with such adoring, eager eyes. . . .

"I guess you've heard about O'Brien," she said.

"Yes, it's awful."

"I wonder why the murderer put the AA book next to O'Brien's body. Rodriguez was curious, too. It seems so . . . garish."

"And exhibitionistic. As though the killer wanted to be sure to get credit for both murders."

Jean hadn't thought of that. She suddenly remembered Betty admitting that she was a born exhibitionist. "I can't help myself," Betty had said. "I enjoy shaking my tits at all those panting guys."

But what possible reason did Betty have to kill either Daniel or O'Brien?

"I wonder if everyone at Clean Slate will blame this murder on me, too," Jean mused. "I certainly hope not. I don't intend to be anyone's scapegoat any longer."

Bob took her by the shoulders. "I'm glad to hear that, darling. I'm glad you're not going to worry about what they think of you at Clean Slate. The hell with them."

"I wouldn't go quite that far," she said. "I'd still like to think they're my friends, but if they don't want to be I refuse to let it get me down."

They were in the living room where Thelma had left

a tray of hors d'oeuvres. Jean was about to spread some cheese on a cracker, when Bob drew her toward him on the sofa and kissed her so passionately that she felt her toes tingle. The cracker dropped silently to the thick carpet. She hadn't been kissed like that in a long time; she could taste the yearning on his lips and feel herself responding in kind. Her body suddenly felt hot, defenseless, melting.

"You don't have to worry about anyone else," he whispered. "Just worry about me. Be with me. Care for me. Love me. Will you do that?"

No one had ever spoken to her with such tremulous urgency before. She didn't know what to say, how to respond. The expression on his face was deadly earnest, his eyes more intense than ever. She had a terrible urge to laugh.

"Do you understand how much I want you?" he asked. "How much I love you? Will you let me love you, Jean? I can, darling, and I want to. I've wanted to for a long time. I can't begin to tell you how happy you made me last night . . . ecstatic. . . ."

"I'm glad. I was happy, too."

"Will you make me happy again tonight? You're the only one who can, you know. Will you let me be your horse again, sweet darling Jean, will you?"

She glanced nervously toward the kitchen, half-expecting to see Thelma come running into the room with a catastrophe of some kind on her hands. Whenever a guest had been invited to dinner, it was Thelma's habit to experience culinary tragedies. If they didn't actually occur, she invented them. The last thing Jean wanted was for Thelma to find her locked in Bob's embrace, oblivious to the world.

"What's the matter?" he asked.

"I thought I heard Thelma."

"I didn't hear anything."

"I must be wrong. Sorry."

A tremor of irritation passed over his face.

"Why don't you let her go home?" he said.

"Go home? But we haven't eaten, Bob. She hasn't served dinner yet."

"I don't care about food. You're all I care about, darling. Can't you get that through your head? We can grab a bite later."

"But I did invite you for dinner," she reminded him. "And Thelma has been in the kitchen all day. She takes a great deal of pride in her cooking."

"Oh, very well." His tone was one of annoyed resignation. "If you insist."

"You're not being a very gracious guest," she said. Then she took a good look at him. "What do *you* want to do?"

"Surely you know."

"You'll have to control yourself. Thelma's feelings would really be hurt if we skipped dinner."

"I'll wait." He smiled at her in forgiveness. "I'm not an animal. I just thought it would be lovely if I could look at you naked now. I can't get you out of my mind, I want so badly to see you naked again, to see you standing there the way you were last night when you had just removed your stockings and your body glimmered in the shadows. Tonight I want to keep the lamp on so I can really see you in all your loveliness, your voluptuousness, your skinniness. You're both skinny and voluptuous at the same time, did you know that?"

"My thighs," she said involuntarily. "They're too fat."

"They're gorgeous, and when you wrap your legs around me like you did last night, I can feel all of your strength. It's very exciting. You don't know how exciting. Will you let me keep the lamp on, darling Jean? Will you?"

"If you want to."

"I'd like to eat you under the table at dinner, I would just sit on the floor and you wouldn't even have to pay

153

attention to me. You could enjoy your dinner while I enjoyed you." He looked at her face to see her reaction. "It's too bad Thelma is here. I want to please you so much. Now. Later. Forever. I want to please you as much as Daniel did."

The name startled her. "Please let's not talk about Daniel. It's not a good idea."

"No, it's not good to keep harping on murder, but I wasn't referring to that. I meant Daniel, the man, the lover, not Daniel the corpse. He was so handsome, you must have loved him a great deal. Did you?"

"I've already told you I did."

"And yet he treated you badly, betrayed you. I wouldn't do that. Do you think you can love me as you loved him?"

"I don't know. How can I tell?" She felt that everything was getting out of hand. "What a strange question. I've just met you."

"You're making me jealous of him."

"Jealous?" She stared at him incredulously; he did not flinch. "Of Daniel? But he's dead, there's nobody to be jealous of."

"Memories." It felt as though his fingers were burning into her shoulders. "What you and Daniel did together, what you said to each other, the way he made love to you. I want you to tell me everything, so I can learn what he did that pleased you so much."

"Tell you?"

"Yes, I want to know." The muscles in his face grew tense, his face seemed to darken. "I want to be able to see everything the two of you did together, and then I can do it better. Now do you understand?"

His voice was soothing, hypnotic. Jean felt as though he were casting a spell over her. What he was saying was unreal and lewd, yet she could almost believe that she would comply with his wishes. It was like being drawn slowly, inexorably into a web of someone else's deepest dreams and lingering there, a stranger glazed with curiosity.

"You needn't worry about my pleasure," he crooned. "I take that as it comes. *You.* You're the important one, to be catered to...."

A moment later she was in his arms, his hands under her long crepe dress (was this why she hadn't worn a stitch of underwear tonight?), exploring, probing, caressing, and she was starting to feel her breath come in quick short spurts. She mustn't, Thelma, the pork roast, she couldn't bear the excitement, and she didn't dare ask him to stop, it was too late to stop now. If only Thelma stayed in the kitchen, if only Bob had waited until after dinner, they were having lime sherbet for dessert. If he stopped now she would kill him, but he wasn't stopping, he was going faster, rounder, wetter, and when she came she screamed and cried in his ear wordlessly....

"Did I do that better than Daniel?" he asked afterward, smiling at her.

❦ 11 ❦

Jean woke up suddenly in the middle of the night. She was having nightmares about O'Brien's murder. Anxious, unsettling scenes lingered in her mind and she felt her heart pounding.

"What's the matter, darling?" Bob sat up beside her. "Can't you sleep?"

"I was just remembering something. Betty is afraid that the murderer plans to kill each of us in turn. She thinks we might be dealing with a lunatic."

"You shouldn't pay attention to other people's fears."

"But it's not like her to be frightened. Normally, she's very courageous."

"Hard as nails, you mean."

In the darkness she could hear the sharp hostility in his voice.

"Don't you like Betty?"

"Not at all, never have. In fact, I wish you weren't so friendly with her. She's tough, mean, a real ballbreaker."

"That's not true. You don't know her. That's only her facade."

"You could have fooled me," he said tersely. "I'd steer clear of that woman, if I were you."

"But she's my friend. And she's been very helpful and supportive in the past."

"Yes, darling. The past." He took her in his arms again, and his arms were surprisingly strong. "Now you don't need her any longer. You have me, and I can take much better care of you than that lesbian."

"Betty isn't a lesbian!" Jean said, appalled by his misinterpretation. "She might even be getting married soon."

"To whom? A lady wrestler?"

"Now you are being foolish. To Peter, of course."

She thought of the murderer meticulously arranging the AA book next to O'Brien's slashed body. Bob had called the act exhibitionistic, and she agreed with him. What was it that Daniel said a long time ago?

"An actor and a criminal trial lawyer are not so dissimilar as they may seem. Basically, they're both showoffs."

Showoffs, exhibitionists.

Peter was an actor.

"Did you ever make love to Betty?" Bob asked, starting to caress her breasts, her belly, her thighs. "You can tell me. . . ."

Friday, March 3

Bob made love to her again toward morning. She was awakened out of a sound sleep to feel him going down on her, and she had an orgasm by the time she fully awakened. His lips glistened with her juices as his head emerged from under the blankets.

"Did Betty used to do that?" he asked. "What's it like being with a woman?"

She was too contented and too sleepy to bother arguing with him.

"You're silly," was all she said, wondering where he got these strange ideas. "And insatiable."

"Aren't you?"

"If I am, you brought it out in me."

It was true, she'd never been this steamed up before. She wanted him all over again right now. His eyes gleamed with pleasure when he realized it, and he pushed her over on top of him.

"Wrap your legs around my head," he said. "I want to feel them alongside my body. Stretch out, yes, like that. Now I can see straight up you and through you. My God, you're beautiful, exciting. Can you come again, darling? Don't try, just let me help you."

To her amazement, she came again. He was a miracle worker, she thought, drifting back to sleep, still in his arms. She loved the way he held her so close, so tight, it made her feel so safe. . . .

As soon as he had left for work, she took out her suspect list. In light of O'Brien's death and what she recently learned about some of the Clean Slate people, parts of the list were all wrong. When she came to Bob's name, she hesitated. Her instincts told her he was innocent, but clear dispassionate reason suggested many doubts. After much revision, the expanded list now looked like this:

Group #1 (Most-likely suspects)	Motive	New Facts
1. Laura	Jealous of Daniel marrying Constance.	Loved Daniel, has jealous, bitchy, possessive nature; not sure if lying about romance with TV star.
2. Peter	Possibility of old feud with Daniel ignited.	Actor's exhibitionistic nature ties in with style of O'Brien's murder.
3. Francine	Jealous of Daniel's other women & forthcoming marriage.	Let Daniel photograph her in compromising pose. Never came to CS meeting prior to day he was killed.
4. Bob	To have clear field with Jean.	Shows intense feelings of competition & jealousy toward Daniel.

Group #2 (Next most likely)	Motive	New Facts
5. Betty	To avenge rejection of Jean.	Admits to exhibitionistic nature. Bob considers her ballbreaker (both victims men.)

A VERY CAGEY LADY

6. Hugh	?	Definitely lying about own alcoholism. Attendance at meetings highly suspect.
7. Drunk	?	Definitely was drunk day Daniel was killed. Showed up at CS for first time that day.
8. Vander-bilt	Hatred of WASPs.	None.

Group #3 (Least most likely)	Motive	New Facts
9. Marcel	?	Daniel killed by nicotine sulfate & Marcel smokes pipe. Pipe tobacco rich source of nicotine.
10. Business-man	?	None.
11. Renee	?	None.
12. Eleanor	?	None.

Group #4 (No longer suspect)	Motive	New Facts
13. Constance	None	Truly loved Daniel, wanted to marry him, had no motive to kill him.
14. O'Brien	None	Dead. Extremely unlikely he killed Daniel, ...ce both murders c...mitted by same pe...

What struck Jean most of all about the list was how much work she still had to do, how many people she knew nothing about. The fact that Hugh was not an alcoholic bothered her most of all at the moment. Maybe if she called Rodriguez, she could find out where Hugh had been Wednesday night when O'Brien was killed.

Then she realized something.

Out of the twelve remaining suspects on her list, some of them must surely have airtight alibis for Wednesday night. What a help it would be to know which ones could conclusively account for their time. What a fabulous time-saver. Because anyone who couldn't have killed O'Brien, couldn't have killed Daniel either. She picked up the telephone.

"Good morning, Mrs. Neelie." Rodriguez sounded surprisingly self-assured, considering that he now had two unsolved murders to deal with. "What can I do for you today?"

"Actually, Detective, Rodriguez I was calling to offer my services."

"Really? In what capacity?"

"I've found out something that I think you would be interested in. It's about Hugh. I've learned that he's been coming to AA meetings under false pretenses."

"You mean, he's not an alcoholic," Rodriguez said flatly. "Is that what you're trying to tell me?"

Jean was more than slightly taken back. "You know?"

"Yes, we even know why he's been going through the motions. The poor man is scared stiff. It seems that alcoholism runs in his family. Both his parents died of it, and so did an older brother. Hugh feels that by going to AA and listening to the horror stories, he might be able to ward off the disease. He looks upon Clean Slate as preventive therapy."

"It's a peculiar form of therapy. I saw him drinking red wine at a restaurant Wednesday night. *After* eight o'clock, I might add. But I guess it explains why he never talks at meetings or discusses his problems."

"Sure, his problems haven't happened yet and he's hoping they never will." A tone of amusement crept into Rodriguez' voice. "In case you were wondering, Mrs. Neelie, Hugh says he was working at his salon Wednesday night, *before* eight o'clock. You know, around the time O'Brien was killed."

"He *says?*"

"Mr. Hugh claims he was combing out a very glamorous celebrity between seven and seven-thirty. But when we checked with the lady, she recalls having left there before seven."

"She should know," Jean said.

"Ordinarily, yes. But this lady's on drugs, her memory is unreliable. She may be right, she may be wrong."

"Weren't there any other people at the salon who would remember? Employees?"

"They'd all gone home. Hugh worked late as a special favor to this woman."

Dead-end street, Jean thought. Which meant that Hugh stayed on her suspect list. Although now that she knew why he was coming to Clean Slate, he didn't seem quite so questionable as before. She moved him from Group #2 to Group #3, then glanced at the four names in the first group: Laura, Peter, Francine, and Bob.

"I imagine that O'Brien's death has everyone at Clean Slate pretty shook up," Rodriguez said. "Nasty business, stabbing."

"I don't know how they're taking it. The only person I've seen since it happened is Bob. Yes, he was extremely upset." She realized now that wasn't true; Bob hadn't shown any particular distress. "I had dinner with him again last evening."

"Well, well. A little romance developing there?"

"You sound like my friend, Betty. She likes to play

cupid too. Underneath that brittle exterior beats a very romantic heart. It may be hard to believe, but it's true."

"I believe it. Isn't she going to marry that Peter fellow?"

"How did you find out?"

"I had to check up on everyone's whereabouts Wednesday night. Peter and Betty happened to be at Sardi's. He was proposing to her."

"Then neither of them could have killed O'Brien," Jean said, thinking out loud.

"I wouldn't go quite that far. I'd say it was most unlikely Miss Lathrop killed him. As for Peter, that's a different story."

"What do you mean?"

"He showed up at Sardi's, late. How late, we don't know, can't be certain. That's the problem. You see, Sardi's is extremely busy between seven and eight because of the before-theater crowd. The waiter who served them says that she was there first, twiddling her thumbs for quite a while before Peter showed. The reason the waiter specifically remembers the incident is because he suggested that Betty have a drink and relax, and she nearly bit his head off."

"It sounds like Betty," Jean remarked. "Doesn't the waiter have any idea what time Peter got there?"

"Close to eight. That was the best guess he could make, give or take a couple of minutes in either direction. I don't like it, it's a little too tight for comfort."

Jean remembered Betty saying at lunch: "He's sneakier than you might imagine." Did Betty suspect Peter, too? Was that why she wanted to postpone the wedding? Not because of the one-year AA restriction, but because she was afraid of marrying a killer?

"At least I'm not your sole suspect any longer," Jean said. "And for whatever it's worth, my money is on Laura. I think she did it."

"Impossible!" Rodriguez snapped. "She was working overtime at the network. They were taping a special."

"Are you sure?"

"I'm positive."

Jean couldn't believe it. Of all the people at Clean Slate, she disliked Laura the most and would have felt the least sorry to see her convicted. But suddenly Laura was no longer a suspect. Ruled out. Just like that. Jean felt a terrible sense of uneasiness; Laura had been her ace in the hole.

"As for you, Mrs. Neelie, you're still in the running," Rodriguez said. "So is your boyfriend."

"Bob?"

"He says he was home shaving when O'Brien was killed."

"Is that so unusual? We were going to dinner that evening."

"Yeah, I know. What's unusual is that his first name is really Eugene."

There was a click and the line went dead.

Jean sat and stared at the telephone for a long time before she could actually move. Her head was swimming, but her heart felt frozen. She thought of Daniel's eyelids fluttering wildly, of him slumping over in his seat, and the one word coming out of his mouth. *Jean. Gene.* Which? Why? Down below on Lexington Avenue tiny dots were moving along the sidewalk, going about their business. Only a few minutes ago she felt active and energetic, her mind filled with investigative plans for the day. Now those plans seemed unimportant and trivial, in light of this latest piece of shocking news about Bob.

Why had he lied?

A moment later she picked up the telephone and resolutely dialed Marcel at home. He was a retired language teacher, living with his wife of many years in Murray Hill. Marcel sounded sleepy when she reached him, but

JOYCE ELBERT

as soon as he realized what she wanted the fuzziness left his voice. A new wary tone set in.

"Lunch today?" he said.

"Yes, I thought you might like to come here."

Jean could hear him inhale his pipe. Did pipe tobacco contain enough nicotine to be distilled into a lethal dosage? What if the killer hadn't bought the poison at a garden store? What if it was home-brewed? She wondered if that was chemically possible.

"This is very kind of you, my dear Jean, but . . . how can I put it . . .?" Marcel fumbled.

"I'd like to talk to you," she said, before he could wiggle out. "It's very important."

Still it took a few minutes to persuade him to accept her invitation, and she suspected it was only his Gallic chivalry that kept him from refusing outright. Even Marcel thought she murdered O'Brien. She no longer knew what to think. Why had Bob said his name was Edwin?

"À bientôt," Marcel said sounding like a trapped rat.

Thelma arrived a few minutes later, complaining about the subway crowds, the weather, and her arthritis.

"Remember that shrimp-and-feta-cheese receipe you wanted to try?" Jean asked her. "Well, today is your big chance. I've just invited a very discriminating Frenchman over for lunch."

"I don't have enough time," Thelma protested. "I haven't even done my marketing yet."

"Of course you have enough time. We're not going to eat until two."

"What should I serve with the shrimp?"

"Risotto and a green salad, please."

"I'd better hustle," Thelma said emphatically. Then she added, "That guy last night was kind of cute. I think he's in love with you."

"Really? What makes you think that?"

"He could barely eat for looking at you. At first I fig-

164

ured he didn't like pork, but then I took another gander at him and it wasn't the pork. It was you. He couldn't take his eyes off you. What happened to your other boyfriend? That actor? Is he still in the Midwest?"

Thelma never read the newspapers or watched the news on TV. She claimed that stories about violence kept her awake nights.

"He moved to California," Jean said.

"That's too bad. He was cute, too, and more friendly than this one."

𝕒2𝕤

Francine had never before realized how much confusion, commotion, and plain general inefficiency could occur as the result of her secretary being out with the flu. Why, oh why, had the wretched girl chosen today to call in sick? There was so much work to be done.

Just a few minutes ago, the promotion manager had complained about not being able to find their press releases for April. It was the sort of thing Francine's secretary routinely kept a copy of in her files. But *where?* Try as they did, they couldn't locate it. Twenty minutes shot to hell and now it was almost lunchtime.

As president of her own manufacturing firm, Francine took a great deal of pride in personally overseeing a smooth operation from the design of the jewelry itself down to the executive end of things. But today made her realize how dependent she was upon her secretary. In addition to all the other delays, her desk was piled high with correspondence which should have been taken care of by now. Francine sighed and picked up the dictating microphone.

Her first letter was to one of her chief suppliers, berating him for his latest and most outrageous price hike. As she spoke, she glanced occasionally at the repair man in the adjoining glass-enclosed office. He was fixing her secretary's typewriter, which had broken down yesterday afternoon at about the same time the girl began to complain of a headache and chills. It was as though everyone and everything were coming apart at the seams all at once.

The repair man seemed to be taking forever, Francine noted with disgust. Like her own employees, he was paid by the week and not by output, so why should he rush? It was only management who rushed, sweated, and broke their necks to get work done, not labor, that was for damned sure. Her telephone rang several times before she realized she had to answer it herself. Jean Neelie greeted her at the other end.

"I'm looking for a second sponsor," Jean said, after the amenities. "My present one, Betty, has been helpful but she's not always available when I need her. Like at night. She works then. I was wondering if you'd be interested."

Francine smelled a rat, but decided to be cool.

"You've never heard me speak at meetings," she said. "And you know nothing about the way I've handled my sobriety. It's strange that you should choose me. I mean, we've met only once."

"One gets intuitions," Jean mysteriously replied. "Could we talk about it a little more this afternoon? Or perhaps tomorrow?"

In the midst of all her office problems, Francine had nearly forgotten about the upcoming weekend. She now wondered it it had been a mistake to accept the last-minute invitation.

"The weekend is out," she told Jean. "I'm going away."

"How about Monday, then? Will you be at Clean Slate?"

In the next office, the repair man was double-checking the typewriter to make sure it operated properly. Francine felt a twinge of misgiving: perhaps she had judged

166

him too harshly, too unfairly. The weekend was a good idea at that. She needed to be treated as a woman for a change, *a female*, or she would turn into a harridan before she knew it.

"I normally don't go to Clean Slate," she told Jean. "The only reason I went on Tuesday was because Renee was scheduled to talk, and she's a friend of mine."

"I thought it might have been because Daniel was back in town."

Francine felt her jaw tighten at the sound of that name. She swirled her head from side to side to ease the tension, and could hear the sound of her own earrings tinkle. Made of silver and stained glass, they had proven to be one of the best-selling designs.

"Daniel?" she said. "What does he have to do with it?"

"I was involved with him, too," Jean confided. "I know what a charmer he was. I'm just sorry I ever let him take my picture. The cops won't let me alone now."

Francine was very interested to learn this. It meant that despite her worst fears, she wasn't Rodriguez' sole suspect.

"You, too?" she said. "The police have been driving me nuts, particularly that PR detective with the macho manner. His latest shtick is wanting to know where I was Wednesday night when that Irishman got knocked off. Can you beat that? You'd think I had nothing else to do but run around New York, killing recovering alcoholics."

"I'm in the same boat. I was taking a bath when O'Brien was murdered. That didn't go over big with Rodriguez, you can be sure."

"Neither did being at the movies. Did you see *An Unmarried Woman*?"

"I walked out after seven minutes."

So had Francine; her secretary told her the rest of the plot.

"That's what I should have done," Francine said. "Dreck. What woman in her right mind would turn down Alan Bates? Anyhow, go and prove you were at a movie at the time you said you were. Lots of luck. Let's see. How about getting together after work on Monday?"

"Sure."

After Francine had hung up, she jotted down the appointment in her book. It made her feel better to know that Jean didn't have a checkable alibi for Wednesday night either, *a lot* better. . . .

⁂ 3 ⁂

Jean hung up, feeling very pleased with herself. Even though she had found out what she wanted to know, she would keep Monday's appointment. Maybe by then she'd have other questions for Francine. Right now she had only one more call to make, but when she tried Betty's number the line was busy.

While waiting, she picked up the *News*. O'Brien's murder was on the front page, the headline reading: "2ND AA MURDER." And there was a photograph of O'Brien slumped over in a corner of his kitchen where he fell after being knifed in the back. He was wearing his Spanish cowboy hat. Jean shuddered and turned to Liz Smith's gossip column.

There in the first paragraph was an item about the co-hostess of *People Talk*, the beautiful ex-model with whom Rick was supposed to be having an affair. According to Liz Smith, Monique was getting a divorce to marry *the producer* of her TV show. Liz Smith emphatically denied that there had ever been a romantic attachment between Monique and Rick, despite what she termed "rumors to the contrary."

Which could mean that Rick had been involved with Laura all along, as Laura claimed. Or it could mean he was a happily married family man, as his publicity people claimed. As informative as this latest piece of news was, it did not answer the question about Rick and Laura. But there was no need to check up on Laura any longer, Jean reminded herself. Laura had been working at the network when O'Brien was killed. Laura could not be the murderer.

She dialed Betty again. The line was still busy.

⊛4⊛

Eleanor was looking at resort clothes at Saks, before walking over to Clean Slate. Shopping was the most effective way she knew of distracting herself from any kind of anxiety, and Rodriguez' phone call made her feel extremely anxious. But she was damned if she'd give into it. The fact that she had been at O'Brien's apartment Wednesday evening didn't mean that the police could pin this murder on her. Let them *prove* she had killed him! Let them try! Unfortunately, Rodriguez acted as though he intended to do just that.

"I'll be talking to you again," the detective had said ominously, in parting. "Don't leave town."

Okay, she thought now, as she fondled a terry afterswim coverup, she would wait until Rodriguez fell on his face trying to solve the double crime and then she would take off for Barbados. It would be good to get away from New York, the remains of winter, and this whole unsettling murder business. The only reason she hadn't gone to the Caribbean in early February (as she did every year) was that she'd fallen so hopelessly in love with O'Brien she couldn't bear being separated from him.

What a laugh. Her anger swelled at the memory of her own foolishness. When would she grow up and stop chasing men who didn't want her? O'Brien made his feelings perfectly plain Tuesday afternoon, when they were all at the coffee shop talking about Daniel's murder. He had not equivocated in publicly informing her that he was not interested; in fact he went babbling on and on, humiliating her in front of the others.

Even then she was incapable of taking no for an answer. It was as though she deliberately sought more humiliation, for why else had she invited herself to his apartment Wednesday evening if not to allow him to humiliate her one last time? He laughed at her on Wednesday, called her a pathetic caricature of a woman, said that she repelled him. Eleanor could still hear his hateful words.

Like a lot of Irishmen, O'Brien loved the sound of his own voice, he didn't know when to shut up. That was why he'd been killed. He knew too much about the empty aspirin bottle. It was stupid of him to have shot his mouth off about it, very stupid, Eleanor thought with grim satisfaction as she turned her attention to a slinky emerald green sarong.

She tried to imagine how it would look on her once she had a smooth Caribbean suntan. Marvelous, sexy. And maybe for once she would meet a man who thought she was terrific (not pathetic), a man she did not have to pursue, a man who would pursue her, send her flowers, perfume. . . . What a refreshing change that would be, and what an ego boost. God knows, she needed her ego boosted after O'Brien's deflating, infuriating, insulting rejection.

"The hell with you Mr. O'Brien," she muttered. "You got exactly what you deserved."

A saleswoman appeared at her side. "Did you say something, madam?"

Eleanor smiled graciously. "I was just wondering where I could try on this lovely sarong."

☙5☙

The minute Jean walked into Clean Slate, she knew how the Christians must have felt during Roman times. Between the announcement of her innocence yesterday and Betty's confirmation of it, people were tempted to suspend judgment about her. But with O'Brien's murder in today's paper, the collective attitude had turned suspicious and unfriendly once more. Jean could feel the tentacles of their hostility, and all of her suppressed rage suddenly bubbled over.

"Why does everyone think I'm guilty?" she lashed out. "What reason would I have to kill O'Brien? Can anybody answer that? Or are you going to stand around whispering and smirking among yourselves, you horrible cowards?"

Her outburst stunned them and for a second nobody spoke. They looked at each other furtively, uncertainly, as though their accusatory thunder had been stolen.

"Maybe O'Brien saw you poison Daniel," Vanderbilt suggested at last.

"*Maybe?* Do you mean you're not even sure I poisoned him, and you're ready to hang me without evidence?"

Laura smoothly cut in.

"Look, Jean, it's obvious that you're the only one who had a motive to kill Daniel. And if you killed Daniel, then you killed O'Brien too. Besides, it's not up to us to find the evidence of your guilt. It's up to the police."

"But you could have given me the benefit of the doubt, couldn't you?" Jean regarded the group with contempt. "I tried so hard to become accepted here, I

171

wanted everyone to like me. Now I wonder why. I no longer give a damn what any of you think, you're all a bunch of weak insensitive fools. And what's more—what's even worse—is that one of you is the murderer!"

Shaking with anger, she marched into the bathroom to wash her face and put on more makeup. Why had it taken her so long to get angry in public? In the past she was only capable of revealing anger when she was drunk. Then it would come pouring out, all of her pent-up frustrations and rage. When she was drunk she could shout and scream in public, but never at the right time, never at the moment she first felt furious, only afterward, seven rum collins afterward. She went through a rum period right after Frank's sudden death.

Coming home from the funeral, she got out of the limousine and walked straight into the liquor store on Lexington Avenue. In her black mourning clothes, she asked to have three bottles of Bacardi light and three Bacardi dark sent to her apartment. *Immediately*. Her in-laws, sensing that something was amiss, had come in with her. She never liked Grace and Henry but was always nice to them for Frank's sake, cordial, the properly behaved daughter-in-law.

"Don't you feel well, dear?" Grace asked nervously.

It was June, the beginning of summer, the beginning of her descent into alcoholic oblivion.

"I'm going to make some rum collins," she replied.

"A good idea," Henry said, trying to pretend that it was.

Upstairs she mixed a quart of rum collins in the cut-glass pitcher she always used for lemonade and brought it into the living room, having first belted down some undiluted rum straight from the bottle. The funeral services had been long, the ride out to the cemetery even longer, she hadn't eaten since yesterday, and the first drink tasted marvelous, it blotted out the reality of Frank's death.

172

"Here we go," she said jovially.

She generously filled all their glasses with the collins mixture and swallowed hers quickly, feeling the sweet, tart, lemony rum tickle her insides. Despite the summer weather she was cold from lack of sleep and food, her eyes itched, and her mind was frozen with shock of her sudden widowhood. As she drank, she began to thaw out. She kept on pouring and drinking, mindless of Grace and Henry. The next thing she knew she was screaming at them, telling them how much she resented them.

"You never liked me for myself, did you?" she cried. "You liked my money, my background, the fact that I would cater to your precious son. But I was plain, not the beautiful daughter-in-law you would have wished for, not the charming, fashionable woman you hoped Frank would marry. Oh, how you patronized me!"

They were staring at her, dumbstruck.

"I never liked you either. I always thought you were both cheap and tasteless, clumsy social climbers. I don't like the values you instilled in your son, the godlike self-image you gave him. I haven't liked you for the last fifteen years, Grace and Henry, and I sincerely hope to never lay eyes on either of you two fucking leeches again."

They fled. She continued orating and drinking. Hours later she woke up undressed in bed, and staggered into the darkened kitchen to mix another batch of rum collins. . . .

6

"Jean, we've been looking for you," Peter said. "Betty and I have something to tell you."

The anteroom at Clean Slate was deserted except for

173

the three of them. The others had gone inside to take seats for the meeting, which was due to start shortly.

"What is it?" she asked.

"We're engaged," Peter grinned, turning to Betty. "Show her the ring, hon."

Betty shyly held out her third finger, left hand. A large square-cut diamond sparkled in the dim light of the basement room. Betty had obviously not expected it because her red polish was chipped, the nails somewhat grimy.

"I wish Peter had warned me in advance," she said. "I would have gotten a manicure."

"It's beautiful, Betty. Congratulations to you both. Am I invited to the wedding?"

A hurried glance passed between the two of them.

"Oh, you're invited," Peter said caustically. "I just can't tell you when the happy event is going to take place. It seems that my fiancée isn't as eager as I am to tie the knot. I can't even pin her down to a tentative date. Do you think that's fair, Jean?"

"Engagements are supposed to be fun. Relax, Peter."

"Relax? Ha!" He pointed to the ring. "That's why I can't account to the cops for my time Wednesday night when O'Brien was knocked off. I was out shopping for this gorgeous piece of ice before dinner."

"Didn't any of the sales clerks remember you?"

"Window-shopping, not shopping shopping. By the time I got to the stores, they were all closed. I didn't make the actual purchase until yesterday. Rodriguez looked at me kind of fishy when I told him that."

Jean didn't wonder.

"He looked even fishier when I said that I'd gone to see a certain theatrical director prior to my window-shopping spree."

"I don't understand."

"Neither do I. This guy was supposed to be home, waiting for me, but when I got to his place nobody was there. According to Rodriguez, he'd taken off for Bucks County the day before."

"You mean, you were stood up on Wednesday?" Jean asked.

"Yes, and the director himself has admitted it, he apologizes for the inconvenience." Peter laughed unsteadily. "Can you imagine calling it that? I'm being suspected of murder because of that absent-minded faggot, and to him it's only a lousy inconvenience."

"I think the meeting is starting," Betty said.

As they filed into the larger room, Jean wondered if Peter was telling the truth. He certainly seemed eager to have his excuse believed. Too eager, perhaps. Up front Constance rapped on the desk for silence. Next to her in the speaker's chair was Eleanor, who for once was without her knitting.

"Welcome to the Friday, twelve-thirty meeting of Clean Slate," Constance said.

Jean suddenly realized that Bob was nowhere to be seen. It was not like him to miss a meeting, and she wondered what could have happened.

"And now here to share her experience, strength, and hope with us is Eleanor," Constance said.

Eleanor's eyes darted nervously about, her usual galloping anxiety more intensified than ever.

"At the moment I don't feel as if I have very much strength or hope to share with anyone. That's one of the reasons it's good for me to speak today. O'Brien's murder has disturbed me very much, especially since I was the last person—well, next to last—to see him alive. I visited O'Brien Wednesday evening. In fact, I was at his apartment about an hour before the police say he was killed."

Without knitting to keep her hands busy, she twisted and pulled at her fingers.

"The reason I went there is because I had a problem that I hoped O'Brien could help me solve. A romantic

175

problem. I got to his place about six o'clock, he made coffee, and we talked. It felt good to get my troubles off my chest, and I must say O'Brien was sympathetic. Extremely sympathetic, we'd always been close. Then he said he was expecting somebody so I left. That was at six-thirty. I remember the exact time because there's a neon clock right outside his window. I didn't pass anyone on the way downstairs, and I don't know if his visitor was a man or a woman. He didn't say. *Just a friend.* I've told all this to the police, but they keep asking me if I'm sure I left at six-thirty. . . ."

Eleanor's voice broke and it took her a moment to regain her composure. Then she began to describe how she became an alcoholic, how grateful she was to AA, how she'd be in the gutter without it. Another alibi accounted for, Jean thought, realizing how anxious both Eleanor and Peter were to exonerate themselves.

"My name is Stanley and I'm an alcoholic."

The tired-looking businessman who had sat next to Betty on Tuesday was back today and taking part in the open-discussion meeting.

"I can appreciate the kind of distress you've been under," he said to Eleanor. "The cops have been on my back too. I guess I'm considered a pretty fishy customer showing up here for the first time when Daniel was killed, and then not being able to prove I was on the Long Island Railroad when O'Brien was killed. But honest, folks"—he broke into a wide, good-natured grin—"I didn't do it."

Jean decided that if she just kept her ears open, she would eventually find out where everyone had been at the time of O'Brien's death. Stanley was on the Long Island Railroad, Betty was waiting for Peter at Sardi's, Peter was window-shopping for an engagement ring, Bob was at home shaving, Eleanor was leaving O'Brien's apartment, and Francine was at the movies. But so far only Laura could actually prove that she was where she said she was.

Jean realized that Vanderbilt was speaking.

"The fuzz have been around to see me, too. But my alibi for Wednesday night is beautifully well documented, it's a jewel! I was having dinner at my mother's. What's more there was a fire in the building, so I've got both the firemen and the cops as witnesses as to where yours truly was when the poor bastard was annihilated. And I must say it's the first time in my life that I've been grateful to slum landlords for charging rent to live in one of those firetraps. If the damned thing hadn't gone up in smoke Wednesday night, Rodriguez would probably be accusing me of murdering O'Brien. The jails in this country are crawling with blacks who've been accused of crimes they didn't commit; I hope you people are aware of the injustices taking place in these United States."

The meeting went on.

Jean wondered what could have happened to detain Bob. She hoped it was nothing more than a minor agency problem. Next to her Peter had his arm around Betty, and the young woman seemed to have relaxed a little. She looked more peaceful now as she rested her head in the crook of Peter's arm. Jean wished that Bob had his arm around her this very second. She wished they were making love. She wished she had no reservations about his innocence. But his jealousy of Daniel was so intense that at moments it frightened her. She had never encountered such fierce possessive jealousy before, and while it was flattering she also saw how easily it could get out of hand, erupt into anger, resentment, violence. Bob told her that his ex-wife used to play around in order to arouse his jealousy.

"She liked to torment me," he said last night. "She had kinky sex habits—threesomes, two men and herself, or one man and a woman. She wasn't choosy, it depended on which she thought would make me the maddest. When I wouldn't go along with her swinging scenes, she accused me of being jealous. I wanted her to myself, she said. Is that so unusual? Once when she'd been gone all weekend, I threatened to break her jaw but I never even touched her. She laughed and called me an impotent creep. It was why we got divorced. She was too far out for me."

There was still no sign of Bob by the time the meeting ended at one-thirty. Jean was getting her coat when Betty approached and invited her to lunch.

"Peter is taking me to the Russian Tea Room for a champagne celebration," she explained. "And we were hoping you could join us."

"Thanks. I would have loved to, but I've invited Marcel to my place."

Betty lit a cigarette. "Really? What's the occasion?"

As much as Jean wanted to tell Betty the truth, she was afraid to since both she and Peter were still suspects on her list.

"I'm considering taking French lessons," she said.

"But you know French. I've heard you speak it."

"I mean, advanced French. I've become very rusty and could use a refresher course."

Betty's cigarette fell to the floor and she awkwardly bent over to retrieve it. As she did so, a wide rip zigzagged clear up her shapely left leg.

"Damn! There goes another pair of pantyhose. For a dancer, I sure am a klutz."

When she straightened up, Jean saw how bleak she looked, how wounded. What she had mistaken for relaxation a few minutes ago was in reality a kind of frozen pain. Impulsively, Jean put her arms around her friend and tried to kiss her on the cheek. But true to form, Betty averted her face.

"Please don't," she said in a choked voice.

In the background Peter was talking to people, smiling

and cheerful, unperturbed. The contrast between the two was remarkable.

"Betty, what's the matter?" Jean asked.

"You heard Peter before. It's the date for the wedding. He doesn't want to wait."

"Didn't you explain how you felt about being sober for an entire year before you got married?"

"The time element," Betty mused. "Of course I explained. He still doesn't want to wait. What do I do now?"

"I suppose you could marry him."

For the barest of seconds Jean had the feeling that Betty was going to tell her something, but then changed her mind.

"If I could marry him, I would marry him," she said enigmatically.

Peter came over and hugged his fiancée, whispered something in her ear, tried to charm a smile out of her. But even when he succeeded, it was a wan smile, pale and begrudging. Across the room, Jean saw Marcel motion to her about leaving. She hated to go, not knowing what was disturbing Betty, what had happened to Bob. . . .

❧ 7 ❧

In the cab ride uptown, Jean and Marcel spoke about how he was coping with his recent semiretirement. She asked if he ever got bored, or missed the large college classes that he had traded in for private tutoring.

"Bored, *jamais*. But every once in a while I find myself thinking about some of my former students, and wondering whether they are making progress. A good teacher is something of a father, *tu comprends*. Protective and caring."

Jean was trying to imagine Marcel in the role of a cunning and dangerous *maquisard*, attempting to outwit the Nazis in the Second World War. He seemed so homey, so paternal. Of course he'd been so much younger then, it was easier to be daring. But would a man like that ever forget how to kill? Ever truly lose the taste for it?

"You had a mysterious phone call, Mrs. Neelie," Thelma said, when they arrived. "The gentleman wouldn't leave his name, but he sounded funny. Like maybe he'd been drinking. He did mumble something about Circe, though."

"*Drinking?* Are you sure?"

"He sounded pickled to these old ears," Thelma said with disapproval.

It must be Bob. Last night he called her Circe, kidded her about turning men to swine. She was horrified. That's why he hadn't shown up at Clean Slate, he was on a bender. Since joining AA, nobody she knew had fallen off the wagon, but she had heard the horror stories about less fortunate people. They were legion at AA. Some straightened themselves out at detoxification and rehabilitation centers, some died. One man who'd been sober for twenty years went on a binge recently, and ended up in an insane asylum. A speaker at Clean Slate once explained that alcohol was especially dangerous after a long period of sobriety, because alcoholism was a progressive disease. Even when you weren't drinking, your illness gradually became worse and worse, your tolerance for liquor lower and lower. Sometimes it proved fatal. Bob hadn't had a drink since 1969.

"The gentleman is going to call back later," Thelma said, glancing suspiciously at Marcel.

"I hope you like shrimp," Jean said to him, for Thelma's sake.

"*J'adore les crevettes.*"

"He loves shrimp," she translated.

Thelma sighed in martyred triumph. "Thank the Lord. Luncheon is served."

Marcel pronounced the shrimp-tomato-and-feta-cheese dish *magnifique*, much to Thelma's delight.

"Dining at home is not taken seriously in these days of quick snacks and frozen foods," he told Jean. "Do you do this often?"

"Thelma usually cooks for me three evenings a week. I regret to say that Wednesday was not one of those evenings, or she could have vouched for my whereabouts when O'Brien was murdered."

"Yes, you are in a very grave situation. I must confess that I, myself, have harbored thoughts about you I am not proud of."

"But *why?* Why does everyone suspect me? Do I seem like a murderer to you?"

"Ah." The Frenchman shrugged. "It is not what you seem like. It is as Laura said: you had the motive to kill your lover after he left you for another woman."

"I certainly don't have the temperament. And what motive did I have for killing O'Brien? Or haven't you considered that?"

"Certainly I have considered it. Motive. It is one of the most intriguing aspects of this entire sordid matter. You will pardom me if I suggest something?"

"Go ahead."

"I do not mean to be cruel, you understand. It is a hypothesis. Let us say that O'Brien saw you put the poison in Daniel's coffee cup, and then he tried to blackmail you: your money in exchange for his silence. What would happen next? O'Brien would have to be killed, *n'est-ce pas?*"

Jean had never thought about blackmail; it sounded like something that only happened in sleazy movies, not in real life. Did people still blackmail other people? She supposed they did.

"Is that the general opinion at Clean Slate?" she asked.

"That O'Brien was trying to blackmail me, and therefore I killed him?"

Marcel nodded. "Everyone knows he was short of money. Everyone knows you have money. *Voila!*"

"If that's really why O'Brien was killed—because of blackmail—then there shouldn't be any more deaths. The killer will feel safe now, secure."

Marcel's features sharpened as he spoke. "No, there should not be any more unpleasantness, unless someone tries to trap the killer."

"What do you mean?"

His face had lost its familiar softness, it looked different.

"Trying to trap a killer can be a very dangerous pastime if you are an amateur." Marcel now looked as foreboding as he must have when he was waging guerilla warfare on the Nazis. "It could result in an unfortunate third death."

Jean felt her mouth go dry. "You mean, for the amateur?"

"But of course," he caustically replied. "For whom else?"

The man sitting opposite her was no longer the nice kindly man Jean knew from Clean Slate. Another personality had taken over, a more ominous one. A minute later the telephone began to ring. As she went to answer it, she realized that her heart was pounding.

☙ 8 ❧

Eleanor.

That was the name on Marcel's mind, it had nearly been on his lips a minute ago when he spoke about the danger of trying to trap the killer. He felt sure now that Eleanor was the killer, and that eventually Jean would come to realize it, too. She was out hunting, sleuthing, that much was clear to Marcel. In order to get herself off the hook, Jean was apparently determined to find the murderer on her own. The naive little fool! He shuddered to think of the risk she was taking.

It was undoubtedly why she invited him to lunch—to pick his brains about the two homicides. There was plenty he could say against Eleanor, but he never would. Jean was safer not knowing; Eleanor could be deadly when crossed (only Marcel knew *how* deadly), and if she ever suspected that Jean was onto her there was no telling what might happen. A third murder, perhaps as he just got through warning her. Jean dead. Marcel shuddered.

Eleanor hadn't stopped after she bungled the first one, had she? To Marcel's way of thinking, O'Brien was her target from the start, Eleanor's very own target born out of unrequited love and abysmal rejection. For O'Brien not only spurned her advances, he laughed at her. Marcel could still hear him at the coffee shop on Tuesday.

"If that scarf is for me, I think you should know that I hate the color red."

"It *was* for you," Eleanor said pointedly. "Once."

When Marcel heard Eleanor admit today that she'd been at O'Brien's apartment only an hour before his death, he felt certain she was guilty. What an incredibly stupid woman. Yet bold, without scruples, unrelenting. She poisoned Daniel's coffee by mistake, the clumsy cow, but did that stop her? No, she went right ahead and stabbed an unvigilant O'Brien to death the next day. Marcel prayed that Jean would forgive him for making up stories about blackmail, for pretending to suspect her of both crimes. For the sake of her own safety, he had to pretend. The less she knew about Eleanor, the better. Still, he felt like a traitor.

He helped himself to more of the delicious shrimp-and-feta-cheese concoction, and sighed. He did not like this business. He thought he was through with murder and traitors a long time ago. He had had his fill of it.

"*C'est suffit*," he now mumbled to himself.

His ill-advised affair with Eleanor took place several years ago when he was still drinking. Eleanor was drinking then, too. Irresponsible drunks, both of them. It was summer, and Marcel's wife had gone to Provence to visit her parents. To make extra money during his summer vacation, Marcel signed up a handful of students for private French tuition. One of those students turned out to be the expensively dressed, sexually eager Eleanor, who was between husbands at the time. After the first lesson, she asked him to her apartment. He politely refused, afraid to get involved with this hard-looking woman, wishing his wife were not on the other side of the Atlantic. Warm weather brought out the sensual in Marcel, and even though Eleanor was hardly his type he could feel her strong, almost repellent attraction.

"Keep away from her," he told himself.

One day when he was feeling especially lonely and vulnerable, she suggested they go to a nearby cocktail lounge for a nice cooling drink.

"Just one," she said, smiling at him, her mouth like a barracuda's. "Come on, Professor. It will do you good. You need to relax."

That was the beginning of the catastrophe. He deluded himself into thinking he could have one gin and tonic, and walk away. But of course they went on drinking, talking, he became conscious of her lusty jokes, the way she gazed into his eyes, the way she invited his overtures. In the end he asked the barracuda back to his apartment and made love to her in the same bed he shared with Marianne (afterward, his only dim consolation was that Marianne slept on the other side).

Even worse than making love to Eleanor was the fact that they continued to drink in the apartment, having picked up a bottle on the way. If not for that bottle, he probably wouldn't have started reminiscing out loud about his days in the Resistance. How one of the members of his *réseau* was captured by the Nazis and tortured . . . Pierre, the radio operator. . . . How he cracked under the inhuman strain and gave the enemy all the information they wanted. . . . How shortly afterward Marcel and the others were picked up for questioning and still more torture when they wouldn't talk. . . . How he, Marcel, managed to escape while the others were systematically killed . . . one by one . . . as the luckless Pierre was forced to watch. . . .

Eleanor listened to him, intrigued. Then the idiot laughed.

"Oh, you escaped, you were a hero!" she said happily. "How thrilling and adventurous. I never would have guessed you led such an eventful life once. The quiet French professor."

"It didn't seem very thrilling at the time," he said dryly. "I felt ashamed that I was the only one of my group to survive."

"If anyone should be ashamed, it's Pierre, not you. You should be proud. You were more clever than the others, resourceful."

"That kind of cleverness is not something one brags about."

"I won't tell a soul," she reassured him, misunderstanding. "You can count on me to keep quiet."

"There is nothing to tell. It happened many years ago, another lifetime, I'm sorry I mentioned it."

She still refused to understand. "I won't tell your wife," she said coyly.

It was only then that Marcel realized what he had let himself in for, and when he sobered up he cursed his own foolishness. His marriage meant everything to him, he cherished and adored Marianne. Why had he gotten involved with this gross, vulgar woman? He vowed never to see her again outside of the classroom. After two months of being avoided by him, Eleanor picked up the telephone and told Marianne everything. She made sure to describe all the details of his Resistance days, as proof of their intimacy. Being a practical Frenchwoman, his wife did not run out the door or speak of divorce, but there was a coldness between them for a long time. Marianne felt betrayed, and he could hardly blame her. If he hadn't been drunk, he kept thinking, it never would have happened.

Eventually, he turned to AA for help. Eventually, Marianne forgave him and their life went on as usual.

When Eleanor turned up at Clean Slate one day, Marcel was sorely tempted to switch groups, but he'd gotten attached to this one, he knew everyone, felt comfortable there. He talked it over with Marianne and she persuaded him to stay.

"You like Clean Slate, your friends are there. They have been good to you. Don't give it up for that one. Besides, if she has stopped drinking, she will be a different person. Just as you are different."

Marianne was wrong. Eleanor wasn't different. She was still the same grasping bitch, she did the same terrible things, she just did them sober now. And when Marcel saw her set her cap for O'Brien, he wanted to warn the Irishman about what she was like. But by the time he got around to it, it was too late. Eleanor had gotten there first. O'Brien lay sprawled on the kitchen floor, a knife in his back.

That was why Marcel hadn't gone to the police with his suspicions about Eleanor—he was too afraid of being implicated himself. Marcel was the friend that O'Brien had been expecting Wednesday night.

Bob's voice was so thick with alcohol that it took Jean a minute to be certain it was really him on the telephone.

"Where are you calling from?" she asked.

"Mars. I'm in a bar on the planet of Mars. Or is it Mercury?"

She finally managed to get the exact address from him.

"I'll be there as soon as I can. Don't leave. Do you understand?"

"What I don't understand is where you've been all afternoon. Are you trying to avoid me, darling? I called you earlier. Are you cheating on me, sweetheart?"

She could see Marcel in the dining room, opening a pouch of tobacco and filling his pipe. Thelma had left the pyrex coffeemaker on the table, and Jean watched the dark liquid slowly drip through the filter as Bob raved on. The coffee, which was the same rich chocolate brown as Marcel's tobacco, complemented the vase of yellow daisies, the apple green tablecloth. . . . As a painter, it was a play of colors that Jean could appreciate.

"You still haven't told me where you've been," Bob persisted.

"I went to Clean Slate, and I was very worried when you didn't show up. I was afraid something terrible might have happened."

And it had. But this was not the time for recriminations.

"I love you, Jean. I only got drunk because I'm so afraid of losing you. You mean everything to me. I've never loved a woman the way I love you, not even The Rabbit."

"We'll talk about it later," she said, wondering who on earth The Rabbit was. "I have to go now."

"Is someone there with you?" His voice held a note of alarm. "Are you with another man?"

Marcel glanced curiously in her direction, and she wondered if she should tell him that Bob was in trouble. Marcel would prove helpful in a situation like this, but she no longer trusted the Frenchman.

"I'll see you shortly," she said to Bob, hanging up.

Bob had seemed so sane and steady in his sobriety, and now this. *An alcoholic is always just one drink away from a drunk* was a popular warning at Clean Slate. Jean had never before realized how true a statement it was.

"Is something wrong?" Marcel asked solicitiously, when she returned to the table.

"I'm afraid so. I know it's very rude, but I'm going to have to cut our luncheon short. A friend of mine has had an accident."

It was the truth, she thought, as Marcel graciously bowed out, expressing his regrets.

When Jean got to the bar on Third Avenue, it was dark and deserted except for Bob hunched over a martini trying to engage a bored bartender in conversation. The first thing that hit Jean was his breath. Good God! Had she smelled like that when she was drinking? Why didn't anyone tell her?

"I've been trying to get him to go home for the last hour," the bartender said. "Maybe you'll have better luck. I hope so because I'm going to eighty-six him after this drink."

"Come on, Bob," she said. "Let's take a cab and go to my place. I want to talk to you."

He smiled in what he apparently thought was an engaging manner, not realizing that his eyes were glazed and his mouth wetly slack.

"You're talking to me right now, darling," he said in slurred tones. "I was afraid you wouldn't get here. I was afraid I'd lose you."

On pretext of going to the ladies' room, Jean went to the rear of the bar to telephone Thelma.

"Make a big pot of black coffee and close the blinds in the living room. I'm bringing home a very drunk man."

"I knew this wasn't my day when I got out of bed," Thelma moaned. "Lord, give me strength."

When they got to Jean's building, she told Bob to wait in the taxi a moment.

"I want you to help me get a friend of mine upstairs," Jean said firmly to the doorman. "He's quite intoxicated."

"But, Mrs. Neelie, I can't leave my post."

"Under the circumstances, Albert, I think you can."

He looked at her, surprised by the new authority in her manner. "Yes, m'am."

Between them they managed to get an unsteady Bob into the apartment and onto the sofa. Thelma was standing by with black coffee and a disapproving look on her face. Only Clark Gable seemed jubilantly happy by all the commotion. He alone was not put off by the overpowering smell of gin that seemed to ooze from every pore of Bob's body. The smell was probably familiar to Clark Gable, Jean thought grimly; he would have remembered it from her. She sent Thelma into the bathroom for an old bottle of Librium, which she had fortunately saved. If she gave Bob two tranquilizers every four hours for the next sixteen hours, it would calm him down and cut the craving for more alcohol. For the normal person that was a very high amount of Librium and not to be recommended, but Bob's system was manically speeded up now.

She looked at her watch.

It was ten past four, which meant she would have to stay awake with him until eight tomorrow morning. Even if he passed out, he would come to soon afterward and be in a bad way, suffering withdrawal symptoms. Librium helped to ease both the psychic and physical pain.

Her doctor had used the treatment on her some years back, and it worked. Temporarily. She stopped drinking for a couple of months, then in time drifted back to it. It wasn't enough to just stop drinking, AA taught her how to cope with sobriety. Bob was lucky, he'd had years of that invaluable indoctrination. The main thing was to get the booze out of his body and not leave him alone.

"Also, please bring me a pitcher of cold fruit juice," she told Thelma. "And be sure we have plenty of juice on hand. Gallons."

Thelma muttered something about running a charity ward, then said: "Should I make up the bed in the spare room?"

"No. Mr. Edwards will sleep with me."

Thelma raised an eyebrow. "Whatever you say, Mrs. Neelie."

Even though she wouldn't get much sleep tonight, she could not let Bob out of her sight. Alcoholics were resourceful, crafty, and if she didn't keep a constant eye on him he would sneak out to a bar or liquor store at the first opportunity. She decided to be crafty, to.

"They're vitamins," she said, handing Bob the two Librium. "To make up for missing lunch."

He had apparently never seen the green-and-black capsules, because he swallowed them without a fuss, grinned, and made a muscle with his upper arm. He also gulped down a large glass of orange juice before realizing there wasn't any gin in it.

"I asked you for a screwdriver," he said accusingly. "You went to get me one. What's going on around here, anyway?"

"I'm trying to take care of you, sweetheart."

His craving for a drink conflicted head-on with his craving for her exclusive attention. What he really wanted was for her to nurse him through the night with a bottle filled with gin.

"Can't you put some gin in this orange juice?" he

190

pleaded. "Come on, honey, just a little shot. You have one, too."

"I don't think so."

Suspicion started to creep over his face.

"Why not? Why can't I have one little drink? If you cared about me, you'd give me a drink. It's not so much to ask for, one teensy weensy shot of gin, that's all I want."

Thelma popped in briefly to see if Jean was all right, then withdrew, shaking her head in bewilderment. To a nonalcoholic, what Jean was doing must have seemed quite incomprehensible, but it wasn't as self-sacrificing as it appeared. By helping Bob through this ordeal, she was helping herself at the same time—to remember what it was like.

"I'm going to get the shakes if I don't have a drink!" he shouted suddenly. "I'm going to get the DTs. Don't you have any compassion? Don't you know what will happen? Come on, darling, just show me where you keep the booze."

"I don't have any. I poured it all out a long time ago."

This knowledge threw him into a state of panic, terror.

"*Poured it out?* Are you crazy? What's going to happen to me?" He leaped up. "I'm getting out of here. I'm going to a bar. I can't stay here like this." He looked wildly around for his coat which she had hung up. "Where's my coat? You've hidden it, haven't you? The hell with it. I don't need a coat. I need a fucking martini."

Jean was sorry now that she let Marcel leave.

"Why did you tell me your first name was Edwin?" she asked, as he reached the door. "Why did you lie to me, Bob?"

He stopped, his mind distracted. She could see him trying to think fast, and she could see him failing.

"Is that what I said?"

191

"You know you did."

"It was only a little white lie, that's all." He slowly came back. "So I said my name was Edwin, and it's really Edmond. So what?"

"So it's not Edmond. It's Eugene. Or should I call you *Gene*, as Daniel did just before he died?"

He sank into the sofa, his eyes filled with fear.

"You've got it all wrong. Daniel didn't mean me, he wasn't talking to me. I swear it."

"Then you admit your name is really Eugene?"

"Yes, but it's not the way you think." He implored her to believe him. "I didn't kill Daniel."

"Why did you lie to me?"

"I was afraid that if you knew the truth, you'd think I was guilty . . . I was afraid the cops would think so too. But Daniel didn't mean me when he said *Gene*. We were only casual acquaintances. . . . How could he know that was my name . . . everyone at Clean Slate calls me Bob. It was just my immediate panic that made me lie. I was scared, Jean . . . scared I'd lose you before I even had you to lose. . . ."

Jean didn't know what to say. Not that he'd explained, it did seem extremely unlikely Daniel had meant him. Who *did* Daniel mean? The question still hadn't been answered.

"I feel a little woozy," Bob said. "Can I lie down?"

The Librium had begun to work.

"Come on," she said. "Thelma's made up the bed. Maybe you can take a nap, and then we'll have dinner."

He smiled gratefully. "Sure."

❧ 10 ❧

Afterward she returned to the living room, ate some of Thelma's homemade apple cake, and smoked a cigarette.

It was dark outside, peaceful, the sky filled with shimmering stars. From the kitchen came the delicious smell of a stew. A man was sleeping in the bedroom. Clark Gable lay curled up at her feet. In spite of the disturbing events of the day, Jean felt oddly secure. Living alone might be less of a hassle, but it was also more barren. She missed the intimacy of sharing her life with a man. No wonder she had stayed married to Frank for fifteen years, even though their relationship was far from ideal. Had he not been killed in that auto accident, she probably would still be married to him. Ideal relationships were one in a million.

"The drunk's first name?" Rodriguez said, when she got him on the telephone. "It's George. Why do you ask, Mrs. Neelie?"

"I was thinking of what Daniel said before he died."

"And you wondered if he could have meant the drunk. *Gene. George.* They're similar, but not that similar. What are you trying to do? Solve this case by yourself?"

"Would that be so unusual, considering that I'm the most likely suspect?"

"Unusual? No. I've seen amateurs take a crack at it before. With very dismal results, I might add."

"Perhaps I'll surprise you."

"Go right ahead," he said sardonically.

"Whoever placed O'Brien's AA book in his own blood is an exhibitionist. Why don't you suspect Peter? Actors are exhibitionists by nature. And you told me yourself that he can't prove where he was when O'Brien was killed."

"I never said I didn't suspect Peter. I suspect everyone. But remember, Mrs. Neelie, you can't prove where you were that night either. And Peter's name doesn't even remotely sound like *Jean.*"

"Isn't it possible that Daniel meant something else when he said that?"

"Such as?"

"Maybe it was the beginning of a sentence. Like: 'Jean, I'm dying.' "

"I doubt it. You haven't seen as much of death as I have. People think amazingly fast when they know it's the end. They don't have time for the amenities. Whatever comes out of their mouth at the last minute is highly significant. And especially when they realize there's been foul play, as I'm convinced Daniel did."

"Maybe he just *thought* I poisoned him," she said. "A dying man can make a mistake, you know."

"If he did, we'll find out." Rodriguez sighed with fatigue. "By the way, how are you and Mr. Edwards getting along?"

"Just fine," Jean replied evasively. "And that reminds me. There was no way Daniel could have known about Bob's name being Eugene. They were hardly more than acquaintances."

"True. However, there's Constance."

"What does she have to do with it?"

"She works at the same agency Bob does, and they're very good friends. Doesn't Bob call her Connie?"

"Yes," Jean said, knowing she was walking into a trap.

"What do you imagine Connie calls him? Go ahead, Mrs. Neelie, take an educated guess."

Her heart sank. "Gene."

"That is correct. Now considering Daniel's intimate relationship with Miss Caruthers, do you still think he didn't know Bob's real first name?"

Click. The line went dead. Rodriguez sure had an effective way of signing off, one that was absolutely guaranteed to depress her. She went to her desk and took out the suspect list. Next to Bob's name, under the "New Facts" column, she penciled in the notation: *First name Eugene, Daniel aware of it*. With the inclusion of those two facts, Bob now appeared more likely to have killed Daniel than anyone else. Was it possible O'Brien had spotted him in the act, and tried to blackmail him? If so, then the man passed out in her bedroom had murdered two innocent people. Jean just couldn't believe it. After a few minutes, she made a note on a separate piece of paper. It read:

> *Important.* People who have not yet accounted for where they were Wednesday night when O'Brien was killed:
>
> 1. Marcel
> 2. Renee
> 3. George (the drunk)

What amazed her was that she'd let Marcel get away this afternoon without asking him that simple question. It was the only reason she'd invited him to lunch. To find out his alibi for Wednesday night. In looking back now upon their conversation, it was clear that Marcel had been manipulating it right from the start. By putting her on the defensive, he neatly avoided being questioned himself. But what possible reason did Marcel have to kill Daniel and O'Brien? She would have to talk to him again and be more clever next time. The Frenchman was a much tougher customer than she had imagined.

"Jean!"

It was Bob calling from the bedroom. She slipped the list back in the desk drawer, and went to see what he wanted. He was sitting up in bed, the covers flung on the floor, a wild disoriented look on his face.

"How did I get here? What's going on? What happened? What time is it?"

He'd had a blackout. Jean wondered what he remembered last.

"It's nearly eight o'clock."

He glanced out the window. "At night?"

"Yes." She once went through the same confusion herself and knew how terrifying it could be. "You've been drinking all day, Bob. About an hour ago, you decided to lie down and take a nap."

"*Drinking?* But I'm an alcoholic. I can't take a drink."

"Well, you did," she said gently. "Lots of drinks. Don't you recall being at a certain bar this afternoon?"

"Bar?" He held his head in his hands, trying to shut out the painful light from the bedside lamp. "Oh, my God, yes. Vaguely. Jesus Christ, what have I done to myself? I can't believe I started in again. I've been sober for nine years. Why did I do it?"

"Because you were afraid of losing me."

"Is this some sort of joke?" He stared at her in disbelief. "Of course I'm afraid of losing you, but that's no reason to get drunk after all this time."

"I know it isn't." She saw him leap out of bed and get into his clothes. "Where are you going?"

"I need a shot. I'm shaking like a leaf. Look at that." He held out his trembling hands. "I can't quit cold turkey. Not like this. Not without medication."

"Do you want to go to a hospital?"

"No, goddamn it. I want a drink."

"You'll only be compounding the damage you've already done," she reasoned.

"I don't care. I'm going to jump out of my skin if I don't have a drink. You remember what it's like. I'll go crazy."

She did remember, unwillingly. The agony that he was experiencing now could never be adequately described, words were insufficient. Nobody would believe it about alcoholics, although for some reason they believed it about junkies. Maybe because heroin was illegal and had such sinister associations, whereas alcohol was looked upon as a convivial, socially accepted part of life. And yet the withdrawal from alcohol was gruesomely painful. The only fast way to ease that pain was to take a drink. The slow way—to stop drinking altogether—was so excruciating, that few people were able to withstand it without a crutch of some kind.

"I have tranquilizers," she said. "In fact, I gave you two earlier. That's why you were able to sleep a little. I can give you two more right now. They'll cut the craving for liquor."

He hesitated, the shirt over his head.

"I've only had sedation in a hospital. And then, by injection. With doctors monitoring it."

"That's why I asked if you wanted to go to a hospital, I can call Freeport."

He sat down at the edge of the bed, half dressed. "Do you really think I could dry out here?"

"Yes, because you were drinking for less than a day. Otherwise, I wouldn't attempt it."

"Would you be willing to put up with me? You know how rough it can be."

"I'm willing."

"How long will it take?"

"The worse will be over by tomorrow morning. Providing you can sleep tonight. Do you think you'll be able to eat dinner?"

He held his stomach. "The thought of food makes me sick."

"It helps to eat. Even if you have to force it down."

"I just hope I don't throw up."

"It's not the worst thing in the world, Bob."

His face had a gray, unhealthy cast. "No. For us the worst thing is booze."

They looked at each other, two people who'd been through the same hell and remembered every pitfall along the way to recovery. She knew how desperately he wanted a drink this very minute. He wanted that more than anything in the world: more than her, his health, more than life itself.

"I'm game," he said, starting to get undressed again.

"Do you have a robe I can wear? I'm afraid to keep my clothes on."

She went to the closet and got out her after-bath poncho.

"Here. It's big enough for the two of us."

"You're giving me ideas," he said, attempting a smile. "Thanks, darling."

If he kept his clothes on, he might run out the door and into a bar as soon as he felt the pressure build up. Undressed, he was much safer. It was a good sign that he recognized the danger and wanted to protect himself.

"This is fine," he said, pulling the poncho over his head. "I'm all ready for bed-check."

Playing the invalid was a sort of self-protection, too. People felt sorry for invalids, they didn't suspect them of any harm—except against themselves. Jean sighed. She felt totally lost and confused. Maybe she would never catch the murderer. Maybe Rodriguez never would either. A cloud of depression settled on her shoulders, weighing her down as she thought of the long night ahead. Then she felt Bob's hands around her waist.

"Would you like to make love?" he said.

"Can you? I mean, do you really want to?"

He was unbuttoning her dress, the expression in his eyes familiar to her by now.

"I'll show you how much I want to," he said.

❧ 11 ❧

"You're so good to me," Bob crooned. "In every way. You take care of me, you're really concerned about my well-being."

"Of course I am. I was very upset when you called from that bar, drunk."

"No, I don't just mean about my drinking. I mean everything. The way you're ready to make love whenever I want. I've never had a woman like you."

"You're pretty unusual yourself," she said truthfully. "I didn't think you'd be able to, after all you had to drink. That's why I was so surprised when you suggested it."

They were resting before dinner, the lamp beside the bed turned on. He would not let her turn it off anymore, he wanted to watch her every move, see her every vibration, anticipate her every orgasm. Despite the fact that Frank and Daniel hadn't been exactly remiss in the art of lovemaking, she had to admit that Bob outdid them both. His desire to satisfy her knew no bounds. There was nothing he would not do if she requested it, no fantasy was too foolish or feeble for him to comply with, whether it was imitating the French accent of his handsome movie-star look-alike, Alain Delon ("We French invented all this, you know), or painting her breasts with chocolate syrup (Thelma wondered why they wanted the can of Hershey's) with Cool Whip for the nipples. He was not only ready to comply, he was reluctant to give up his life's work.

"All I want to do is please you," he had whispered later. "Do I make you happy?"

"Yes, in a strenuous sort of way."

"What does that mean?"

"You're so intense. Sometimes I feel as though I can't breathe."

"Am I smothering you with so much love and attention?"

"Yes, a little."

"I want to smother you, darling. I can't get near enough to you. Don't you understand? I want to be inside your skin every minute, that's why I'm able to become aroused even after all that booze. Because the thought of being in you is so thrilling, feeling you, loving you, holding you. I loved the way you didn't let me go running out to a bar before, when I was acting so crazy. I love the fact that you were concerned enough to look after me. Never look at another man, will you? Will you promise that you'll never look at any other man? Promise, sweet, darling Jean."

It was easy to promise in the heat of passion, but even as she did so she felt a twinge of regret. During dinner Thelma took Bob's lack of appetite personally, and said she wished that everyone enjoyed her cooking as much as that afternoon's guest. Jean tried to signal her to shut up, but to no avail.

"That man *liked* good food," said the anxious-to-please Thelma. "I wish more people around here did. Maybe if they didn't gorge themselves on chocolate syrup first . . ."

"Who was here this afternoon?" Bob asked as soon as they were back in bed. "You didn't tell me you'd invited anyone for lunch."

"It was only Marcel."

"Did he make love to you?"

"Bob!" She burst out laughing, still thinking it was funny. "Don't be ridiculous."

"Jealousy is never ridiculous," he said solemnly. "The thought of you with another man makes me sick. I couldn't stand the thought of Marcel touching you, he's old enough to be your father. Why did you invite him to lunch? You could have invited me."

Matters were definitely getting out of hand. But try as she did, she couldn't seem to make him forget Marcel and what he considered to be a suspicious interlude.

"Even if I wanted to have lunch with you," she said, "you had disappeared. And besides, I was anxious to talk to Marcel."

"Why? About what?"

"Why everyone at Clean Slate is so convinced I'm guilty."

"So it's Clean Slate again, is it? I wonder how many

men there you've gone to bed with, besides Daniel and me."

"Stop it. This is ugly. I won't have this conversation. I won't have you talking to me this way. It's hideous. What's the matter with you?"

He became the paragon of apology. He begged for her forgiveness. He said it was a terrible mistake to accuse her of promiscuity. He said it was just a joke, anyway. He said he was getting hot all over again.

"Please don't be angry at me," he pleaded. "I didn't mean to offend you, darling. I just got carried away. I'll make it up to you."

He took her in his arms and began to kiss her. He was so warm, his kisses burned her mouth; their bodies wet and sticky from before felt as though they were pasted together. She couldn't remember when she hadn't known him and she couldn't imagine not knowing him forever. He'd become part of her. And at the same time there was a quality about him that revolted her, his pleading, cajoling, his jealous needs which were shameless in their demands and expectations. Then he was inside her and it felt marvelous. Suddenly, he said: "You were sexually happier with Daniel, weren't you?"

"Oh, my God, you're doing it again."

"Doing what?"

"Comparing. Trying to compete. I hate it."

"I'm sorry if I upset you. I was just curious. I want to know what Daniel did that you liked so much. Tell me so I can do it, too. I want to hear you tell me in careful detail, don't leave anything out. Tell me while I'm fucking you . . . go ahead, darling, *tell* me."

To her own astonishment she did, and felt immediately ashamed. Bob had drawn her into his shadowy world of possessiveness, and if she let him he would devour her inch by inch. She didn't know what to do. She was becoming dependent upon his particular brand of all-consuming attention, it catered to her insecurities. She

was becoming hooked on it, and soon she would need to
hear how lovely and beautiful and desirable and sexy she
was more than he would need to say it. The prospect
frightened her, and she broke out of his embrace.

"Darling, what is it? Have I done something wrong?"

"No, I'm just tired. Let's go to sleep.

"Are you sure I haven't—?"

"For God's sake, I just want to sleep! I'm tired."

"Okay."

"I didn't mean to shout. I'm sorry."

"It's all right. I've worn you out."

"Yes, something like that," she said. "Good night."

"Sleep well, sweetheart."

She could have sworn she heard a tremor of despair in
his voice. The next thing she knew the room was totally
dark and she heard him groan in the blackness.

"I'd give anything for a drink."

Poor Bob. She could sympathize with his craving, and
it occurred to her that maybe all they had in common
was their struggle against alcoholism. That and their
voracious sexual appetites. On the other hand, it was a
lot more than most people had.

"How about some cake and cocoa instead?" she asked.
"And two more Librium."

"Whatever you say. I feel awful."

The gin was still taking its physical toll, and his
blood-sugar level was probably very low right now. She
had tried to get him to eat more of the lamb stew at dinner, but he said he was too nauseated. She watched him
picking up the pieces of vegetables rather than the meat,
and mashing them with his fork. A long time ago she
had determined that alcoholics weren't chewers, their
toothless infantile urges never giving way to the adult
ones that normally followed. Among Clean Slate people
the foods typically preferred were baby food in consis-
tency: ice cream, moist cakes, puddings, mashed pota-
toes, cheeseburgers, anything with whipped cream. It

was one of the reasons she had Thelma cook for her three times a week. She was afraid that without the grown-up meals Thelma prepared, she would sink into the kind of mushy-eating pattern so typical of most alcoholics.

"That tasted good," he said, finishing the cake and cocoa. "I feel much better now. Thank you, darling."

"Try to get some sleep," she said, turning over on her side. "You'll be fine in the morning."

He kissed her gently on the back of her neck, passing his hands over her smooth shoulders, down her spine, down her legs. She drowsily shook off his touch.

"Go to sleep," she murmured.

"I was hoping. . . ."

Sometime later she was suddenly awakened by the sound of him racing to the window. She was in time to see him open it and stare seventeen floors down to Lexington Avenue below. She ran up behind him and locked her arms around his waist, pressed her head against his warm back.

"What is it, Bob?"

"I wish I had the nerve to get it over with."

"It's the alcohol talking. You don't mean that."

"Yes, I do."

"But why? Only a little while ago you seemed so much better. Your hangover was going away."

"It's not the hangover." His voice sounded strangled. "It's you. I realize that you'll never love me as much as I love you."

"And that's why you want to kill yourself?"

"Does that seem so very odd to you?" He turned around and faced her. "It seems perfectly reasonable to me. When you pushed me away before, I felt so alone and miserable. Without you, I have nothing."

"That's not true. And besides, you're not without me. I'm right here."

"Here in body, but do you still want me? I can see

your breasts in the moonlight, I'll see them in my dreams. I want to kiss them right now . . . please let me, please come back to bed with me and let me kiss you everywhere."

"Kiss me right here, standing up."

He was thrilled by the command. He got to his knees and began to work his way up her moonlit-bathed body.

"You make me so happy," he murmured, his face buried in her.

Saturday, March 4

❧ 1 ❧

Now the sun's first rays were trying to push through the bedroom's heavy drapes. Jean had closed the window and drapes after Bob was safely asleep. He was still asleep, for which she felt thankful. The longer he slept, the more sobriety time he compounded. She slipped out of bed and joined Clark Gable who was patiently waiting for her in the kitchen.

"I'm sorry I had to lock you out last night," she said to the poodle. "But I didn't think Bob would want you around."

Clark Gable covered her face with kisses and wagged his tail furiously. No wonder people kept pets, she thought, they forgave you everything. She was putting the kettle on to boil when Bob walked in, freshly shaved. He smelled nice and lemony.

"I don't even like to sleep without you," he confessed. "It's too lonely."

"How about some juice?"

"Sure. Fine."

It had been quite a while since she shared the morning with a man. Daniel was too restless to relax and usually went jogging in Central Park. Frank frequently worked on briefs. But Bob seemed content to sit at the kitchen's tiny café table and watch her be domestic.

"You look gorgeous without makeup," he said.

"Thank you." She handed him the juice. "How do you feel today?"

205

"A lot better, but still slightly punchy."

All in all he'd had eight Librium, and cumulatively they packed quite a wallop. She wondered how much he remembered about their moonlit lovemaking, or whether it happened for him in some kind of drug-induced haze. As though reading her mind, he said: "You were beautiful last night with the moon on you. I'll never forget it. For me it was the best so far, but it's going to get even better. Pretty soon you'll want me as desperately as I want you. I'll *make* you want me."

His erotic references seemed garishly out of place in the clear morning light, and she wished he would not keep harping on the same subject. He was beating it to death.

"Maybe we can go to a meeting later," she said, trying to clear the air. "You really should, you know. After yesterday's slip, it's the most constructive thing you can do."

"But Clean Slate doesn't meet on weekends."

"There are plenty of other groups. Clean Slate isn't unique."

"I'm glad to hear you say that, darling." He took her hand and kissed the palm, thrusting his tongue deep inside it. "You used to be too obsessed with those people. What happened?"

"I resent them for thinking I killed Daniel and O'Brien. You weren't there yesterday, but we had quite a confrontation. O'Brien's death has made them all slightly crazy."

He finished the orange juice.

"I've been thinking a lot about those two murders, and I'm pretty sure I know who's responsible. But if I tell you, you're not going to like it."

"Tell me anyway."

"Do you promise not to get angry?"

"Stop playing games, Bob. Just tell me."

"Okay. Your friend, Betty."

"I've considered Betty, too," Jean said reflectively. "But she doesn't add up. It's extremely unlikely that she even had the opportunity to kill O'Brien. And why would she want to kill Daniel?"

"In my opinion, she had a motive to do away with them both. A strong motive. She was jealous of them."

"I don't know what you mean."

"You were pretty friendly with O'Brien, weren't you?"

"Yes. Why?"

"That's all Betty would need to set her off. A man who liked you. He wouldn't even have to love you, as Daniel did. She'd be jealous of me this very minute, if she could see me here with you. Now do you understand?"

"No, not at all."

"Betty is in love with you, darling."

Jean felt as though he were playing a bad joke on her. Either that or he'd lost his mind. What did the psychiatrists call it? Transference. He was transferring his own feelings of love and jealousy to Betty.

"Are you serious?" she asked.

"Perfectly. And it's not as far-fetched as you imagine. I've seen the way Betty looks at you when she doesn't know she's being watched. It's all there in her eyes—admiration, desire, lust. You're just not conscious of it."

"I guess Peter's not conscious of it, either."

"What's that supposed to mean?"

"Peter has given Betty an engagement ring. They're going to be married."

"I find that very hard to believe. I can't see Betty, the ballbreaker, as anyone's wife."

"Well, she's going to be Peter's, so you're obviously wrong. And there's something else. I told Betty last Sunday that Daniel was leaving me. Therefore, even if she were 'in love' with me, as you claim, she would have no reason to kill him on Tuesday. She knew it was over between us."

"She could have killed him out of sheer plain bitchiness. That woman despises men, and make no mistake about it. The trouble with you, darling, is that you're too close to the situation to be objective."

"Bob, I *know* Betty."

But did she? What did she really know about her friend? Very little, actually. Betty's background was a rough sketch of fly-by-night jobs in the Midwest, taking care of a terminally ill mother, and a terrible descent into alcoholism when her mother died. There were a lot of loopholes, a lot of inconsistencies. Such as Betty's job as a topless dancer. With her antagonistic attitude toward men, it seemed odd that she had chosen such a sexist line of work. Still it appeared to suit her, so who was Jean to say? And when it came to being a good friend, Betty was unsurpassed.

A couple of months ago Jean was having a hard time staying sober; Daniel had just gone on tour and she missed him very much. She frantically called Betty late one evening, afraid that she would start drinking again. Betty cut short her date with Peter and raced over to spend the rest of the night in Jean's apartment, talking and kidding with her. They had watched the sun come up together, exhausted from lack of sleep, but Jean was sober. For that alone she would always remember Betty as a caring, loving person. Hardly the description of a cold-blooded murderer.

"We've been cooped up here since yesterday," she said now to Bob. "Maybe we should go somewhere for brunch. What do you think?"

"Anything you want, darling. First a meeting, then a nice quiet meal together. It sounds good to me. I still remember those bloody-mary brunches that restaurants try to entice you with on weekends. You know, one free bloody mary with your choice of entree. I used to delude myself that I went because it was such a great bargain. Not because I wanted to start boozing early."

"We all deluded ourselves about our drinking."

"You, too?"

"Sure. On Saturday I insisted upon cooking breakfast for my husband. I pretended I was being a good wife and I wouldn't hear of Frank pitching in to help. I purposely kept him as far away from me as possible. I didn't want him to see the glass of straight vodka that I had sitting right here in the sink. I used to cover the glass with an old sponge, so it didn't look conspicuous. By the time we sat down to eat, I was bombed out of my mind. I wonder now if Frank ever knew."

She realized that Bob was staring at her curiously.

"You said that you only became an alcoholic *after* your husband died."

And there it was, her greatest self-delusion exposed at last. She felt naked, as though her clothes had been ripped away and the body underneath was covered with canker sores. Of course she drank while Frank was alive, not as much as she would later on, but certainly enough to have warned her of her growing dependency upon alcohol. There'd been so many warning signs, like making an important ritual over their predinner cocktails when Frank couldn't have cared less . . . only going to the homes of those friends who drank considerably themselves . . . blacking out in the guest bathroom of the Hendersons, and Ginnie finding her on the floor with her hand over the side of the tub . . . belting down a couple of quickies before Frank came home in the evening . . . watering the bottles so he wouldn't guess . . . paying the liquor bills herself so he'd have no idea how much was actually being spent each month (a lot).

To all of this she had turned a blind eye. For years.

"I guess I didn't feel as though I had any justification for my drinking while Frank was still alive," she said now. "Supposely, I had what any woman in her right

JOYCE ELBERT

mind could wish for. A handsome, successful husband, a career of my own, a lovely home, money, health, a good life. Yet, secretly, I was miserable and insecure about everything. I refused to confront Frank with his unfaithfulness. I was scared that if I did, he'd up and leave me. So I drank to forget it. I also drank to forget what a rotten painter I thought I was. I used to drink in the studio, so that if a picture didn't turn out right I'd be too glazed to care. Alcohol softened everything, it blurred the edges, lessened the pain."

"It's easy to find an excuse to drink," Bob agreed. "Like my going off the deep end yesterday. I was afraid that you'd find out my name was really Eugene, and I would lose you."

Alcoholics seemed to have more irrational fears than most people, she thought, and then during the process of drinking they became even more afraid. Alcohol itself was a morbid mind-twister, feeding one fear upon another.

"You haven't lost me," she said. "And I wish you would stop worrying about it. I'm here. We're together. And everything's going to be all right."

"Is it?" The anxious expression was back on his face. "When I hear your talk about your husband, I realize how many years there were when I didn't know you, when you were with another man—in his arms, thoughts, when he was in *yours*."

"You must stop torturing yourself like this."

"I can't."

"You mean, you don't want to."

"Why should I want to? It's only natural to realize that you were loved before you met me, it's only natural to be jealous of the others. Would you have me any other way?"

Maybe he was crazy. "Yes!"

"Then you obviously don't care for me very much."

Jean was at her wit's end, she didn't know what to do,

what to say, how to deal with his stubborn one-track mind. She was still thinking about it when to her great relief, the telephone began to ring.

☜ 2 ☞

Betty was so upset that she had to dial Jean twice before she got the number right. The first time she'd been connected with a funeral parlor. Eerie, she thought, looking again at the anonymous letter that had just arrived in the morning's mail.

> RETRACT YOUR DEFENSE OF THAT BITCH, JEAN, OR YOU'LL BE DEAD NEXT. P.S. YOU NEVER RECEIVED THIS, UNDERSTAND?

Betty understood all right, but she couldn't cope with the situation by herself. She needed help, advice, comfort. If she and Peter hadn't argued so bitterly yesterday, he would be here with her right now. Instead he had gone away for the weekend, leaving her vulnerable to letters that threatened her life, damn him.

"I have to see you," she said when Jean answered the phone. "It's very important. Can you come over here right away?"

"What's happened? You're not drinking, are you?"

"No, no. Nothing like that. Look I'd rather not explain on the phone but it's urgent."

After a moment's hesitation, Jean said: "Bob is with me."

"Bring him along, I don't mind. In fact, he might be of help."

"Help about *what?*"

"I just received a very strange note from the murderer," Betty said. "No signature, but a weirdo message. Please hurry."

"We'll be there as soon as we can."

"Thank God."

Then she hung up, trembling and cursing Peter all over again.

☙ 3 ❧

Bob angrily confronted Jean.

"What's all this?" he wanted to know. "Why are we rushing off to Betty's so suddenly? I thought we were going to have brunch, and then go to a meeting."

"We can do that afterward. Betty is frantic." She explained about the letter. "You don't mind, do you?"

"Of course I mind!" he snapped. "So Bettty received a crank letter, so what? It sounds pretty fishy to me, and yet you're putting her wishes before mine. I got drunk yesterday, I need to go to a meeting, you were right about that but now you're playing favorites. Why is Betty so goddamned important anyway?"

"She's my friend."

"Friend?" he said in a nasty voice.

"I don't know what you're trying to imply, but Betty has been kind to me when I've had problems. Now she's in trouble."

"She's in trouble, all right. You know, the fact that she's marrying Peter doesn't mean she can't also be in love with you."

Jean felt her patience give way. "I thought we dropped the subject."

"Why does the mere mention of it make you so angry?"

"Because what you're suggesting is ridiculous."

212

"No, it isn't. It happens all the time among homosexuals. They marry for appearance, for convenience, but it doesn't stop them from falling in love with members of the same sex."

"I'm sure that's true of many people, but not in this case. For instance, where would it leave Peter? Have you thought of that?"

"He might be gay, too. A lot of theater people are."

"Bob, honestly!" She was exasperated. "Will you stop it!"

He flushed. "It makes me feel uneasy to have a woman for a rival."

"A rival? You can't be serious. Are you saying that you're jealous of *Betty?*"

"It might strike you as preposterous, but I'd be jealous of anyone who loved you. Don't you understand what I'm saying, Jean? Don't you understand what I'm trying to tell you, darling?"

She couldn't believe it. "But surely not a woman, a friend . . ."

He stood up and grasped her by the shoulders, his voice urgent and compelling.

"You still don't know how much you mean to me. How much I love you, need you, depend on you. I couldn't stand the thought of losing you to anyone else. Anyone. Man, woman, it doesn't matter. What matters is that I don't want to live without you. That's why I was going to kill myself this morning. Because I thought I *had* lost you. I was afraid you would never care for me again, never let me touch you again, the way you turned your back on me and went to sleep. It's been so long since I've felt like this, darling, so very long since I've loved someone with all my heart. Now do you understand?"

The veins on his neck were taut, his eyes filled with a burning-passion. He called it love. In the clear morning

213

light, Jean called it pathological jealousy. Madness. Rodriguez had tried to warn her about him. Daniel had called him *Gene*.

"Yes," she said. "I understand."

ॐ 4 ॐ

Rodriguez had been sitting at his desk for several hours, staring at a piece of paper. He could not make up his mind as to why O'Brien was killed. What it boiled down to were three simple questions which he'd written on the piece of paper.

1. Had the murderer meant to kill O'Brien right from the start? If so, Daniel's death was a mistake—the poison had erroneously been put in the wrong cup of coffee.

2. Or was O'Brien murdered because he knew who the killer was?

3. Or were they dealing with a mass murderer who intended to knock off everyone at Clean Slate, and chose Daniel and O'Brien at random to be the initial victims?

It was an interesting and infuriating puzzle.

The first possibility made a lot of sense (all of those identical white plastic coffee cups), except for one important fact. Daniel obviously knew he'd been poisoned. That was why at the end he'd said *Jean* or *Gene*. And Rodriguez not only had Francine's word for it, Jean herself—who couldn't hope to gain anything—admitted it. Meaning Daniel's death was intentional. Had to be.

Rodriguez wrote a large "No" next to the first possibility, and moved on.

If O'Brien was murdered because he knew who the killer was (and either threatened to tell the police, or wanted money to shut up), then the murderer would feel safe now and there'd be no more deaths. That struck Rodriguez as extremely logical but on a gut level something nagged him, told him that the killings weren't over yet.

He wrote 'Maybe" next to the second possibility and frowned.

What was he saying? That he believed the third possibility: that they had a Richard Speck–type maniac on their hands? Yes, somehow he did. It was only a hunch, but if he was right, then Jean Neelie was innocent. She didn't belong in a nut category. Rodriguez suddenly realized that he wanted her to be innocent, he liked her.

He wrote "I think so" next to the third possibility, stared at the piece of paper, and wondered what Bob Edwards was doing that very minute. He didn't trust the son of a bitch, but so far he had nothing on him. All that Edwards was guilty of was not being able to prove where he was when O'Brien was killed, and not admitting up front that his real name happened to be Eugene.

Jean. Gene.

No matter which way Rodriguez turned, there was no denying that the last word out of Daniel Streatham's mouth held the key to the killer's identity. He picked up the phone and dialed Edwards' home number. No answer. Then he dialed Jean. Doubly no answer. Maybe the two lovebirds had gone to the movies.

Jean. Gene.

Rodriguez picked up the phone again and dialed Marcel. The Frenchman knew something he wasn't telling, and Rodriguez intended to find out what the hell it was.

☙ 5 ❧

Betty lived in the West Fifties. It was only a short cab ride from Jean's apartment, and she shook the entire way. Bob thought she was getting the flu.

"Bundle up, darling."

She didn't contradict him. So many things now seemed to add up. . . . Running into Bob accidentally the day after Daniel's death . . . or was he following her, obsessed with her even then? Believing his theory that Daniel might have been killed by mistake, as he tried to convince her that was why a second murder seemed likely. Attempting now to make Betty appear guilty of his own lovesick obsession, for it was what he called *love* that drove him to kill Daniel in the first place. And afterward poor O'Brien, whose only crime was liking her. . . .

"Darling, we're here."

His voice snapped her out of her chilling reveries, and she allowed him to help her from the taxi and into the lobby. What she felt like doing was running away and calling Rodriguez.

"I've found out who the killer is," she would say.

But what would she say after Rodriguez arrived?

"I want you to arrest this man for murder. Do I have proof of his guilt? Of course. He's pathologically jealous."

The police couldn't help her and she didn't know who could. In the midst of her dilemma it struck her as ironic that she'd gone to AA for a solution to her problems, and instead she had found murder and more problems than she ever dreamed possible.

"Darling, do you realize that you're still shaking?" Bob felt her forehead. "You should have said something before we left the apartment. I don't want you getting sick on me."

"Betty will have aspirin."

"Why the hell did we come here anyway?" Just the mention of Betty's name made his bad spirits return. "We'll get this over with fast and then it's back home to bed for you. Today you can be the invalid. I'll take good care of you."

The prospect of finding herself alone with him again

was quite horrible, appalling, and Jean shivered even more. Only this morning she had let him make love to her, now she was afraid of his touch. Betty welcomed them, wearing a long apricot lounging gown and high-heeled marabou mules.

"Thanks for getting here so fast. I appreciate it, you guys."

Bob grunted something, and looked around at the apartment. Jean had forgotten how intensely feminine the furnishings were. There was a lot of crushed velvet, pinks and mauves, fur throws, richly embroidered lamp-shades with tasseled pulls, a boudoir effect actually. The crowning touch was a full-color Renoir reproduction, framed in gilt, showing four voluptuous nude girls enjoying themselves in an outdoor bath. A heavy scent of perfume hung in the air.

"Is she kidding with the decor?" Bob asked, after Betty disappeared into the kitchen.

"Not at all. She's very proud of it."

"What's it called? Early Bordello?"

Jean smiled in spite of herself. Why Betty should have strived for something so flamboyantly female escaped her. She felt there was no need to gild the lily, but Betty didn't share her views on restraint. She reappeared minutes later carrying a tray of coffee and pastries. Instead of her usual instant brew, Jean was surprised to see a drip pyrex identical to her own. Perhaps Betty's palate was improving, she thought.

"Here's the letter," Betty said. "The envelope is post-marked New York and dated yesterday afternoon. It could be from anyone at Clean Slate."

"Yes, it could." Jean reread the typewritten message, as she sipped the delicious coffee. "You must be scared stiff."

"I am. There's only one thing I don't understand. Why should my defense of you have made the murderer so furious?"

"Maybe you've upset his apple cart," Jean said as Bob continued to stare at the floor.

"What do you mean?" Betty asked.

"As long as everyone thought I was guilty, the murderer could walk around feeling fairly safe. But by defending me the way you did, you planted doubts in people's minds, possibly got them thinking . . . if I'm not the killer, then who is? What you've done is put the real killer in danger of being found out. Or so he thinks."

Betty was staring at her in confusion.

"I don't understand your logic. Nobody at Clean Slate is in doubt about you, they're all convinced you're guilty. My defense of you didn't carry any weight in the long run. Don't you remember how hostile they were yesterday?"

Jean remembered. But Bob hadn't been there yesterday, he was out "getting drunk." His last contact with Clean Slate was Thursday, when Betty spoke so eloquently on her behalf and people were moved to suspend judgment. There was no way he could have known that after O'Brien's death the tide of opinion would turn drastically against her, until she told him so this morning. And by then it was too late. He'd already mailed the note.

"Has Peter received a similar message?" Jean asked.

"I wouldn't know." Betty flushed. "He's away for the weekend. We had a fight yesterday and he took off for the Hamptons. He owns a house there."

"I wouldn't be surprised if he finds an anonymous letter in his mailbox when he returns. Peter has been nice to me, too. He didn't defend me outright, the way you did, but he's been warm and friendly."

"Are you saying that the murderer is out to silence *anyone* who likes you?" Betty asked.

"That's the way it's beginning to look."

Betty turned to Bob. "You should have been included in the mailing, in that case. Were you?"

"I don't know. I haven't been home yet. I slept over at Jean's last night."

Bob, as the murderer, began to come into clearer focus in Jean's mind.

He cruelly planned to eliminate everyone who was close to her, everyone she liked, all her friends. She had repeatedly told him how much she cared about the opinion of Clean Slate people, how much their goodwill mattered to her, but in light of his possessive jealousy that meant nothing. He wanted her to himself, *all* to himself. Daniel and O'Brien had already been dispensed with, now Betty was next—if she didn't watch her step. And Bob wanted Betty to know it; he was probably enjoying himself this very minute, reveling in Betty's fear and confusion.

"What am I supposed to do now?" Betty said. "Get up at Clean Slate and say that my defense of Jean has been a big mistake?"

"Yes," Jean said firmly. "Say you've changed your mind and you feel I'm guilty after all. And be convincing. Your life might depend on it."

"Is that all the murderer wants from me? My condemnation of you? It doesn't seem like such a big deal."

"People get satisfaction in strange ways."

They both regarded her curiously.

"Somebody doesn't want me to have friends. Writing notes like this is a good way of insuring that I won't. No matter how much certain people might like me, they aren't going to jeopardize their own lives by remaining on close terms with me."

"Then we're dealing with a very ruthless person," Betty said, sipping her coffee. "And I think I know who."

Jean felt transfixed. If Betty accused Bob, there was no telling what might happen. She heard her own voice quietly say: "Betty, can I trouble you for some aspirin? I'm not feeling too well."

"Sure." Betty got up. "How many do you want?"

Jean got up, too. "I'll come with you."

The minute they were inside, Jean locked the bathroom door and heaved a sigh of relief.

"What is it?" Betty said, perplexed. "You look weird."

"Bob."

"He is acting strangely, I agree. What's wrong? Have you been arguing? I was hoping that after what you went through with Frank and Daniel you might have struck oil at last, but I'm beginning to see—"

"Goddamn it, shut up and listen to me. *Bob is the murderer.*"

There was absolute silence for a moment as the two women stood in Betty's orchid bathroom, staring at each other.

"Bob?" Betty said at last. "I thought it was Francine."

"It's Bob, I tell you."

"Are you certain?"

"I'm positive."

"Why haven't you called the police? What are you doing bringing a murderer here?"

"I don't have proof."

Then she told Betty everything, beginning with Bob's jealousy of Daniel.

"Does he know that you suspect him?"

"No," Jean said. "He seems immune to everything except his own feelings."

"Murderers usually are. They're egomaniacs, in a twisted sort of way."

"Never mind the analysis. The question is, what should I do? He's going to suggest that we leave and I go home to bed. I've been pretending to be sick."

"You're not going anywhere," Betty said firmly. "You're staying here."

"But what excuse should I give? You don't know him."

"All you have to do is go into my bedroom right now and lie down. This door connects to it, so you don't even have to pass through the living room. I'll explain that you don't feel well and are resting. If he should try and wake you, act drowsy, groggy. Don't come to. Fake it. I'll say that you need to sleep. Eventually, he'll go home and then we can decide what to do next."

Jean flung her arms around Betty and kissed her before Betty could pull away.

"I don't know what I'd do without you."

"Don't be silly. That's what friends are for."

"Bob wouldn't understand that. He can't get it through his head that two women can simply be friends and nothing more. Would you believe that he thinks you're a lesbian?"

Betty grinned. "You're joking."

"No. Honest. And I'll tell you something else. The reason he doesn't think Francine is the murderer is that he would like me to believe *you* are."

Betty burst out laughing. "You sure can pick them can't you?"

❧ 6 ❧

Bob was fuming as he walked out of Betty's building.

That damned dike was absolutely the last straw! No man should have to put up with this much, he thought, counting them in his head: Frank, Daniel, O'Brien, maybe Marcel, and now Betty. His rivals for Jean's love and attention. He hadn't been kidding earlier when he told Jean that he thought Betty was a lesbian and a murderer. She didn't fool him with that stagy note, which, as

221

far as he was concerned, she'd sent to herself to throw them all off the track.

But Jean believed her. Jean was with her right now. He couldn't get it through his head that Jean would prefer Betty to him; it was shattering, it was crazy, he felt quite deranged as he stumbled out into the chilly street trying not to think about what the two of them were doing this very minute, naked, in each other's arms, kissing, caressing. . . .

He turned the corner and began walking north on Broadway past the theaters and gaudy shops, Beefsteak Charlie's and the Mony building which told the time, trying all the time not to see the vivid pictures in his mind; it was disgusting what they were doing (shades of The Rabbit) but it thrilled him just the same, and as he started to walk faster the pictures started to move faster, they became more jagged, more surreal, more satisfying . . . an arm here, a bare leg there, glistening thighs, breasts upturned, hair entangled, polished toenails in the air, lipsticked mouths meeting, other mouths opening wide, wider, ah yes, breath coming harder. . . . Bob walked still faster, he felt as though he were choking, dying, as he heard Jean's cry of pleasure and saw Betty's triumphant smile, that fucking redheaded bitch had taken his place but he didn't even want to kill her, she wasn't important enough to bother killing or hating, he realized suddenly; none of them were because there could always be replacements. No, it was Jean he hated, Jean who was harming him, Jean whom he wanted to kill . . . first her, then himself. . . . He kept on walking. . . .

❧7❧

Betty returned to the bedroom a few minutes later.

"He's gone," she said. "He was mad as hell, but he

222

left. I wonder why he wants you to think I'm the murderer."

"So that I don't think it's him. Also, he's jealous of you. I've explained that."

"He might have a point, you know. Telling you to suspect me. Until the murderer is apprehended, we should all be on guard. It's horrible to go around suspecting your friends, but at this stage how can we be sure who's a friend and who's an enemy?"

"I can," Jean said loyally.

"You're too damned trusting. For all you know, I could have killed them both. I might not even have needed a motive. I might be insane. You read about cases like that all the time. No motive. The killer just felt something come over her."

"You're talking rubbish, and you know it."

"Yes, I am," Betty admitted. "Why don't you call Rodriguez and tell him about the threatening note? Although frankly, I'm not sure Bob sent it. You might be making too much of his jealousy, blowing it way out of proportion. Lots of men are jealous without being killers."

"But it fits," Jean protested.

"Does it? My feeling is that Bob doesn't have what it takes to pull off two premeditated murders. He's not smart enough."

"You still think it's Francine, don't you?"

"Yes," Betty admitted, "I do. I always thought it was one of Daniel's women, who got fed up finally and killed him. And Francine fits the picture. O'Brien probably saw her do it, so she had to shut him up. Now she's running scared. What better way to protect herself than to force me to implicate you?"

"It's really not much protection."

"Don't forget that Francine was the first one who mentioned the aspirin bottle after Daniel was killed. How come? I mean, isn't it strange that she would have

223

known exactly how the murder took place when nobody else did? The reason she knew is because she poisoned him herself."

"I still think it's Bob."

"Think what you like," Betty said, "but please relay my suspicions to Rodriguez. If he's going to start asking more questions, he might just as well start with Francine."

"What makes you think she's such a genius in the murder field? From the way you've described her, she sounds pretty klutzy to me."

"I have my reasons."

Jean didn't know how to respond to that enigmatic statement. It seemed to her that Betty was being very whimsical and self-indulgent in her choice of murderers, very unfair, and she wondered what Rodriguez' reaction would be. She wished she knew how close he was to wrapping up the case. Her own efforts so far had been pretty pathetic. Private eyes were supposed to find fascinating leads and clues, trails that conveniently ended on the murderer's doorstep, but all she had found to date were a lot of inconclusive maybe's. She could not even prove her darkest suspicions about Bob, and Betty was no help with her adamant doubts. Perhaps she would fare better with Rodriguez, but when she called the precinct he wasn't there. She left a message for him to call her back.

"You should have said it was an emergency," Betty reprimanded her. "I mean, it's not every day you catch a murderer."

"Maybe I'm wrong. All your talk about Francine makes me wonder if I know what I'm babbling about, accusing Bob. What if he's innocent? What if I'm just being hysterical?"

"And what if it's Francine?" Betty sat down at the vanity table and began to brush her hair. "Rodriguez could have a little chat with her, shake her up a bit.

Who knows? She might panic and confess, and it would be all over.

Jean was still wondering if she had blundered in her logic, imagining that Bob was the murderer. Only a moment ago she had been so certain, but now she could feel the insidious doubts set in.

"Rodriguez wouldn't be able to talk to Francine today, even if I got hold of him," she said, absent-mindedly "Francine is away for the weekend."

Betty stopped brushing her hair.

"How do you know?"

"She happened to mention it to me."

"I didn't know the two of you were so chummy. She didn't also happen to mention *where* she was going, did she?"

"No. Just away." Jean noted the expression of alarm that had spread across Betty's face. "Why are you so interested in Francine's weekend plans?"

"Because I suspect they include Peter. I think she and Peter are together in East Hampton. Now you know why I consider her smart. She made sure I'd find out about them."

"But you and Peter are engaged to be married," Jean said, trying to digest this latest surprise. "He was so happy yesterday when he gave you the ring. I don't get it. Is there something I've missed?"

"There sure as hell is, but I don't know how to put it." Betty took a deep breath. "I'm not certain I can explain it, so that it makes any sense. In fact, I'm not even certain I should try."

"Try to explain what? What are you talking about?"

"I can't tell you. It's too freaky."

"For God's sake, Betty, what is it?"

"Peter and I have never—made love."

Jean thought that after the tumultuous events of the past week nothing could catch her off guard anymore, but she was wrong.

"Why haven't you?" was all she could think to say.

"I hope you're ready for this one."

So did Jean. "Shoot."

"I'm a virgin."

After what felt like a long time, Jean managed to nod her head in some semblance of comprehension.

"You're flabbergasted, right?" Betty asked.

"I honestly didn't expect it. There aren't too many virgins walking around New York these days. Or anywhere else for that matter, I'm told."

"Particularly not many thirty-four-year-old virgins," Betty said bitterly, looking at herself in the bedroom's full-length mirror. "But there I am, folks, a true original."

"Do you want to talk about it?" Jean asked, sensing the extent of her friend's desolation. "You might feel better."

"There really isn't very much to say. It's a common enough story. I was brought up in a very strict Lutheran household. My mother drummed it into me that sex out of wedlock was sinful, and by the time I decided it wasn't, I was too afraid to take the plunge. I was afraid of being laughed at for my ignorance, particularly since I looked so experienced. I mean, I always *looked* hip, like I knew the score. . . ."

It was the first time Jean had ever seen Betty cry, and it was painful to watch. The sobs came in harsh animal sounds, as though they'd been held back for years. Jean put her arms around her friend until there were no more tears left and Betty was worn out. Her eye makeup was streaked and clownish-looking, and up close her features seemed to have lost their femininity, with the outpouring of her shameful secret.

"This is a hell of a time to be a recovering alcoholic," Betty joked. "I'd cut off my right arm this very minute for a good stiff brandy."

"So would I. Why don't you go wash your face and I'll scramble some eggs?"

Betty managed a smile. "Thanks, pal. Make some more coffee, too, would you? In case you didn't notice, I finally got around to buying the real stuff. Your admirable influence."

"I did notice. It tasted delicious."

Jean realized that so many things which had seemed contradictory before now fell into place. Betty's hostility toward men was due to her fear of them. Her reluctance to set a wedding date was also due to fear. And because she lacked confidence in her womanhood, she went overboard to prove it. She dressed too provocatively, used courtesan touches in her apartment, titillated men for a living.

"There are English muffins and jam in the fridge," Betty called out.

"Relax. I'll find everything."

Although the new drip coffeemaker was an exact replica of her own, Betty did not have Thelma to keep it spotless. The bottom was slightly but stubbornly discolored. Jean cleaned it as best she could, still thinking about her friend's ambivalent personality. Beneath that exterior of sexy toughness must lay deep feelings of doubt and vulnerability. Was it because of those feelings that Betty imagined Peter was spending the weekend with Francine?

"No, that's not why," Betty said when they were in the living room, eating scrambled eggs. "The reason I think they're together is that it wouldn't be the first time Peter has gone off with another woman. But in the past, he always told me who it was. He confided in me. Ever since he met Francine, he's changed. He's become sneaky."

Jean was still trying to absorb the fact that Betty was a virgin. "Sneaky? How?"

227

"This weekend, for instance. I asked him if he was going away by himself, and he wouldn't answer."

"That hardly proves he's with Francine."

"No, except she's the one we had the fight over. I wanted to know if he had screwed her, and he refused to tell me. Now you say she's away for the weekend, too. Doesn't it strike you as suspicious?"

"Not at all. A lot of people go away for the weekend."

"You don't understand. Until Francine came along, Peter and I had an arrangement. I didn't expect him to be faithful to me. Under the circumstances, how could I? All I asked was that he not get emotionally involved with any of his women. And he didn't. He was careful."

"When did Francine come along?"

"Ah! The very day Daniel was murdered. Peter spotted her just before the meeting started and he was entranced, intrigued. I saw it all in his eyes immediately. He trailed off after her just as the meeting was about to begin, he forgot I was there. Then later at the coffee shop you mentioned her name in connection with the empty aspirin bottle, and Peter lit up like a damned Christmas tree. It never occurred to me then that Francine was the murderer. I just viewed her as a rival, and I was damned right. Peter hasn't been the same since. I wouldn't be surprised if he was falling in love with that bitch. She's probably terrific in bed."

"Even if she is, it's obvious that Peter is in love with you. He gave you an engagement ring only yesterday. He's pushing you to set a wedding date. Those aren't the actions of a man who's falling in love with someone else. Don't be irrational, Betty."

"Why *has* he given me an engagement ring? Why *does* he want to marry a woman he's never gone to bed with? That's what I find irrational."

Jean remembered being a virgin herself when she met Frank. Frank had laughed at her at first, said that nobody was a virgin anymore, called it ridiculous, but she sensed that in a certain way he liked the idea, approved of it. After they were married, he admitted she was right.

"Deep down, every man wants to have gotten there first," Frank said. "It's primeval. No matter how sophisticated we may act, part of us is still at the savage stage. We want to brand the woman, make her ours alone, and by sexually getting there first that's what we do. There isn't a guy in the world who doesn't secretly object to second-hand goods."

Sixteen years later and in light of women's lib, it was a very chauvinistic remark. But Jean wondered whether many men didn't still feel that way today, even if it was unfashionable to admit it. Sex was so available now, so easy to come by, it must have lost a lot of its previous mystery and intrigue. Perhaps to Peter, Betty's being a virgin was a refreshing change from all the women he met who were ready to rip off their clothes at a moment's notice.

"Has it ever occurred to you that Peter might be old-fashioned?" she said. "That he cares for you so much, he's willing to wait until after you're married? It could also explain why he wants to get married so urgently. Because he *does* love you. If I were in your shoes, I wouldn't keep him waiting too long."

"How does he know that I won't be a total washout in bed?" Betty persisted. "How do *I* know? I've never even gotten undressed in front of Peter." Betty went on. "Do you believe that?"

"At that point, I'd believe anything."

"Of course he's seen me topless at work."

Jean giggled. "But not bottomless."

"What's so funny?"

"I'm sorry. I mean, you are going to marry the guy. It seems strange that he's never seen you without clothes."

"I'm a strange person," Betty said.

8

Marcel had gone to an afternoon concert, but Rodriguez was having an interesting chat with his wife, Marianne. She had proven to be very affable, very cooperative, and very understanding when it came to her husband's private tutoring, for instance. Rodriguez wasn't sure that an American wife would be so intelligent about certain things.

"Sometimes my husband will pretend he is with a student, when perhaps—" Marianne's eyes sparkled with mischief. "And even then, I am not altogether certain. He is getting to be the old professor, I don't begrudge him his harmless little flirtations."

"But you are sure he was with a student the night O'Brien was killed?" Rodriguez said. "That was no pretense?"

"Oh no, she is a charming young girl of whom Marcel is very fond. She cannot afford to pay much, but she has the ear for language." Marianne tapped her own ear. "It is a quality that always impresses my husband. Marcel is a poet at heart."

A poet and an ex-guerilla, Rodriguez thought.

"Does Marcel have any idea who killed O'Brien?" he went on. "When I asked him directly, he insisted that he knew nothing. But I believe he suspects someone. Do you know who?"

Marianne shook her head. Her hair was dark, curly, somber.

"No, I do not concern myself with these matters."

Her mood had changed too abruptly for Rodriguez to buy it.

"Anything you tell me will be held in the strictest confidence, I assure you."

"There is nothing to tell."

"Ah, but there must be or you wouldn't look so troubled. You are obviously an honest, conscientious woman who wants to see justice done. Don't you want this murderer caught? He's killed two innocent people, he may kill again. You might be able to prevent that if you would only tell me what you know."

Her face grew very grim.

"Very well. I think my husband suspects . . . Eleanor. *Tu connais*, the divorcée. . . . There, I have said it!"

Rodriguez knew all about the ancient affair between Eleanor and Marcel. Eleanor had proudly told him of it, boasting, pleased with herself and her ability to make trouble and cause unhappiness.

"Eleanor?" Rodriguez said. "But why should she want to kill Daniel and O'Brien?"

"Possibly because they rejected her. She does not like the rejections, that one, no. She thinks she can lure any man she desires, it is a sickness with her. *Au fond*, she has a hatred for the men."

"A sickness, yes."

Rodriguez was thinking. Sick people were known to kill, certainly, yet he couldn't see Eleanor in that extreme a role. She was probably a genius at disrupting other people's lives with her greedy need for attention; he could see her going from man to man, situation to doomed situation, creating chaos all around her. But when it came to murder, Eleanor faded right out of the picture. She was too frivolous to be a murderer.

"Then you are certain that it is Eleanor your husband believes to be guilty?"

"I am not saying he is right," Marianne protested. "Please do not misunderstand. Marcel is not the Sûreté, he only has his personal suspicions. . . ."

Her voice trailed off, she seemed to be thinking of something else, going back in time, tears came to her eyes. Why? Who was she crying for? Certainly not the woman her husband had once had an affair with behind her back. Then for whom were these tears being shed?

231

"What is it?" Rodriguez asked as gently as possible.

"I am remembering old wounds, they are often the hardest to forget, to heal. I am thinking of how Marcel was after the war, when he would wake up at night having terrible dreams about the killing, the Nazis, the torture; he was tortured by them, you know."

"I didn't realize."

"He was tortured and he told them everything they wanted to know. He gave them information that led to the slaughter of every member of his *réseau*. Marcel has never forgotten what he did, he has never forgiven himself, he still sleeps with the light on, he is still afraid. . . ."

"Afraid?"

"That he will be accused once more of murder."

"Once more? I don't understand."

"In his heart he knows that he murdered his Resistance friends, and he carries with him the guilt of their death. A traitor's guilt. But in his mind, he can never admit that he was responsible for their dying. It is too much for him to bear, that they perished because of him. He always blames Pierre, the radio operator, for their death. To this day, he insists it was Pierre who gave them away, Pierre who murdered them."

Rodriguez was beginning to comprehend.

"Just as he now says it was Eleanor who murdered Daniel and O'Brien?"

Marianne nodded, weeping.

"Yes."

9

Rodriguez finally called in the late afternoon, and Jean told him about the threatening letter Betty had received.

"I hope you still have it," he said.

"Well, of course. You don't think we'd be stupid enough to throw away the evidence, do you?"

Instead of answering, he said: "I'll be right over. Stay there."

Rodriguez' visit was brief and he was unusually taciturn, as he listened to Jean's suspicions about Bob and Betty's about Francine.

"What are you going to do?" Jean finally asked.

"Poke around, talk to them both, check out typewriters. Make sure you lock the door after I leave, and don't open it to anyone. Do you understand?"

They both realized that he was taking the note very seriously.

"That settles it," Betty said. "I'm not going to work tonight. I refuse to leave Jean alone."

"Leave *me* alone? But you're the one who received the threatening note. You're the one who's in danger."

"More's the reason why I shouldn't be on public display tonight. One of the other dancers wants tomorrow afternoon off, and I can arrange to switch with her. I'm exhausted, anyhow."

"Good," Rodriguez said. "Just one more thing, Betty. Be sure to follow the note's instructions. Denounce Jean at Clean Slate as soon as you can. And if Peter receives any threats, call me at once."

Jean was glad that she had decided to sleep over at Betty's, rather than return to her own lonely apartment. She phoned Albert, the doorman, and asked him to walk Clark Gable, then she and Betty watched television and managed to eat some dinner. Neither of them had much of an appetite; Jean was too disturbed about Bob, and Betty about Peter, to be hungry. Although their fears existed on totally different planes, the mutual distress was one more bond in an already strong friendship.

"There are some nightgowns in the bottom bureau drawer," Betty told Jean. "Please help yourself."

Betty had insisted that Jean should sleep in her bed,

and she would sleep in the living room on the sofa. Jean refused at first, but finally, reluctantly gave in. It had been a long day and she was too tired to argue. All she wanted to do was fade into oblivion, forget, be at peace. But instead of that, she found herself troubled by a series of nightmares. The worst was the last. She dreamed that she woke up in the middle of the night and had to go to the bathroom. Still groggy, she groped her way toward the connecting door. As she opened it, she gasped. The person urinating at the toilet was naked, grotesque, unbelievably freakish.

"Please excuse me," Jean said in her dream. "I didn't realize anyone was in here."

The person turned around to reveal a face contorted by rage. It was Betty's face.

"How dare you? Out! GET OUT!"

Jean fled.

She woke up in a cold sweat sometime later, the dream still vivid in her mind, horrifying in its bodily detail. She wondered if she had screamed in her sleep and disturbed Betty. But when she went to look, Betty was curled up on the crushed velvet sofa, softly snoring. Jean tiptoed back to bed, knowing she would be awake for the rest of the night.

Sunday, March 5

❧ 1 ❧

Sunlight was streaming into Betty's pink-and-mauve living room, throwing a cheerful glow over the two women. Both of them were wearing robes, sipping coffee, and reading the *Times*, but there the similarity ended. Jean had dark rings under her eyes due to lack of sleep, whereas Betty appeared rested and refreshed.

"I had a ghastly dream last night," Jean said looking up from the art page. "I think I might have screamed out loud. Did you hear me, by any chance?"

"I wouldn't hear an earthquake, kid. You don't know me when I sleep. Dead to the world, it runs in the family." Betty's face was buried in the magazine section. "What did you dream about?"

"Actually, it was a nightmare about you."

"Really? What was I doing?"

"I can't quite remember." Jean found herself unable to repeat the horror, even in the calm sanity of daytime. "It's not important, it was only a dream."

The sound of the telephone suddenly pierced the room. The two women stared at each other, alert and on guard.

"Bob," Jean said.

"Peter."

"If it's Bob, I definitely don't want to talk to him."

As Betty picked up the receiver, Jean ran to stand next to her so she could hear the caller's voice.

"Hello," Bob said. "I'd like to speak to Jean."

"She's not here."

"Where did she go? She wasn't feeling well when I left yesterday. I hope she's not worse."

"She feels fine. She went home."

"No, she didn't. I called her apartment and there wasn't any answer."

"That hardly proves she's with me."

"I know she is, Betty, so why don't you just put her on the phone?"

"Because she's not here."

"You're lying."

"Would *I* harbor a murderer, after receiving such a frightening note?"

"She's not the murderer." A string of enraged obscenities followed, ending with, "You are, you rotten dike."

Betty replaced the receiver and looked at Jean.

"Your boyfriend has a foul mouth."

"He's not my boyfriend; he's crazy."

Betty studied her a moment. "You really mean that, don't you?"

"Yes. That's what I was trying to tell you yesterday in the bathroom, when I felt so convinced Bob was the killer." She sank into a mauve silk chair. "Shit. What are we supposed to do?"

"We could call Rodriguez."

"We called him yesterday. What do we tell him now? That Bob is angry and wants to talk to me? Big deal."

"What do you plan to do this afternoon, when I go to work?" Betty asked.

"Maybe check out the Guggenheim." Jean glanced at the art page again. "They have a new exhibit, it sounds interesting."

"You can come back here afterwards, if you want to spend the night. I've got an extra key."

"No, thanks. I have to face my own apartment at some point. And besides, I can't leave Clark Gable alone for too much longer."

236

"I imagine you'll be barraged with phone calls from you-know-who."

"Yes, I imagine I will be. But that's another thing I have to face, isn't it?"

"You're becoming very courageous all of a sudden."

"It's not all of a sudden. I've been practicing for thirty-five years."

❧ 2 ❧

Bob felt positive that Jean had stayed overnight at Betty's and he was infuriated at being unable to talk to her. He wanted to explain . . . how much he still loved her, how sorry he was if he had (in any way) offended her, how frightened he was for her. Being with Betty was dangerous in more ways than one, and Jean didn't realize it. Jean was afraid of the wrong person; it was Betty she had to fear, not him, Betty who had the ability to corrupt and demoralize, to turn Jean against him.

His rage of yesterday was still there, but under control now. Yesterday, when he blindly walked all the way home from Betty's, he hated Jean, wanted to kill her. Now he could almost laugh at his childish urge for destruction. He even wanted to kill himself afterward, as though that would solve anything. Silly, that's what he'd been. It was the little visit from Rodriguez, a few minutes ago, that made him see how self-defeating it would be to give into anger.

"The note that Betty received was typewritten," Rodriguez said. "Do you have a typewriter here at home?"

"No, I don't."

"What about at your office?"

"My secretary has one, of course."

"Did you type that note on your secretary's machine?

237

Don't bother to lie, Edwards, because my men are on their way now to check it out."

"It's Sunday, the building is closed."

"Just answer the question."

"Of course I didn't type the stupid note. You don't really think I killed Daniel and O'Brien, do you?"

"Never mind what I think. Did you kill them? Well? Did you?"

Bob's mouth had fallen open in dismay. How could Rodriguez seriously suspect *him?* He'd been so careful to wait until Daniel was out of the way before he approached Jean, he had timed everything with such clocklike precision, even O'Brien's death couldn't have come at a more opportune moment—Jean clung to him for safety when she heard about it.

"No, I didn't kill them," he said.

"Then why did Daniel say 'Gene' at the end?"

"I don't know. I've already told you I have no idea. Maybe he meant *Jean Neelie.*"

"Are you accusing her of being the murderer?"

"Certainly not." Bob turned red. "Betty's the murderer. Why don't you go check her typewriter?"

"Because she doesn't have one."

"She could have borrowed one, or rented one, or stolen one. I'm positive that she sent the note to herself."

"Oh, you are?" Rodriguez was looking at him with suspicious eyes. "Then you're convinced Betty killed both men?"

"Yes."

"If that's the case, why didn't Daniel say 'Betty'?"

"Maybe he made a mistake. Maybe he *thought* that Jean put poison in his coffee. Dying people have no monopoly on accuracy, you know."

"I don't think he made a mistake. And I don't think he meant Jean. I think he was saying 'Gene.' I think that just before Daniel died, he remembered something . . .

perhaps seeing you turn around in the meeting room, leaning over toward him. . . . Is that when you dropped the poison in his coffee cup? You were seated diagonally in front of him, you could easily have done it when he was lighting a cigarette, when he was distracted. Or did you do it in the anteroom, before the meeting started?"

"I didn't poison Daniel," Bob said quietly. "And I didn't stab O'Brien. You're barking up the wrong tree."

"O'Brien was sitting at the end of Daniel's row, behind you. He could have seen you turn around and do your stuff, then tried to blackmail you. It fits, Edwards."

"It might fit someone at Clean Slate, but not me."

"Really? We'll see."

After the detective left, Bob realized that he never should have shouted at Betty on the phone this morning. It was stupid to curse her like that, stupid to show rage or act angry; they would think he was violent. That's what goddamned Rodriguez was waiting for: an act of violence from him. Well, he wouldn't give the creepy bastard that satisfaction. Even though he was being suspected of murder, he would remain cool. No more phone calls and no more accusations. He would handle the matter with kid gloves from now on; he would show them that love (not hate) was his overriding concern.

A little while later, he put on his olive-green windbreaker and left the building.

⊛ 3 ⊛

Jean decided to walk to the Guggenheim Museum on East Eighty-ninth Street. The day was muggy in spite of the low temperature and her body felt heavy; it seemed to stubbornly lag behind with every step she took. She had thought that the walk would do her good, wake her up, but by the time she reached her destination she felt exhausted.

She stopped on the park side of Fifth Avenue and looked around, convinced that she'd been followed. That fear tired her even more, particularly since there was no one suspicious in sight, just a few kids on skateboards, couples out for a Sunday-afternoon stroll, teenagers in packs, a man in a wheelchair, and the obligatory shopping-bag lady. Was one of Rodriguez' men lurking behind a Central Park tree? Jean decided that she was being paranoid, yet she could not shake off the uneasiness.

Across the street the Guggenheim boldly ballooned out among its starchy uptight neighbors, a gigantic concrete snail that had proven to be Frank Lloyd Wright's crowning achievement. The remarkable structure never failed to impress her, it was so different from every other museum she had seen, so absolutely outrageous. She still remembered the prolonged controversy back in the fifties between Wright and the New York City building authorities, who objected to the unorthodox design. Thank God they had lost.

She remembered attending one of the museum's grand openings in 1959 with her parents. She was only sixteen then and awed by the exotic crowd of painters and sculptors in evening clothes who strutted up the continuous spiraling ramp and were met by champagne and hors d'oeuvres on each floor. A famous surrealist arrived in a satin emerald-green dress shirt with a parrot to match, and proceeded to feed his parrot pâté, shrimp, and watercress. By the time Jean and her parents reached the dizzying domed top, almost one hundred feet above, they felt quite intoxicated.

"I'd hate like hell to have an exhibition here," her father commented, looking around him. "The competition would be ferocious."

"What competition?" Jean wanted to know.

"Anyone who shows in this place is competing with the master himself. With Wright. His genius is everywhere. There's no way you can outshine him, you've entered his domain. And that's the way he intended it, the shrewd devil."

"I agree," her mother said. "You can feel Wright's presence, it's engraved in the concrete. It's awesome."

The words spoken nearly twenty years ago struck Jean as insightful now as then, and she realized how privileged she was to have been born the child of such unique parents. Most of the time she took her artistic heritage for granted, abused it, neglected it, failed to honor it, but every once in a while she became aware of the gift that had been bestowed upon her, the responsibility to achieve, to create. It was golden, exquisite, she must not treat it so shabbily in the future. She suddenly thought of her unfinished landscape and realized what was wrong with it, why she had not been able to finish it until now. It was because the view of the city no longer coincided with her own personal one, it was too desolate, too forlorn; it was a view that had been forged out of feelings of isolation and defeat, feelings she no longer shared.

Jean paid the admission fee and went in.

The museum was crowded, but strangely quiet. All around her people were talking, yet their voices did not carry. It was as though their conversation drifted right up to the domed top and out into the sky above, leaving the people below in spiraling, weightless, noiseless, colorless space.

The lack of color struck her forcibly. Except for a blue pool of water near the entranceway and a red mobile descended from an upper floor, the museum was bathed in neutral earth tones which managed to swallow up everyone and everything inside it. Even Louise Nevelson's huge black sculpture was dwarfed by the sculpture of the museum itself. Jean felt tiny, invisible, unimportant. Her parents had been right, she thought, walking toward the elevator.

"Sixth floor," she told the operator.

For it was starting to come back to her, how to enjoy this strange place and not feel overwhelmed by it. The enjoyment lay in the journey downward from the top; that was when a sense of giddiness set in, as you moved down that long, curving, slippery, cantilevered ramp which never seemed to end, that was the *fun* of the Guggenheim, the childish joy of it, sliding down. Jean felt sorry for those people who didn't know the secret and were slowly climbing their way upward, floor by floor.

"This is the sixth," the elevator operator said.

The minute she stepped out, Jean felt olympian. She walked over to the absurdly low railing and looked at the blue pool and red mobile far below, at the specks of humanity streaming in, at a child's yellow balloon, at a familiar olive-green windbreaker. The person inside it was gazing up, craning. It was Bob! She was right about being followed; he'd followed her from the moment she left Betty's all the way here. How else could he have possibly known where she would be this afternoon?

"I must not panic," she said to herself.

If she grabbed the next elevator, she might just manage to miss him. Or, she might walk right into him. It depended upon his own plan for finding her. At the moment he was standing still, peering upward, undoubtedly trying to spot her mink cape on one of the ramps. She moved back out of view, toward the paintings on the sloping walls. She felt hot, her palms were wet. Did he know that she suspected him of murder? Had Rodriguez told him about her suspicions? Was that why he'd followed her? Becauss he was angry with her for blowing the whistle on him?

Modern Masters In France, it said on the wall.

Jean moved toward the canvases of Van Dongen, Delaunay, Gleizes, Gris, one by Vlaminck called *Under the Bridge*, one by Chagall called *Birthday*, in which a woman with a bouquet of flowers was being kissed by a man flying through the air half upside down, a slew of Miros, early Picassos, Matisse, Derain, Picabia, a large hermaphroditic nude by Kupka (man? woman?), a long-necked Modigliani next to a short-necked Soutine, both women with their hands clasped solemnly in front of them, both painted in the late twenties. She rounded the bend and found herself on the fifth floor, Bob next to her, short of breath.

"Jean," he said, laying an arm on hers. "I've got to talk to you. Wait."

"No."

"Please."

"Let me go."

Several people turned around to glance at them, a few smiled, no one understood that he was dangerous, that he had killed two men. The expression on his face now was dark, menacing. Was that how he'd looked before he poisoned Daniel? When he stabbed O'Brien in the back? Did he want to kill her because she had told Rodriguez about him?

She broke his grasp and started to walk faster, there were so many people in her way, so many paintings, now all by Mondrian, oils, drawings, gouaches, geometrics and bright colors, straight lines and a right angle . . . that was the world of Mondrian, Mondrian at the Guggenheim. She was sliding down the ramp now, she could feel the eerie possibility of falling, sprawling, her heels were too high to descend gracefully.

"Jean! Stop!"

His voice was lost in the high dome of the museum, but she saw his desperate, determined face coming after her. . . . She was on the fourth floor, paintings flew past her eyes, the third floor. . . . Did he mean to kill her at the Guggenheim? Did he have a knife? What if he suddenly pulled out a gun and shot her?

As hysteria gripped her, she veered left on the second floor toward the Justin K. Thannausen wing, a little cluster of rooms off the main ramp, enclosed but not safe, for he had followed her in and was trying to catch up with her. How clumsy he was, how odd; he appeared so trim and graceful but he didn't know how to snake his way through museums. It was a special talent, he lacked her invaluable experience. Still he wouldn't give up, he was like a charging bull with only one goal in mind, stubborn, obsessed. He kept on coming, she kept on fleeing without actually running. . . . Certain paintings leaped out at her demanding recognition. Raoul Dufy showed her a man in top hat seated on a horse and called it *"At the Circus,"* Leger offered a cubistic *Woman Holding a Vase* . . . lots of blue and black there. The floors in the Justin K. Thannhauser wing were parquet, sound, secure, yet she was caught in a treacherous cul-de-sac along with Renoir's still life of flowers and Pisarro's beautiful *Hermitage of Pointoise*. People sat quietly on benches in the middle of the cluster of rooms she was encircling. . . . She left Bonnard's *Dining Room on the Garden* behind her, left Bob to rush into a group of students with a guide intoning artistic wisdom about Manet, Degas, Gauguin, a marvelous Rousseau called *The Football Players*, and now she was back on the main ramp again and it felt more slippery than ever. Bob had caught up with her at last, he reached for her moist hand, and she began to run, to fall, down down like a child, sliding down Frank Lloyd Wright's sliding pond of a museum, with Bob finally picking her up off the floor.

"Why did you do it?" she cried, her heart still galloping.

"Because I love you."

You killed Daniel and O'Brien because you love me?"

"Killed?" His tormented eyes peered into hers. "I didn't kill anyone. I *followed* you here because I love you, because I want to be with you, help you. That's what I meant."

"Liar!"

"It's the truth, darling. You must calm down."

"Liar! Murderer!"

"Please, dear."

"Homicidal maniac!"

And their voices drifted right up to the top of the dome and out into the blue Sunday-afternoon sky.

❧ 4 ❧

From time to time Francine sneaked glances at Peter's face as they zoomed along the Long Island Expressway, en route back to the city. She was still in a state of minor shock, and no wonder. The weekend had been a combination of deep sexual disappointment, outrage at being subjected to Peter's blundering experimentation, and finally an almost maternal concern about his sad problem.

"Oh, my God," she said Friday night when they were in bed, in East Hampton. "You don't know how to fuck. You haven't the foggiest idea. What am I doing here? Why did you invite me? What the hell is going on?"

"I think I'm gay," was the muffled, embarrassed response.

"You think? Why didn't you think of that before you asked me to go away with you for the weekend?"

"I did think of it. That's precisely *why* I asked."

The light was beginning to dawn. "You mean, you're using me to find out if you can make it with a woman? Is that what you're saying?"

Peter nodded. "In a nutshell."

And this was the man who was supposed to have saved her from becoming a boss lady. Boy, could she pick them. Francine didn't know whether to laugh or cry.

"Hey, wait a minute," she said. "What about Betty? You're engaged to her, surely the two of you must have . . ."

"No. Never."

"I can't believe it."

"Well, it's true."

"But it's unheard of for a couple who are going to get married never to have made love. It's outrageous. What does Betty say?"

"She wants to wait until after we're man and wife."

"That's bizarre. Does she know you're with me this weekend? Or doesn't she care?"

"She would care very much if she knew, she'd be quite jealous. Perhaps more jealous than most women. You see, Betty is very unsure of herself sexually. Like me, she has problems in that area."

"Are you saying she's a lesbian?"

"Not actively, but on some level, well, yes, I think so. I think she's attracted to Jean, for instance, but I doubt if she would ever do anything about it."

Francine shook her head in disbelief. "If Betty's a lesbian, and you're gay, why do you both want to get married?"

"Because it's not quite that simple, I'm not *totally* gay. I was married before, you know, and the sexual part was damned good, I enjoyed it a lot. It's just that I'm out of practice now, I haven't been with a woman for a long time. That's why I want to be good for Betty. I'm very much in love with her even if she is a little dikey."

"A little dikey sounds like a little pregnant."

"Only if you perceive people in either black or white terms. The point is that Betty and I are ideally suited for each other, because we're both pansexual."

"Is that what they're calling it these days?"

But her sarcasm seemed to escape Peter, who had mentally soared off into another plane.

"The idea of marrying a virgin appeals to me a great deal," he said dreamily. "It seems so pure, so romantic, so old-fashioned."

"It sounds decadent as hell to me. A virgin! This is too much. I'm going home."

She leaped out of bed.

"But it's the middle of the night and you're in East Hampton," he said, snapping out of his reverie. "There aren't any taxis here, there aren't any trains at this hour. Please don't leave me, Francine, I need you. Please. Let's try again, I'm sure I can do better if you would only help a little, refresh my memory, guide me. . . ."

"Listen, buster, I never signed up to give a weekend course in sex education."

And yet she had stayed, and helped. And little by little Peter improved, so that by this morning he was acting at least one-quarter male and masculine, he was certainly trying, there was no denying that. But it was difficult for him, it did not come naturally, and she wondered about his ex-wife.

"Oh, she was a virgin, too," Peter explained. "So she had nobody to compare me with."

"Well, I do," Francine said spitefully.

"I'm sure."

"Don't look so bleak. You've improved a lot since we got here."

"Have I really?"

"No question about it, you'll be okay on your wedding night. What I'm curious about is why you picked *me* for the job."

"You have know-how. It shows. I spotted it the minute I laid eyes on you at Clean Slate."

Know-how, but not know-why. After he was asleep, Francine began to wonder if she didn't possess some masochistic streak that drew her to impossible men. Peter hadn't been the first, and she suspected that he wouldn't be the last. This disturbing pattern had emerged innocently enough.

After her divorce several years ago, she became soured on love and romance, bitter, and she sought men who were just as bitter and disillusioned as she, men who only wanted to run to a lot of discos and be distracted. That was fine with Francine. She would just as soon boogie and hustle the night away as spend that time in bed, in love, in misery. And if at the end of a long disco she and whoever did happen to find themselves in bed, they were usually too stoned or too drunk to do much anyway. Or if they could do something, it didn't amount to much. Francine didn't really care, even when some of the sexual entanglements veered toward the comedic.

Like the time she ended up in a motel in Virginia with a jewelry buyer from South Carolina, who was determined to fuck her in the ass. He kept telling her *not* to turn over on her stomach, which she didn't understand at first. But he knew what he was doing, old Charlie did; only just when she thought everything was going to work out okay, he became maudlin. She had never before (or since) been fucked in the ass by a man who sobbed continuously throughout and called her by his ex-wife's name. Lana.

"Oh, Lana, darlin' baby, when you wiggle your hips like that, I could die."

And this with a Southern accent to boot. Oh well, Francine decided it was exotic, that was the way to look at it. But while she was looking at it, she couldn't help wondering where these men were getting her, a boogie and a hustle and a fuck later, and slowly, gradually (without even seeing it) her needs started to change and deepen, yet the men did not. They remained the same: divorced, disillusioned, desperate.

After Charlie from South Carolina, she met Herbert from St. Louis. Despite the fact that his ex-wife had ruined him financially, Herbert was no crier. He buried his grief in grass. Francine and he used to get so stoned on grass and white wine that often they fell asleep in the middle of lovemaking, and once when they woke up he could not get it out.

"Locked in forever," Herbert lamented.

"But it's morning, I have to go to work."

"So do I, sugar. It's not my fault it won't move. Maybe it's happy where it is."

Eventually it moved, and Francine went to work, and thought a lot. She had managed to delude herself that because she was working so hard to build up her jewelry-design business, she didn't have time for deeper, longer-lasting relationships. Her work demanded her best energies, she reasoned, and love would just have to take a back seat. What *was* love, anyway? She thought she loved her husband yet he turned out to be having an affair with their accountant, then the two men disappeared with all the money in the couple's joint-savings account. The hell with that sentimental claptrap known as love, Francine had decided.

Yet late at night when she found herself lying beside a drunken stranger—or looking at *it* lodged inextricably within her—the barrenness of her life would hit her hard ("Don't worry, it's gonna move soon, I can feel it," Herbert had tried to reassure her). She was thirty-one, smart, beautiful, financially independent, yet except for her thriving business she had nothing: no man of her own, no children, no family, not one emotional commitment to anybody ("Lana, I love you!" she could hear

Charlie cry in anguish); and worst of all she suspected
that she'd forgotten how to love, it had been so long
since she allowed herself that precious privilege. Then
Daniel came along.

A mutual friend sent him to Francine Creations, Inc.,
where she had just completed a new line of cuff links for
men: *champlevé cloisonné*, and silver.

"They're very handsome," Daniel said, admiring the
range of intricate designs in her showcase.

So was he. She rarely sold to retail clients, but there
were occasional exceptions. Daniel proved to be one of
them.

"I need them for a dress shirt," he explained. "My
wife insists I get dolled up for this year's Emmys."

"Have you been nominated for an acting award?"

"Hardly." He laughed with pleasure. "But I am an actor. I didn't realize it showed."

"It's like electricity. Other people can feel the charge."
She smiled right into his cornflower-blue eyes. "It's an
extremely magnetic quality."

"You're very kind."

And very foolish, as it turned out. She was in bed with
him by that afternoon, but it took a while longer before
he asked her to pose. She had seen the pictures in his
studio, and being something of a closet exhibitionist
thought she could do better than most of the girls he'd
already photographed. She certainly had a better body
than most of them. Daniel agreed when he saw her
naked for the first time.

"Your skin is like marble." he said.

"So is my heart," she joked.

Because it wasn't. It had become a tender heart again,
vulnerable, ready to be broken by someone with Daniel's
persuasive charms. They spent three blissful weeks together, during which time Francine remembered what it
was like to fall in love. The fact that they were both

recovering alcoholics was another bond between them—it made her trust him.

Daniel was still living with his wife at the time but had his studio on Thompson Street, and they met there every evening after she got through work. First they would smoke some grass, then she would pose for him, and afterward they would make love, the photography sessions having excited them both to a feverish pitch.

Francine could see why she was so turned on. In the daytime she was a cool woman executive with a business to run and employees who were dependent upon her; but at night she could relax, shed those responsibilities, and change into a seductive, desirable, exciting female whose only concern was to please Daniel. It was heavenly relief to play the subservient role for a change and be completely at his disposal, defer to his whims, obey his decisions. Even when the photo sessions started to become pornographic, she didn't object. In fact, she found herself more sexually steamed up than ever, and afterward their lovemaking transcended all inhibitions. She did things she had never done before, and Daniel photographed everything.

"When I gave up booze, I became addicted to pornography," he said. "What the hell. It's cheaper, more fun, and I don't get hangovers.

She saw no harm in what they were doing; it was a private matter concerning only the two of them. Then one day he startled her by suggesting group sex. Francine was upset and vehemently refused.

"Don't be such a prude," he teased her.

"It's not a matter of prudishness," she explained. "I don't want to share you with anyone else."

"Share me?" he laughed. "You're sharing me right now with my wife and girlfriend."

"Girlfriend?" Francine said, feeling sick.

"Yeah, she's pretty wild and goes for women. She'd

know just what to do with you and you'd love it, honey. I want to see your two bodies together. I want to see her face buried in your cunt. Now wouldn't that make a lovely picture?"

Francine ran to the bathroom and vomited. The purge seemed to clear her brain as well. She wondered if she'd been out of her mind, letting him take all those incriminating photographs. Why hadn't she realized what she was letting herself in for? He could humiliate her, blackmail her, ruin her business career if he ever spread those pictures among her clients. She would be the laughing-stock of the jewelry-design business. She would be bankrupt, all those years of hard work down the drain. Maybe if she spoke to him, reasoned with him, paid him off . . .

"There's no way you can buy those pictures back," he said, amused by her request. "They belong to me, honey. I paid for the camera, the film, the processing; the pictures are mine. I don't want your money, I don't need it."

"Then just give them to me."

"Sorry, no dice."

"But Daniel, I'm so ashamed."

"There's nothing to be ashamed of, honey. I'm not going to circulate them all over town. They'll remain in my own personal collection, I promise. They'll only be seen by other beautiful women who want to get high on that sexy body of yours. Are you sure you won't change your mind about meeting my girlfriend? She could be here in ten minutes. She really digs brunettes."

That was nearly a year ago. Since then Francine had tried everything to persuade Daniel to either sell her the negatives or destroy them, but to no avail. She knew that she would never rest easy as long as they remained in his possession. She made her last desperate pitch just before he went on tour with *The Iceman Cometh*. But she must have gotten him at a bad time, because instead of his usual jocular refusal he became nasty and threatening.

"Look, Francine, you've been on my back for months now and I'm sick of it. One more call like this and I guarantee that I'll personally PLASTER your photograph in the centerfold of *Hustler*. I know exactly which shot of you I'll choose. Remember the one where your clitoris is sticking out about five inches?"

She heard that he was back in New York via the AA grapevine, and went over to Clean Slate on Tuesday to see the bastard. She would ask him for the return of those pictures one more time. Maybe the Midwest had mellowed him, maybe he would be in a more receptive mood. If not—

Francine was afraid to imagine what she might do. She was very, very angry.

∂5∂

As Betty put on the glittery g-string in the club's dressing room, she found herself thinking about Peter's weekend. Had it been a success? She prayed not. She couldn't bear the idea of him making love to Francine, and the more she thought about it the more it sickened her. She should never have let him know how jealous she was of Francine. It only made the bitch more attractive to Peter, more desirable.

She stood up and shook her breasts at the floor-length mirror, did a few energetic dance steps, made sure that her g-string was secure, and then decided there was time to give her toenails an extra coat of polish before she had to go on.

She chose plum frost and began to apply it carefully, artfully. In the murky light of the dressing room, her toes began to shimmer and shine. *This little piggy went to market.* . . . How did that old nursery rhyme go? She hated thinking about her childhood, it had been such an unpleasant one. It was so painful to wish for a life that seemed out of reach, but within the past year everything had changed thanks mostly to Peter . . . darling Peter. *This little piggy ate roast beef.* . . .

Maybe when she returned home tonight, there would be a call from him, maybe he would ask to come over. Then they would sit and drink hot chocolate, and talk. He would tell her everything that happened over the weekend, and she would tell him about the threatening note.

"It was only a stupid fling with Francine," he would say. "It's you I love."

"Then protect me," she would say. "I'm afraid of becoming the murderer's next victim, terribly afraid."

And Peter would hold her close, tight, he would try to distract her by talking about the Broadway play that still was not cast. Betty had a strong feeling that in spite of his doubts and uncertainties, Peter was going to get the lead, become an acclaimed actor, make a lot of money. Then she would quit this sordid job which had outlived its appeal a long time ago, and devote herself to Peter's well-being.

One of Betty's earliest dreams was to be a happily married woman, a housewife who worried about washing-machine cycles and how to turn leftovers into appetizing main-course meals. As a child, she used to devour the women's magazines even though her parents teased her mercilessly about this preoccupation with domesticity, femininity. Grownups could be so cruel, so unfeeling. But now all that was in the past (she reassured herself), she only had to wait a few more months before the time element permitted her to marry Peter and see her dreams come true. Maybe they would buy a cottage somewhere in the country, she could sew curtains, *and this little piggy stayed home.* . . .

"Pinch your tits," the owner of the topless club said, standing in the doorway. "They're looking a little wilted today. And shake it, will you? You're on in three minutes."

Betty wiggled her wet toes. "I'm coming."

"So is your devoted audience. I can smell it all the way from here."

Monday, March 6

When Jean left for Clean Slate, she timed it to get there just as the meeting started. That way, she could avoid another unpleasant encounter with Bob. After yesterday's chase through the Guggenheim, she never wanted to see him again.

"Can't I come home with you?" he had pleaded as they dusted themselves off from the fall down the ramp. "I need to talk to you. You're in a lot of danger, associating with Betty. I want to help you, Jean, I love you."

"The only way you can help me is to stay out of my life. It's all over, Bob. It really is."

"But why? What have I done? Tell me."

"Just let me alone."

Then she ran out of the Guggenheim and into a taxi before he could catch her. When she got home, she ignored the ringing telephone, and eventually it became silent. Clark Gable was delighted to have her back, and to make up for her twenty-four-hour absence she cooked a small steak for him and a larger one for herself. The funny thing about the poodle was that he liked his steak the same way she did: rare, with Worcestershire sauce, and smothered with fried onions.

"The trouble with Clark Gable is that he thinks he's a real person," Jean said, hugging him. "Doesn't he?"

Although she went to bed early, she couldn't sleep. She was too disturbed about Bob's erratic behavior, too apprehensive as to what he would do next. In the morning there was a call from Betty.

"You were right about Peter receiving a threatening note," Betty said. "It was waiting for him when he got back from East Hampton. The message was: 'Stop being so friendly to that bitch, Jean, or you'll be dead next.'"

"Bob doesn't leave one stone unturned, does he?"

"What I don't understand is how he can pretend to love you, and then do something like this."

"I've told you. He's crazy."

"You know, Jean, Peter and I have been talking. We both resent having our hand forced by the killer, we resent being intimidated by him. If we do what he wants, then neither of us will publicly speak to you again."

"You'll do even better than that. You'll get up at Clean Slate today and say exactly what that nut wants you to. I couldn't bear the thought of anything happening to you or Peter because of me. Not after what's already happened to Daniel and O'Brien. Okay?"

"Okay," said Betty reluctantly.

From time to time Bob turned around trying to catch Jean's eye, but she pretended not to notice. The speaker had just finished giving his qualifications, and Constance threw the meeting open for discussion. The first person to raise her hand was Betty, who promptly retracted her previous defense of Jean.

"I'm no longer certain she's innocent," Betty said in a clear but troubled voice. "And I'm sorry that I defended her in the first place. It was misguided of me."

A startled silence followed, and then the meeting continued as usual. Several people sneaked hasty glances at Jean, and next to her Laura was smirking with satisfaction. Although it hurt to realize that Laura was pleased, Jean felt glad that Betty's condemnation of her had been accepted at face value. It made Betty's position safe. To insure Peter's safety, they had decided that he would cut Jean dead today.

"With a friend like Betty, nobody needs an enemy," Jean now whispered to Laura.

"I notice that Peter isn't talking to you either."

"I'll live."

Knowing Laura, the exchange would be all over Clean Slate in no time. Jean hoped that Bob was satisfied with his insidious handiwork. When the meeting ended everyone seemed to scurry out fast, except for Bob who approached her swiftly.

"I hope you're feeling better today," he said. "Because I'd like to talk to you."

"I feel fine. Now will you please excuse me?"

But he blocked her way.

"No, goddamn it. The least you could do is tell me what I've done. Did I offend you? If so, just tell me how and I'll never do it again, I promise."

"You didn't offend me."

"Then why are you avoiding me?"

"I'm not avoiding you." In the empty room every sound was magnified, and she wondered if he could hear her heart pounding. "I have a class at the Art Students League in a few minutes, and I don't want to be late."

"How about dinner this evening?"

"No."

"Jean, I love you and I want to be with you tonight."

"I'm sorry, I'm busy."

"I hope you're not planning to see Betty. She's dangerous, she sent that note to herself. I've already told Rodriguez so."

"That's ridiculous."

"Then you *are* seeing her?"

"Certainly not. Betty is severing our friendship until this whole thing blows over, and I don't blame her. She doesn't want to get killed, and neither does Peter."

"You don't really believe that crap about their lives being in danger, do you?"

"Of course, I do. You read the note yourself. Anyone would be frightened."

"Betty's really got you coming and going, doesn't she?"

No, you do, Jean thought angrily.

"Okay, you're busy for dinner. I'm not even going to ask who the lucky person is, although I'm dying to know. Maybe I am possessive, but it's only because I love you so much. Would you meet me after work, just for a little while, darling?"

"Absolutely not."

"I could be at your place around six. You seem so tired, so drawn. I'd make you feel better, you remember how well I do that, don't you? Don't you want to feel better, sweetheart?"

"I'm meeting Francine at the Algonquin after work. Now will you kindly step aside."

"You mean, you'd rather see Francine than me?" he asked in utter astonishment.

"I don't like to break appointments."

"Only hearts," he said, walking out in a rage.

She waited until she was certain he had gone, then she went into the anteroom for her cape. Maybe it was a tactical mistake to have refused to see Bob later tonight. How was she going to trap him into confessing if she continued to avoid him? Suddenly, she realized that she was not alone. George, the drunk, was standing next to the coat closet. He seemed to be waiting for her.

"Excuse me," he said, darting forward. "I'd like to have a word with you."

Close up, he was much younger than she had thought, probably only in his mid-forties. Years of heavy drinking had lined his face and broken the blood vessels, coarsened the features, aged him about fifteen years.

"Yes?" she said, curiously. "What is it?"

259

"It's about that fellow who was poisoned here. Daniel. I just wanted to say that I don't think you did it."

"That's very kind of you. But everyone else seems convinced I'm guilty. How come you don't?"

"You weren't frightened."

"What's that?"

He shook his head and smiled, as though at a private joke. Like many alcoholics, he had neglected his teeth for years.

"It's a funny thing when you're pissed out of your mind, the way I was that day. You pick up on certain remarks that a sober person would overlook. Know what I mean?"

She nodded. "Yes, I know."

"Most drunks do. It's like you have a sixth sense. I remember Daniel telling the group how he had a mean, vindictive nature that he was trying to overcome. He hadn't overcome it yet, he said, and that's why he doubted if he could forgive anyone who'd harmed him in the past. It was the part about him being harmed that registered with me at the time. Then the next day he was poisoned."

"Just a minute," Jean said. "You couldn't have heard Daniel say that. He spoke here on Monday and you didn't show up until Tuesday, the day he was actually killed."

"No, m'am, you've got it wrong. I was here on Monday, and many times before that. I used to drink at the bar around the corner, and I'd come in here whenever I started feeling too guilty. But I always stood in the back of the room, that's why you didn't notice me. On Monday I didn't stay for the whole meeting. I left right after Daniel's speech."

"Please go on."

"The point I'm trying to make is that I have a mean, vindictive nature just like Daniel. And I nearly got myself killed once as a result of it. I tried to get even with the guy who ruined my marriage, and he beat me up so bad that I was taken to the hospital. That started me thinking. What if pretty much the same thing happened to Daniel, only he wasn't as lucky as me? What if the person he had it in for saw it coming and decided to protect himself? Forewarned is forearmed, as they say. So he went ahead and poisoned Daniel at the next opportunity."

"That's a very interesting theory. But even if it's true, how do you know I'm not the person Daniel had it in for?"

"Because I saw the way you were looking at him when he spoke. As drunk as I was, I'll never forget the expression on your face that day. It was all pain and love, but no meanness there and no fear. The murderer had to be afraid. You weren't."

"You saw all that in my face from the back of the room?" Jean asked incredulously.

"You'd be amazed at how much emotion there is in a profile. And you weren't still, you know. You fidgeted, moved around in your seat. It was easy to see what you were feeling."

"That's very observant of you. What else did you see? Did you see fear in anyone's face?"

"If I'd been looking for it, I might have. But nobody told me there was a murder in the making that day, no m'am."

A murder in the making, she thought afterward. It was a provocative phrase. If George was right, it meant a fast murder, one without too much advance planning. She had assumed differently. She'd been thinking about it over the long weekend, and her idea was that Bob would have tried to concoct a perfect premeditated crime. He was a premeditated kind of person. He wouldn't have minded waiting all those months for Daniel to return to New York. The delay would have given him time to work out every detail of the careful poisoning, and make it foolproof.

But what if she was wrong and it didn't happen like that? What if the killer hit upon a spontaneous scheme at the last minute, exactly as George had reasoned? It was a disconcerting possibility. It meant Bob was innocent.

Jean left the brownstone and started to walk over to the Art Students League on West Fifty-seventh Street. The weather felt raw with the promise of more snow, and people she passed looked irritated. So was she. George's theory had upset her neatly formulated ideas about Bob, who'd been a regular at Clean Slate for well over a year. If George was right, the murderer only showed up there for the first time on Monday.

She tried to think back to Monday's attendance. But it was impossible a week later to remember exactly who'd been present. And besides, anyone might have slipped in (as George did) and gone unnoticed by her—but not by Daniel. The sudden sight of his old adversary could have rekindled Daniel's memory and prompted all that dangerous talk about revenge. Yes, she could see it happening. The veiled verbal threats on Daniel's part leading to quick retaliative action on the part of the other man. If George was right, Daniel had more or less talked himself into his own murder. It was a rather startling idea.

❧2❧

Jean spent the rest of the afternoon sketching nudes at the Art Students League, her mind flying all over the place. The model who was posing today reminded her of Betty. She was tall and full-breasted, with the same kind of long red hair falling softly over her shoulders.

It made Jean think of the dream she had Saturday

night, although somewhere in the back of her mind it seemed too vivid to be a dream. But she knew that was ridiculous. She couldn't have walked into Betty's bathroom and actually *seen* that grotesque carnival apparition, it was impossible. . . .

When she left the League, it was after five and already icy cold and snowing again. Francine had made a reservation for the two of them in the lounge of the Algonquin Hotel on West Forty-fourth Street. What Jean liked best about the lounge, aside from its convivial living-room atmosphere, were the little gold bells on each table that you rang when you wanted a waiter. Francine was there ahead of her, wearing a crimson pants-suit and drinking Perrier water.

"I have a wild craving for a bullshot," Francine admitted. "Their bullshots are out of this world. I still remember them."

Jean remembered her famous dinner at the Algonquin, when she ended up with her face in the red spaghetti sauce. It was shortly after Frank died and she had bravely decided to go to the theater one evening, have dinner out, try to make the best of her new life. Between acts of the play she had ducked into a nearby bar and drank martinis, aware of the fact that she was the only unescorted woman present. By the time she got to the Algonquin, she was feeling very sorry for herself. It was a Saturday night. This was how it would be from now on, she thought, going to plays alone, dining alone, living alone. She barely managed to choke down the hot appetizer. Red wine on top of the martinis made her lachrymose, and by the time the spaghetti arrived her self-pity was spilling over. Life was too painful to be borne. The maitre d' had to lift her face out of the marinara sauce and escort her to the door, as other diners looked on, astonished.

"You didn't ask me here to talk about being your

sponsor, did you?" Francine said after Jean had ordered a tomato juice. "I figure you want to compare notes about Daniel. Am I right?"

"I hope you're not angry."

"Why should I be?" Francine shrugged good-naturedly. "I don't mind talking about the bastard. Did he give you a hard time, too?"

The room was warm and bathed in a rosy light, definitely the wrong atmosphere for talking about hard times, Jean thought, as she leaned back in the plush easy chair. Next to them a distinguised man in homburg and dark glasses was enjoying a fragrant pot of tea.

"I loved Daniel," Jean said, "and he dropped me without any warning. Right after he got back to New York. I was stunned. I had no idea he was such a liar, such a cheat. It wasn't until after he died that I learned about that filthy photo collection of his." She flushed, remembering Francine's picture. "I'm sorry. I forgot that you and Daniel were once . . ."

"I was once a schmuck, but don't apologize. It's all water under the bridge. Yes, I posed for him, I'm ashamed to say. Daniel could be very charming and persuasive when he put his mind to it. Of course, he didn't always have to exert himself to get what he wanted. Some women are more depraved than he. Constance, for instance."

At the sound of the name, an image swam into Jean's head. The crisp and efficient chairwoman of Clean Slate, with her tailored outfits and smoothly groomed hair, her restrained manner.

"But Constance is so proper," she said.

Francine's earrings tinkled throughout the room.

"*Proper? Constance?* She's kinky as can be, she took a lot of those photographs herself. She's AC/DC, in case you didn't know. Constance and Daniel used to have a lot of fun with some of the girls in those photographs, that was a big part of Daniel's appeal for her. He got her the girls, he was her pimp. Count me out on that one, incidentally. I don't swing both ways and I don't go for groups. But Constance is so decadent that she would have made it with two kangaroos and let Daniel photograph them in the act."

Jean just sat there and wondered where she had been all her life. In what kind of ivory tower had she been hiding to be shielded from these unsavory revelations? How could she have been so blind, so naive, so trusting?

"I don't know what to say," she blurted out at last. "You must think I'm an incredible fool to find Daniel's behavior so shocking. But I *do* find it shocking. What made him act like that? Do you have any idea?"

"As a matter of fact, I do. If these quirks can ever truly be explained. Did Daniel tell you much about his early years?"

The man in the homburg ordered a second pot of tea and a piece of raisin cake. He spoke with a familiar French accent. It was much less guttural than Marcel's, more suave.

"The only thing Daniel told me," Jean said, "was that he grew up in a small town in Ohio and wanted to be a lawyer. Then something happened in college that affected him deeply, and he switched to acting. He never told me what caused the switch, only that he started drinking heavily around then."

"I know what took place, but it's not a very pretty story."

"I'd like to hear it, anyway."

"Okay," Francine said. "Danny was a virgin when he entered Ohio State at the age of seventeen. He'd had no experience with women at all and he was very self-conscious about that, very scared of the big event. This is by his own admission, remember. One of his college buddies discovered the truth somehow, and the very night Danny was going to get laid for the first time this guy managed to herd half the campus into the next room. Anne, the girl Danny had lined up, was in on it, too. They all thought it was a great practical joke. You know the kind of collegiate insensitivity that passes for humor."

"What did they do?"

"At the big moment, just as Danny was about to stick it in her, suddenly through the dormitory wall comes this thunderous roar of voices: 'HIP HIP HOORAY FOR DANNY, DANNY IS GONNA FUCK ANNIE. CAN HE? CAN HE?'"

"Oh, my God."

"Being nervous to start with, of course he couldn't. Not only was he impotent, but he was impotent to the ears of thirty of his classmates listening in the next room to his humiliating failure. Daniel told me that it took three more years before he was successfully able to make love to a woman. And in the meantime he was so traumatized, he couldn't concentrate on his studies and eventually he dropped out of school. That meant the end of his dream about becoming Clarence Darrow, which is when he turned to acting. You don't need a college diploma to be an actor."

"Or a Cassanova," Jean said.

"Right. Daniel never got over his early sexual failure, and in time he turned it into a need for sexual triumph. An obsessive need. Once he could do it, he couldn't stop doing it. There were never enough women for him. He told me that if he lived forever, he would never forget the guy responsible for staging his humiliation, and he would never forget those voices coming through the wall, shouting 'CAN HE? CAN HE?' I think he must have heard those voices every time he was about to seduce a new woman."

"Perhaps seduction was his way of trying to quiet the voices."

"But they were never quieted permanently. They never could be. And so he had to begin all over again

266

with a new woman, a new seduction scene, a new challenge to be met, several women at once, anything to drown out those taunts."

Jean looked around at the tables of attractive, well-dressed people sipping their predinner drinks. The man in the homburg was signaling to the waiter for his check. In the Rose Room the maitre d' was placing fresh carnations on all the tables. It was so pleasant and civilized. She found it hard to believe that she had just listened to a modern-day horror story with far-reaching overtones. For Daniel had died at thirty-six, still affected by events that took place nearly twenty years before.

"I wish he had told me," she said. "It would have explained so much."

"He would have been too proud to tell you, too afraid you would think less of him. Too ashamed. He could tell someone like me, because I didn't count."

Jean caught the quick flash of bitterness in the almond-shaped eyes.

"Being a hybrid means that neither whites nor Orientals will identify with you. And when men don't identify on that kind of deep racial level, well . . . how can I put it? You're not taken seriously. It's as though you're okay for fun and games, but you don't bleed like they do. Even my husband was that way. I converted to Judaism to be accepted by him, but it didn't work. He still saw me as a kind of racy, slutty half-breed. So now I'm the only Chinese American Jew I know."

Francine was so different from what Jean had imagined, so much more sympathetic. She thought of Betty's theory about Francine killing Daniel in a moment of vindictive rage, but it didn't fit the picture of the woman sitting opposite her. At the next table the man in the homburg was putting on his velvet-collared Chesterfield and leaving. As he crossed the busy lounge, a young boy raced by and knocked the gloves he was holding from his hands. The man bent down to pick them up in a gesture that reminded Jean of someone, but she couldn't think who. It had been a disconcerting evening and an informative one, but something still bothered her. Constance.

"All things considered, it seems odd that Daniel was planning to marry Constance," she said. "Don't you think? Or am I being naive again?"

"*Marry Constance?*" Francine burst out laughing. "You've got to be kidding. Where did you ever get such a screwball idea?"

"You mean, he *wasn't* going to?"

"Of course not," Francine said emphatically. "Who told you that he was?"

"Let's see. Rodriguez mentioned it first, and then Laura confirmed it."

"The two stooges. Don't you see what happened?"

"You mean, they only repeated what Constance told them?"

"Obviously. Has to be. Daniel wasn't cut out for monogamy. Once was enough for him, he would never walk into that trap again. And for that matter, I don't believe Constance wanted to get married either. It was just convenient to say so after Daniel was killed."

"Then she made it all up."

"Sure."

"But why?"

"So nobody would suspect her of murder. Would a woman in love kill her future husband? Certainly not. What motive would she have?"

Jean shook her head sadly. "And I believed her."

"Apparently you weren't the only one."

Jean remembered eliminating Constance's name from her suspect list after hearing her make that touching speech at Clean Slate, about how she and Daniel were going to live in California, how part of her died when he did, how picking up a drink could not bring him back to life. . . . How convenient it had been for Constance to say all that without Francine present to contradict her or call her a liar, how convincing Constance had sounded.

"I'm not saying that she did kill Daniel," Francine added. "But she sure as hell went to a lot of trouble to remove all suspicion from herself. Constance is a shrewd one, don't underestimate her."

"I won't again," Jean promised.

❧ 3 ☙

In the taxi going home Francine kept turning around to see who was in the cab behind her, but the person slouched down in the back seat was bathed in blackness. She could have sworn that she was being followed.

On a rational level, she knew she was being silly, yet she couldn't shake off the uneasiness. *Daniel's ghost is following me*, she thought, as the other taxi lagged and wavered and faltered. Her own driver was so incompetent that any car would have darted past them long before now. Unless, of course, the other driver was incompetent too.

When she got to Sutton Place there was no sign of the lagging yellow cab, no sign of anyone except the familiar night doorman who tipped his cap to her. Francine lived in the kind of sleek, modern, expensive building that O'Brien had been dreaming about just before his death. The lobby with its subdued murals and discreetly placed palm trees was softly lit and soft underfoot. Francine felt herself relax in this familiar territory; it had been a long day and she was glad to be home.

She picked up the mail and stepped into the empty elevator. One of the letters came as a surprise: it was from her ex-husband who had recently gotten a job teaching at a small Midwestern college. She read a few sentences and cursed out loud. The nerve. The arrogance. How dare he? He was asking for a one-thousand-dollar loan: "I can't think of anyone else to turn to, he wrote. "You not only have the cash, but I know what a generous person you are . . ."

Why didn't he turn to their accountant? The jackass he'd run off with, when the two of them swindled her out of all the money in their joint-savings account? What had happened to that pretty liaison, Francine wondered, as she viciously tore the letter into shreds. Maybe she had been generous once, when she first started to make money. She didn't know how to say no then. Being a successful career woman carried so many guilts and bonuses with it, it was such a new and unsettling role, that lending money was a simple way to ease her conscience. It was like saying to the world of men: "Of course I'll share what I have with you. I probably don't deserve to have it anyway."

But that was a long time ago, and people no longer took advantage of her; she didn't let them. She had learned. She worked hard for what she earned, and she wasn't about to give it away to some freeloader—ex-husband or not.

She put the key in the door, and another unpleasant surprise awaited her. The apartment was in the same state of chaos as when she left this morning. Newspapers and magazines and clothing and overflowing ashtrays were everywhere in the living room. Unwashed dishes sat in the kitchen sink. Her entire spring wardrobe lay on the bed. The bathroom was dank. Her maid had stood her up.

Francine sank into a white leather armchair and wondered why maids did not like to work for women; they seemed to resent it, as though they expected other women to fend for themselves. This was the fourth maid she was having trouble with, yet the bachelors she knew got along just fine in this respect; they were babied by their maids, coddled, and catered to. One faithful family retainer even baked chocolate cakes and cookies for her poor helpless employer, a banker with a heart of steel.

Francine kicked off her shoes and decided to start in the kitchen. Take out the garbage and turn on the exhaust fan, wash the dishes, put away her spring wardrobe, empty the ashtrays, throw out all the newspapers and magazines, mop the bathroom floor. . . . She worked quickly, efficiently, and had just returned from a fast trip to the incinerator when the telephone rang.

She took it inside where she could put her feet up on the stripped bed. Like the rest of the apartment, the bedroom was done in black and white with occasional touches of red. Here, the drapes were made of fine red silk which reminded Francine of a ship's sails at sunset. Peaceful.

"Hello," Jean said. "I just thought of something. Remember what you told me tonight about that guy at college, who caused so much trouble for Daniel? The one who staged his sexual humiliation?"

"Yes," Francine said. "What about him?"

"I know this is a long shot, but do you by any chance remember his name?"

Francine drummed her long fingernails on the ebony night table. "Daniel did mention it once."

"It might be important. Please think."

"Let's see . . . I'm positive I know it. Daniel really despised that bastard. . . . Was it Jerry? George? No. Oh wait, I've got it," Francine said triumphantly. "It's Gene."

At that moment the red silk drapes moved, and a familiar figure emerged from behind them. Francine gasped. Somehow the man did not seem real. Frozen with terror, she watched as he slid toward her, a gun in his hand, and motioned to her to replace the receiver. As she did so, she heard Jean's voice thanking her for the important information.

271

"Please," Francine implored the intruder. "Please don't."

He didn't answer. His face was almost sad as he aimed the gun directly at her and slowly pulled the trigger. The last thing she heard was the sound of her tinkling earrings being drowned out by a powerful roar, the last thing she felt was her chest being ripped apart.

❧ 4 ❧

Constance lived in a brownstone around the corner from Bloomingdale's. The apartment was charming, homey, exactly the opposite of what most people expected of her. It had a brick wall, hooked rugs, an oak dining table (now set for two), and a working fireplace. Outside it was still snowing heavily, but in here it was warm, pleasant. She threw some more logs on the dwindling flames, poured herself a cup of herbal tea, and sat down to wait.

Constance hated being kept waiting. All her years as an executive secretary made her appreciate people who were unfailingly punctual, and in the past Bob had never been late. Not to anything she could remember, and certainly not to a home-cooked meal. He had stopped by her office that afternoon and asked what she was doing later. Since she'd been hounding him all week about getting together, she promptly invited him to an Italian dinner.

"You bring the spumoni for dessert," she said.

"Gladly, *signorina*."

Daniel's death left her feeling alone and unappreciated, a situation she found unbearable. She thought of all the people she could call, the parties she could arrange, but without Daniel to join in the raunchy festivities, they suddenly didn't interest her. The group sex they had enjoyed together would not be the same if she were to attempt it without an interested receptive partner. The kick would be gone. What she needed was a man to replace Daniel, and although she remembered how jealous and possessive Bob could be, she also remembered how anxious he was to please. Perhaps over the years he had become less medieval in his approach to sex.

"One person just isn't enough to satisfy me," Constance used to tell him. "I need variety, I crave it. Don't you?"

"I don't like the idea of sharing you with anyone. It appalls me. I want you to myself, all to myself."

But people could change. She had once been a naive little farm girl, believing in monogamy and marriage and spending the rest of her life with one person. Now she couldn't imagine spending the rest of the *month* that way. Being with one person became so tedious after a while. You were locked in your head, in your conversation, in your lovemaking. Even Daniel had become tedious after the first few weeks, and that was when she suggested they ask one of the girls in his photographs to come over.

"She can spend the night with us," Constance urged him. "We'll have fun."

Daniel was surprisingly agreeable and after that it started to be a ritual with them. A wild erotic ritual which Constance enjoyed and savored even more than he did (she would think about it all day long as she sat behind her mahogany desk, the efficient secretary). She was never jealous when she saw Daniel making love to another woman, doing the same things that he did to her. Instead she got excited and joined in. There was always room for a third party to delve into the tangle of arms and legs and gaping openings. Near the end, though, Daniel became competitive with her, resentful and accusing.

"You're a degenerate!" he lashed out at her not long

273

before he went on tour. "I thought that having a third person around would be a little extra titillation for you, but now I see that she's the whole show. It's the girl you really want. *I'm* the one who's the extra titillation. You're degenerate, corrupt."

"Is the pot calling the kettle black?" She laughed.

But Daniel did not laugh along with her, he refused to be mollified. His resentment toward her grew and festered, her bisexuality became a hurtful thorn in his side. And to her surprise he announced one day that he was having an affair with Jean Neelie.

"You're kidding," was Constance's first reaction. "I don't believe it. She's too damned plain."

"Not with her clothes off, she isn't. She's very exciting, but even more than that I have her undivided attention in bed. I don't have to share her with a horny, insatiable bitch like you."

"You're jealous of me," Constance said. "You know that I make women happier than you do, and your ego can't take it. You can't stand the fact that they get more pleasure from me than from you. I'm right, aren't I?"

He became enraged. She had obviously hit a sore spot.

"Just stay away from Jean," he warned her. "She's not like the others. She's straight, and I want her to remain that way."

"You have nothing to worry about. Little Miss Squaresville isn't my type. She probably douches with Mr. Clean."

"Let her alone," Daniel said. "Save your filthy thoughts for someone else."

"It sounds like you're falling in love," Constance mocked him.

"Maybe I am."

Constance didn't care for that, not one bit. Daniel's active participation had made their parties exciting; now he was threatening to pull out and leave her stranded.

"You'll get bored with Jean," she predicted. "I give you one month, tops."

"I don't think so. She's the first woman I've ever met who truly satisfies me. I'm sorry, Constance, but that's the way it is."

Constance was infuriated, enraged. Men like Daniel were not easy to replace. True, there were a lot of guys eager to make the orgy scene, but the majority of them were unattractive and unappetizing. They couldn't function sexually on their own, they were for the most part emotional and physical misfits. And even though Constance preferred making love to a woman, she only enjoyed doing it in the presence of a handsome, appreciative man. A man like Daniel. Other women felt the same way. Daniel was a big attraction, he drew the women in, photographed them, and fucked them before turning them over to Constance. Yes, he would be very hard to replace indeed.

And then he left on that Midwestern tour, his romance with Jean still going strong. Constance missed him. She wrote to him while he was gone, begging him to change his mind about Jean and come back to her. *I may not be able to offer you the same kind of exclusivity that Jean can*, she had written, *but in my own way I do love you.*

Daniel's reply was that *her way* no longer appealed to him. He called it a dead-end road, with no satisfactions for him now that he'd been with Jean. He said that when he returned to New York, he was going to ask Jean to marry him. That did it! Constance got on the next plane to Chicago and walked into his hotel room a few hours later.

"Are you serious about marrying that jerk?" she demanded. "Because I'll never let you do it. Never. I want you back, Daniel, I need you. I want things to be the way they used to. Don't you remember the fun we used to have? Remember that tall brunette who brought her twin sister along—"

"Forget it," Daniel said, cutting her off. "I'm not interested. That's all in the past, I don't want to live that way again. It's over for me, I've outgrown it. Please try to understand, will you?"

"Outgrown it?" She laughed. "You can't, it's impossible. We're alike, we belong together. We enjoy the same things, we always have. You'll never be happy with Jean. Never!"

"We used to be alike," he said gently. "And you're wrong. I *will* be happy with her. I'm happy now."

"I'll tell her everything," Constance finally said. "I'll show her the pictures we've taken. I'm sure she'll be quite interested in your diverse sexual tastes. Believe me, she'll get an eyeful."

He turned white. "You're not serious."

"Aren't I? Try me. Try me and find out."

"Anyhow, you couldn't. Those pictures are in my possession."

"I have a negative of every single one."

He stared at her, trapped. "I don't believe you."

"That's your privilege, but you'll discover when it's too late that I'm telling the truth. You never should have given me a key to your studio, lover. I doubt if Jean will want to see you again, after she gets a look at some of your cuter perversions. Remember the time we hired that dog act for a night? I think you once said Jean is quite a dog lover. . . ."

He was staring at her with hatred. "I'd like to kill you."

"I'm flattered. But what you're going to do instead is get your ass back to New York, break off with Jean, and return to Momma's loving arms. Isn't that right, sweetheart?"

In the end, she had won. Well, almost. On Sunday he got rid of Jean, but later that day he came over to tell Constance that he was getting rid of her too.

"I don't want you anymore," he said coldly. "And

there's no way you can hurt Jean now. I just did that. But you and I are through, so you can take your negatives and shove them. I never want to lay eyes on you again, Constance."

When she saw him die two days later, she wasn't even sorry. He had outlived his usefulness. But she did have to cover herself in case the police became suspicious. And that was when she decided to inform everyone at Clean Slate about the make-believe wedding plans. She was sure they would believe her. Jean could be counted on to tell the truth about breaking up with Daniel, but Constance felt bound by no such morality. And furthermore, she knew that Laura would gullibly back her up. Laura would never believe that Daniel wanted to marry Jean—no one would, Constance figured. Laura would simply assume it had to be Constance. It was a brilliant idea, and she made a note in her engagement calendar. Under March 17th, she penciled in: *Marry Daniel today*. Then she smudged the pencil mark a little, hoping the cops would buy it.

At eight-fifteen, Constance was still waiting for Bob. She was sorry now that she had asked him to pick up the spumoni, if indeed that's what was causing the delay. All she knew was that the eggplant parmigiana was rapidly turning to cardboard, the antipasto was curling at the edges, and her salad had wilted. She wrapped everything in aluminum foil and impatiently looked at her watch again. Forty-five minutes late and that idiot didn't even have the courtesy to telephone.

5

By the time Detective Rodriguez and his men reached Francine's apartment, it was eight-thirty and she was barely alive.

A bullet had pierced her chest and blood trickled down the front of her crimson pants-suit, red upon garish red. She was lying on her stripped bed, next to the white princess telephone. The receiver had been replaced by Francine herself, Rodriguez soon discovered, which meant that he was once more left without a set of fingerprints anywhere. And without a murder weapon. When he called Jean back, she asked if Francine had been able to identify her assailant.

"She did mumble something," Rodriguez said, watching the ambulance stretcher take away the still-breathing woman. "*Homburg*. At least that's what it sounded like. Does it mean anything to you?"

"The man at the Algonquin! But how? Why?"

"What are you talking about?"

She described the distinguished-looking man in the homburg and dark glasses, who'd been sitting next to them.

"And you have no idea who it was?" Rodriguez asked.

"He was pretty well covered up. I realize now that it could have been a disguise."

"Wasn't there anything familiar about him? Anything at all?"

"The way he bent down to pick up his gloves, when he was leaving. It did remind me of someone, but I can't think who."

"And yet you saw him at such close range."

"He was probably wearing makeup in addition to the hat and dark glasses. In a way, I didn't see him at all."

"Then it could have been a woman."

"I don't think so. He moved like a man. He left the lounge shortly before we did. He probably went straight to Francine's building and was waiting for her when she walked in."

"Who knew that the two of you were planning to meet at the Algonquin?"

"That's what I'm trying to remember."

278

She delved back to the earlier part of the day, the Clean Slate meeting, that provocative conversation with George, painting nudes at the Art Students League. Nothing there. Yesterday? She had spent it with Betty, never mentioning her appointment with Francine. Betty would have been too upset to learn that her best friend was chummy with the woman she suspected of sleeping with Peter, not to mention of murdering two innocent people. Betty's suspicions could be laid to rest now, Jean thought grimly, wondering if Francine was going to live, wondering how the man in the homburg knew they'd be at the Algonquin.

"The strange part of this business is that I was trying to reach Francine earlier," she heard Rodriguez say. "I wanted her to come down to the precinct for questioning."

"Why? About what?"

"My men were following through on those threatening notes that Betty and Peter received, and guess what? They were both typed on Francine's secretary's typewriter. Two hours ago, I thought I had this damned case wrapped up with a big red ribbon."

"There must have been a mistake," Jean said. "Francine is obviously innocent."

"There was no mistake. Her secretary's machine was definitely used to type those notes. It's conclusive. We also checked out the equipment in Mr. Edward's office. No soap. So now I'm back where I started."

Bob. He knew she was meeting Francine at the Algonquin, she remembered now. How he'd badgered her after Clean Slate about seeing him later, how she said she couldn't because she had an appointment with Francine. She even told him where. He must have gotten to the lounge ahead of them and arranged to be sitting close by, carefully disguised. That phony French accent. Of course, it was the Alain Delon imitation transplanted from the bedroom ("We French invented all this, you know").

The only thing she couldn't understand was why Bob had panicked and decided to follow Francine home. What had Francine said at the Algonquin that made him decide to get rid of her? Jean didn't know, but Bob seemed to have a penchant for following women. She still recalled his crazed pursuit of her through the Guggenheim. Also, the man in the homburg was five feet nine or ten, the right height for Bob, too short for Peter, too tall for Marcel.

She verbally erupted into the telephone.

"Okay, Mrs. Neelie, here I am at your beck and call," Rodriguez said minutes later, addressing her in person. "Now, what's all this about you suddenly knowing the murderer's identity? I hope you haven't gotten me over here on a wild-goose chase."

"You won't think so after you hear what I have too say."

She took him into the living room. Rodriguez kept his coat on while Jean quickly filled him in on the sequence of events she had just finished piecing together.

"So you see, Bob has to be the murderer," she concluded. "It all fits. Francine being shot, everything. Bob must have ordered her to replace the telephone right after she got through telling me the name of Daniel's nemesis at college. Gene. Bob's own name. He must have realized then how truly dangerous she was. So he shot her and ran."

"There are certain inconsistencies."

"Such as?"

"If Daniel had known Bob at college, known him as Gene, why would he have waited so long to turn vengeful? Why didn't Daniel do whatever he was going to do before he left for the Midwest? He certainly had plenty of opportunity, they saw each other at Clean Slate all the time. It doesn't make sense."

"No it doesn't, but—" She suddenly remembered something. "When I called Francine at her office last week, she told me that her secretary was out sick and her typewriter was broken. Francine said that the repair man was due to arrive shortly, and that was Friday. Those threatening notes were postmarked Friday. Do you get the picture I'm getting?"

"You mean, it was a put-up job? The repair man was really Bob in disguise?"

"Why not? If he could pull off that distinguished-homburg act at the Algonquin, why couldn't he carry a tool kit and masquerade as a typewriter-repair man?"

"And while he was supposedly fixing the machine, he typed both notes," Rodriguez theorized.

"Exactly. Francine never would have suspected it was Bob. Nobody notices what repair men look like."

Jean felt her excitement build, then momentarily abate as she remembered that Bob was out getting drunk on Friday. But he could have gone to Francine's office first (he admitted that he hadn't gone to his own office), then changed back to his regular clothes and hit the bars afterward. Getting drunk might have been a deliberate ploy on his part, an alibi for where he was during the early hours of Friday. He'd done a good job of getting smashed, so good that she had taken him home, felt sorry for him, let him make love to her.

"If Bob used the secretary's typewriter, he must have had her cooperation," Rodriguez mused. "I'll have my men get onto her first think in the morning. She should be easy to break down. She probably only did it for money, and a small amount at that."

"I don't understand." Jean stared at him. "Aren't you going to arrest Bob?"

"Mrs. Neelie, Mrs. Neelie." Rodriguez shook his head. "I *can't* arrest the man. What we have now is inconclusive evidence. But I will get him down to the station and make it plenty hot for him, I assure you. We'll check on his college background. If that fits with Daniel's, we might have something. And if we're really lucky, Francine's secretary will be able to identify him as the guy who bribed her. After that, he should crack." Rodriguez got to his feet. "If he's the killer."

"You're the most stubborn man I've ever known." She walked him to the door. "What about Francine? Do you think she'll pull through?"

"I'm afraid not." Rodriguez' mouth twisted. "I received a call just before I came over here. She was DOA when they got her to the hospital. She never stood a chance. I'm sorry."

After a moment, Jean said: "So am I."

"I hoped I wouldn't have to tell you. It's the one part of my job I despise."

"She was a nice person," Jean said, trying to assimilate the news of this latest death. "And if it weren't for me, she'd be alive right now."

"You can't start blaming yourself."

"How can I help it? It was my idea to meet for a drink, my idea to dredge up the murders, my idea to call her after I got home. If I'd never made that call, she never would have told me the murderer's name. Bob only shot her after she said *Gene*. I remember hearing the sound of her earrings just as she spoke his name. That must have been the moment he surprised her. If I had let Francine alone, she wouldn't be dead this very minute."

"You don't know what might or might not have happened. Try not to be too hard on yourself. It can't bring her back."

"That's what's so terrible. What kind of gun was she shot with?"

"It looks like a thirty-two."

The possibility that Bob had had a gun in his possession all this time horrified Jean. She wondered where he'd gotten it.

"I'll be leaving now," Rodriguez said. "I want you to stay home, alone. No visitors. Understand?"

"Don't make it sound so ominous."

"It is ominous. A third person has just been killed. Take this, it's my home number." He handed her a slip of paper. "I don't think you'll need it, but hang onto it anyway. Just in case."

"Are you trying to tell me that my life is in danger?"

"No, not unless you do something stupid. Like trying to talk to Mr. Edwards before we can get to him. You're not planning any bravado tactics, are you, Mrs. Neelie?"

The shock of Francine's death was just sinking in. The guilt. The senseless waste. Jean suddenly felt very tired.

"No, no bravado tactics. The events of tonight have been quite enough for me."

"Good. Then you're going to leave everything to us from now on. No more snooping around, right?"

"Right."

He looked at her skeptically. "Promise?"

"I promise, I promise."

"Good girl. Try to get some sleep. That's the best thing you can do for yourself right now."

After the door closed behind him, Jean realized that she liked Rodriguez even if he was overly cautious. Tonight was the first time he had seemed concerned about her safety, which meant that he finally believed she was innocent . . . and in danger . . . and maybe he was right. It would be stupid to take chances. She wouldn't even walk Clark Gable herself, she would ask Albert to do it.

"I know you don't like being walked by Albert," she told the poodle. "But you have no choice."

Afterward she made supper and couldn't eat it. Then she tried to watch television and couldn't do that either. She felt too jumpy. How easy it was to be fooled by a handsome, sexy, sympathetic stranger. Just because Bob was a recovering alcoholic like herself, she had let him enter her home, make love to her, sleep in the same bed. He could have murdered her in her sleep. She glanced at the slip of paper Rodriguez gave her, as though for reassurance. It was lying next to the telephone. A minute later, the telephone began to ring. *What if it was Bob?*

✤6✤

"Hi!" Betty said cheerfully. "I've been trying to get you for ages. First there wasn't any answer, and then your line was busy. I have some absolutely marvelous news. Peter just landed the lead in a new Broadway play."

"Oh Betty, that's wonderful." What a relief it was to hear aboout something good happening, for a change. "You must both be delighted."

"*Delighted,* she says. We're out of our minds with sheer, unadulterated ecstasy. Me, even more than Peter. You don't imagine that I was looking forward to supporting my future husband, do you?"

"I shouldn't think so," Jean said, smiling at the idea. "Not you."

"Not me, is right. The play is supposed to open on Broadway in the fall, and I've convinced Peter to set the wedding for just before opening night. That way, if the play's a huge success, he can't accuse me of marrying him for his money. And at this point, the fall seems a long way off. It will give me time to prepare."

"You mean for the wedding?"

"Yes, I'm still jumpy about the prospect of marriage. But I'll have been sober for a year then, so I'll feel more relaxed about the time element."

That time element certainly meant a lot to her, Jean thought. She'd never known anyone at AA to take it so seriously, so literally.

"The play is a light comedy, and I think Peter will be

wonderful in it," Betty said, the sparkle back in her voice. "I've seen him do comedy, his timing is excellent."

Jean suddenly remembered how unhappy Daniel seemed last Monday after he spoke at Clean Slate, how defeated-looking. At the time she couldn't understand what had caused that air of failure. Now she began to wonder if, possibly . . .

"Betty, do you know if Daniel happened to be up for this same part?"

There was an uncomfortable delay before Betty replied.

"Yes, as a matter of fact he was. Peter told me it was the main reason he returned to New York ahead of schedule. To read for it."

"When did Daniel actually audition?"

"On Monday. The day before he was murdered."

"And how did it go?"

"According to Peter, Daniel was brilliant. But Daniel thought otherwise. He was very depressed after the audition."

"You knew about this all the time, yet you never mentioned it to me. Why not?"

"Isn't it obvious?" Betty took a deep breath. "I didn't want there to be a shadow of a doubt in anyone's mind that Peter had a motive to kill Daniel. They did have a falling out once over a part in a play, and it could seem like it was happening again. I was trying to protect Peter. He didn't kill a soul, Jean. I know he's innocent, Francine is the murderer."

"I'm afraid not."

"What do you mean?"

"Francine is dead. She was killed less than an hour ago. She died on the way to the hospital."

"Oh, no!" Betty screamed. "Not another one!"

Betty became even more distraught than Jean would have expected. She tried to calm her down, but Betty kept babbling about mass murderers, and who at Clean

Slate was going to be next, and why were the police so incompetent, so stupid, so *worthless?*

"You don't have to be afraid—" Jean began.

"Not afraid? Are you crazy? Who *wouldn't* be afraid? There's Francine dead as a doornail. Why? I know she was a bitch, but who would want to shoot her? I simply can't believe this has happened. I'm terrified. Does Rodriguez have any kind of lead at all?"

"That's what I'm trying to tell you. There's nothing to worry about any longer. The police are picking Bob up for questioning."

"Picking Bob up?" Betty said slowly, uncomprehendingly.

"For questioning," Jean repeated. "Suspicion of murder. It's all over. Or will be very shortly."

It took a minute for her message to sink in.

"So you were right," Betty said at last.

"It's one of the times when I wish I were wrong."

"It was Bob from the start." Betty sounded as though she still could not believe it. "I wouldn't have thought he had the brains, the guts. He seems so dull and ineffective. Yet you were right. You know, it's a peculiar thing about murderers. . . ."

Betty rambled on but Jean had stopped listening. She was remembering what Betty said just a few seconds ago and trying to figure out how . . . No, it was impossible, it didn't add up. . . . Over the telephone she heard Betty's voice urgently drawing her back.

"Jean? Are you there? Are you okay?"

"I'm sorry." She unconsciously braced her shoulders. "I must be more tired than I realized. Sleepy."

"Of course you're tired. It's been a hell of a night for you, but we can all rest easy now that it's over. I still can't believe it, you know. The murderer caught at last. It's almost too good to be true, isn't it?"

286

Jean was thinking of the man in the homburg, bending down in the lobby of the Algonquin to retrieve his gloves.

"Yes," she said. "Almost."

Tuesday, March 7

❧ 1 ❧

Jean did not sleep all night. She sat up in bed, thinking and making a list. But this list bore no resemblance to her previous ones of Clean Slate people and their supposed motives for murder. This was a series of questions with tentative answers, not conclusive but promising enough to keep her thoughts flowing in one direct line of reasoning.

Yes, she finally, exuberantly decided! This was the way it must have happened. And for these reasons. It was easy now to understand why the murderer had so tantalizingly eluded her and the police, but the masquerade at the Algonquin made her see that a much more ingenious masquerade had been parading before her eyes all the time.

Light was creeping through the heavy bedroom drapes, and it was Tuesday. Daniel had been killed exactly one week ago to the day, and it seemed appropriate that on the date of this grim anniversary she had at last unraveled the mystery of his death.

"Come on, Clark Gable. It's time to rise."

The poodle looked at her skeptically, and dug his nose into the blankets on the bed. But Jean was already in the bathroom, washing her face and getting dressed. She had to make two phone calls as soon as the hour was respectable enough. Without all the props surrounding the identity of the murderer, the truth was quite simple. It had been staring her in the face all along.

288

"Sometimes your mother isn't very bright," she said to Clark Gable, who had followed her into the kitchen. "But you love her anyway, don't you?"

The poodle whined.

As Jean fed him, she realized that in order to do what she had to she must have faith in herself. Blind faith. Nothing else mattered at this moment, except the conviction that she was right and could prove it. For the first time in her thirty-five years, she truly understood the meaning of self-confidence. It was a heady emotion, more exhilarating and intoxicating than liquor had ever been.

She no longer needed liquor. She was no longer the shy unassertive person she'd been a week ago, the one who was afraid that without Daniel she couldn't function and would go unnoticed. Not anymore! Her ability to do things on her own and do them *well* had come as the most wondrous surprise of all. That she was actually about to solve a triple murder case filled her with immense pride.

At ten to nine, she decided to phone Hans at his laboratory.

Hans was an old chemist friend of her parents, and she wondered why she hadn't thought of getting in touch with him before. Probably because the chances of what she was now considering seemed too remote and implausible, and she was afraid of being laughed at. That fear was gone now.

Hans turned out to be very familiar with the properties of $C_{10}H_{14}N_2$, otherwise known as nicotine sulfate. He answered her questions with amused skepticism.

"I thought you were studying painting," he said at last. "Since when have you become interested in the subject of toxic poisons?"

"Since a friend of mine was poisoned," she said, filling him in on the salient facts about Daniel's death. "And you're certain that a lethal amount of nicotine can be extracted the way I've described?"

"I've been a chemist for thirty years. I'm positive."

Jean could hardly believe that her wild hunch had just been verified by a bona-fide authority. The blood rushed giddily to her head.

"Thank you, Hans. You've been very helpful. One more thing. It sounds so simple to poison somebody like this. How come it's not done more often?"

"What makes you think it isn't?"

"You never hear about it."

Hans chuckled, the cynical scientist.

"Just because you don't hear about it, doesn't mean it's not being done. Too often the nicotine goes undetected, particularly if the victim was a heavy smoker. That might have happened with your friend if the aspirin bottle weren't found. It was careless of the killer to leave it lying around like that."

Careless, Jean wondered. Or too rushed for time to be able to make more foolproof plans?

"Mrs. Neelie, you're dressed so early." Thelma had just arrived, complaining of a toothache. "Is something interesting going on?"

"That remains to be seen."

Thelma grimaced. Between her toothache and the prospect of an unpleasant surprise, she knew that disaster was imminent.

"Does it have anything to do with your new boyfriend? Mr. Intoxication?"

"It certainly involves him," Jean said.

"I hope he's not blotto again. He polished off a whole can of chocolate syrup last time. I've just replaced it."

Thelma had come from the supermarket and was unloading her purchases on the kitchen table. Jean spotted a bottle of Ivory Liquid among the groceries.

"Is that what you clean the coffeemaker with?"

290

"Yes, it does a good job." Thelma eyed her employer with suspicion. "Why?"

"I wondered if you had to scrub a lot."

"Scrub? No, not at all."

"And yet it's supposed to be a gentle cleanser. They're always recommending it for baby clothes, aren't they?"

It was the wrong thing to have said, she realized a moment later as Thelma confronted her in horror.

"*Baby clothes?* You're not pregnant, Mrs. Neelie, are you?"

☙ 2 ❧

Jean's second telephone call and first visit of the day was to Betty. When Betty opened the door, she was wearing plum pajamas and a matching silk robe. Spotting the Saks hat box that Jean carried, she asked what was in it.

"An icebucket I bought Thelma for her birthday. She doesn't like it, so I offered to exchange it for her."

"You're too damned good-natured," Betty said. "Come on in and have some coffee. You look like you can use it."

"I can. I haven't slept all night."

The pyrex coffeemaker, identical to Jean's own, sat on a metal trivet. Cream, sugar, and a dish of cheese Danish completed the breakfast for two. After Betty had served them, she said: "I still can't get it through my head that Bob was the murderer. I felt sure it was Francine. Do you realize that one of your lovers was killed by another?"

"Maybe next time I'll listen to you." Jean managed a smile. "You always said I had lousy taste in men, right?"

Betty laughed. "Right."

❧ 3 ❧

When Jean left Betty's, she ducked into a telephone booth on the corner. To her relief, Peter was at home.

"I've called to congratulate Broadway's next big star," she said. "Do I get a ticket to opening night?"

"What on earth are you talking about?" a puzzled Peter asked.

❧ 4 ❧

Jean's next stop was the Forty-second Street Public Library where she was in luck. She found the book she wanted in the biography section and checked it out at the desk. Then she set off for the police station. Detective Rodriguez was not especially pleased to see her, and even less pleased when she explained what she wanted him to do.

"Is this some sort of joke, Mrs. Neelie?"

"Not at all. And if you could have the results by the time Clean Slate meets at twelve-thirty, I'd appreciate it."

Rodriguez sat behind a cluttered desk, the overhead light showing the fatigue on his face. He was in his shirtsleeves, his tie pushed to one side.

"Do you have any further instructions?" he asked. "Or will that be it for the day?"

"As a matter of fact, there is one other thing. Could you check Ohio State's records for the following name? I think you'll find that this person entered college the same year that Daniel did."

Rodriguez jotted down the name with mild surprise.

"He wouldn't, by any chance, be related to a certain Clean Slate member, would he?"

"In a way."

"I don't know why I listen to you," the detective snapped.

"Because you suspect I might be right. And would you please hurry? I'm afraid."

"Of what?"

"A fourth death."

Before Rodriguez could ask her what she meant, Jean was out the door. He sighed in frustration and turned his gaze to the pyrex coffeemaker sitting on his desk.

"Amateurs!" he said.

But despite himself, a shade of uncertainty colored his voice.

❧ 5 ❧

It was twenty past ten when Jean emerged from the police station and headed straight for the nearest luncheonette. She felt dry and thirsty after all the coffee she'd drunk at Betty's, and ordered an ice-cream soda.

Then she opened the library book and began to read the story of one person's relentless search to find himself. She did not think she would be as moved as she was, but the way the author unflinchingly bared his soul made her understand the fierce upheavals he had to contend with during the course of treatment. And afterward. She became so engrossed in the poignant odyssey that she nearly forgot about the next call she had to make.

There was a telephone in the rear.

"I'm sorry," Bob's secretary said. "Mr. Edwards is out sick today."

When Jean tried his apartment, there was no answer. She waited while the phone continued to ring. Still no answer. Starting to feel panicky, she dialed the advertising agency again and this time asked for Constance Caruthers.

"I was wondering if you know where Bob is," Jean said. "It's very important that I talk to him."

"Haven't you done enough talking already?" Constance snapped. "If you had checked Bob's whereabouts before alerting the police yesterday, you would have found out that he was at my apartment when Francine was killed. And what's more, I can prove it, you damned fool!"

"I'm sure you can. *Mrs. Edwards.*"

There was a gasp at the other end of the line, and then a dial tone. Jean paid for the ice-cream soda and left. Where could Bob be? She had to speak to him before he showed up at Clean Slate and ruined everything.

Then she remembered Friday and the Third Avenue bar.

❧ 6 ☙

It was a little past noon when Jean arrived at Clean Slate, alone. All of her efforts to find Bob had failed and at last she gave up, depressed by her bar-room search.

"Have you seen Betty?" It was Peter, looking troubled. "I've been trying to get her on the phone since receiving that crazy call from you, but there's no answer."

"She's probably on her way here right now."

"I can't imagine why she would tell you that I was set to do a Broadway play when no casting decision had been made. It's not like Betty to jump to conclusions."

"I'm sure she'll be able to explain."

"You look like you're waiting for somebody yourself," Peter said.

"Bob."

It was a half-truth. She was also waiting for Rodriguez. The detective's absence meant that either he hadn't yet gotten the lab report, or that he hadn't *tried* to get it. Perhaps he thought she was barking up the wrong tree. Jean knew otherwise; she had never been so sure of anything in her life. She tapped her foot, trying to control her impatience.

Then she spotted Bob coming through the door, wearing an old raincoat, red-eyed, unshaven. He looked tired but sober, and several people stared at him curiously. By now, word of his arrest had spread through Clean Slate, and Jean could imagine people's confusion upon seeing him there. It was exactly what she had hoped to avoid.

"Where have you been all morning?" she asked him. "I tried to call you."

"Home. Getting some sleep."

"I was worried half to death. I thought you were at a bar, drinking."

"Isn't it a little late in the day to be concerned about my well-being?" he asked coldly. "You should have considered that before you went running to Rodriguez with tales of my being a homicidal maniac. Do you know what it's like to be cross-examined half the night for three murders you did not commit?"

"I'm sorry."

"The damage has been done. Your lack of faith in me was a real kick in the head. I didn't think you loved me, Jean. I'm not a complete fool. But I thought you knew me a little better. I'm a gentle person; violence and cruelty are not part of my makeup. I don't hurt people. They hurt me. Like you have."

"Don't you think you hurt me, too?"

"Not *I*. What have *I* done?" His eyes shone with martyred torment. "My only crime was to love you too much. But you defiled my love by your hideous suspicions."

"What about your suspicions? That Betty and I were

lovers? That I preferred Daniel's lovemaking to yours? It was awful, the way you kept hounding me for the truth and all the time you were lying yourself. Why didn't you tell me that Constance was your ex-wife?"

"*Who told you that?*" he said angrily.

"Nobody did. At least, not in so many words. But Francine's description of Constance and your description of your ex-wife were almost identical."

"What difference does it make if Connie and I used to be married? That was a long time ago, it's nobody's business."

"It just seems like a very peculiar omission."

"She asked me not to breathe a word to anyone." He had turned sheepish. "She was ashamed of me for being such a square. After we were divorced, she sometimes let me hang around, providing I didn't mention our marriage. I used to watch her and other guys make love. She liked it when I got jealous and mad, it excited her. She fucked like crazy then."

His eyes glazed in memory.

"But she never told this to anyone, not even your precious Daniel. That bastard. Daniel didn't know we were married either. It makes me laugh to think he actually believed that Connie was going to marry him. She never would have, she wasn't in love with Daniel. But you were. You'll always be in love with him. And you accuse *me.*"

"You're getting us mixed up, Bob. It's you who'll always be in love with Constance."

"Do you think so?" He became reflective. "Maybe you're right. She's the only woman who understands me."

"Speak of the devil."

Constance had just arrived. She glanced contemptuously at Jean, then crooked her finger at Bob.

"I'd better go see what she wants," he said.

"Yes, run to your Rabbit."

But he was gone and did not hear her.

Jean felt relieved that their affair was over, that she would never again be subjected to his jealous demands and insatiable needs. Getting involved with Bob had been a terrible mistake, but she could console herself with the fact that it was a short-lived one. At least she had put an end to the unpleasantness fairly fast.

"The meeting is about to start," Peter said to her. "Aren't you coming in?"

She turned toward the street door, but there was no sign of either Rodriguez or Betty.

"I hope she hasn't had an accident," Peter mumbled as they went inside and took their seats in the large room.

Vanderbilt was a few minutes into his talk about how he had become a falling-down lush, when Jean suddenly stood up and walked out. Peter glanced at her curiously but she avoided his gaze, hailed a cab on Madison Avenue, and gave the driver her home address. Her heart was pounding. *Why was she going home? Why had she left the meeting so soon?*

She didn't know. She was obeying some wild instinct that she felt too afraid to question.

✇7✇

Jean heard Clark Gable bark as she turned her key in the door. He nearly threw her over, jumping and leaping at her, wagging his tail, joyously happy to see her.

"What's the matter, Clark Gable? I've only been gone a few hours. Where's Thelma?"

Suddenly she knew that Thelma was not there, and that someone else was. Her heart stopped pounding and became strangely still as she look up and saw Betty standing on the threshold of the living room. Betty was wearing a violet tweed suit, a violet cashmere sweater, her hands resting in the side pockets of her skirt.

To Jean's own amazement, her voice sounded normal.

"Betty, what a nice surprise. What are you doing here?"

Betty's voice did not sound normal, it was like steel.

"What have you done with it?"

"Done with *what?*"

"Don't play dumb, Jean. You know what I'm talking about."

"Really, I don't." She mustered up as much sincerity as possible. "Betty, what is this? What's gotten into you?"

"You switched coffeemakers on me this morning. I realized it after you left my apartment. My own was slightly chipped."

"Switched coffeemakers?"

"You weren't returning a birthday gift for Thelma in that Saks hatbox. You had your own drip pyrex in there. Then when I went to the john, you switched it with mine."

Jean swallowed. "Why would I do a crazy thing like that?"

"You tell me."

"I can't. I mean, there's nothing to tell. I really was exchanging something for Thelma. By the way, where is Thelma?"

"At the dentist. Her tooth was killing her. I gave her the rest of the afternoon off." Betty smiled slyly. "I said you told me to. Now walk over to the door and lock it."

"I certainly will not."

Betty's right hand came out of her suit pocket. It held a revolver pointed directly at Jean's head.

"I think you will. Lock and bolt it. Right this instant.

Jean had never had a gun pointed at her before, she'd never even seen a gun before. Its effect upon her was riveting. She locked and bolted the door in a flash.

"I didn't know you owned a gun," she said.

"I stole it from O'Brien." Betty's voice had gone flat, her eyes were strangely blank. "I didn't want to kill O'Brien, but he left me no choice."

"What about Francine?"

"That seductive, conniving bitch had it coming. Betty snapped out of her blankness. "As for you, I'll kill you too unless you do exactly as I say. I want you to go into the living room. Then I want you to sit down on your precious heirloom sofa, and explain how you got wise to me. Come on. *Move.*"

It was a strange procession: Jean walking in front of Betty, the gun jabbing into her back, and Clark Gable solemnly glued to Jean's side. The dog knew she was in danger, she thought; it was amazing how they knew.

She sank into her parents' Duncan Phyfe sofa, wondering what they would think if they could see her being held captive by her best friend, a dangerous criminal. Betty sat down in Frank's old rocker.

"Talk," Betty said. "I want to know how you figured it out. And don't bother denying that you did, or I'll blow your head off this minute."

Jean was terrified. The more she confessed to knowing, the greater danger she would be in. If she didn't speak, Betty would kill her. If she did, she would surely be killed after she finished relating how clever she'd been. Clever!

"What the hell are you smirking about?" Betty wanted to know.

"I've been too smart for my own good."

"That's a fact." Betty took out a cigarette and lit it, inhaled deeply, never removing her eyes from Jean. "Cagey is what you are. A very cagey lady."

"Not as cagey as you."

"Cut the crap and start talking. I want to know everything. Start with motive. What motive did I have for killing Daniel?"

Jean realized that her only chance for remaining alive was to ramble on as long as possible. Perhaps at some point, she'd be able to figure out how to extricate herself from this insane situation. She took a deep breath.

"Daniel was killed because the murderer was afraid of him," she began. "Daniel knew too much about the murderer's past, he posed too much of a threat."

"The past." Betty's hand, holding the gun, trembled for a moment. "No matter how we try, we never escape it. We're all victims of our lousy pasts. But I want to hear about Daniel. I want to, hear how he put himself in jeopardy. Because that's what he did."

"I know," Jean said softly. "When Daniel spoke at Clean Slate last Monday, he unwittingly verbalized a blueprint for his own murder. He admitted that he was a very vindictive man, who would get even with anyone who ever harmed him. *No matter how long it took.* That's what made George wonder whether a stranger showed up last Monday, the day before the murder, and heard Daniel confess to this dangerous trait of his."

"Who the hell is George?"

"The drunk."

"Every schmuck gets into the act," Betty said. "Go ahead."

"If a stranger had showed up and he was an old enemy of Daniel's, what would his reaction be? Fear. He'd realize that he stumbled into a potentially dangerous situation, and his major concern would be how to protect himself from Daniel's vengeance. Providing the stakes involved were high enough, he might have felt that murder was the best protection of all."

"But there was no stranger at Clean Slate on Monday." Betty had a cat-and-mouse smile on her face. "I wasn't a stranger. Nobody was. It was just the usual group of people."

"I know. That's what I couldn't understand. Francine,

300

Stanley, and Renee only showed up for the first time on Tuesday."

"You left out George."

"No. George had been with us many times in the past. He'd stand in the back where nobody saw him. George is quite sneaky."

"Also, quite screwy. If there was no stranger on Monday, then his theory is wrong."

"What was wrong was the way I'd been looking at the time element," Jean said. "The murderer didn't have to be a stranger to Clean Slate before Monday, merely someone who had never seen *Daniel* before Monday— someone who joined our group during Daniel's three-month absence. There was only one person who fitted that description, Betty."

Betty turned pale. "But if I'd never seen the creep before, why would I want to kill him?"

"Oh, you'd seen Daniel before Monday. You knew him as Daniel Roland a long time ago. The two of you were buddies at college. You were the one who urged his classmates to play that terrible practical joke on him. Unfortunately, the joke backfired and Daniel suffered for years afterward. Emotionally, sexually, professionally. He dropped out of school due to poor grades, and was forced to give up his dreams of becoming a criminal trial lawyer."

"I had those same dreams, myself," Betty said mournfully.

"The Carl Cappolino case. I thought so," Jean mused. "Without a college degree, Daniel couldn't get into law school and eventually he turned to the theater. But as much as acting suited him, he never forgot the person who had such a humiliating, disabling, and far-reaching effect upon his life. Not only did Daniel never forget him, but being the kind of vengeful man he was, he resolved to get back at him one day. If their paths ever crossed again."

301

Betty's voice was barely a whisper. "So?"

"When Daniel returned to Clean Slate last Monday after a three-month absence, he was stunned to see one person there. His old college nemesis, the guy who damned near ruined his whole life. Daniel spotted him right away—"

"*Him, him,*" Betty interrupted mockingly, desperately. "You keep referring to a *him*, to a *guy*. Do I look like a *him?*"

"Not anymore," Jean said, just as the telephone began to ring.

❧ 8 ❧

"Step on it," Rodriguez told Detective Adams. "And don't wait for lights. Just *go*."

He leaned back in the car, praying that he would not be too late as he was with Francine. If he'd put a tail on Francine, she might never have been killed. Putting a tail on Jean had crossed his mind, but after arresting Bob last night he no longer thought it necessary.

What a fool he'd been. Jean's not answering the telephone a few minutes ago made him apprehensive, suspicious. Nobody at Clean Slate knew why she had left the meeting so abruptly, or where she'd gone. But Rodriguez had a hunch she'd returned home.

"Murder at AA," he said out loud. "Can you beat it?"

Detective Adams, contending with heavy midday traffic, didn't answer. She was too busy trying to get uptown as fast as possible.

"Who would think of a bunch of reformed drunks harboring a potential murderer?" Rodriguez said. "Nobody. That's who."

He felt his stomach burn. This case had turned into one of the most unusual of his career, one of the most labyrinthian he had ever tried to unravel, and he had to admit that without Jean Neelie's help he would still be in the dark about solving it. She deserved a medal of some kind, an award for ingenuity; the whole thing was so far-fetched, so gothic, so Krafft-Ebing.

But to his surprise, the name she'd given him earlier today checked out with Ohio State's admission records. The suspect had attended college at the same time Daniel did. There was no question of it.

"Who is the murderer supposed to be?" Adams asked him. "You've never told me."

Rodriguez did not like Adams. He considered her frivolous, incompetent, a token cop to pacify the women's liberation forces in the city. From the minute the AA case started, he had managed to get rid of her. Fortunately, their superior saw eye-to-eye with him and derouted Adams to some obscure drug crime.

"I'm not sure about the murderer's identity," Rodriguez said. "Only the next victim's."

"I doubt that. I think you've been keeping me in the dark on purpose. I think—"

"Get ahead of that fucking postal truck." He felt as though his stomach were on fire. "Or we're going to be stuck in this traffic forever."

"I'm doing my best."

"Then start praying."

"What for?"

"That we'll be in time to prevent another killing."

⑨

Betty had collapsed into hysterical tears, yet still managed to hold the gun aimed at Jean. Distraught as Betty was at Jean's knowledge of her transsexuality, she seemed intent upon keeping her captor a terrified captive.

Jean could see her wavering between the urge to pull the trigger, and the urge to describe all the horrors she'd been through. Fortunately, the latter won out.

"Not long after I quit college, I decided that nature had really played a dirty trick on me," Betty said. "I *hated* being a man. That's when I moved my mother and myself to Detroit, and severed ties with old friends. Then I went through a course of medical treatment that precedes the actual sex-change operation. You can't imagine the agony."

"Yes, I can. I've been reading about it." The book Jean took out of the library that morning was the memoirs of a well-known English transsexual. "Is that why you worked at all those transient, temporary jobs in the Midwest?"

Betty dried her eyes with a lace handkerchief.

"Yes, although financially I didn't need to work. My mother died and left me a lot of money, which was why O'Brien thought he could blackmail me. But I took those temporary jobs for something to do while my appearance was changing. It was a slow but sure process and I couldn't risk being observed by the same people over a period of time. The hairiness began to disappear, my voice got higher, my breasts developed, my skin became smoother."

Suddenly, her voice reverted to its old intimate tone of friendship. "That's when I became an alcoholic, Jean. The strain was too much for me. I was afraid."

"Of what?"

"That I'd never fool anyone in my new role . . . that I'd never be accepted as a woman . . . that I'd never . . ." Her voice broke. ". . . find a man to love me."

"But you did. You moved to New York, joined AA, and found Peter."

"Peter. Yes." Her eyes grew dreamy. "And for a while I thought I'd succeeded. I thought I had gotten away with it. Then Daniel showed up last Monday, a ghost out of the past. I knew he would blow the whistle on me." Betty sounded very bitter now. "We had a moment alone at Clean Slate and he said that he recognized me. He said he knew everything."

"But how?" Jean asked. "So much time had passed."

"Apparently he had traced me to Detroit years ago and paid off someone in my doctor's office to tell him what I was doing there. So he knew about my decision to switch sexes all along, but then he either lost interest or lost trace of me. Until he showed up at Clean Slate on Monday and saw me there, transformed outwardly, a new person. But to Daniel, I was the same old trouble-maker he wanted to get even with. I knew he had the provocation to tell Peter what I really was. I knew I would lose everything that mattered, everything I'd worked so hard for, unless I acted first. . . ."

Jean wondered where Rodriguez was that very moment. Had he gotten the lab report yet? She wondered what would happen if she suddenly jumped up and tried to get the gun away from Betty. But Betty was bigger, stronger than she, and Betty had nothing to lose anymore. She had cold-bloodedly killed three people. What difference would a fourth make? It was hard to believe that this tearful and pathetic woman sitting opposite her had caused so much destruction, been responsible for so much human waste. And yet she didn't doubt that Betty would kill her too, if provoked.

Jean could only pray that the police lab had reported positive nicotine stains on the bottom of Betty's cof-feemaker. Then Rodriguez would realize she'd been right. But would he realize she was in danger? Would he arrive in time to save her life? She shivered.

"One of my fly-by-night jobs was a lab assistant," Betty said, standing up, her voice breezy now. "Did you know that?"

"No."

"Didn't figure out everything, did you?" she teased.

305

"It was a control lab for testing insecticides—among them nicotine sulfate—so I got pretty familiar with the killing dose. Remember my old inventor friend I told you about?"

"You mean, tennis rackets for cheating?"

"Right!" Betty laughed loudly, her mood swings becoming more severe by the second. "He was brilliant, that guy. He came up with this oddball way of extracting nicotine sulfate in a coffeemaker. 'Nicotine coffee,' he called it. Can you beat it?"

Jean forced herself to laugh. "It sounds ingenious."

"It was. I knocked off Daniel, didn't I?"

"How did you do it, Betty?"

"Simple." Betty twirled the gun from one hand to another, showing off her dexterity. "After the Clean Slate meeting last Monday, I bought a drip coffeemaker and a pouch of pipe tobacco. Do you know that old joke about the customer asking the shopkeeper if he has Prince Albert in a can? The shopkeeper says yes, he does. And the customer says: 'Then let him out!' "

Jean joined Betty in raucous laughter. A moment later, Betty was serious again.

"When I got home Monday afternoon, I put the tobacco in the top of the coffeemaker and poured boiling water over it. The liquid that dripped through the filter was honey in color, and deadly poison. I dropped it in Daniel's coffee the next day, when we were all in the anteroom. Nicotine sulfate is bitter, but not when mixed with black coffee. So Daniel drank it and died minutes later, *exactly* as I had planned. And with fourteen possible suspects present, besides myself." Betty grinned triumphantly. "I'm pretty ingenious too, you know."

There was only one thing Betty hadn't counted on, Jean thought. That with his last breath, Daniel would try to name his murderer. And he did try. But in his by-then demented state of mind, he unthinkingly reached back to the adversary he'd known at college. . . .

"You goddamned clever bitch." Betty started to scream, a high wailing sound. "How did you know that I was *Gene?* You don't think I'm going to let you live knowing that, do you?"

❧ 10 ☙

Detective Adams pulled up in front of the sedate, well-kept apartment building just off Lexington Avenue, and Rodriguez jumped out of the car.

"Homicide," he told the startled doorman. "Lieutenant Rodriguez. Is Mrs. Neelie home?"

"Yes. She went up a little while ago. Is anything wrong?"

"Is she alone?"

"No, Lieutenant. A friend arrived before her."

"What friend?" Rodriguez snapped.

"A Miss Lathrop—"

"Is there an entrance to her terrace from the roof?"

"The roof?" Albert scratched his head. "Sure, but why don't you ring the bell first? It's apartment 17—"

Rodriguez was out of sight, running down the hall to the elevator. As soon as he managed to make the shallow leap across the building's rooftop onto Jean's terrace, he heard the blast of a gun somewhere inside the apartment. He silently began to pray. *Jesus, Joseph, and Mary* . . .

❧ 11 ☙

"It was pretty damned courageous of you to have switched those coffeemakers," Rodriguez said to Jean as they arrived at Clean Slate. "It's a miracle you're still alive."

307

A miracle? Jean wondered. Or had Betty been incapable of killing the person who represented what she most wanted to be? *A real woman.* By killing Jean, it would have been like killing the personification of her own yearning and striving.

"Let me handle the explanations," Rodriguez said. "You're in no condition."

She nodded, feeling very tired now, drained.

The meeting had just ended as the two of them entered the large room. Jean caught a glimpse of Peter, looking forlorn, as though he had somehow guessed the worst. Rodriguez held up his hand, and began to explain the events of the last nine days to the startled group. From time to time, there were gasps of shock and bewilderment.

"It's all over now," Rodriguez finished. "Betty took her own life a few minutes ago, before we could stop her. Considering the kind of prison sentence she faced, perhaps it's for the best."

Afterward, everyone solemnly trouped around the corner to the coffee shop, still talking about the murders. Jean and Rodriguez sat together at a booth, as various Clean Slate people came over to offer congratulations and apologies to Jean. Only Bob and Constance were missing, having gone off by themselves.

"If it weren't for you, dear Jean," Marcel said, "we would all still be wondering which one of us was going to be killed next. *Un mils pardons* for our foul suspicions."

"It hurt to know that everyone thought I was the murderer," she said. "I can't tell you how much."

"Shall I let you in on a shameful secret? I never believed you had killed anyone. I suspected Eleanor all along. If I'd had any guts, I would have told the police."

"It's not guts you don't have," Eleanor said. "It's balls." She turned to Jean. "I was the one who made that anonymous phone call the day after Daniel was killed."

She lowered her voice. "*Daniel lied to you. He never intended to go back to Laura.*"

Jean could smile now at the confusion. "And I thought it was Constance."

"No, it was my silly way of getting even with Daniel. I wanted to make sure that you remembered him unkindly. He wouldn't have liked that. He loved you so much."

"Loved me?"

Rodriguez cut in.

"There's something you should know, Jean. I had a little talk with Constance earlier, and as I had surmised, Daniel never intended to marry her at all. That stuff about a wedding and moving to California—it was a total fabrication."

"That's what Francine said. She claimed that Constance invented the wedding to keep the police from suspecting her of murder."

"True. But there's another tidbit that even Francine wasn't aware of. Daniel had planned to marry you."

"Daniel . . . and me . . . married?" she said, incredulously.

"Yes, Constance forced him to break off with you by threatening to show you certain incriminating photographs. Daniel didn't want you to see them. He didn't want you to see him in that light. In his own way, he must have cared for you very much, Mrs. Neelie."

Jean felt a great sense of relief. It was as though a terrible wrong had just been corrected. One of the things that had bothered her most was trying to reconcile her impression of Daniel with that of other people's. She'd always seen him as such a wonderful person, and yet when anyone else spoke about him he emerged as such a monster.

It made her feel better to know that her judgment wasn't entirely wrong—much better.

❦ 12 ❦

It was three o'clock, and Jean and Rodriguez were just finishing lunch. All of the Clean Slate people had left the coffee shop, with the exception of Peter. He sat at a table alone, looking bleak and forlorn, and they invited him to join them.

"Thanks." He moved over. "I still can't believe that Betty is dead, that she was the murderer."

"She had everyone fooled," Rodriguez said. "Her method of extracting nicotine sulfate in a coffeemaker was brilliant. In all my years on the police force, I've never heard of anyone doing it that way. How did you figure it out, Mrs. Neelie?"

"I have a keen eye for color. When I saw Marcel's pipe tobacco lying on my dining table next to a pot of coffee, I couldn't help noticing they were both the same rich chocolate brown. Then I started thinking about how easy it was to extract the essence of coffee just by pouring boiling water over it. And I wondered if the same thing wouldn't work with pipe tobacco."

Rodriguez reached into his pocket for the Tiffany gift he had purchased earlier today while waiting for the lab report to come through. He handed Jean the small blue box.

"This is for you, for being so smart. Go ahead. Open it."

Nestled at the bottom of the tissue paper was a gleaming sterling-silver trowel.

"Thank you," Jean said, touched.

"It's quite serviceable. My wife loves hers."

"Then your wife really *is* a gardener. I thought you made that up after you discovered I had a garden. Tell me something. Did you really think I killed Daniel?"

"Let's just say that I had a damned good case against

310

you, at the beginning. But I would have been sorry if you turned out to be guilty. I'm sorry about Betty. She wasn't your classic criminal."

"Betty was as much a victim as a murderer," Peter said, tears in his eyes. "When did you first start to suspect her, Jean?"

"When she phoned me last night, after Francine was killed. Betty referred to Francine being shot, but I had never said how she died. That got me wondering. I didn't see how Betty could be the murderer, because I was still convinced Bob had done it."

"You mean, Betty sent those threatening notes to me and to herself?"

"Yes, Bob was right about her all along," Jean said. "But his credibility was so poor that neither Rodriguez nor I believed him. Betty bribed Francine's secretary to let her play typewriter repairman on Friday. That morning you gave Betty an engagement ring. But when she showed it to me later, her fingernails were grimy and the polish was chipped. In her rush to change clothes and get to Clean Slate on time, she forgot to wash her hands."

"Poor Francine," Peter said. "She never hurt a soul."

"That's not quite true," Rodriguez pointed out. "She hurt Betty in the most vulnerable place of all. Her insecurity as a female. Betty was jealous that you found Francine desirable, and she wanted to get rid of her. Having her accused of the murders seemed a perfect way."

Jean thought of Betty's desperate attempts to be feminine . . . the long wavy Rita Hayworth hair, always wearing skirts and dresses, never pants, working as a topless dancer, even her boudoir of an apartment . . . all props in her search for the womanly self she longed to be.

"How did Betty find out that you and Francine were going to the Algonquin?" Peter pressed her.

"She must have overheard me tell Bob yesterday at

Clean Slate. The meeting had just ended, the room was empty, and voices carry there. Betty was probably up front getting her coat when I spoke to Bob. Afterward she went to a men's store for that homburg, affected a phony French accent, and was waiting for us at the hotel. She was afraid that Francine might know something incriminating, and she was right. Francine knew about the Ohio State incident."

"After Betty followed her home and killed her, she went back to her own apartment and phoned me immediately. She pretended that she'd been trying to call me for hours. She acted very excited. You had just gotten the lead in a new Broadway play! It was a foolish lie, but by then she was desperately afraid I would put all the pieces together."

Peter sipped his coffee. "But how did you figure out that Betty had once been a man?"

"By accident," Jean said. "When the man in the homburg bent down at the Algonquin to retrieve his gloves, it reminded me of someone. The gesture was familiar. Last night I realized it was exactly the way Betty bent down, to pick up a cigarette or other stuff. She ripped her pantyhose doing it once, too. She ripped her pantyhose the day Daniel was killed, and I wondered if she'd bent down to pick up something then. *Or to throw something away.*"

"The empty aspirin bottle," Peter said.

"Yes. Don't forget the wastebasket was difficult to get at. Also, men bend down differently than women. That's why Betty kept ripping her pantyhose. Her body was still moving in the way that felt most familiar to her. That of a man. Afterward, it didn't seem too far-fetched to wonder if her real name was Gene."

"Didn't you ever suspect something was wrong?" Rodriguez asked Peter.

"If I was suspicious of Betty, it was due to all the contradictions in her nature. Working as a topless dancer, and yet refusing to make love to me. Desperately wanting to get married, and then hedging about setting a date. Acting so super-feminine, but showing such a violent hatred for men."

"I couldn't understand her hostility toward men either," Jean said. "Now I see that other men represented the part of her she was trying to get rid of, the part she despised, the part that had caused her so much unhappiness. Whenever Betty went into one of her antimale tirades, it was because she felt uncomfortable in her new identity, threatened by it."

"Is that why she wouldn't let me make love to her?" Peter asked. "Because she didn't *feel* womanly? Not that I really objected. I didn't mind marrying a virgin. But it is curious."

Jean and Rodriguez exchanged hasty glances, which Peter failed to intercept.

"Betty was very unsure of herself," Jean said. "She never even let me kiss her on the cheek because she was afraid that her skin might be rough."

"But it wasn't," Peter said. "And having had the operation, she *was* . . . a woman. . . . Wasn't she?"

To Jean's relief, Rodriguez took over.

"Physically, yes. But emotionally, she hadn't yet made the adjustment, and she was afraid she couldn't. Can you imagine playing the masculine role for years, and then having to switch to the feminine one? It must have been awful for her, the fear that she would make a fool of herself."

"Or even worse," Jean said. "Lose you in the process."

"If only she had trusted me enough to tell me the truth," Peter said regretfully. "She wouldn't have lost me. We would have worked things out together, and none of these tragedies need ever have happened."

Tears streamed down his face.

"We could have gotten married. I really loved her,

you know. You may consider me the biggest fool in the world, but in my eyes she was always a woman."

❧13❧

After Peter had left, Jean and Rodriguez confronted each other.

"Do you think we did the right thing?" she asked.

"I don't see what good it would have done to tell him."

"No, I suppose not."

Jean was thinking of her last minutes alone with Betty, before she blew her brains out. Betty's final words would haunt her forever.

"I know that Rodriguez is on his way here to arrest me. I know that the lab found nicotine stains at the bottom of my goddamned coffeemaker. But I refuse to go to prison, Jean, I couldn't face it. Where would they decide to put me? In with the men, or in with the women? Either way, it would be a cruel joke, grotesque. It wasn't a bad dream you were having that night when you stumbled into my bathroom and saw me there, half male, half female. I blame the doctor in charge of my case for refusing to operate until I had completed one year of sobriety. If only he hadn't been so stubborn about the time element. . . ."

Rodriguez smiled wryly at Jean.

"I didn't get a chance to tell you this before, but the nicotine stains came out negative. Too much time had passed."

About the Author

About herself, Joyce Elbert says:

"A VERY CAGEY LADY is my eighth novel and first thriller. I have never been able to guess the murderer in anyone else's book, so I decided to write my own. People are always asking where I get my ideas. I got the one for A VERY CAGEY LADY when I was having a drink with an acquaintance in London. In the midst of a rather routine conversation, this person suddenly told me an astonishing secret that none of our friends could possibly have gleaned. I was so shocked that I couldn't speak. I hope that when you come to the end of A VERY CAGEY LADY, that's how *you* will feel."

Big Bestsellers from SIGNET

☐ **THE REBELLION OF YALE MARRATT** by Robert H. Rimmer.
(#E8851—$2.50)*

☐ **COME LIVE MY LIFE** by Robert H. Rimmer. (#E7421—$2.25)

☐ **LOVE ME TOMORROW** by Robert H. Rimmer.
(#E8385—$2.50)*

☐ **PROPOSITION 31** by Robert H. Rimmer.   (#J7514—$1.95)

☐ **THURSDAY, MY LOVE** by Robert H. Rimmer. (#E7109—$1.75)

☐ **A GARDEN OF SAND** by Earl Thompson.   (#E9374—$2.95)

☐ **TATTOO** by Earl Thompson.   (#E8989—$2.95)

☐ **CALDO LARGO** by Earl Thompson.   (#E7737—$2.25)

☐ **DANIEL MARTIN** by John Fowles.   (#E8249—$2.95)†

☐ **THE EBONY TOWER** by John Fowles.   (#E8254—$2.50)

☐ **THE FRENCH LIEUTENANT'S WOMAN** by John Fowles.
(#E9003—$2.95)

☐ **THE DHARMA BUMS** by Jack Kerouac.   (#J9138—$1.95)

☐ **ONE FLEW OVER THE CUCKOO'S NEST** by Ken Kesey.
(#E8867—$2.25)

☐ **THE GRADUATE** by Charles Webb.   (#W8633—$1.50)

☐ **YOUR CHEATIN' HEART** by Elizabeth Gilchrist.
(#E9061—$2.25)

* Price slightly higher in Canada
† Not available in Canada

Buy them at your local bookstore or use this convenient coupon for ordering.

THE NEW AMERICAN LIBRARY, INC.,
P.O. Box 999, Bergenfield, New Jersey 07621

Please send me the SIGNET BOOKS I have checked above. I am enclosing
$_____ (please add 50¢ to this order to cover postage and handling).
Send check or money order—no cash or C.O.D.'s. Prices and numbers are
subject to change without notice.

Name _____

Address _____

City_____ State_____ Zip Code_____
Allow 4-6 weeks for delivery.
This offer is subject to withdrawal without notice.